BLESS YOUR HEART

BLESS YOUR HEART

LINDY RYAN

MINOTAUR BOOKS
NEW YORK

This is a work of fiction. All of the characters, organizations, and events portrayed in this novel are either products of the author's imagination or are used fictitiously.

First published in the United States by Minotaur Books, an imprint of St. Martin's Publishing Group

www.minotaurbooks.com

Design by Meryl Sussman Levavi

The Library of Congress Cataloging-in-Publication Data is available upon request.

ISBN 978-1-250-88888-4 (hardcover)
ISBN 978-1-250-88889-1 (ebook)

First Edition: 2024

1 3 5 7 9 10 8 6 4 2

Dedicated in loving memory to

Royce Pennington Evans (1919–1991)

Jimmy Darlon Miller (1943–2002)

Ethel Ruth Evans (1919–2005)

Linda Ruth Miller (1943–2014)

PROLOGUE

Edwin Boone

Edwin Boone was not the kind of man to be intimidated by a walk in the dark.

He wasn't the kind of man to cower in the face of anything, really. Country-born and cornbread-raised, Ed was the kind of man those softer, yellow-belly types he saw out around town liked to call *good ol' boys*. He had enough marbles to know the term was meant as an insult, but Ed had never been able to riddle out why. It wasn't like there was anything wrong with attending church every Sunday. Paying your bills in hard-earned cash and thanking the Good Lord every night to be an American.

Men from Ed's generation were just made of sterner stuff, he often reasoned. More grit and less gravy. Just the way it was. He had, after all, served two tours in Korea, fighting a war against communism on the other side of the globe and making it back home when over thirty thousand of his brothers-in-arms had not. Nothing thickened the soul and hardened the gut like watching a man bleed out in your arms, and by Ed's own approximation, he'd done that very thing no less than a dozen times. Maybe more.

Probably more, he thought and shrugged. Probably a *lot* more.

Ed's memory wasn't quite what it used to be, not that it mattered. All of those men were dust in the ground now. Hell, almost everyone Ed had ever cared about was dust in the ground—his brother, his best friend. His favorite dog. His wife. He'd buried more friends and acquaintances these last few years than he could remember. If it hadn't been for the little one-by-two-inch cuts of newspaper he clipped from their obituaries and kept in a pile on his bedside table, Ed would have forgotten their names just as easily as he'd forgotten those of the men who'd died in his arms.

All except his wife's, of course. Her name was imprinted on his soul, her memory embedded in the gold wedding band Ed still wore on his left hand, in the faded tattoo inked on his left biceps. She'd been a good woman, his Darlene. Good until the very end.

Better than you ever deserved, Ed thought.

After the war, Ed had gone straight back to the small, rural southeast Texas town where he'd been born, married his high school sweetheart, and worked every shift his boss would give him at the Fair Store. When he'd saved up enough money, Ed had bought a scratch of land on the edge of town and built a home. He'd raised three kids, seven dogs, and more feral tomcats than he could count on that land, and in all those years, he'd never seen anything more frightening on his midnight rounds than the eyeshine of a coyote caught in the beam of his flashlight.

And so tonight, like every other night for the past forty-odd years, Ed tucked his Smith & Wesson Model 686 into the holster on his hip, put his old white Stetson on his head and a toothpick between his teeth, and went out to survey the flat, dry, pine-trimmed expanse of his property.

The night ran warm, even by late-August standards. Sticky. Ed licked the taste of it from his lips. Hot days of summer didn't give way to cooler weather this far south easily. The heat's long, humid fingers clung to the air long after the Texas sun had set, sometimes all the way through dawn. Ed could count on one hand how many times he'd seen snow in these parts—maybe three if he stretched back far enough. The last was two years ago, February '97. A good bit of ice had moved in, left a bunch of folks across the county without power and a whole lot of trees on the ground. Ever since, the heat had seemed to be making up for it, reclaiming its territory like a dog gone to rut. Tonight felt hotter than usual though, the air turned heavy by fog that had rolled in with twilight. Even the cicadas were quiet. Between the heat and the stick and the haze, the night sucked at Ed's skin, pulling at him hungrily, like it could peel the flesh from his bones.

Could just hang it up and go on back home, he thought. *Maybe catch a rerun of M*A*S*H*. But a few minutes of discomfort was no match against forty years of routine, and so he continued on into the thick, hungry dark.

The beam of Ed's flashlight skittered through slim pines and midnight mist as he walked. A sharp crack sounded, the snapping of a tree branch, and something dense and low to the ground scurried across his line of vision. Ed stopped short, palm sliding to the revolver holstered on his hip, pulling loose the leather strap. Whatever had moved obscured itself in the layers of shadow near the small barn at the edge of his property. He squinted into the darkness, tried to make out a shape or catch the gleam of nocturnal eyes, but Ed's vision was almost as bad as his memory. Animals he didn't pay much mind. Cats or raccoons, maybe even a coyo—

Crack.

The branch hit the ground, somewhere off where it was too dark to see, and the flutter of wings taking flight beat against Ed's eardrums. Shadows blurred in another rush of movement and the toe of his boot stumbled forward. For a split second, he thought he'd seen something shuffle in the dim—a pair of men's feet?—and his heart stuttered in his chest. He had half a second to register the image, but then he blinked, and when he looked again, it was gone.

An owl hooted somewhere in the distance, and Ed's heart flipped again.

Memory's going and now your mind's playing tricks on you, he chided himself. *Better not tell anybody you thought you saw someone sneaking 'round in the dark. They'll haul you off. "There goes old Edwin Boone, crazier than a sack of frogs in a thunderstorm."*

Ed swung his light over the barn in a final inspection. Nothing. His hands fell away from the holster, and he tongued at the toothpick between his lips, letting air slip out between his teeth to ease the pressure building in his chest.

A stinging sensation prickled on his arm. Ed slapped at the tickle of tiny insect legs, then held the light over the spot, but the smear of red insect blood he expected wasn't there. Instead, a faint buzzing in his ear, followed by another prick beneath the brim of his hat. Ed clamped a hand on the back of his neck, rolling his fingers to feel for the bug. This time he got the little nugget.

"Damn mosquitos," he muttered. "Hasn't even been any rain goin' on three weeks, but they're still out, eatin'—"

His words fell off as he studied the body in his palm. Black and gray, striped thorax, bright red eyes. Unease rose in Ed's throat. Flesh flies didn't typically bite living things but preferred to feast and lay their eggs on the dead. Didn't make a lick of sense to find one crawling up his arm. He wiped the insect on his pantleg and made a mental note to check in the morning for expired critters. Maybe a coyote had dragged in a kill, and that's what had the raccoons in a frenzy, taking their spoils up into the trees.

Wouldn't be the first time, he considered. This was the country, after all, and didn't any place know the cycle of life better than farmlands on the edge of nowhere.

Ed lifted his boot but didn't get it down before a thud from behind startled him back to stillness. Then came the sound of tussling, followed by the high, pinched scream of a dying animal. He spun on his heels, facing back in the direction of the barn, his eyes darting to where he'd seen the shadow slip into the dim overhangs of the small structure.

Ain't no damn raccoon. He aimed his light at the building, jerked the gun free, held the barrel at eye level. Even with the cataracts, Ed was a dead shot, but a shiver escaped down his spine nonetheless, tingling all the way to his toes.

"You're trespassing on private property," he called out into the dark. "Come on out from behind the barn. Let me get a look at you."

When nobody emerged, Ed inched forward. The heels of his boots thundered on the grass beneath his feet. The night felt too quiet, too still. Every sound pulsed in the dark. Sticky sweat beaded along his upper lip, and Ed resisted the urge to pull the handkerchief from his back pocket and dab it dry.

"This is private property, and I am within my rights to shoot you on sight," he called. "Don't make me have to tell you again. Come on out from behind the barn."

A form peeled itself from the shadows. Drew itself up from the ground. Crept into the strips of thin gray haze.

Ed made out a head, shoulders, two arms. Not an animal, this thing walked on two feet. Upright. A man slugged forth, arms outstretched as if pulling his body along with them. One ankle dragged on the ground, the foot twisted at an unnatural angle where it slid immobile behind the leg.

Cold rushed through Ed, freezing the tips of his fingers where they grasped the grip of his gun. A bead of sweat dripped onto his lip. He swallowed salt.

"That's close enough, buddy," Ed warned, when the man was no more than twenty feet away. He could smell the stench of wet earth and something else. Something foul.

"Ed," rasped the man. He ambled forth, still dragging one foot at the ankle.

Only one man said his name like that, drawing the lone syllable out into two, and the sound of it cut through the panic swelling in his belly. Ed lowered the revolver. He'd last seen his neighbor Clyde Halloran at church this past Wednesday, helping himself to a nice chunk of brisket from some fundraiser put on by the Symphony League of Southeast Texas. He'd thought then Clyde looked a little green around the edges, but that was about as good as one might expect for a man a day older than God—and drunker than Cooter Brown.

"Clyde, you damn near scared the piss out of me."

The older man shuffled forward with stilted, uneven steps. He was now fifteen feet away, the sound of Ed's name squelching into the muggy midnight air like soft cheese forced between splintered teeth.

Ed lifted his light to see the old timer's face and bit back a surge of vomit. The sick sheen he'd seen four days ago did not compare to the way Clyde looked now. His cheeks bloomed in ruddy patches against pale, clammy, shriveled flesh, smudged with dirt and dried blood. Sightless eyes bulged from their sockets, and crooked chips of teeth jagged downward between parted lips wet with fresh red. An ugly wound gaped in the side of Clyde's neck, the surrounding flesh black from blood drain.

What in God's name? Ed's lips fumbled for words, making and then dropping sounds before they could push their way off his tongue. The coldness he'd felt before hardened around him, freezing him in place.

Clyde kept moving. Dragging.

Ten feet.

Ed's vision tunneled around the figure that had once belonged to his neighbor. To his friend. He recognized the odor Clyde carried now—he had smelled it before, back when he'd been a boy working on his daddy's cattle farm. Back when he'd buried men who had died on the other side of the world. This was the smell of dead things, of blood and body fluids mixed together and left to rot in the sweltering Texas hot.

Eight feet.

"Clyde, stop!" Ed tried to take a step back, but the heat-brittled ground caved in under his boot and the heel stuck. "For cryin' out loud—*stop*."

For a blink the Clyde-thing stalled, almost as if it recognized something in Ed's words, but then it ambled forward, faster now, closing the distance between them.

Ed lifted his gun, cocked the hammer with his thumb. His hand shook, but his voice knew better. "Stop, damn you."

Five feet.

He aimed at Clyde's center of mass, his hand shaking so bad his long shirtsleeve shivered. *God forgive me*, Ed thought, and pulled the trigger.

Four feet away, the thing that had once been his neighbor—his *friend*—stumbled backward as the round caught in its chest, but then fury coated the creature's eyes and it pitched forward, tackling Ed to the ground. They thrashed about, the gape-mouthed, monstrous thing strong and unyielding even though maggots wriggled where the metal had ripped open mottled flesh. Ed had time to think, *How can a dead man be so strong?* before teeth clamped into his neck.

A dozen unformed thoughts floated through Ed's mind as the Clyde-thing ate out his life—raccoons, obituaries piled on his bedside table, Darlene—and then he lay in the creature's arms, stared up at the moon-full, midnight sky, and died.

CHAPTER 1

Snow Leger, August 1999

The body resting in the coffin at the front of the empty chapel had once belonged to Mina Jean Murphy, aged fifty-five years and seven months. Wife to Burton and mother to Clarice, Reagan, and Jeb, Mina Jean was the founding member of her neighborhood's Red Hat Society. She had been the kind of woman other women gossiped about behind her back—mostly because they were jealous and didn't have much else to talk about, and not because Mina Jean had ever done anything more scandalous than tip the tart at Marble Slab Creamery ten percent instead of twelve. She'd possessed both the nicest car and the prettiest lawn in all the West End side of town, as well as a husband who dutifully handed over his checkbook but otherwise kept to himself.

Unfortunately, Mina Jean had also had an aggressive smoking habit. She'd sneaked her first L&M cigarette from her mother's purse as a girl of sixteen, and all the chilled ambrosia salad and lean fish in the world couldn't combat the cancer that had started growing in her lungs with that first inhale. Neither had the efforts of the pricey pulmonologist she'd been seeing in the city who couldn't make heads or tails of her condition. The result of this was that Mina Jean had ended up having her hair teased around her head on a coffin pillow at Evans Funeral Parlor on Monday morning rather than brunching at the Symphony League of Southeast Texas's ladies' luncheon, as had been printed in her itinerary.

Snow Leger had tended Mina Jean's hair for decades, and today was their final appointment. Ladies of a certain age, Snow's clients had a habit of passing away with shocking regularity. Styling dead women's hair had bothered Snow once, but she'd learned families found it easier to grieve when they recognized the body in the casket. Ensuring her clients went to their eternal resting place with their hair done up properly gave everyone a measure of comfort, Snow included.

She lifted Mina Jean's silvery-blond bangs with her comb, then held the hair in place while she doused it with hairspray. Mina Jean had been one of her chattier clients. So far, Snow had bitten back her usual questions of *How are the kids?* and *What's old Burton been getting up to?* no less than thirteen times.

Thirteen is such an unlucky number, Snow thought. *But then I guess any number can be unlucky.*

Poor Mina Jean died at only fifty-five. Snow was already forty-eight herself.

She smoothed a stray strand of wiry blond back into place and gave it another spritz, keeping the back of her warm, living hand from touching Mina Jean's cool, dead forehead. Snow had never gotten accustomed to the way the dead felt. Frankly, she didn't care to.

"Well, Mina Jean, dear, it's almost time for your last party," she said, plucking a piece of fuzz from the dead woman's bright paisley burial dress and adjusting the set of the brooch on her chest. "All that's left to do is get your face on."

Aside from hair, everything from the moment the body was brought in from the morgue until it was covered up with earth was conducted in-house at Evans Funeral Parlor by the family's elderly matriarch, Ducey Evans; her daughter, Lenore, only a few years Snow's senior; or Lenore's daughter, Grace, born right after they swore in JFK. It had been that way so long even Snow, who knew almost as much about everything going on in the county as had Mina Jean Murphy, couldn't remember it ever being any different. Ducey's mother had once run the parlor, but Pie Evans had passed so long ago that even Mina Jean hadn't had any good gossip to hand down. The Evanses' business was a generational one, passed from daughter to daughter.

"You've done up Mina Jean real nice, Snow." Ducey Evans gave Snow's shoulder a reassuring pat as she settled into a chair beside the casket stand, short curls damp against her cheeks. The aging matriarch popped a butterscotch candy between her lips with an audible *pop*, then pulled her bifocals from the bridge of her nose and tucked them into the front pocket of her blouse. "She always liked her bangs teased up like that, ever since she was a girl. Poor thing spent her entire life tryin' to grow into her hair."

Snow considered the ample height of Mina Jean's bangs. "I made them extra poufy on account of the special occasion," she said. Another stray hair had sprung loose, and Snow sealed it back down with a generous douse of hairspray. "Let me see how you're settin' up, Ducey, dear."

She set her comb and the Aquafina canister down on the pew beside her beauty kit, then tugged on a pair of pink nitrile gloves as she shifted to stand behind Ducey's chair. Snow checked the instructions on the pink and gray Fanci-Full Color Rinse bottle, glancing at the pendulum clock anchored on the chapel's back wall.

"Oh, I'm sure it's fine," Ducey said, the words wet around the hard candy in her mouth. "Not much you can do to ruin hair when you're my age."

"Well, we don't want it coming out blue," Snow teased, "unless that's what you'd prefer. And if that's the case, I'm sure I've got something better than a rinse."

The old woman flapped her wrist in dismissal, but Snow knew better. Ducey Evans might have worn a baker's apron stained with Lord-knew-what the same way people wore a lucky shirt, but she was still a woman who looked after herself.

Lenore Evans stepped into the room, her arms laden down with a spray of lilacs, lavender cremones, and a single white rose. "Mama's hair used to be so black it was almost blue—"

Ducey jabbed an arthritic finger toward the ceiling. "Raven black."

"Daddy's, too," Lenore went on, as if she hadn't heard her mother. She laid the flowers on top of the organ near the casket and fingered the edges of her cropped ginger bob. "He used to tease that I got my auburn hair from the milkman."

Coming in behind her mother, Grace, the third member of the Evans family, carried a bunch of spotted lilies and a red vanity case of mortician's makeup. She set the flowers near the spray and the case on an empty pew, watching Lenore tuck and pinch the blooms that had crumpled during transport. Once the spray was appropriately primped, Lenore stepped aside and Grace rolled up her denim shirtsleeves, then wrapped the funeral bouquet in a ribbon the same purple hue as the dead woman's dress.

Ducey set her glasses back into place as she watched the younger Evans women work. "Royce was always fussy about his hair," she said, turning over the candy in her mouth with her tongue as she spoke. "Man took better care of his hair than most women I ever knew, always combin' and conditioning. When he started to go gray, he took to colorin' it—never could stand the look of it otherwise, no matter how thin his hair got." She chuckled. "He kept what little he had left as black as shoe polish 'til the day he died."

Snow laughed, patting Ducey's shoulder before she stepped away to finish packing her things. Grace set the flowers aside and moved to take her place over Mina Jean, vanity in tow.

"I remember that," Grace said as she clicked the case open. "In fact, I remember coming in one day and finding Papa Royce in the kitchen, reading the newspaper and wearing nothing but a robe and slippers and a Lady Clairol processing cap. He was so embarrassed." She smiled at the memory. "Started hollering for Ducey and trying to scurry out of the kitchen before the image could stick in my memory, I guess."

"That was Daddy." A smile fixed itself on Lenore's face as she teased the petals of the white rose into place. "Of course, your daddy never had any hair to worry about," she told Grace. "Jimmy came out of the womb bald and left the world the same way. Never bothered to grow hair in the years between."

"Never bothered to grow much of anything but a big beer gut and those pretty weeds outside," Ducey grumbled, nodding at the white rose still clutched in her daughter's hand as Snow towel-dried her hair. "But he was a good man."

Lenore cut her eyes at her mother as she stalked to the clock on the chapel's back wall, pushed the key from her pocket into the keyhole, and cranked even though the weights were already tight.

"We've known some good men," Grace inserted, rustling through her vanity case. She arranged cosmetic compacts and tubes, thick-bristled brushes, a pair of scissors, and foam sponges on a cloth next to Mina Jean's obituary photo. "Papa Royce, and Daddy," she said, "and . . ."

Her voice trailed off and Snow tightened her lips into a reassuring smile. The man who'd given Grace Evans a daughter hadn't stuck around long enough to be a father, so the list was short. What had that fella's name been? Stephen? Simon? It was just on the tip of her tongue, something with an S—

"When Jimmy died, I thought for sure you girls would sell this place," Snow said, observing Grace as she held each of her tubes and powders up to the dead woman's face, carefully selecting the right colors to match Mina Jean's complexion. "I can't imagine how much work it must be for the three of you, handling everything you do."

The first butterscotch finished, Ducey popped another hard candy in her mouth and stood, pushing her vacated chair back to its place against the wall. "What else would we do, sit at home and play canasta?" She shook her head and shoved her glasses up the bridge of her nose. "I've got better things to do than sit around and rot 'til somebody puts me in the ground."

"Now, don't go getting yourself worked up, Mama," Lenore warned. "You remember what Dr. Hicks said about your blood pressure." She thumbed the clock key back into her slacks pocket, eyeing a butterscotch candy wrapper that had fallen on the floor. "*And* about all that darn candy."

Ducey wagged her index finger. "Don't sass me, Miss Priss. I'm eighty years old—I've earned the right to say what I mean to say."

"And the candy?"

The old woman gave her daughter a hard look and pursed her lips. "Well, I reckon I've earned them, too."

Lenore bent and snatched the offensive candy wrapper from the carpet. She waved the cellophane at her mother, then balled it up in a piece of tissue and stuffed it into her other pocket without remark.

Snow put her palms up. "I don't mean any offense. I'm just saying, it's a little funny, isn't it—a bunch of women running a funeral parlor? If it were me, I'd turn this place into something more . . . uplifting. Maybe a nice little boutique."

Ducey's tongue clicked against her dentures. Her green eyes fizzed like poison, but Lenore's warning about her blood pressure had struck a chord and so she kept quiet.

"Oh, I don't think it's that strange at all, really," Lenore told Snow, her voice cool. "We Evans women like to think of ourselves as caretakers. Making sure the people of this community are laid to rest well taken care of is our way of showing gratitude. Everyone deserves that kind of care and dignity, and so that's what we do—what Evans women have always done."

Grace nodded in agreement as she worked on the dead woman's face. Ducey made a *harrumph*ing noise but didn't disagree.

"I'd never thought of it like that," Snow admitted. She watched as Grace applied a pencil to Mina Jean's eyebrows, filling them in just the way the woman would have done. "I'd always thought it a very manly business, what with all the embalming and messy things you must have to do." She thought of body fluids—blood and guts and organs on tables—and shuddered.

"Oh, it's actually very feminine," Grace mused. "A funeral parlor isn't all that different from a beauty salon—hair, makeup, a new outfit, a little pampering." She flicked the tip of a mascara wand against Mina Jean's lashes, pulling the skin at the corners of her eyes tight so the liquid didn't smear. "Besides, think of all the things we put ourselves through on a normal basis to feel pretty and presentable. It really isn't all that different once we've passed on; we just need a little extra help, is all."

"Especially the way we do things here." Lenore stepped up beside her daughter in front of the casket, a faint smile quirking at the corners of her lips. "We take our time, do things naturally and respectfully, and avoid embalming or disturbing our clients' bodies. No sense in any of that. We simply make them look their best so their loved ones can say goodbye, and then we lay them to rest."

Grace lifted a tube of lipstick from her tray, popped off the cap, and twisted the cylinder to expose a stick the same smoky red as Snow's new manicure.

Lenore slapped at her daughter's hand. "Oh, don't you dare, Grace Ann! Mina Jean never would have worn that shade."

"She always complimented me when I wore it. Besides, it's so fashionable." Grace nodded in Snow's direction. "Look, Mama, Snow's nails are painted a similar color."

Snow lifted her hand as proof, admiring the deep shine of her manicured fingernails in the chapel's low light. The dusty shade had become a hit since some model wore it on the runway, or so she'd heard. "Chanel *Vamp*," she said. "Though I wish they'd named it something more alluring, maybe *Merlot* since it's such a nice burgundy."

Ducey adjusted her glasses. "They ought to call it what it is—*oxblood*," she said. "Used to be a dye. They'd use animal blood to color fabric, leather, paint. Went on bright red and turned brown as it oxidized."

Lenore wrinkled her nose and clamped her hands against her hips. She considered the lipstick Grace still held beside the dead woman's lips. "It looks like someone ran a black marker over red polish."

"Oh, leave it alone, Len," Ducey said. "Mina Jean liked a good drama. She'd love to know she left people with their chins waggin'—it'd give her a good laugh."

Snow watched Grace trace Mina Jean's lips in bright red liner, fill in the lipstick, dust with setting powder. More stray strands of hair fluttered around in the air above the woman's face.

"My goodness," Snow muttered, reaching for her hairspray again. "I've never seen hair fly away with so much spray in it, not even during a hurricane."

Grace and Lenore had stepped aside and were too busy listening to Ducey to pay Snow any mind as she inched back toward the open casket.

"Put me in pink lipstick or blue hair if you want when I go," the old woman was saying, "but bury me with my brassiere on and I'll haunt you."

"*Oh.*" Snow had moved away to work from a distance. This close, the view was . . . different. She stalled, her hand rising to flatten against her bosom. Her heart stuttered under her palm, restarted.

"What's wrong?" Lenore's voice sounded far away.

Snow could feel the weight of the Evans women's gazes on the back of her neck. "Nothing, I just thought . . ."

She tugged at her earlobe. She couldn't bring herself to say that she'd thought she'd seen Mina Jean stir. How foolish would she sound? Dead bodies didn't move. Their hair didn't flutter.

It must have been a trick of the light is all, she told herself. The casket's feet faced the chapel exit, the crisp morning light playing over Mina Jean's features through the parlor's stained glass windows.

"Everythin' all right, Snow?" Ducey's family formed a semicircle at Snow's back.

A lump had risen in Snow's throat and she swallowed it down. "I'm just amazed at how . . . alive she looks. If I didn't know any better, I'd think Mina Jean had just laid down for a little catnap, is all."

Grace's face darkened, then she blinked into a smile and beamed at Lenore. "I do good work, don't I, Mama?"

"Yes, you do," Lenore said.

Snow attempted a smile. *All this talk about taking care of the dead has you spooked, you silly cow*, she thought. Yet, when she looked back down at the body in the casket, she could swear she saw the dead woman's left eye twitch. Swear she saw Mina Jean's chest rise as if the woman took a breath.

Snow nearly jumped out of her skin when Lenore's hand touched her arm. She almost screamed when the bell on the front door chimed.

"Why don't we go on up front and get your check?" Lenore's bone-thin fingers steered Snow away from the casket. "And I'm sure you need to be getting on to your next appointment. It's a lovely day outside."

"O-okay." Once she'd taken a few steps toward the parlor's entrance, Snow's heart seemed to beat normally again, her pulse no longer hammering inside her ears. "I'll see y'all later."

Ducey and Grace stood side by side between Snow and the casket, obstructing her view. They waved her off with lazy wrists and friendly smiles.

"You take care now, Snow," they said.

At the threshold, Snow cast one final look over her shoulder. It was just a body in the casket at the front of the chapel, nothing more. Just Mina Jean Murphy, rest her soul. Her eyelids didn't flutter. Her chest didn't rise. The poor dear was as dead as they got.

CHAPTER 2

Lenore Evans

Deputy Roger Taylor stood in the lobby of Evans Funeral Parlor, wringing his mudpie-brown uniform hat and looking about as comfortable as a turkey one week before Thanksgiving when Lenore arrived in the lobby with the beautician. She sighed and forced on a smile.

"Be right with you, Roger," Lenore said as she ushered Snow to the front desk.

Roger's voice was thin. "Take your time, ma'am." The deputy gave Snow a small nod, but she didn't return the greeting.

Lenore handed the younger woman a check from the blotter on the desk, taking note of the line of sweat beaded along her upper lip. Her skin had faded to the color of meringue and her eyes had gone glassy. "Are you okay, Snow, honey?" Lenore asked. "You look like you've seen a ghost."

Snow snapped blue-shadowed eyelids open wide. "I don't know. I just . . ." She shoved the check into her jeans pocket and shook her head. Her cheeks flushed as red as her fingernails. "I must be tired, is all. Allergies."

"Ragweed pollen is terrible this year." Lenore did her best to sound polite. "Why don't you go on home and get yourself a cold compress? Put something on the television and rest. You'll feel good as new in no time, and I'll call and check on you later."

"All right." Snow's voice was as thin now as Roger's had been. "I think that's a good idea."

Lenore ushered the younger woman out the double front doors, then stood inside the doorway, holding the doors open as Snow walked down the sidewalk toward her powder-blue coupe. Roger's reflection waited in the glass beside Lenore's, the two watching as Snow packed her beauty supplies in the trunk, then situated herself behind the steering wheel, shut the driver's side door, and pulled the seatbelt across her chest. When the little car's ignition roared to life, Lenore let out the breath she'd been holding and allowed the entry doors to fall closed. There'd been a strange feeling in the pit of her stomach when she woke up this morning—something not quite right, though she couldn't put her finger on it. Now the late-morning air felt dense, the same way it did before a thunderstorm rolled in, even though the day was just as hot and sunny as it always was this time of year. Hotter, actually.

Too hot.

"Hot summers bring cold winters," Lenore mused aloud, fanning at herself. "If this season's any indication, we might have snow come Christmas. Hopefully nothing like that ice storm a couple of years back." She remembered the Great Freeze of '97. The cold, the trees. Her rosebush had barely survived, the bright white blooms paling to a frosty gray.

Thank heavens. If her rosebush had died . . . Lenore stiffened. It hadn't, and there was no sense worrying over it otherwise.

Roger cleared his throat behind her. "Yes, ma'am."

Lenore watched in the door's reflection as the deputy's knuckles turned white where he clutched at his hat. There was something thin about the man this morning, but it wasn't just his voice—or his waistline, which she'd noticed had diminished in small increments over the past several weeks. He turned and peered through the open chapel door to where Ducey and Grace still tended to Mina Jean.

Most people look better when they're in love, Lenore thought, but Roger Taylor had been lovesick for so long the emotion had taken a toll on him. The man was the bravest deputy the sheriff's department had—more than enough to be sheriff, if that old coot Buck Johnson would give up and retire—but the poor thing had never quite summoned up the courage to ask Grace out.

Of course, neither had any other man in town. Not that Grace would have agreed anyway. Her hands were too full taking care of her daughter, Luna.

Roger's reflection went stiff. One hand uncoiled from the brim of his hat to jerk in an awkward wave—swiping once left, once right. Grace must have caught him looking.

Lenore turned her gaze to the blue coupe outside. Snow didn't look back as she took a left out of the funeral parlor's parking lot and drove away. Only one other vehicle remained in the front guest lot, and it wasn't a sheriff's department Crown Victoria. A nondescript white minivan with the word CORONER emblazed in large black letters on the hood sat running in the spot reserved for incoming deliveries.

Lenore's lip twisted. "Nobody called to let me know we'd have another body coming in today."

"Bit of a special circumstance. Thought I'd drive this one over myself." Roger shifted his weight and trained his eyes on the tasteful beige carpet at his feet. Thirty years on the force and even in the roughest moments, the deputy's bedside manner still beat Sheriff Johnson's. That man had been born with a heart full of holes.

"Everything all right?" A bead of perspiration trickled through the little hairs on the back of Lenore's neck, and she swept back to her desk, busying her hands with putting away her ledger so she didn't wipe at the sweat. People expected funeral directors to be calm, cool, and collected at all times, and Lenore prided herself on upholding that standard. Besides, she was no flighty bird like Snow Leger.

She was an Evans—even if she was sweating her hairspray out at half past ten in the morning.

"Well, as right as it can be, considering," Roger said, his fingers playing along the brim of his hat, still clutched in his hands. He nodded at the van outside. "Afraid there was an incident last night. The body's . . . well . . . not in the usual shape."

Shape? As far as Lenore was concerned, all bodies had the same general form—a head, a torso, two legs, and two arms. Not all pieces made it to the grave all the time, but they did more often than not, and the few exceptions, well . . . Lenore angled herself so she could see the chapel over Roger's shoulder. Ducey shot her a questioning look and Lenore shook her head at her mother. She had everything under control.

The clock key pulled heavy in Lenore's pocket as she cleared her throat. "Car accident?" she asked.

Roger cleared his. "Not exactly."

"Suicide?"

"No, ma'am."

Silence choked the air and Lenore bristled. "Making a lady guess isn't very gentlemanlike, Deputy Taylor."

Roger cleared his throat again. "I'm sorry, Lenore," he said. "I just haven't quite figured out how to prepare you for what you're about to see."

Lenore screwed on a prim smile. "I've been in this business for a long time, Deputy, and I promise it's not as pretty as you think. I don't think there's anything I haven't seen yet."

"This one's . . . unique," the deputy insisted. "Looks like some kind of animal attack, but the coroner's never seen bite marks like this."

Something in Lenore's gut curled at the mention of bite marks. She thought of limbs, unattached. Skin, loose and sagging. *Thin.*

"Body's torn up. Most of the throat's gone," Roger went on. "There's a lot of blood loss—Quigg thinks that's what killed him, even with the wounds." His recital of the details complete, the deputy's eyes made a quick dash to his boots. "Could be we've got a rabid animal on the loose, but animal control hasn't gotten any calls."

The strange, looming sensation Lenore had felt all morning closed in around her, sucking the breathable air from the room. She hadn't wanted to consider it when she'd seen the color drain from Snow's face, but if what Roger was saying was true, then it wasn't a ghost the poor woman had seen in Mina Jean's casket. The very fact they'd *found* a body in such bad shape that the good deputy had seen fit to deliver it himself meant that Godawful Mess had already started.

Again.

Lenore straightened her posture, raised an eyebrow, and digested the man's words with an imperious swallow. "You're saying this just happened last night?"

"Best we can tell. Time of death right about midnight."

"And Quigg has already released the body?" Lenore glanced at the clock on the wall above her desk and felt the second hand tick under her skin. The old coroner was the sort who took the long way around a shortcut, sometimes twice. To have brought the body in and signed off on it so quickly was highly unusual.

The body's not in the usual shape, Roger had said. "Yes, ma'am."

Lenore bit back a sigh. In this case, unusual might well be a close cousin to lucky. "Quigg didn't want to do an autopsy?"

Roger's eye twitched. Sweat stained the collar of his white undershirt. "No family to ask for one."

"If there's no family to arrange a service, and the coroner's office has already signed off, we cremate the body within forty-eight hours," she reminded the deputy. "Often twenty-four."

"That's fine," he said, twisting his hat. "I don't expect you'll want to hold onto this one any longer than is necessary anyhow."

"Who is it?" Lenore held her breath and waited for the name.

"Edwin Boone."

Lenore's knees rattled under her, and she grasped the edge of the desk to keep steady. Like Mina Jean Murphy, she'd known Edwin Boone since grade school—nearly fifty years. He'd been sweet on her, but she'd fallen head over heels for Jimmy Stewart and he'd married Darlene Newcastle. The last time Lenore had seen Edwin was at Darlene's funeral four, maybe five years before. Lenore had given him a hug and her phone number, but Ed hadn't called. There hadn't been any reason to.

"We found him out near his property line on Farm Road 121," Roger said. "Had his gun in his hand, looks like he even got a shot off—there was an empty casing in the cylinder. But if he hit something, we haven't found it yet." The deputy raked a hand through sweat-matted brown hair, laughed at something that wasn't funny. "I never saw Ed Boone miss a shot in my life, not even with his eyes closed. He put a .357 Magnum round in something, and whatever it was kept going."

Hand still in his hair, the deputy flicked his gaze to Lenore. "That sound like a rabid animal to you?"

"I'm afraid I wouldn't know." Farm Road 121. Lenore tried to think of who else had homesteads out on the fringe of town, but her thoughts were cloudy and unfocused, like a jigsaw puzzle dropped on the floor.

The coroner's never seen bite marks like this.

Could be we've got a rabid animal on the loose.

Are you okay, Snow, honey? You look like you've seen a ghost.

The wooden cracks of stiff limbs splintered over Roger Taylor's shoulder. Lenore kept her eyes locked on the deputy, holding his gaze so he wouldn't turn to see hands claw upward into the air in the room behind him, see nails bite into skin as the dead woman tore at her own jaw. Faint squelching noises echoed across the open space. The sickening split of cartilage. The snap of bone tearing loose from flesh. Red poured over purple, the remains of artfully applied lipstick lost as, in the chapel across the hall, Mina Jean Murphy sat up in her casket.

CHAPTER 3

Luna Evans

Even though she was technically still going steady with Andy West, Luna Evans couldn't help but smile whenever she saw Crane Campbell. She'd been dating Andy ever since he broke up with Amelia Jordan last spring, but lately, Luna had noticed Alison Haney looking at her boyfriend like she was next in line. This would have bothered Luna a lot more two weeks ago.

But that was before Crane moved to town, Luna thought.

Crane wasn't nearly as handsome as Andy. The new boy had a narrow, Disney-villain mouth and his greasy black hair hung to his shoulders, but he spoke like a poet, and whenever he looked at Luna, she felt like she was the only girl in the world. When Luna and Andy had first started dating, Andy would sneak out to tap on her bedroom window, either late at night after her mom went to bed or early in the morning before his paper route. Now, she couldn't even remember the last time he'd tapped on her darkened windowpane, or she on his—at least not since before his mom made him start volunteering at the Symphony League, which coincidentally was where he'd gotten cozy with Alison, a debutante.

So much for stealing late-night kisses like in the movies. Luna's mom had installed the security alarm on her bedroom window for nothing.

Andy had once told Luna she was his forever, but apparently forever wasn't quite as long as she'd thought. Wouldn't even last until her sixteenth birthday just a couple of months away. If she made it 'til then, anyway. Exactly how many nights could a teenage girl go without sleep? Bad dreams were one thing, but over the past several weeks, Luna's nightmares had descended to a new low. Blood, teeth, shadows. Nasty stuff worse than any horror movie she'd ever seen. The memory of the dreams waited behind her eyelids and made her shiver with each blink. They haunted her even now, in the safe bright glare of midafternoon.

In any case, Luna wasn't worried about forever, and Crane Campbell didn't seem too bothered about cutting out of school early. So, when Luna saw him ditch algebra, she'd grabbed her backpack and followed him to the mall.

There weren't a lot of shoppers out at this time of day. Outside of Luna and Crane, the place was mostly empty, save for a few young moms pushing baby strollers and the old people who got their daily exercise walking laps up and down the long, air-conditioned corridors. The foam soles of their orthopedic tennis shoes squeaked in time with the elevator Muzak pumping at low volume through the PA system. The sound grated on Luna's nerves as she shadowed Crane through the music store, around the food court, and down the aisles of a small, badly lit shop that sold band T-shirts and trinketry emblazoned with marijuana leaves.

Don't let him see you. He'll think you're a stalker or something. Luna adjusted her pace and fell back, pretending to be interested in an ugly FIMO clay incense dispenser.

In Books-A-Million, Luna watched as Crane slunk through fiction and memoir, then hovered like a forlorn spirit in the occult section. The selection was meager, with more shelf space allocated to religious texts and self-help manifestos—both better sellers in the conservative South. What few books did exist in the occult section were mostly glossy paperbacks on New Age spiritualism, a selection of titles penned by authors with names like Marina Medici and Silver RavenWolf.

Crane thumbed through a few pages of a bulky, hardcover text—*The Writings of Aleister Crowley*—then set it aside in favor of a slender paperback volume with a stark black cover. He tucked the book inside his trench coat pocket, smoothly, as if it had been there all along. When he appeared to be heading toward the bookstore exit that led out of the mall, Luna took a shortcut through the magazines and beat him outside.

Be cool. Luna positioned herself just beyond a blue metal trash can, leaned against the brick wall until heat sizzled her back, and crossed her arms over her chest. Her backpack was too heavy, and she tossed it to the ground, then picked it back up and hung it off one shoulder. She scraped at the corner of her lips.

Just when she thought Crane must have changed direction and headed back into the mall's interior, his tall, lanky form slid through the bookstore doors and out into the midday sun. He shielded his eyes with one ringed hand and stared in Luna's direction.

Her heart squirmed up into her throat. Beat in her neck. She licked her lips and tasted peaches—the aftertaste of her lip gloss. Luna didn't like peaches, but Andy did.

Crane took a step closer, his combat boots thudding on the concrete. Scents of patchouli incense and tobacco smoke pulsed off his all-black clothes, swirling around him like small planets stuck in orbit. Luna sank into his gravity.

"Hey." Crane's voice rumbled in a rich, deep baritone. "You got a cigarette?"

Did she? No, of course, she didn't. "No, sorry."

"Doesn't matter." Crane reached into the trash can's ashtray crown and plucked a butt from the ashes with long, spindly fingers tipped in black polish.

Luna watched, mesmerized, as he put the butt between his lips and lit the end with a lighter from his pocket. She'd never seen a guy wear so many rings in real life. She stuffed her hands in her jeans. Why hadn't she thought to paint her nails black? She'd have to buy a bottle of polish at Claire's.

Crane took a puff of the foraged cigarette and exhaled smoke. "You're Luna, right?" he asked. "We have algebra together."

"Yeah. Luna Evans." She swallowed her pulse and tried not to feel stupid for introducing herself like they were in the third grade. "You're new here, right? From Colorado?"

Another puff. He nodded and took another step closer.

Rumor said Crane's real name was Robert, but nobody called him that except Mr. Tucker, the tenth-grade economics teacher who called everyone by whatever he thought their name was, even if he usually got it wrong. He'd called her *Lunar* twice so far. He'd also given her detention for correcting him. Today would be her second no-show. If Tucker couldn't bother to learn her name, then she couldn't be bothered to surrender what little free time she had—which, between school and her daily duties at her family's funeral parlor, was practically nonexistent.

Idle hands make the devil's work. Something she'd heard once. Maybe from Tucker, but more likely from Nana Lenore.

Still puffing, Crane drew so close Luna could see dirty-blond roots in his dark hair. His eyes were brown flecked with green. There was a tiny dimple in his left cheek. A scar on his right.

"Love kills," he said.

She blinked. "What?"

Crane stretched out one black-tipped finger and tapped the Sid Vicious button pinned to her backpack strap—*Love Kills.*

"Oh. Yeah." *Duh.*

"Sex Pistols are cool," he said. "For a punk band."

Luna shrugged, tried not to blush at how *sex* sounded on Crane's lips. She'd never actually listened to any of the Sex Pistols' albums, but the tragic romance between the band's bassist and his girlfriend was cooler than *Romeo and Juliet*, and Hot Topic didn't sell Shakespeare buttons anyway. She'd bought the Sid and Nancy button when she'd seen it, along with a handful of others that looked cool and a Rainbow Brite one she actually liked. They'd been four for a dollar fifty, affordable on her meager allowance.

Crane bit the cig between his teeth, speaking around it as he parted the folds of his black leather trench coat to reveal sweat-stained pits and a black Type O Negative band shirt faded gray by too many turns in the wash. "You should check these guys out. Peter Steele is a giant among men. Figuratively *and* literally. The man is almost seven feet tall, and he can sing—if you don't mind songs about death."

She didn't. Considering her family owned a funeral parlor, death was sort of a family business. Should she tell Crane that?

"Cool," she said instead. Maybe she'd pick up a Type O Negative CD when she got the nail polish. Her mom wouldn't approve of either, but that didn't matter to Luna any more than skipping school did to Crane. Then again, her mom wouldn't approve of Crane. Not by a long shot. Neither would Nana Lenore or Ducey. Her grandmothers practically interrogated poor Andy when they'd met him, and it wasn't long afterward that her mom had bumped her curfew up to sunset, bought Luna a pager to keep tabs on her, and put up that stupid window alarm system so she couldn't sneak out after dark. Her mother and grandmothers had treated her like a ticking puberty time bomb since her thirteenth birthday, but something about her first real boyfriend had sent her mom over the edge. Grace Evans's little girl was growing up, or whatever.

All that and Andy was harmless—like a puppy. A sweet, goofy puppy who had stopped leaving notes in her locker and kept insisting he felt too sick to talk on the phone. Maybe all her mom's rules had finally pushed him away, or maybe Alison Haney's big dumb debutante doe eyes had finally pulled him in.

Luna struggled for something to say while Crane smoked, settling on, "So, why'd you leave Colorado and move to this dump? This town is super boring. Nothing exciting ever happens here."

"Didn't want to." Another puff. "Had to because of Columbine."

Luna's eyebrows twisted. Four months ago, two boys had opened fire in their high school, then turned their guns on themselves. "Because of the shooting?"

Crane nodded, his facial features puckering around his inhale.

"Did you go to that school?"

His expression darkened. "No, but that doesn't matter. I was driven out just the same. Persecuted. People thought I was part of the 'Trench Coat Mafia.'" He lifted his hands to form air quotes, lips sucking in air around the cig. "And a Satanist."

Luna had not considered either. She surveyed his pale skin and painted black nails, wondered what else he had tucked into his jacket pockets besides a stolen book and a Bic lighter. Should she be scared? She wasn't.

"Are you?" she asked.

Crane's eyes studied her from between the greasy curtains of his hair. The ember of his cigarette sparked red-hot as he pulled at it. The silence between them swelled until it was hotter than the midday sun.

"To worship the devil implies one must first believe in God and Satan," he said. "I don't believe in, either. Therefore, I cannot be a Satanist."

He paused for another drag. Exhaled in a ring of smoke. "I'm Pagan."

"Oh." Luna was not entirely sure what Pagans believed in, though she assumed they must believe in something. She did know the term Wiccan, because she'd also skimmed the books in the Books-A-Million occult section, searching for books about dream meanings. If there were answers to the weird, frightening things she saw in her dreams, they'd be there. So far, though, zilch. "Is that like . . . a Wiccan—a witch?" she asked. "Or, a warlock, I guess, since you're a guy?"

"Not a warlock." Crane's voice was firm. Slick around the edges. "A warlock is an oath-breaker. A deceiver. Male Wiccans are called witches, too—it's gender-neutral. But I prefer the term 'ceremonial magician.'"

"Oh." Luna's cheeks were on fire. She definitely knew nothing about ceremonial magicians, whatever they were, and her ignorance felt a lot like stupidity. She diverted her gaze to the pavement at her feet, digging the toe of her Converse into a crack in the cement. "So, you, like, practice magic?"

God, he'll think you're such a loser, her inner voice moaned.

"*Magick*," Crane clarified, "with a *ck* at the end. And, in a manner of speaking, yes."

His words were accented with another flash of red-hot light that pulled Luna's eyes up from the pavement.

"Cool," she managed.

Crane gazed at her with new interest as he removed the cigarette from his lips and twisted the butt between his fingers. "I can tell you more sometime, if you're interested. I sense you could be a powerful witch, especially with a name like Luna."

"I don't know." Luna cringed and tried for flippant. "I don't think my name means anything, probably something my mom picked out of a name book. My middle name is Royce. It was my great-grandfather's name, but my nana says it's okay for girls, too."

The fire on her cheeks was in full blaze now. She wanted to melt into the crack in the sidewalk. *No way* she'd just said that.

Crane ignored her. "You do know who Luna is, don't you? She's a Roman goddess, the divine embodiment of the moon."

Luna felt the prickle of Crane's gaze as it swept from her head to her feet and back. She liked how he said Luna *is* the goddess of the moon, not *was* the goddess of the moon, although *divine embodiment* gave her pause when Crane's gaze passed over the soft pudge of her stomach. Thighs that couldn't pull off a pair of pleather pants to save her life.

"You look like a Luna," Crane said when his eyes met hers again. He winked, the corner of his mouth twitching into a half-smile.

Luna tried to pin the corner of her lips down but failed. Her whole body burned as red and hot as the tip of Crane's cigarette. "Thanks."

Before she could say anything else, a rusted hatchback blaring industrial rock squealed to a stop at the curb. The driver had dreads and looked too old to hang out with high schoolers. Crane jerked his head at the car, then looked back at Luna. He pulled one last drag from the butt, dropped it, and snuffed out the ember with the toe of his boot.

"Want a ride?"

Yes. "No, I've got to get back to school before seventh period," Luna said. "If I don't show up after school on the bus, my mom will kill me."

Just wait 'til she finds out I've been flirting with a "ceremonial magician."

Crane shrugged and pulled open the passenger door, letting loose a thick cloud of bitter-smelling smoke. "See you later, Moon Girl," he said, then slid into the car and shut the door behind him.

CHAPTER 4

Grace Evans

Grace Evans had just finished mopping the laboratory floor when the front door of Evans Funeral Parlor chimed open again. She wondered if the deputy had come back, but then school bus tires squealed in the distance as the driver let off the brakes and pulled away. The sound of Luna's footsteps propelling her down the hallway followed, and Grace dunked the filthy mop head into a bucket of soapy, pink water before her daughter reached the lab.

She breathed a sigh of relief. They'd cut it close. It had taken several hours to get things back in order after . . .

After Mina Jean.

Grace shuddered at the memory, still too fresh in her mind to be anything other than present, than *now*. She saw the dead woman rise out of the casket, eyes blank before she reached up, tore at her own jaw, and ripped out the stitches Ducey had sewn in to keep her mouth closed. Lenore had managed to distract the deputy with the details of delivering a new cadaver while Grace and Ducey took care of the dead woman, but Mina Jean's rising, followed by the arrival of Edwin Boone's mutilated corpse, marked the start of something that would only get worse before it got better.

A lot worse.

Grace had known something was wrong when Mina Jean's freshly sprayed hair had begun to flutter, though she hadn't been able to say anything with Snow in the room. By the time she'd gotten to the woman's lipstick, Mina's skin had grown so hot the stuff melted on her mouth. Legends always made one think the dead were cold when they came back, but they weren't. They were warm. Warm and soft and so very close to alive, which only made it more terrible—especially when the dead in question was someone you'd known.

Maybe even loved.

Herding the dead woman out of the chapel and into the sterile environment of the lab while she slurred Grace's name had been difficult enough. Plunging a pair of sewing scissors through the heart of the woman who'd been her classroom mom all through elementary school, distinctly horrifying. The act got easier, but never so much that it didn't still hurt. How would she face Clarice Murphy, her childhood friend, at tonight's visitation knowing she'd just skewered a trocar into her mother's chest? It didn't matter if Mina Jean was dead. She'd been upright when Grace stabbed metal through her heart.

"You know it wasn't Mina Jean," Ducey had reminded her. "It's not them, no matter how much we think it is, or how much we want it to be. They're long gone. This is just what's left."

Lenore had tensed at that, and Grace, too. Ducey was adamant that the soul didn't stick around after death, but she'd known dead that still carried life inside their eyes.

A fifteen-year-old memory flashed through Grace's mind, one in which she, Lenore, and Ducey were coated in a salty stew of tears and blood. The body of a man she'd loved more than anything in the world laid dead at her feet, her heart shattered beside him. Her mother had cried the death wail of a broken heart, and Ducey had covered her eyes. Luna, just a few months old and barely aware she'd just lost someone special, had been crying.

And it had all been Grace's fault. Love wasn't salvation for Evans women. It was a curse.

Grace fingered the scar carved into the top of her left wrist and pushed the memory away. The Godawful Mess of that night would not happen again, and the mistakes that had led to it—

Over my dead body, she thought, then shivered at the irony. If history repeated itself, she would probably not survive it a second time. Cats had nine lives, but people had one—two, if they had the bad fortune to rise again.

"Hey, Mom." Luna stepped into the room and dropped her backpack on the freshly scrubbed examination table. Her nose scrunched. The chemicals they'd used to clean up after Mina Jean were cloying, but the acrid stink of bleach was still better than the coppery tang of blood.

Grace scanned the room—had she missed a drop, overlooked an incriminating handprint? Seeing nothing, she faced her daughter. "Have a good day at school?" she asked.

Luna jerked the bag's zipper, the noise so uncomfortably like the sound of Mina Jean's mandible separating from her flesh that Grace's jaw ached. The girl pushed a strand of dark hair behind her ear but didn't look up. "Sure. Great," she said, nose still wrinkled. "Everything good here?"

Grace dunked the mop bucket into the closet, swished until bubbles rose and obscured the pink-tinged water, and shut the door. "Of course."

Why did she bother to lie? Why now, when the truth was so very close, scratching at the surface, desperate to show itself? *Because the truth never stays buried*, Grace thought. No, but perhaps she could delay it just a few minutes longer. "How'd you sleep last night?" she asked.

A groan. "*Fine*, Mom."

The skin of Luna's nose leveled back into place—a lie smoothed over, tucked inside the tangled, sweaty sheets Grace laundered from the girl's bedroom. Grace knew Luna couldn't sneak out at night through her window anymore, not since she'd installed the alarm and given her daughter one more reason to stay mad at her, but she couldn't guess what kind of monsters might come unbidden into her dreams.

"I'm just checking in, hun," Grace managed around the lump in her throat. "I worry about you. You've got circles under your eyes."

"It's hot on the bus. I sweat. Things smudge." Luna rubbed at her eyes as if to demonstrate. "And you don't have to 'check in' every day. I said I'd tell you if I couldn't sleep." She walked to the door joining the lab to the chapel, peeked through at the few floral displays and framed portraits stationed near the podium. "I thought Mrs. Murphy's visitation was today?"

"It is."

"Then why is the casket closed?" Luna's lips curled into a mocking grin as she lowered herself into a chair at the end of the counter and crossed her arms over her chest. "Did you mess up her makeup?"

Lenore's clipped tone breezed through the hallway door one step ahead of her. "Your mother did a lovely job with Mrs. Murphy," she said. "Don't be sassy, Luna, honey. It's not ladylike."

Luna sucked her teeth as Ducey came into the room next, a bright yellow coroner's tag clenched between her index and middle finger. She hung the tag on cooler number three, adjusted her bifocals, and cast a meaningful glance at Grace first, then Lenore.

We don't have long, the look said. There wasn't a timer on when the dead would rise, but in Grace's experience, the quicker the death, the sooner the return.

She put one palm over her stomach and clutched at her neck with the other, recalling the terrible wound she'd seen on Edwin Boone's throat. Roger had said a rabid animal might have gotten at Ed, escaped with a bullet hole big enough to take down a bear, but the Evans women knew better. Animal control hadn't caught anything because they weren't going to catch anything—at least nothing that would fit in their flimsy, chain-link holding area down at the county pound. Had Mina Jean's body come in as ruined as Ed's, they'd have been prepared. The fact that Mina Jean had risen unmarked while Edwin Boone's head had nearly been separated from its shoulders meant things were already escalating.

Someone else had taken a chunk out of the poor man's neck.

Someone else still out there, feeding.

Some*thing* else, Grace corrected. *Just what's left.*

She wiped her palms against her jeans and avoided making eye contact with her daughter as Luna pushed herself off the chair and ambled over to the cooler. Luna's hand reached for the yellow tag.

"Who's the new guy?" she asked.

"Don't open that!" The words shot out of Grace's lips like lightning, and Luna froze mid-step. She pivoted on her heels, aiming hard, midnight-dark eyes on her mother.

"It's not like I've never seen a dead body before, *Mother*," Luna snapped. She pointed first at one grandmother, then the other. "I've been helping Ducey here since I was five, even though you and Nana Lenore said I was too young."

She had been too young. Too young to tell her the truth, but old enough to keep a close eye on. Coming of age meant something different for Evans women, different still for Luna. Grace swallowed and tried to say something, but her tongue was too coated with shame to form words. She cast a pleading glance at the other two women. Did the yellow tag on the handle of cooler number three shiver, or was it just her imagination? It was all happening so fast. *Too* fast.

The yellow tag fluttered, and this time Grace saw it, a slight flick of the edge.

Edwin Boone was waking up.

Lenore cleared her throat. "Luna, why don't you go on and head to the break room?" She took a step closer to the cooler, putting her thin frame between it and Luna. "Get yourself a cold soda water and get busy on your schoolwork."

"Don't have any."

Panic soaked through the thin calm in Grace's voice. Another flutter. "Sweetheart, I really think—"

"Oh my God, what did I do now?" Luna spun on the heels of her black and white canvas shoes, the thick rubber soles squealing on the freshly mopped floor. She emitted a low growl, flung her hands out at her sides. "It's like you're all trying to get me out of here."

"We are," Ducey cut in. She slid a butterscotch between her lips, rolled it against her teeth, the tip of the infant trocar she kept tucked in her apron pocket gleaming in the fluorescent lab lights. "Now go on—*git*."

Umbrage moved across Luna's face, but the look slipped as a loud *boom* erupted from inside cooler number three. The yellow tag came loose and flittered to the ground like a falling leaf.

Shuffling from inside the cooler followed, sending undulating, metallic waves reverberating throughout the small room. A loud shriek—the sound of fingernails scraping against steel—screamed behind the metal door.

Inside the cooler, a man groaned. Dull black fluid leaked from the edges of the metal door, oozed down the steel surface, puddled on the tile. The stench of rot crept into the air.

Luna jumped in shock. Another groan sent her sprawling to the floor and scrambling backward on four limbs. She gawked at the cooler.

"Wh-what i-is in there?" she stuttered.

Lenore's lips thinned into a line. "Edwin Boone."

Breath caught in Grace's chest as Luna's eyes turned toward her. Round with confusion, they held no spark of petulance in them now, no piss and vinegar and all the other stuff teenage daughters were made of. Just fear—wide, worried, wondering fear.

Her voice cracked. "Mom?"

Bang, bang, bang.

"*Mom?*" Luna's voice sliced through the room. "Why is Mr. Boone locked in the cooler?"

I'm so sorry, baby, Luna wanted to say. Instead, Ducey's words came back to her and she said, "It's not Mr. Boone. Not anymore."

"*What*?" Luna's eyes went wide, her lips forming a circle.

Lenore twisted a tuft of ginger hair at the base of her neck. "Luna, I think it's best if—"

BANG. BANG. BANG.

"What is going on?"

Luna's voice stung Grace's ears. She reached for her daughter, but Luna pulled away, folding in on herself like a wet paper towel. Her eyes screamed, the fear in them too big, too eager, too *interested*. Grace fought not to look at the doorway, at the safety of the hallway beyond. She couldn't be in the room the first time her daughter put down one of the restless dead. Her heart couldn't take it.

On the other side of the room, Ducey popped another butterscotch into her mouth, pulled the metal spike from her apron, and folded her arms over her chest. "Girls," she said, "no sense sugarcoating it now. It's time we let Luna see what's become of ol' Edwin Boone."

CHAPTER 5

Luna Evans

A large crack shuddered against the walls of the narrow metal cooler. The sound sparked down Luna's spine like a dynamite fuse, zinging to the tips of her toes to burn the soles of her feet. Words rushed up from her stomach in its wake, tumbling over her tongue, her lips.

The room swam, pulling Luna under. She swallowed, cleared her throat, then swallowed again. "Wh-what?"

The word fizzed on her tongue. Edwin Boone, the cranky old man who spent his weekends on his front porch yelling at everyone who drove by doing one mile over the speed limit? Stuffed inside the morgue cooler, banging to be let out? Only bodies awaiting funeral preparations went in there—bodies brought over from the coroner's office.

Examined.

Declared dead.

Luna spluttered. Blinked. "*Why?*"

Another bang from inside the cooler sent a fresh deluge of noxious black fluid pouring through the seal on cooler number three. The rancid odor of raw meat and metal slapped Luna. The knot tightening in her stomach turned to pudding, and she pressed a hand over her mouth to suppress a gag. Luna watched the fluid sludge down the shiny surface to join the puddle widening on the stark linoleum floor.

BANG.

The oozing fluid had soaked through the coroner's tag, turning the bright yellow pale and viscous, like a scab. Nana Lenore snatched a paper towel from the roll on the counter and spritzed the sheet with spray bottle bleach, then swiped away the once-yellow tag. Luna took in the color the paper had left behind.

What looked black at first was actually red: deep, crimson red, tinted the suffocated purple of death. The black sludge leaking down the cooler walls was blood. Dead blood from something still inside, still moving, still—

BANG.

It took a few attempts, but Luna managed to pry open her mouth. When she tried to speak, her great-grandmother's voice came out. The sound grabbed Luna, thrust the heavy feeling from her legs back up into her belly so hard it clogged her throat. She took a step backward, coughed the taste of chlorine.

"I don't know why you're bothering with that right now, Len," Ducey snapped. "There's just gonna be a bigger mess."

Nana Lenore's jaw tightened, but she shook her head and folded the bloodied paper towels and coroner's tag into a neat bundle. Clenched them in her fist so hard drips bled on the tile.

"Doesn't mean we should just leave it, now does it?" she snapped, stepping across the room on the toes of her loafers to deposit the towels in the trash bin. "No sense leaving it for someone to step in. It's not—"

Ducey clicked the butterscotch against her teeth in warning, like a rattler lifting its tail.

"Sanitary," Nana Lenore finished, noticing the drops that had rained from her fist.

Candy apple–red nails lighted on Luna's forearm and she recoiled, cradling her arm as if she'd been wounded. The color was too bright, too vivid, to not hurt. Had the touch burned? Stung? She couldn't tell.

Her mother's face was suddenly in front of hers, but her voice sounded far away. "I'm going to go freshen up Mina Jean." Grace tapped her fingernails along the top of Luna's arm, the beat faster than her words. Her mother's eyes looked at Luna's forehead, her chin, but never at her eyes. "People will be arriving soon for the visitation."

Visitation?

Grace blinked too fast, a smile too weak to hold up the corners of her eyes wrinkling in the periphery of Luna's vision. "Unless you want me to stay with you?"

"You go on, child," Ducey's voice answered on Luna's behalf. "We can handle things in here."

Luna stared after her mother. This didn't make sense. Everyone was so calm—how could they be so calm? Everyone except her mother, who left the room without looking back.

The person in the cooler—Mr. Boone?—banged again. The sound pummeled against Luna's ribs. Something was rotting behind the locked cabinet door of cooler number three—rotting and yet still shuffling around.

Mr. Boone.

Luna lowered her hand from her mouth to her stomach, tried to inhale without tasting death, and braced herself. "Why is Mr. Boone locked in the cooler?" she asked, her voice almost normal.

Ducey's cataract green eyes sparked behind the lenses of her bifocals as she squinted in Luna's direction. She shrugged as if settling an internal argument. "To keep him from getting out," she said.

"Wh-why is he b-bang . . . ?" Luna couldn't finish her sentence. The stink was so bad she could taste the words decaying in her mouth.

"He ain't bangin'," the old woman yelled over the noise. "He's knockin'."

"Knocking?"

"You'll just confuse her more, Mama," Nana Lenore cut in. She turned to Luna, raising her index finger when Luna opened her mouth to protest. She pointed to the bookshelf in the corner of the room, shelves stuffed full of medical texts and raunchy paperbacks Ducey liked to read while working. "Luna, dear, we need to take care of Mr. Boone. No matter what we say now, it won't make a lick of sense, and we don't have time to fiddle around. So stand over there and wait quietly, and let's discuss this when we're done, okay?"

BANG.

Luna jerked, then nodded. Anything to get the banging—*knocking*—to stop. The smell to go away. She watched with increasing anxiety as her grandmother set her backpack on the floor, then wheeled the metal examination table in front of the cooler, pushing it right through the spot on the floor where Edwin Boone's sour blood had pooled. Once Nana Lenore had brought the slab broadside along the cooler's doors and fixed the wheels in place, she positioned herself so the locker door would shield her when it opened. The door and the table would pin in whatever was in the cooler, and keep it from coming out.

Ducey made her way to the lab sink, where she set the trocar on the counter and rolled the sleeves of her blouse to her elbows. She twisted her wedding ring around her finger, then slipped the band off, deposited it in her shirt pocket, and patted it secure.

"One of the settings is loose," she explained when she caught Luna's eye. "I don't need a stone gettin' lost in Ed. Poor Royce would roll over in his grave."

"Mama, that's not funny." Nana Lenore's voice came out breathy. "You shouldn't say things like that. Not about Daddy."

"Oh, don't be such a stick in the mud, Len," Ducey shot back. "Humor is good for the soul. You don't live to be as old as I am without learning to laugh at the mess life throws at you."

Nana Lenore went stiff. "Well, we're as good as we're going to get," she said and clamped her hands on her hips. "Luna, honey, it's not pretty but I need you to watch—it'll help things make sense later. Y'all ready?"

Finally, words, *actual words*, made purchase on Luna's tongue. "Ready for what?"

Another rush of bangs came from inside the metal cooler.

Edwin's knocking hammered Luna's pulse up into her throat. The last time she'd seen the man he'd fussed at her for not returning the shopping buggy at the Market Basket to the corral. *Kids these days*, he'd grumbled, and Luna had thought then how it was no surprise he lived all by his lonesome out on the edge of town where nothing but tumbleweeds and stray dogs bothered to go. She'd wondered how long it'd be until he kicked the bucket.

Now he was bleeding dead blood from the inside of a funeral parlor cooler and banging to be set loose.

Her knees shook so loudly she couldn't tell what was Edwin Boone's knocking and what came from her own body. Nana Lenore's hand was on the cooler door handle before Luna managed to get another word past her own pulse. It flew out sharp, a dagger in the air.

"Wait."

Both of her grandmothers swiveled to look at her.

"What . . ." Luna gestured around the room, startling herself when a pair of metal scissors in her hand confronted her vision. When had she picked those up? Had her mother handed them to her? They looked like the pair Grace kept in her mortician's makeup case, which Luna only remembered because she thought it odd to keep scissors with cosmetics. "What do you mean 'we're ready'? You're going to just open the door and let—"

She stopped. What was she supposed to call the thing inside the cooler? They'd said it was Edwin Boone, but whatever it was didn't smell like a man. "What's gonna come out when you open that door?"

Luna jumped when she felt Ducey's wrinkled hand on her shoulder. She hadn't realized she'd stepped farther into the room as she spoke, closer to the cooler and away from the relative safety of the bookshelf. The taste of acid filled her mouth, the carbonation from the soda she'd downed during lunch still potent on its return trip up her throat. Something bitter burned her tongue. She thought of Crane, cigarette smoke seeping through his thin, grinning lips.

Her great-grandmother spoke slowly, the way she had when Luna was a kid. "We're fixin' to open the cooler so we can take care of what's left of Edwin Boone," she said, lifting the metal spike up where Luna could see it, "but you don't need to worry. We'll explain everything—" The old woman stopped, pursed her lips together, considering. "Well, I reckon we'll explain as much as we can, after. Only thing you need to know now is that we've done this before—and it's somethin' you're gonna need to learn how to do, too."

"With a trocar?" Luna eyed the mortuary instrument in the old woman's fist. The giant metal needle featured a sharp awl at one end of its hollow tube, a suction-topped handle at the other. Most of the trocars in the lab were several feet long and meant for adult-sized bodies, but the one Ducey carried in her apron was only a little over twelve inches. A child's trocar, made for reaching up through a little kid's skull.

The man in cooler number three banged on the metal wall again, and the rattle ricocheted up Luna's spine. Another bang, and the cooler slammed against the wall hard enough to chip paint. How exactly were they planning to use the trocar on Edwin Boone?

"I thought those were for draining body fluids," Luna said, stabbing the sharp end of the scissors at Ducey's trocar.

Ducey flipped the instrument so the tool pointed at the linoleum. "They're useful for a lot of things."

"Mama." Nana Lenore sounded impatient.

Unable to speak for fear of losing what was left of her lunch, Luna nodded. The pulse in her throat beat in time to Edwin Boone's knocking inside the cooler walls.

The old woman motioned Luna back as she padded over to the drain grate centered in the floor. "You get on behind me," she instructed and raised the trocar like a slasher movie villain. "He won't be goin' anywhere, but better safe than sorry."

Luna's words were practically a screech. "You're going to *kill* him?"

"Oh, child," Ducey clucked. "Ol' Edwin Boone's already dead."

The floor swam under Luna's feet. She blinked hard when she heard the handle twist against the cooler door, the scratch of metal as her grandmother pulled the slab out just enough that the man's head emerged from the dark. Then she braced herself, gripped the scissors, and wished like hell she'd gone to detention.

At first glance, Edwin Boone looked like any other body lying on his back inside the cooler slab, head positioned at the door like any other body they'd slid in to await preparation for burial. Then he moved, stink and sound coming off him in a way no thing, living or dead, should have. Luna recoiled, inching backward until her feet bumped against the bookshelf, but she couldn't tear her eyes away from the figure swallowed in the cooler's shadows.

Don't scream, an inner voice commanded, the same one that had criticized her for acting so dumb in front of Crane Campbell earlier this afternoon.

It's not Mr. Boone. Not anymore.

We need to take care of Mr. Boone.

Ol' Edwin Boone's already dead.

Edwin Boone rolled his face toward the light, two milky, unfocused eyes bulging from wrinkled skin turned the pale, slate hue of death. Ragged groans tore between the old man's gnashing teeth and gaping jowls as black fluid oozed from a wound on what was left of his neck to pool around his head. Broken flesh flapped around the hole like a second mouth as the man writhed on the slab. His movements were sluggish and heavy, accompanied by scratching and sucking sounds of skin against steel as he struggled to unpin his arms in the narrow space. The meaty stink hung like a cloak over him, billowing directly into Luna's nostrils with each movement.

Luna's mouth hung open, bitter bile slicked against the backs of her teeth. She'd thought a scream would slip out, bubble up from the depths of her stomach, but nothing came. Her vision tunneled, limbs going numb as she stared, transfixed, at the thing on the table. Something rippled under her skin.

A phantom aftertaste rose in her mouth, sweet and faintly metallic.

Across the lab, Nana Lenore held herself pinned against the metal tray so it wouldn't slip and allow Edwin Boone to move about. The man twisted on the slab, arms pressed against his sides in the belly of the cooler. Luna felt a tug in her gut every time his skin sucked against the metal.

Nana Lenore stared unaffected down at the body on the metal tray. "Oh, Ed," she said.

Bloated and bruised, Ed's tongue lolled from his open mouth while his eyes rolled in the direction of the voice.

"Lenore," he croaked. "*Len . . . nore.*"

"I'm so sorry this happened to you." Pity softened the hard lines of Nana Lenore's face. "You were a good man, and a good friend."

"Lenore." Fingernails raked into the interior walls of the cooler as Edwin Boone struggled to get his arms free. His neck mouth pursed, his voice becoming harsher from the effort of speaking with the wound in his throat.

Ducey clicked her butterscotch against her teeth and stepped closer to the cooler. "You know better than to talk to them like that, Len," she said. "Just gets you upset."

"I know, Mama," Nana Lenore said, a hint of irritation curling the edges of her words. "I know."

"You say that every time." The trocar still held high above her head, Ducey used her free hand to pull the lip of Ed's slab out far enough to expose his shoulders.

"Wait!" The word rushed out of Luna like the sludge pouring out of Edwin's throat.

Too late. Ducey plunged the metal spike into the man's heart and Luna felt the stab echo inside her bones.

Black blood poured over the edge of the slab from the hole in the man's chest. Luna watched Edwin's life drain away under her grandmothers' feet. Then she pivoted to the sink and vomited.

CHAPTER 6

Ducey Evans

Ducey Evans ignored the bloody smudge on her bifocals lens as she helped her daughter wrap a fresh sheet around what had once been Edwin Boone and hoist the man onto a gurney. A rose bloomed through the cloth where she'd staked his heart, but the body beneath was still. No more groaning. No more writhing. No more knocking. Most of the blood and other bodily fluids had been wiped away, flushed down the drain in Lenore's manic cleaning. If the stench of rot still hung in the air, Ducey couldn't smell it over the buttery taste of her hard candy.

Course, you've been working on losing your sense of smell since 1976, she thought with a snort. It was hell to get old. It would probably be hell to die, too. She'd seen enough of the good, bad, and ugly of death to know better than to expect her time to come quietly. Things just didn't work that way for Evans women. Never had.

Ducey watched the stain creep across Edwin's bundled corpse. She listened as Luna twisted the lab sink on and splashed water on her face under the faucet. The girl was sucking down gulps of tap water like it was going out of style, but she was still standing. Good sign. Even Ducey hadn't made it through her first encounter with the dead without a good knock to her bottom, but she'd only been a girl then, and her own mother hadn't helped soften the blow. Then again, Pie Evans hadn't earned her nickname by being sweet.

Luna twisted off the sink. "What was *that*?" Pauses punctuated each word as they pushed through her lips to land in Ducey's lap.

"Strigoi." Lenore's tone came out pinched as she tucked the loose ends of the sheet around the body on the gurney.

Every one of Ducey's eighty years pushed against her as she anchored her knees and lowered herself into a hard plastic chair with a deep exhale. "Weak little thing." She pulled a butterscotch from the stash in her pocket and unwrapped the cellophane. "Make a racket," she added as she pushed the candy in her mouth, "but they're slow as molasses when they first wake up."

Luna wiped water from her lip. "A *what*?"

"Come have a look," Lenore said. The girl didn't budge, and she drummed her palms against the front pleats of her pants. "Come on, now. He's perfectly harmless."

Harmless. Ducey gave an extra hard tug on the candy on her tongue. Nothing about the restless dead was harmless.

When Luna had made her way to the gurney, Lenore uncovered Edwin's head and gestured at the dead man's face. She kept the cloth up, careful to conceal the wound in his throat.

"He still looks like a man," Lenore explained, using her index finger to direct Luna's attention as she traced Ed's features. "All strigoi do when they first rise. They come back in the same shape they died in, but with every victim, every soul they take, they mutate—their bodies become more resilient. They gain vitality and intelligence, sometimes even memory. Some become monstrous; their skin pales, eyes turn black, teeth and ears sharpen into points. Others revive until they can pass for human, but they're—"

"Monsters," Ducey interjected from her chair, stabbing a finger into the space in front of her. "No matter what the dead look like or how they act, they're all monsters. And don't you forget it."

Lenore returned the cloth over Ed's head and tucked it gently under his shoulders. "We need to finish this," she told Luna. "Then we'll sit down and talk."

Luna spoke to the bloom in the center of Ed's chest. "You mean it's *not* finished?"

"It's best we don't leave anything that could get up and walk around again," Ducey said. "Once restless, always restless. The only way to be sure they're gone for good is to turn 'em into a pile of dust."

Luna's eyebrows twisted. Released. "The crematorium."

"Precisely." Lenore grabbed the handle at the end of the table and pushed the gurney toward the door. "Come on, Luna. Ducey needs to rest."

"Rest." Ducey rolled her eyes. "I'll put on a pot of coffee. Luna, you come with me. Your nana can manage on her own."

Lenore tensed. "She should see how it's done."

"And she will," Ducey agreed, "but for now she's seen enough."

Fifteen minutes later, Ducey sat in the parlor's small break room, watching as black coffee sloshed over the edge of Luna's mug. The girl set it down on the coaster, then folded her hands in her lap as the filmy black fluid pooled in a half-circle on the table's surface. She might have enjoyed a glass of sweet tea or a soda water instead, but sugary bubbles didn't pair well with this sort of news.

Coffee is better for the nerves, Ducey thought as she sipped from her own mug. *Stiff and bitter. Keeps your eyes open.*

Across the table, Grace looked as if she'd turned to stone. Ducey could hear the sound of gritting teeth. Beside her, Luna cleared her throat. Her long, dark bangs masked her eyes and she brushed them to the side, then spread her hands on the table, bumping the coffee mug and causing a bigger mess.

Lenore snatched a dishrag from the counter with a frustrated sigh. She mopped her granddaughter's spill, then took her place at the small, four-seater table. "Come on, Mama," she said. "No sense in putting this off any longer."

Of course, Lenore and Grace would defer to her. Nobody wanted Ducey's opinion on when to trim the begonias or how to get a blood-stain out of a blouse, but it was a different matter when it came time to bore the next generation with Evans family history.

Ducey took another sip of bitter coffee and pulled a face at the taste. "Just tryin' to think of where to start," she said as she retrieved the flask of brandy from her apron pocket and poured a dollop in the cup. Sloshed it through. She took another sip, clicking her tongue against the roof of her mouth as she savored her swallow.

Luna bristled. "Wait, you *knew* about strigoi"—she pronounced it wrong, a little too long on the *oi*—"or whatever, this whole time?" Another wave of coffee sloshed out of her mug, propelling Lenore back onto her feet and scurrying over with the dishrag. "Why didn't you tell me this before?" Luna asked. "Like, literally *any time* before now?"

Her question was met with silence. Of all the things she could have asked, this was the one they couldn't answer. Not yet, because of all the other truths that would spill out.

Luna swung an accusatory glare at her mother, then fixed each woman in turn with it so they all felt the look's burn. "Is this why Mrs. Murphy's casket is closed?" she asked. "Was she a . . . was she a strigoi, too?"

Lenore winced and Ducey hid a smile inside another sip. Her great-granddaughter might have been scared as all get-out, but she was quick on her feet.

Grace's voice came out in a whisper. "Yes."

Luna gawked at her mother. "Did you, like, kill her, or whatever?"

"I put her to bed," Grace said.

"This is insane." The girl buried her face in her hands with a groan.

Ducey swallowed down the rest of her coffee and set her mug on the table, careful to put a napkin under the bottom so Lenore didn't come fussing over with her rag. A little coffee stain on the tabletop was the least of their concerns right now. Coffee didn't bite. Didn't tear a person limb from limb and drink their soul.

"Life is a thing of balance," Lenore said breezily, "and just like there have always been two sides competing against one another, there has always been something to keep both sides from spilling over into each other." She motioned around the small circular table. "In this case, *we* are that something."

Luna screwed up her face. "Seriously? You're telling me that what I just saw in there was . . . what, *normal*? I mean, I just saw a dead man—"

"Ain't a thing normal about it," Ducey cut in. "But you saw it with your own eyes, child, like you said. You saw the thing that used to be Edwin Boone."

The incredulity on Luna's face melted into angry disbelief. "So, what, our family are monster hunters, or something? Like *Buffy the Vampire Slayer*?"

"Caretakers," Ducey clarified before anyone could get their drawers in a knot over semantics. Her taste buds thrummed, longing for just one more butterscotch—or another swig of boozy bitter coffee, though Lenore would certainly protest if she tried too soon for a second cup—and she ran her tongue across her teeth. "Our job is to take care of the dead, so they don't rise. Sometimes things get a little unsettled and we have to put it right again. That's what we just did with ol' Edwin."

She thought of poor Mina Jean. Edwin. So many others over the years.

As if thinking the same, Grace adjusted her hands atop the table, covering the scar on her left wrist she pretended nobody knew she had. Lenore twisted the dishrag between her hands, knuckles white and cuticles chewed short. Her eyes darted to the westward-facing wall where her garden waited on the other side, the cemetery just beyond.

Ducey cleaned her glasses and waited out the memories.

"Right. Okay." Luna shifted in her seat so the chair leg squeaked on the floor, and chewed at her lip. "I thought the risen dead were, like, vampires or zombies," she said. "Allergic to garlic, can't stand crucifixes and holy water, and only come out at night to eat brains. Stuff like that."

"Vampires and zombies." Ducey scoffed. "The first thing you need to understand, Luna, child, is those old legends get far more wrong than they get right. The creatures we deal with existed long before Bram Stoker or anybody else muddled everything up with their hogwash." Her hand slid to her apron pocket, touched a butterscotch, then rose to adjust her glasses. "Strigoi are ghouls, plain and simple. They're the monster from which every horrible undead creature originated. They are not beautiful. They are not romantic. And they don't give a fig what part of you they can get their teeth into—brains or otherwise, day or night. They are rottin', baleful things, fallin' apart on themselves, especially if they have any loose body parts to begin with, and they know only hunger. Every time they feed, they grow stronger."

She paused to allow her speech time to sink in. When Luna's blinking slowed to a normal pace and the girl no longer looked in danger of fainting, Ducey delivered her most important point.

"You need to understand," she said. "These ghouls are the risen, restless dead, come back to feed on the livin'—and they don't stop until someone puts a stop to them."

Luna stared too long at the table. "What causes them to come back?"

"Nobody knows for sure why they rise," Grace said, "or how everything started, whenever and wherever it began." She chewed the words as she reached across the table to squeeze Luna's hand. Long shirtsleeves hung down over her hand, hiding the scar on her wrist. Grace wore long sleeves, even in summer, to keep that mark covered. "Everything we know is what we've learned over time, passed down from one generation of Evans women to the next," she said. "But no one has all the answers, not even us. We just do the best we can."

"Evans women," Luna echoed. Her pupils dilated, backlit by an inner light bulb. "So *that's* why we own a funeral parlor—to be on the lookout for restless dead? Is it just us here? Why our family?"

"Good questions, but like your mama said, we don't have all the answers." Ducey raked her teeth against the candy dissolving on her tongue. "We know that the dead have risen in this town for as long as it's been a town, and we know the Evans women have always guarded the balance. Reckon that's enough to go on."

"Strigoi"—Lenore clicked her teeth to emphasize the word, redirecting the conversation—"are known as the 'impure' dead." She straightened in her seat, folding the soggy dish towel into a neat square. "The term is old, and needlessly superstitious. At one time, it referred to those born with hair, or tails, that sort of thing. People cursed by witches." She unfolded the towel, refolded. "But that sort of hokum fell out of favor centuries ago."

"*Hokum.*" Ducey snorted. Hokum accounted for at least half of what they knew about ghouls. If there was anything practical about strigoi she, Lenore, or Grace didn't know, it had gone into the ground with Ducey's mother, Pie.

Or—worse—with one of the strigoi.

Neither thought was comforting. Ducey hid her expression behind a sip of coffee and nodded at Lenore to continue.

"In more enlightened times," Lenore said, "we've come to determine those most likely to become restless are people who die suddenly or in horrible ways, those who were terrible people when they were alive, or even souls who have not made peace with their own death."

Luna seemed to consider this. "What about the people they attack?" she asked. Her shoe tapped against the break-room floor. "Is that what happened to Edwin Boone? His neck . . ."

The girl's hand reached up to her throat.

"Usually, if a strigoi takes a victim, they'll come back as well, though no one knows if it's a contagion or just another person coming back from a horrible death." Lenore cut her eyes at Ducey, daring her to disagree. She didn't. "The majority, however, rise from improper burials. That's why what we do here is so important—it's preventative."

"Preventative?" Luna repeated.

"If the dead are satisfied with how they are laid to rest, they have no reason to rise from the grave," Grace explained. "Our job is to make sure those who die are buried properly, and that, should they wake, they will have no desire to remain in a place they no longer belong—and no interest in pulling the living into death with them."

Luna nodded, but her words came out less certain. "Is that why we have all these weird customs?" She waved her hands around her as if summoning a list. "Taking the caskets out of the chapel feet first, never letting tears fall on the body—stuff like that?"

Lenore allowed a smile. "Precisely."

Luna fell quiet again, her brow furrowed as her mental hamster wheel spun. Pieces snapped into place, exposing holes. "But what about Mrs. Murphy? She died from cancer. That's horrible and all, but not sudden or violent. And she's not even buried yet, so what went wrong with her?"

"Nothin' went wrong," Ducey said. "We couldn't have prevented what happened to Mina Jean."

"What does that mean?" Luna asked. "Why not?"

"Mina Jean was already a strigoi when she arrived here. She just hadn't woken up yet," Lenore explained. "That's how it is with these things. Some people simply pass and wake up. Not all strigoi deaths are violent."

"What about, like, embalming them?" Luna asked, which was a fair question.

"Makes it worse." Ducey shrugged. "Don't know why."

Luna chewed on that for a second. "How do you know when someone is . . . going to get restless?"

Grace gave her daughter's hand another squeeze. "There are signs," she said. "Hair moves. Skin gets warm. Sometimes they smile, or snarl. But you don't know have to worry about Mina Jean," Grace added. "She's—" She cleared her throat. "It's been taken care of."

Luna swallowed. "Mr. Boone, did you know he—"

"Don't think of them as *someone*," Ducey cut in. She poured herself a fresh cup of coffee and dumped a healthy dose of brandy into the mug without meeting her daughter's judgmental, ice-cube eyes. "The Mina Jean who rose today was not the same woman you knew, and neither was Edwin Boone, bless his heart. They're nothin' more than ghouls wearing faces that were once familiar."

"I wish you wouldn't call them ghouls, Mama." Lenore's voice was stone. She pressed her spine against the chair and gripped the edges of the table so hard her knuckles strained against the skin of her fingers. "Referring to them as strigoi gives them more dignity."

Ducey swallowed the contents of her mug in one gulp. "You call them what you like, Len. I'll call them what they are. The only dignity afforded them once they rise from their grave is a swift return. And that—" She shot a meaningful look at Luna. "*That* is the problem with ghouls. By the time the first one gets restless, there's more already stirrin', needin' to be put down."

"Mama!" Lenore's hand unclenched from the table to cover her heart. She looked stricken.

"Oh, you know it's true, Lenore," Ducey snapped. "You too, Grace. Let's not put lipstick on a pig and pretend it's the prettiest girl at the county fair. The dead are restless. Mina Jean wasn't the first to rise, and

Edwin ain't gonna be the last. We need to nip this thing in the bud before it gets worse." Ducey hammered her fist on the Formica table-top, then stabbed a finger at Luna. "Knowing what they are and how to keep 'em in the grave is one thing," she said. "No matter how good a job we do keeping them in the ground, sometimes the dead still come back. When they do, you need to know how to handle 'em. You need to know how to kill them and make sure they don't get up again."

Ducey cast her gaze around the room and when no one challenged her, she continued. "Now, the first thing you need to know about ghouls is what to do when you cross one. That's the most important part." She adjusted her bifocals and raised two fingers. "There are two types: Callers and Knockers. Both kinds need you to acknowledge 'em—to invite them in, so to speak, before they can claim you. Callers say your name, and if you answer, you're as good as got. Knockers, like ol' Edwin, they knock on the door of the one they want, and if you answer—"

"You die," Luna finished in a whisper. Her normally fair skin had lightened to the color of buttermilk, her dark hair and eyes sharp in contrast.

Ducey clicked her tongue and shook her head. "You *fight*. Just because these creatures are already dead don't mean they can't die."

Pink bloomed in the white spaces of Luna's cheeks. "I assume crucifixes and garlic don't work?"

Ducey shook her head. "Your great-grandpa tried to get me to carry a gun, but Evans women are blades women. I'm partial to my trocar, but any pointed bit of metal will do. Anything you can stab into the heart or brain." Ducey slid the long metal instrument from her apron and flipped it in her hand as easily as a baton. "Then you cut off the head and rebury the body with the head placed upside down at the feet."

Luna froze in her seat—eyes wide, lips parted, mouth open. Her words took on that stuttering quality again, ill-shaped and bunched together. "You cut off the head?"

"In olden times, people sometimes would bury the body with a silver chain around its neck, or with a blade laid across the throat to keep 'em pinned down, but it's simpler to just cut the whole thing off and be done with it. Total decapitation works best." Ducey shrugged, returning the trocar to her apron pocket while the other three stared at her like she'd just wrecked someone's surprise party. "Truth's ugly, but effective."

"Not all ways of dispatching the dead are so gruesome." Lenore's voice slid like a butter knife through the sudden tension in the room. "Cremating the bodies works just fine, and is much simpler, all things considered. In fact, it may be the best way to combat any spread. Plus, this method leaves behind something we can study and learn from: ashes."

Ducey groaned. "Oh, hell, Lenore. Now's not the time to go on about all your 'experiments.'" It pained her arthritic fingers to make air quotes around the word, but she powered through.

"One historical case involved mixing the ashes of a burned strigoi with water and feeding the mixture to its victims," Lenore went on, ignoring her. "Those ailing from the strigoi's influence were healed."

"Healed?" Luna's eyes grew larger still, threatening to pop out of her skull. "But I thought they were . . . you know . . . dead. Or dead*ish*."

"In theory, the ashes would be applied to a living person, to reduce the chances they too come back or to release them from the strigoi's hold on their soul," Lenore explained. "Not all deaths from strigoi are violent and immediate. Sometimes they feed for a long time, letting their victim waste away until there's nothing left to take."

"A ghoul's idea of dinner at Golden Corral," Ducey offered when lines crawled across Luna's forehead. "A taste here, a bite there. Helps them slip by unnoticed."

Luna's milky complexion soured. "Oh."

"Those being fed on by strigoi may lose their appetite, begin to lose weight," Lenore said. "They sort of fade away, and often appear sick, like they have—"

"Cancer," Grace completed the sentence. She blinked hard. "Like Mina Jean."

"Which means Mama's right: the dead have been rising longer than we've known," Lenore finished. "Whatever siphoned energy off Mina Jean and killed Edwin is still out there." Her eyes drifted to Luna, hung for a beat, before her lips tightened and she went back to folding and unfolding her dishrag.

Luna straightened in her chair. She lifted the cold coffee to her lips and drained the rest, then wiped her lips dry. She cast a measured look around the room, and when her eyes met Ducey's, they were steady. "Making sure dead things stay buried is a family business," Luna said. "The restless dead rise if not buried correctly, and if—*when*—they do, it's up to us to put them back in their graves."

Ducey saluted Luna with her empty mug. "She's a spitfire, our littlest Evans," she told Grace and Lenore. "Just like her great-granny."

Of course, it wasn't only Evans blood running in the girl's veins, and blood—Ducey knew—was thicker than water. Blood was everything.

CHAPTER 7

Snow Leger

In the twenty-two years she'd been doing hair, Snow Leger had never missed one of her deceased clients' visitations.

Never.

Until now.

She had meant to go to Mina Jean's visitation tonight, truly she had. But her heart hadn't stopped racing since she'd left Evans Funeral Parlor earlier that afternoon, and by the time evening rolled around, all the extra adrenaline coursing through her veins had left her worn slap out. She was so tired she'd sat in her La-Z-Boy until her round rear end had begun to bond with the recliner's cushiony leather bottom, which, considering the day's events, was just fine by her.

I did the woman's hair. Isn't that enough? Snow thought, then immediately felt bad for having thought it. Mina Jean had been a lot of things, but she had always been kind, and showing up at the woman's wake to pay her last respects was the least Snow could do.

Still, something in the parlor this morning had spooked her, and she'd spent the rest of the day trying to distract herself from thinking about Mina Jean Murphy's oddly lifelike corpse.

Snow had come straight home from the parlor and changed into something comfortable. Once she'd rescheduled the rest of the day's appointments, she made a nice cup of Earl Grey and a cold pimento cheese sandwich and let herself fall into the comforting drama of her favorite daytime soap opera, just like Lenore had suggested. On *The Young and the Restless*, Victor betrayed Jack to Brad while Katherine spilled the beans about her grandfather to Jill. When the show ended, Snow had dozed through the rest of the *TV Guide*'s afternoon programming, hardly bothering to change the channel until it was time for the local evening news. On Channel Six, Deputy Roger Taylor went on about some mischief down on Farm Road 121. Hadn't he been in Evans Funeral Parlor this morning when she'd left? Snow couldn't remember and she didn't have much time to waste thinking on it before news anchor Penny Boudreaux came on the screen, her bottle-blonde dye job outdone only by the amount of cleavage the floozy thought it appropriate to show on broadcast television.

She's got her nose so high she could drown in a rainstorm. Snow sucked her teeth at the TV, then clicked over to finish the news on Channel Four with handsome Bill Kershaw and catch a glimpse of Vanna White's gown on *Wheel of Fortune* while she touched up her manicure. Before she'd realized it, Mina Jean's visitation had come and gone. To make matters worse, Snow's stomach grumbled. She'd forgotten her supper.

She switched off the television, tapped her oxblood nails on the armrest of her recliner, and thought of the frozen lasagna she'd planned to pop in the oven on her way out the door to the funeral parlor. A fresh gallon of Blue Bell Homemade Vanilla ice cream—Snow's favorite—waited in the freezer for dessert.

"Ten o'clock is just too darn late for all that," Snow muttered aloud to the empty room. Eating a heavy meal at this hour would just go straight to her hips and Lord knows they didn't need the help. "Better make myself a warm cup of milk and get on to bed."

Missing Mina Jean's visitation was one thing, but Snow would never forgive herself if she were absent at the funeral, too. Neither, she considered, would any of the late woman's friends who'd be in attendance to take notice. Social proprietary was about more than just manners in small towns—the wrong kind of gossip could land a gal unemployed.

Considering you don't have a husband to foot the bills, you can't afford to tarnish your reputation, Snow thought. Warding off funny looks was hard enough when she spent so much time around the Evanses.

She pushed herself up from the chair. Her legs were numb from sitting, and she wobbled onto her feet as she made her way into the kitchen, stopping at the small square dining table to jot down a reminder to pick up a sympathy card for Burton Murphy on her way to his wife's funeral in the morning. After draining the leftover water from her tea kettle into the sink, Snow poured in some skim milk from the half-gallon in the icebox and set out a fresh cup and saucer, then reached into her spice cabinet. She had just lit the gas stove and set the kettle on to boil when the motion light on her driveway flicked on.

"What in the world?" Snow peered through the window over her kitchen sink, flipped the overhead light on, off, on again. If anything moved around out in the dark beyond her azalea bushes, she couldn't see it. A shiver raced through her as the window unit in the den clicked on, pumped cold air into the first floor. She pulled her house robe tighter around her chest and leaned across the counter, straining for a better look.

A pair of bright, poison-yellow eyes blinked at her from the blackness outside.

Snow's hand jerked, sending the canister of cinnamon she'd meant to sprinkle into her milk crashing to the floor. Her heart leaped up into her throat, catching her breath on its way. She pressed her palm against her chest. Gasped.

On the other side of the window, the eyes blinked again. This time the blink was followed by a *hoot*, loud enough to be heard through the glass.

"It's just an owl, you silly cow." Snow pushed out a sigh as she snatched a dish towel from the counter and squatted to mop up the spill of brown powder at her feet. *You're as nervous as a long-tailed cat in a room full of rocking chairs.* She let out a little laugh at her own expense. It was no wonder she'd never landed a man; she was too much of a ninny to—

A knock at the door.

Snow's heart attempted a somersault, but she stilled it by putting her hand over her chest. Who on earth would be calling this time of night? Guilty thoughts swam into Snow's head. Had Lenore been concerned when she'd missed the visitation, and dropped by to check in on her? No, that didn't sound like Lenore—Grace, maybe, but not Lenore. Lenore would phone first.

Avoiding the owl's leering eyes, Snow leaned in close to the window over her kitchen sink, trying to peer around to the side door off the den and see through the dense azalea foliage. She flipped the light switch off and let her eyes blur as they adjusted to the dark.

Knock, knock.

A small, hunched figure stood on her porch, hands clinging to the doorframe like its legs didn't work quite right. The motion light on the driveway cast a shadow on the back stoop, but even in the dark, Snow recognized the crooked shape of her neighbor, Mrs. Milner. The old widow's spine curved so severely it nearly bent her in half, the poor dear. She almost never left her house unless in the company of her daughter Petunia, a self-righteous little number who lived a town over. Even then, Mrs. Milner was never without the aid of her walker, an oversized aluminum contraption with tennis balls for feet.

And yet, here the woman was, hunched over in her nightdress, hammering unassisted on Snow's side door as if in desperate need of the last cup of sugar on the planet.

"Well, what in the world . . ." Snow set her dish towel on the sink and straightened her robe, patted down her hair. She checked the clock on the oven. Already half past ten. Mrs. Milner was the type of gal who took supper at two o'clock and put herself to bed by six. She certainly wouldn't have ventured out in the dark if there hadn't been trouble. Something must be terribly wrong.

Snow considered ringing the police as she shuffled in her fuzzy pink socks past the phone in the hallway, but Mrs. Milner knocked a third time, and she decided against it. Better to get the poor old dear in the house and comfortable first, then go from there.

"I'm coming, Mrs. Milner," Snow called, doubtful the old woman could hear through the heavy oak door even if she was wearing her hearing aids, which she rarely did. Said they made her feel old. "Give me one second, dear."

Undeterred, Mrs. Milner knocked again. Louder this time. Urgent.

Mrs. Milner was still knocking when Snow crossed the den to her side door. Snow barely had time to think, *She'll break a finger, hammering like that,* before she pulled open the door and fell backward onto the carpet to stare up in horror at the creature waiting on her stoop.

The thing eyeing Snow from the threshold *was* Mrs. Milner, or at least it had been very recently. Pale knees poked against the hem of her flowered muumuu, as thin fleece house slippers scuffled back and forth on Snow's welcome mat. Cat-eye glasses sparked in the overhead light. The thing even had Mrs. Milner's spun-glass hair and cloudy, cataract eyes. But it wore her skin like old linens, mottled purple and red, and what remained of the woman's mouth had shriveled in on itself like old, rotted fruit. Elbows bent in wrong directions, and chunks of meat were missing from its arms. Its expression was the worst, though, because the look on the creature's face looked nothing like Mrs. Milner, Snow's neighbor for the past decade.

This was evil—dark, venomous, and *hungry*.

"Snow," the Mrs. Milner–thing rasped, its tongue pressing against toothless gums missing their dentures. Black fluid spilled from the cavity of its mouth. Spindly legs curled over the edge of its bottom lip. A spider crawled down its chin. The Mrs. Milner–thing's bloated tongue lolled after it and licked it in.

Dead. Mrs. Milner was dead, but the woman walked, and gurgled, and *moved*.

A ragged inhale of breath. Then, "Snow."

The sound of her name issuing from the creature's mouth scared the bladder out of Snow. Her socked feet caught in the fabric of her robe and her own fluids, and she lost her balance, crashing to the shag carpet. Fire seared in her ankle, but Snow kicked out wildly, ignoring the stabs of pain racing up her leg. The thing didn't flinch, not even when Snow's foot connected with its knobby old knee and brought it down to the ground inside the open back-porch door.

"No, no, no, no." The single syllable beat between Snow's lips in tandem with her heart pounding inside her chest. She was numb with shock, her body stiff where she lay on the carpet in a puddle of her own urine, her ankle bent broken beneath her. Sweat poured down her forehead, mixing with her tears to run in salty rivulets into her gaping mouth.

"Snow."

"No," Snow said. "No, n-n, n—"

Fingers gnarled from decades of arthritis coiled above the sock's hem on Snow's ankle, squeezed until she heard the snapping of old bones. The creature's nails stabbed into the meat of Snow's calf as it pulled itself up her leg, reached for her torso. An index nail bent back, disconnected at the cuticle bed with an auditory *suck*, but still the Mrs. Milner–thing kept digging, kept clawing. Pain flooded Snow's body as the dead woman worked itself on top of her, bringing along with it the musk of sour rot and body oil.

Snow lost all memory of how to move.

Toothless gums gnawed at her skin, desperate to break through, and the Mrs. Milner–thing let out a frustrated growl as its damp gums clamped against Snow's flesh. It reached up, fingernails slicing like glass at Snow's cheek and into her neck. A current of blood rushed from the wound. Warm. Wet.

Mrs. Milner lunged.

Snow opened her mouth, hitched in a great, gasping breath, and finally screamed at the same moment her tea kettle began to whistle on the kitchen stove.

CHAPTER 8

Deputy Roger Taylor

The slight breeze of the late-August morning had already thickened to mud when Deputy Roger Taylor picked up his morning coffee at Jimbo's Java Café. On the advice of his sister, Rochelle, a fitness instructor at the women's gym on the hoity-toity side of town, who lived and breathed by fad diets, Roger had started watching his sugars and counting his carbs. Regardless, whether it was the heat or the lack of sleep, or just the frustration of pulling a double shift and missing Mina Jean Murphy's sunrise funeral, Roger's desire for a sweet pastry won out over his desire to trim his waistline.

Carbs, schmarbs. He'd never even heard of Dr. Atkins. Besides, he'd skipped breakfast. That had to count for something.

"I'll take one of them cream cheese–filled croissants, too," he told the counter girl, keeping his gaze locked on the pastry case so he wouldn't have to see the eyebrow she might quirk at him. This was a trick he'd mastered after many night-shift donut binges as a rookie—look at the food, not at the one slopping it out. Less judgment that way. He'd have plenty enough of that later when he stepped on the scale.

Trust me, darlin', I'm my own worst critic, Roger thought, and pulled at his too-tight gun belt.

The girl behind the counter, a skinny, barely twentysomething with box-black hair named Kim, flumped down the book she'd been reading from and popped her gum as she sacked the pastry. The cream cheese–filled croissant hit the bottom of the thin paper bag with a *thunk*. She set it on the counter beside the cardboard coffee cup filled to an inch below the brim with steaming black liquid.

"Cream or sugar?" Kim's question came out flat, disinterested under heavy-lidded eyes. Like she didn't care one way or the other, or at all.

"Both. Half-and-half, if you got it. And two sugars."

Roger watched as she plopped in two heaping teaspoons of sugar, followed by a thick glug of cream from a pitcher beside the coffeepot. He gave his belly a reassuring pat. *I'll get back on the wagon after the weekend.*

He intended to keep the promise. Eighteen more pounds gone, and Roger would finally summon up the nerve to ask Grace Evans out for coffee. Twenty-one, and maybe he'd ask her to dinner and a movie, a night out on the town. He hadn't yet considered what he might do if she declined—or, for that matter, if she said yes. Either he was an optimist, or delusional. Probably the latter, considering he'd been making excuses for not asking the woman out for the better part of twenty-five years. He'd come close once, but then Grace had shacked up with that fella from out of town. The guy had long since gone, but he'd taken most of Roger's courage with him. Then Grace's daughter had come along, and Grace's father passed, and he'd thought it best to give them their space. The Evans women liked to handle things on their own. They didn't need a man in their business any more than they felt the need to take his last name.

Kim rang up the order and Roger paid for his breakfast. He started to stuff the change in his pocket, but she popped her gum meaningfully and he dropped the few coins into the tip jar instead.

"Have a nice day, Deputy Taylor," Kim drawled, a little saucy on the *deputy* part. Her purple-stained lips worked as she chewed, then popped the gum again.

Roger winced at the sound and nodded a quick goodbye in her direction, noticing her thick black eyeliner for the first time when she dropped her gaze back to the open textbook on the counter. How had the glitz and glam of the eighties turned so bleak that *macabre* became a fashion statement? Hopefully the trend wouldn't catch on, but Snow'd had a rusty shade the color of dried blood painted on her fingernails when he'd seen her at the funeral parlor the day before, so it wasn't just the kids jumping on the bandwagon. Roger had never much cared for horror movies and shock-jock rock 'n' roll. He preferred mettle over metal.

He had just slid back behind the wheel of his patrol car, cranked the AC on high, and taken his first sip of joe when Dispatch Darla's voice crackled over the radio.

"Taylor, we've got a situation at 5445 Garner."

Roger tossed the pastry bag onto the empty passenger seat and grabbed the receiver from the center console, ignoring the one pinned to his shoulder. "Say again?" He'd pressed down the push-to-talk button before he remembered to swallow. Hot coffee poured from his lips, scalding his chest through his shirtfront. He wiped at his mouth with the back of his hand.

This time there was a catch in the woman's voice. "Possible homicide at 5445 Garner Road," Darla said. "You're gonna want to hurry on this one, Taylor. Hinson's on scene and it's . . . well, let's just say it's a bad way to start my shift."

The address clicked. *That's Snow Leger's place.*

The memory, still fresh, of Edwin Boone's throat torn out, eyes locked open wide in terror, flashed through Roger's mind. Animal control still hadn't picked up any problem animals, and he didn't expect they would. Farm Road 121 was way out on the edge of town. Nobody but folks who wanted to be left alone lived out there. Any animal passing through would be long gone by now.

Garner Road was closer.

Too close.

And there were still loose ends out on Farm 121. "Any word on Clyde Halloran?" Roger asked into the mic. No one had seen hide nor tail of Boone's nearest neighbor for almost a week. The town drunk didn't make for the best lead, but it was the only one he had.

"Nothing yet."

Roger rolled his ear against his shoulder. One dead, one missing, and now a fresh crime scene. "Tell Hinson to sit tight," he said. "I'm four minutes out."

Appetite gone, Roger opened his driver's side door and poured his coffee out on the concrete, then tossed the emptied cup to the floorboard along with the pastry bag. He flicked the siren on and floored the gas pedal hard enough to know he'd have to call Jimbo later and apologize for the skid marks his tires left in the parking lot.

He made the trip to Snow Leger's small craftsman in three minutes, twenty-seven seconds flat. Brandon Hinson was on scene, just as Darla had said, and as Roger pulled up, he saw the rookie hunched in the green vinyl chair Snow kept on the wraparound porch, head tucked between his knees like he might see his breakfast again—and not for the first time. The side door of Snow's back porch hung partway open and her two-door coupe was parked in front of Hinson's patrol car, but there wasn't a sign of anyone else at the house. Not that there would be. Snow was unmarried, and proud of it. No pets, no boyfriends—which she always maintained were essentially the same thing.

Roger slung the car into park and shut off the engine, eyed the house through the driver's side window. A thick brown smear had dried into crust on the back steps. Only one substance dried like that once oxygen had its way.

He'd been in a hurry to get to the scene, but now that it came time to heave himself out of his cruiser, Roger's boots stayed rooted to the floorboard. "Get a move on, Taylor," he mumbled under his breath. "Duty calls."

Duty. That word didn't count for much when you were one short, bad walk away from a bloody crime scene with a friend's name on the mailbox. Of all people, why did it have to be Snow Leger? The woman was friendly and kept to herself. Never had been in a lick of trouble, hadn't even gotten so much as a speeding ticket as long as Roger'd been on the force. She certainly didn't deserve whatever fate had left Hinson barfing on her porch.

He sighed and got out of the car. Tucked his thumbs in his belt. "Mornin', Hinson."

The younger deputy didn't raise his head. He passed a hand over his mouth, shirtsleeve straining where his biceps stretched the fabric. "Morning." His voice sounded thick.

Soupy, Roger thought. Not a good sign. Not good at all. But the boy still smelled of the academy—not that anybody ever got used to seeing something like whatever waited on the other side of Snow Leger's door. Once you got past that learning curve, you were either retired, or dead.

Roger sucked in his gut and lowered himself into an uncomfortable squat beside Hinson. He sucked in stale summer morning air, giving his stomach time to settle before speaking. No breakfast, no brunch, and if that dried smear was any indication, probably no dinner, either.

"Mind tellin' me what I'm gonna see when I walk into that house?" he asked.

Hinson wiped the back of his hand over his mouth and lifted his head. "I can tell you what you're *not* going to see," he managed, the words sloshing around on his tongue. "A body."

"I'm *not* gonna see a body?"

The rookie's head gave a violent shake. He sniffed, pulling air into his lungs from the pit of his stomach, swallowing it back down. "Everything that should be *in* a body is in there. Blood. Guts. Even a tongue. But no body. It's just like it—"

He shook his head, letting whatever *it* was die on his tongue.

Didn't much matter. Roger could imagine the sort of scene waiting on the other side of the door from the rookie's reaction. He'd been there once or twice himself. Hell, he'd been there less than forty-eight hours ago, with Ed Boone.

Roger cleared his throat and clapped a hand on the boy's shoulder, biting back a groan as he hoisted himself to his full height. "Breathe from your belly," he instructed Hinson. "Keep your head down. It'll pass. If it don't, aim for the grass."

Grass. Roger tracked a blood-crust trail as he stepped toward the open side door, boots thudding on Snow's porch. The mottled red-brown stain stretched all the way back across the driveway before disappearing into the lawn on the other side of the carport, tracking each footfall in heavy pools that deepened as they moved away, the balls of the feet dark blots of stain. Whatever had come into Snow's house had come from that direction, had gone up the back porch steps and into the house.

Don't look like animal tracks, though, Roger thought. Not a rabid coyote or some other rampaging mongrel. Nothing like that walked on two feet.

Roger eyed what looked like a smudged brown handprint on the door, counted the individual smears of all five fingers, and adjusted his assessment. No, whatever had done this wasn't an animal—wasn't a *what* at all.

It was a *who*.

Whoever had come into Snow's house had come from across the grass. They had come right up to the side door, and—Roger surveyed the larger, rounded mark on the panel—knocked to be let in. Maybe someone needed help? Had been injured and come to Snow for assistance, to phone an ambulance?

No. As he approached the side door, Roger saw there wasn't one track of crusted red. There were three—one coming, two going. A second departing track ran parallel to the first, thinner and crusted brown at the edges.

Mindful of the still-tacky handprint, Roger held his breath, used his elbow to push open the door, and became instantly grateful he hadn't taken a single bite of his sugary brunch. Bile rose in his throat as he stared at the mess on Snow's shag carpet and breathed in metal and ammonia. A thick puddle of red congealed on the surface of the fibers, pooling around torn muscle matter and bits of skin.

And a tongue. Sweet Christ Almighty, there was a tongue. Just like Hinson had said.

Roger backstepped out of the house, nearly slipping in the muck.

"Told you." Hinson had recovered enough to stand and caught Roger's elbow, helping him to get his footing and avoid stepping on a newspaper waterlogged in blood on the stoop.

Roger grunted; he hadn't even seen the damn paper. His stomach lurched as he read the headline. MAN FOUND DEAD ON FM 121, SHERIFF WARNS OF RABID ANIMALS.

The remnants of last night's microwaved Hungry Man dinner crawled up his throat, but he swallowed it down and wiped his mouth with his sleeve. "I've seen drunk driving accidents, suicides, even the occasional homicide," he said, "but I've never seen a scene like this. Not in thirty damn years on the force."

Hinson produced a weak smile and looked glib. "Maybe once in a career is all we get, and either I'm getting my turn out of the way early or you're catching up."

"Maybe so," he told the rookie without conviction. "All right, let's get on with it before the day gets too hot. Sight's bad enough; we don't want to smell it any worse than we already do. Run me through."

Hinson cleared his throat. "Call came in at oh-six-hundred from a pay phone at the gas station up the street about a possible B&E. Paperboy found the scene, ran up there to call it in. Apparently, he noticed the blood streak across the driveway when he came by with the *Enterprise*. Found the side door open and saw blood on the stoop. Poor kid was pale as a ghost when I got here, probably unloaded his breakfast, too, by the looks of things." Hinson's eyes flicked to the pool of his vomit cooling into a crust on Snow's azaleas. "Got his statement and sent him on his way. Suggested he take the day off school. Upgraded the call to possible homicide when I radioed back in."

"Uh-huh." Roger pulled his notepad from his belt, wiped his mouth, and began scribbling notes. "What's the paperboy's name?"

"Andy West."

Roger scribbled down the name. West—he knew the kid. Came from an old family, good people. Some sort of kin to the Murphys, but he couldn't remember if it was on Mina Jean's side or Burton's. If memory served, he'd seen the boy with Luna Evans a time or two. "Anybody else see or hear anything?"

"Not that I've found so far. Haven't been knocking on too many doors yet," Hinson said, pale green eyes sweeping the surrounding areas. His shoulders relaxed when he didn't see anyone watching them on Snow Leger's stoop. "Didn't want to sound the alarm bells before you got here."

Roger harrumphed and glanced at the dinged-up Timex on his wrist. Already half past nine. More like it took the rookie some time to get himself together before radioing back to dispatch. "Good call."

Hinson tugged at his collar. "Closest neighbor is Widow Milner, but doesn't look like she's home," he said. "House is quiet, curtains drawn. Everything looks to be in order, but . . ."

The rookie's voice trailed off.

"What?" Roger asked.

Hinson bit his lip. "The front door was unlocked. That's kind of odd, right?"

"It's a safe town. Lots of folks leave their doors unlocked." Roger elected to ignore the irony in his response. Town was *safe*. Hell.

"I took a quick look inside and . . ."

Roger sighed, holding his breath on the inhale so he didn't suck in the bitter stench of Hinson's puke or lecture the boy about poking his head into someone's home without probable cause. "You took a look inside and what?"

"Well, it might be nothing," Hinson said, "but I noticed her walker was in the den. Wouldn't she need that to get around?"

Roger turned the information over in his mind. "Petunia Milner—Patsy Milner's daughter—lives in the next county over. Comes over regularly. I'm sure Pettie keeps a second walker in her vehicle but make a note."

But Clyde Halloran's disappeared, too, a voice niggled in the back of his mind. The man hadn't been home when Roger had driven over to ask if, as Edwin Boone's closest neighbor, he'd seen or heard signs of trouble. Not that a house three miles down the road rightly qualified as a neighbor, not in this day and age, and not that Halloran hadn't spent his fair share of time drying out at the sheriff's station. Still, two residents dead—or presumed dead, anyway, at least in Snow Leger's case—in the space of two days, and both with neighbors unaccounted for.

Hinson might have been new to the force, but Roger recognized a pattern when he saw one. Quigg's rabid-animal theory had been flimsy at best, with a marksman like Ed Boone. But bipedal footprints on Snow's lawn and a five-fingered handprint on her door told Roger that whatever he was up against—and the two must be related—it wasn't no animal.

"Let's get the place marked off, keep out the looky-loos," he told Hinson. "This is officially a crime scene."

"Should I call it in?"

"No." Roger knew what the rookie was about to say. He'd want to radio in, call for backup, but all that would do was stir up the media and send Sheriff Johnson barreling down his throat. The sheriff should have retired decades ago but still clung to the job with the iron grip of someone who would rather work themselves to the grave than waste away in retirement—or, worse, let someone else assume command. "Right now the sheriff thinks there's a rabid animal on the loose," Roger said, itching at a bit of scalp just under his hat. "Let's take a look around the house before we tell anybody otherwise."

The men didn't talk as they ran yellow police ribbon around Snow's side porch and took a barricade from Roger's trunk to station at the edge of the driveway. Afterward, they walked the perimeter of the house in silence, finding nothing. The crusted trail of blood ran out into the grass and vanished into the morning dew. Snow's blue coupe was unlocked, so they checked the front and back seats, then popped the trunk. Salon supplies crammed the small space full. If anything was out of order, Roger couldn't tell.

He shut the lid, an uneasy feeling forming in his gut. "Let's check inside." Roger watched Hinson's ruddy pallor slide to a sickly green. "Snow keeps a spare key under one of those phony rocks in a pot on her front porch," he added. "Let's use the front door instead of stepping over the evidence."

In the kitchen, they found Snow's purse on the table, keys still inside and cash in her wallet. Other than the smell of burnt milk coming from a kettle on the stove and a hastily cleaned spill of cinnamon on the linoleum, the room was undisturbed. No signs of struggle.

"Looks like she was fixin' herself a cup of warm milk before bed," Roger narrated, his gaze sweeping across the room as he assembled the clues to what were probably Snow's last moments this side of heaven. He peeked through the kitchen window, twisting his head toward the side door. He could see the stoop, but not much else. The view would have been more obscured at night, even with the motion light. Why in the dickens had she not trimmed back the damn azalea bush so she could see better? "Something interrupted her."

Hinson bent over the breakfast table, examining a scrap of paper. "There's a note here to pick up a sympathy card for Burton Murphy. Wasn't Mina Jean's visitation last night?"

"It was."

"Then why would she have a note to pick up a sympathy card?" Hinson asked. "Unless she missed the visitation." He surveyed the room, looked through the kitchen window at Snow's car in the drive. "It almost seems like she came straight home from her last appointment and never left."

"That's what it looks like," Roger agreed, remembering her trunk full of salon supplies. He did a quick mental rundown. He'd seen Snow around 11:00 a.m. the previous day, when he'd gone to deliver Edwin Boone's body to Evans Funeral Parlor. She'd seemed unsettled then, spooked. If Hinson was right, Snow had come home, not bothered to unpack her trunk, and then skipped Mina Jean's service.

Roger had known Snow since school, though she'd been several years ahead. She'd even barbered for him a time or two, along with the rest of the boys at the station who didn't mind a pretty gal lifting up their ears. He knew firsthand how fastidious Snow was with her salon supplies, and how much import she put on attending her clients' final services. What had gotten the woman so flustered yesterday afternoon? And what in God's name had happened between when he'd seen her last and when Andy West had come by on his paper route this morning?

"Radio the station and have Darla send a cleanup crew, but tell her to keep it quiet," he instructed Hinson. "No reporters, no sheriff." For the love of Christ, Buck Johnson better not get wind of this before Roger had some kind of explanation for what in the hell was going on. "Don't go anywhere until I get back," he said.

The younger deputy looked for a second like he might argue, but didn't. "Where are you going?"

"Evans Funeral Parlor."

"Evans Funer—" Hinson blinked. "Why?"

"Because if the timeline you've put together is correct, then I may have been the last person to see Snow Leger alive. Me and one other person." Roger sighed, pulled his notepad from his belt, and scratched down a name on the open page: *Lenore Evans.*

CHAPTER 9

Lenore Evans

Eternal Flame Cemetery was just a hop, skip, and jump across the lawn from Evans Funeral Parlor. The properties weren't combined when the town first zoned the resting places of its residents, but good planning had made them conveniently adjacent for both those who directed funerals and burials, and those who attended them.

Thank goodness for small distances, Lenore thought as she picked up her bouquet of fresh-cut pure white roses and stood, wiping garden dirt from the pleats of her pants. Her knees cracked and the pads of her fingers throbbed from winding the clock in the chapel. *I'm getting too old for this.*

She cast a glance back to the parlor to verify the last stragglers from Mina Jean's funeral had gone. The cordless phone didn't get past the parking lot without breaking to static, and she wouldn't hear it ringing from this distance, but aside from the service, it had been a slow morning. Still, best not to dally too long. Ducey was good at taking care of business, but not at handling the front desk—or anything that involved the general public, for that matter. Her mother didn't exactly give off the sweet elderly lady vibe people expected of a woman her age.

"Well, we each have our own skill set," Lenore muttered under her breath. Each of the Evans women approached her duty differently whenever the situation called for it, but all with equal effectiveness—even if none agreed with the others' methods.

All of us but Luna. Lenore brushed the thought away. Her granddaughter's time would come, just like hers had. Like Grace's. Like all of them.

We've done the girl a disservice, she thought, tightening her grip on the bundle of white roses in her hand, *keeping things from her for so long*.

A kink worked itself into the back of Lenore's neck and she freed a hand to rub at it, digging the tips of her fingers into her skin until her nails started to give way, push too far. Sting.

Yes, they should have told Luna. They should have told her a long time ago.

"Things might be different now," Lenore mumbled under her breath before catching herself. She wet her lips, clicking her tongue as it pulled back inside her mouth. Talking to oneself wasn't proper, even in private. If anyone saw, it might give them the wrong idea.

And Lord knows they didn't need that. Not now, not after how hard they had all worked to put that Godawful Mess of fifteen years ago behind them. Blend into the small town. People had a way of forgetting the past, overlooking the fact every woman in your family bore a daughter in her teens, well after that stopped being the norm, and that you lost all the men in your family within a few months of each other. Everyone gave the Evanses a wide berth, though only Buck Johnson seemed to harbor a special resentment. Of course, he had reason to, didn't he? Still, Lenore could see it in their eyes, when they said hello at the market but looked away just a little too fast, or when the only holiday cards she received were from her doctor's office. When the only people she had to share her thoughts with outside of family were a sheriff's deputy, a hairdresser, and the dozens of clocks her dead husband left behind.

Lenore continued on her trek through the cemetery, careful to avoid pricking her fingers on the snowy roses as she arrived at Mina Jean's final resting place. Dug in the morning's predawn, the dead appreciated a fresh grave the same way that the living enjoyed fresh sheets. Lenore would have preferred to cremate the woman's remains, just in case, to save a sample of her ashes, but the casket had already been covered with moist earth and a thick marble gravestone beset with rolling scrollwork stationed at the grave's head. Burton and his children had taken away most of the flowers, but a few sprays still waited for someone to claim them.

Lenore smiled as she lowered herself into a squat, ignoring the unpleasant tingle in the backs of her knees. The funeral had been lovely. Ducey had wired the dead woman's jaw back into place and Grace had done a remarkable job of concealing the damage with makeup. No one noticed they'd changed her burial dress. The eulogy had been elegant, the music tasteful, and the service had gone off without a hitch from the moment the doors opened until Mina Jean's casket was closed. In the end, the groundsman had poured earth over the coffin just like he always did, not an hour after the last mourner had left, and that was that.

But Snow didn't attend the funeral, a small voice pressed into the back of Lenore's mind. *She wasn't at the visitation, either.*

"It's hardly my responsibility if Snow Leger doesn't have the manners to show up for a service." The words snapped off Lenore's lips before she could stop them. A thorn from the fresh-cut roses pricked her finger and blood beaded on Lenore's skin as she exchanged the red rose a mourner had placed atop the dirt for a pristine white rose from her bouquet. She put the withered bloom in her pocket, suckled at her finger, and reconsidered.

Something had kept Snow from coming, hadn't it?

I'll give her a call as soon as I get back, Lenore promised herself. She had meant to do so last night, but other things—Mina Jean's rising, Edwin Boone's knocking, Luna—had taken her attention. The kink in her neck twinged. Having a sample of the woman's ashes might have given Lenore a clue as to what—*who*—drained her life away, but only if she knew what questions to ask or how to interpret the answers, which she didn't.

Lenore took a step forward and tripped over the toe of her loafer. She righted herself, dusted her hands on her thighs, and made sure her foot firmly touched ground as she continued, taking time to stop on her weekly pilgrimage to Eternal Flame's mausoleum to visit the grave of Darlene Boone, something she hadn't done since the day of the woman's funeral. Darlene and Edwin hadn't had any children to mourn their mother's passing, but Ed had arrived in the cemetery every Sunday after church with a Bible and a fresh bouquet of daisies, Darlene's favorite. He'd settle himself on the side of the double burial plot reserved for him and read a passage from the Good Book to his wife, then refresh her flowers and clasp his hand to the top of her headstone before going on home.

Every week the same, until now.

Lenore felt a pang of grief as she gazed at the blank side of the marker reserved for Edwin. Without her husband laid to rest beside her, the empty half of Darlene's burial bed would stay cold. His ashes, most of them anyway, would soon return to the earth beside her, but his body never would.

Bless his heart. Lenore thought of Edwin calling out from the cooler and put a white rose in each of the Boones' grave vases.

Lenore padded through the cold marble walls of the mausoleum, visiting her daddy's crypt first, then her husband's. Her last two white roses were for them, and she wiped down the stone slabs of their chambers with the rag she'd used to protect her fingers from the flower's thorns, then replaced last week's wilted stems.

"I miss you, Jim," she whispered, pressing her cheek to the smooth stone. If only it were him she was touching, her husband's skin warm upon her flesh instead of the cold touch of death against her face. "I miss you more every day." Tears prickled where they slipped down her cheek. "You and Daddy. I wish I could bring you back to me."

Silence and the memory of her mother's voice were her only answer. *I don't know why you torture yourself, Lenore,* Ducey would say. *There's nothing there for you but memories and dust.*

Lenore righted herself. She wiped her cheek and swallowed her feelings along with Ducey's weekly reprimand, forcing both down like a bad meal. There was still something here—there was still *someone* here. More than her husband's name emblazoned on a marble slab. Her father's etched into a headstone. There simply had to be.

"I'll see you next week," she promised. The quick trek back through the cemetery steeled her nerves, numbed the tingle of unshed tears. Death was hardly worth crying over, not when life was so hard.

When she arrived at the funeral parlor, Lenore avoided the front door and walked around the side of the building to where Jimmy had planted her small garden. He'd always had such a green thumb, her

Jimmy, and he'd suggested having things fresh and full of life around the parlor would be good for the soul.

Jimmy had planted the garden, but Lenore had seeded the white rosebush.

She pulled the wilted flower from Mina Jean's grave out of her left pants pocket, and a small vial of Edwin's ashes from her right. She fingered the bush's stalks where she'd cut fresh white blooms to take to the cemetery, then dropped to her knees in the flower bed to search for the right spot. Somewhere with good sunlight and room to grow. It took a minute, but she found a suitable place, digging into the earth with her hands the same way she'd dug against the kink in her neck—not too deep, just enough for the fresh cutting to take root. She laid the bloom from Mina Jean's grave in the shallow hole, then sprinkled Edwin's ashes over the rose before covering the spot with dirt and a small bit of peat moss.

Lenore watched as the small rise of dirt deflated, her offering accepted.

Hopefully she was wrong. Hopefully Mina Jean had died of cancer, and Edwin Boone had been a fluke, the victim of a rabid-animal attack after all. Hopefully they'd done enough to ward off the one thing they had no idea how to plan against.

Hopefully.

A dark spot blurred in the corner of Lenore's vision. She hadn't noticed it from afar, but here where the blooms met the earth, it was unmistakable. The pearl petals of her roses had faded, their edges wrinkling like old skin. She touched a dying rose, sending pallid gray petals fluttering to the ground as a sheriff's department Crown Victoria pulled into the parking lot, Roger Taylor grim behind the wheel.

The brakes squealed as he put the cruiser in park, let the car idle for one minute, two, before killing the engine. When he finally pushed open the driver's side door and swung his leg out, the thinness that she'd noticed about the deputy the day before was gone. If anything, he looked about as heavy as the hot air pressing against her chest.

Lenore set the edges of her palms against her knees and pushed herself to her feet as the deputy trudged toward her across the parking lot, notebook in hand. She brushed away the dirt on her hands, leaving unsightly brown smears on her slacks. "Deputy."

"Lenore." The man's jaw squared. He didn't take off his hat. "There's something I need to speak with you about—" He looked around, and his voice lowered, even though they were alone. "Inside, if you don't mind."

She attempted a smile, but only her eyebrow lifted. "Something wrong, Roger?"

The man shook his head. His eyes locked on hers, studying her expression in a way that might have made a lesser woman squirm. "When was the last time you saw Snow Leger?" he asked.

Lenore's blood ran cold, ice prickling inside her chest. A part of her had already known something was off, hadn't it, when Snow hadn't shown up at the visitation, at the funeral? The woman didn't miss a service. "I haven't seen Snow since she finished Mina Jean's hair yesterday morning—about the same time you arrived, as I recall."

The deputy's eyes dropped to the notebook in his hand. "You're sure? She didn't attend Mina Jean Murphy's visitation yesterday evening, or her funeral this morning?"

"Not that I'm aware of, but we can take a look at the visitors' log." The man's eye twitched, mirroring the stitch in Lenore's chest. Something about the way he'd asked the questions indicated he'd anticipated her answers. "Roger, did something happen to Snow?"

The man frowned. "Yes, ma'am," he said with a look that Lenore had seen before—in her husband's eyes the night of that Godawful Mess. In Buck Johnson's eyes ever since. "Yes, ma'am. Something did."

CHAPTER 10

Luna Evans

Luna hadn't slept well. In fact, she had barely slept at all.

When she'd left the funeral home last night after cleaning up from Mrs. Murphy's visitation, she thought she'd been okay. Maybe a little excited, even. After all, it wasn't every day you discovered that you were part of a family legacy to guard the balance between life and death, to slay the restless dead, was it?

Then there was the other thing—the feeling that curdled in her stomach but left a sweet flavor in her mouth. She'd tasted it at the parlor, when she'd watched her grandmothers pull Edwin Boone shoulders-first out of cooler number three. The coppery tang had haunted her dreams, thick as syrup on her lips when she awoke this morning.

Like blood, she'd guessed, though she couldn't be sure what blood tasted like.

Every time she'd closed her eyes to sleep, Luna had seen the black slime oozing out of Edwin Boone's mouth, his tongue lolling as he twisted inside the morgue cooler. The reddish-black stain spreading on the sheet wrapped over his body as Nana Lenore wheeled him to the crematorium. In the precious few moments Luna's eyes had managed to stay shut long enough for her to drift off to sleep, nightmares awaited her. Sometimes she flew, her vision cutting across the night. Other times she walked in the dark beneath an owl with white rose–petal wings, but always a knocking would sound, followed by a man-shaped shadow. He would reach for her, wrap his arms around her, until there was nothing but darkness—still, silent, suffocating black. Like being buried alive.

Then came the teeth. So many teeth.

By the time Luna's alarm clock had finally gone off, evidence of the sleepless night bruised the space under her eyes and faint nausea swirled in her stomach. She would have stayed in bed if she could, but if she'd tried to stay home, her mom would have made her go to the parlor to keep an eye on her, like she might burn down their apartment if left alone. So she'd gotten up, told Grace she slept fine like every morning, and gone to school.

Andy hadn't been at their meeting place before school, and by third period Luna assumed he'd called in sick for the second morning in a row. Alison Haney was also a no-show. Maybe the two were playing hooky together. Considering Luna had just discovered the dead were rising from their graves, boyfriend problems were the least of her worries. Still, when she called twice from the pay phone in the cafeteria and he didn't answer, images of Andy and Alison swelled into her thoughts. The swirling nausea took root, rumbling worse and worse as the morning progressed, until when the bell finally rang for lunch, Luna was convinced she might never be able to eat again.

Not that I want to, she thought, recalling what she'd seen yesterday afternoon.

Mina Jean's closed casket.

The gaping wound in a dead man's neck where someone had eaten out his life.

Bodies writhed and shuffled through the high school cafeteria, one mass of teenage spirit and hormones as kids made their way through the food lines. *Like maggots*, Luna considered, watching as two groups of popular kids in brain-gray athletic hoodies and matching joggers squabbled over the table closest to the exit. The din of hundreds of voices ricocheting off concrete walls pounded in her ears, the movement and noise crowding in around her, hungry, hungry—

Like Edwin Boone. Her stomach turned. Maybe she should try to call Andy again. Sick kids slept late, but it was noon. Surely he'd be awake by now.

"Luna Lou!"

A sudden voice calling from behind startled Luna, and she spun to see her two best friends waving from across the cafeteria. She sighed with relief as Dillon Cole and Crystal Shipley wove through the battlefield of tables and students. The closer they came, the more the nightmare of Edwin Boone receded. Eventually, the world settled back into place around her. In the company of her friends, the noise was just the familiar racket of the cafeteria, the wriggling students, the same kids Luna had known since elementary school.

Luna hugged Dillon and Crystal like she hadn't seen them in years, even though she'd traded notes with both before last period.

"What are you guys doing here?" she asked. "Don't you have third lunch?"

Crystal shrugged, trying to look casual and failing. The bright pink glitter she'd smeared over her eyelids matched the butterfly clips in her hair and made her brown skin sparkle. "We had a student council meeting. Plus, we wanted to have lunch with you."

Luna's eyebrow shot up. Dillon might have been prone to mischief, but Crystal was a firm rule follower. "Why?"

"Because you look like a hot mess and—" Dillon grimaced when Crystal nudged him in the ribs. He shrugged one shoulder. "*And* because your supercute boyfriend isn't here today, so we thought you could use some company," he finished weakly.

"Andy's 'sick' again—" Luna's shoulders tensed. "And apparently so is Alison Haney."

Crystal's nose crinkled, but Dillon eye-rolled away the insinuation tucked in Luna's words. "Andy West may have a type, but just because you and Alison are both curvy brunettes doesn't mean he's trading you in." He put his hand to his mouth and spoke through open fingers. "Seriously, Luna, she's the *worst.*"

That made Luna smile—a little. She thought of yesterday's conversation with Crane. Sure, she and Alison shared some similarities, but the other girl wasn't named after a goddess.

The trio made their way to the end of a long wood-veneer table with a handful of open plastic seats, but Luna pulled back when she saw Michelle Bryant and her flock of equally vapid groupies also seated at the table. Michelle was bad enough on her own. The cheerleader was a whole next level of awful when she had the full power of her squad behind her—even if her bestie, Alison Haney, was missing from the gaggle.

Luna turned, hoping to push her friends back out into the cafeteria and away from the danger zone at her back. "Why don't we find a spot somewhere else?"

"There isn't anywhere else." Dillon bristled and sucked his teeth. "What's wrong with here?"

Michelle's nasal soprano cut in before Luna could answer. "Um, excuse me." The girl flicked her wrist, motioning to the three empty seats. "Those seats are taken."

Dillon clamped his hand to his hip, his arm forming a sarcastic question mark that matched the sneer on his face. "Oh, really? Because I don't see anybody sitting in them."

"Look, this is *our* table." Michelle's voice inched an octave higher, and she spaced out her attack while her flock turned their collective gaze toward Luna and her friends, zeroing in for the kill. "We don't want a fag, a fatty, and a freak show anywhere near us." The rest of the table sniggered, and the corner of Michelle's lip curled triumphantly as she swiveled her glare at Luna. "Isn't there a dead body somewhere for you to play with, *Lunie Evans*?" she asked. "Why don't you run along home and play crypt keeper with your weirdo grandmas?"

Satisfied with her slew of insults, the head cheerleader began to apply a fresh layer of bright lip gloss to her pink-lacquered lips. Luna shot Michelle the bird, but the girl just clicked her teeth and kept her gaze trained on her compact mirror.

"Come on," Luna said, "let's—"

"That's a great color on you." Dillon blinked a little too fast, then he lifted his hand, flicked his wrist, and smirked at Michelle. "Twat pink shows off your yellow teeth."

Crap. If Luna had learned one thing surviving as an outcast in a small, Southern town, it was to let the popular kids have the spotlight and stay tucked in the shadows. Now Michelle's eyes bugged, and Luna braced for what was sure to be a dramatic scene—performed right on the main stage of Forest Park High School's cafeteria.

Michelle rounded on Dillon, maw snarled and ready to snap, but then she pulled back, stricken. Her glossy pink lips sealed closed.

"I'd choose your next words very carefully." Crane's deep baritone rolled like warm mist over Luna's shoulder. "You never know who might be listening, or how they might use what you say against you."

Crane emerged from behind Luna and settled himself in the open seat beside Michelle, gazing down at her with a look of passive interest, like a cat observed a mouse before it pounced. The cheerleader's lips fluttered open, closed, and open again as she stared at the much taller boy's long black hair. Black eyeliner. Trench coat. Michelle thrust back her chair, making the metal legs screech against the linoleum floor.

"Whatever, we were done eating anyway," she spluttered, and with a meaningful look and a scrambling of chair legs, Michelle and her gaggle were gone.

Apparently, Crane's reputation preceded him. Even the most popular girl in school didn't want to tangle with a strange goth boy rumored to have connections to the Trench Coat Mafia. If only Luna and her friends could harness the power of their meager reputations and throw it back at their tormentors.

"Impressive." Luna lowered herself into the chair opposite Crane, and the other two moved to open seats vacated by Michelle and her cronies. "I haven't seen anyone tell Michelle Bryant off like that since Emma Daniels butchered her ponytail with scissors in the third grade."

"Too bad Emma moved before middle school," Crystal added wistfully. "Maybe Michelle wouldn't have turned into such a tyrant if she were still around." Her cheeks were still flushed pink as she settled into the chair beside Luna. "She shouldn't make fun of you just because your family runs a funeral parlor. It's not like her mom does anything other than sit at home and day drink."

"And gossip on the phone to *my* mom." Dillon rolled his eyes, still lingering at the edge of the table, like he thought Michelle & Co. might return.

Luna bumped her shoulder against Crystal's. "Kids have been teasing me about the parlor since kindergarten," she said. "It's no big deal. Every town has a funeral business. People are born, people die."

Sometimes they get restless. Luna pushed the thought away.

Crystal's lips curved into a smile, but her cheeks didn't rise. Luna watched her friend fidget in her chair, fussing with her dark hair and the bunch of skin pushing out of the slightly too-small top. One hand lifted to the butterfly clip at her temple and Luna reached out to stop her before she could unclasp it. "Don't let her get under your skin, Crys. You're beautiful, butterflies and all. Bitchy Bryant's just jealous you're confident enough to let your colors show, and she's not."

The girl shrugged, but her hand dropped and her eyes shone a fraction brighter.

"She's right," Crane agreed. "All people like her need is someone to be their reflection. They don't typically like what they see." He motioned at his all-black garb, the ring of black drawn around his eyelids. "Trust me. It takes a lot of confidence to look this good and not care what other people think."

This earned him a real smile from Crystal, and at least three bonus points from Luna.

Dillon lowered himself into the chair next to Crane but didn't make eye contact. He looked up, down, right—keeping his attention trained on anything other than his friends. The tip of his nose had turned as pink as Michelle's lipstick.

"I'm sorry she called you a . . . you know. That was low, even for her," Luna told Dillon. She bent her head, trying to catch his gaze, but the boy turned his head to the side so all she got was his freckled profile, the gleam of his baby blues.

"I wish you could buy thicker skin at The Gap." Dillon's voice was strained with unshed tears, his eyes glassy when he looked at her. He shrugged. He rolled his eyes, adding, "I'd buy *that* in every color."

As abruptly as the cheerleader had abandoned her table, Crane leaned over and pressed his lips against Dillon's cheek with a loud *smack*, earning a gasp from Luna and Crystal, and another series of rapid eyeblinks from Dillon. Crane laughed and put his arm around the boy, cloaking him in a sheath of black leather. He blew kisses to each of the girls across the table—and anybody else he caught staring.

Dillon's eyes went wide. "Oh my *God.* I can't believe you just did that."

Murmurs tap-danced around the room, but Crane kept his arm boldly around the other boy, proudly giving the finger to anyone brave enough to look in his direction.

"People who hate themselves don't know how to love other people," Crane said with a grin. "I happen to love myself, and I'll gladly tell everyone else what I think of them, too, if they care to ask."

"Someone should tell that to my dad." Dillon's words were sharp, but the pink had moved from his nose to his cheeks and the ghost of a smile played on his lips. He planted a quick peck on the side of Crane's face in return. "Of course, coming out of the closet just pissed him off. Wait until he hears I kissed Marilyn Manson in the cafeteria. He'll have a heart attack."

"Things will get better at home, too," Luna offered, reading between the lines. Her family could be difficult, but at least they always loved her for who she was. Which was kind of ironic, wasn't it? Considering she'd only just discovered who they really were.

What else haven't they told me? she wondered.

Across the lunch table, Dillon rolled his eyes. "Well, they can't get much worse."

"What about your sister?" Crystal asked. "She's still on your side, right?"

Dillon shrugged. "Yeah, Kim's cool." A smile tittered at the edge of his lips. "When she's not hanging out with Stripper Cop. *Seriously* don't know what she sees in that guy."

"It's kind of weird she's dating a cop," Crystal said, delicately. "She's not, like, the biggest fan of law enforcement. Or, you know, rules in general."

"It's the uniform." Something twinkled in Dillon's eye, sparkling like the glitter on Crystal's cheeks. "One hundred percent."

Inspired by Crane's public display of affection, Luna leaned to the side to rest her head on Crystal's shoulder and nuzzled into her neck.

"You're so weird," Crystal teased as she pat Luna's head. "What's gotten into you today?"

"I don't know," Luna admitted, pulling herself upright. "I had a strange night and a sort of terrible dream, and it's nice to forget about it for a second."

Three friendly faces nodded back, and Luna smacked her palm against her forehead. "Oh!"

She'd gotten so caught up in what was happening that she hadn't thought to introduce Crystal and Dillon to Crane. The act was kind of pointless, considering there wasn't a person at school who didn't know who Crane Campbell was, and Dillon had already essentially made it to first base with the school's newest student.

"This is Crane, by the way," she said. "He just moved here from Colorado. Crane, this is Crystal and Dillon."

Crane bowed his head. His arm was still around Dillon's shoulders, and he gave Crystal a slight wave with his free hand, but his eyes never strayed from Luna. His lip twitched. "Now that we're all good friends, tell me about your dream."

Luna's breath caught in her throat. "It was nothing. Just a stupid nightmare."

"My favorite," he said.

"Fine." Luna sighed. She bypassed the weird shadows lurking in her nightmares. "All my teeth were falling out. Like, my mouth was full of loose teeth. There were so many—way more than I actually have, you know?" She shuddered at the memory and tried not to let her thoughts land on any of the other terrors of her most recent dreams. "Every time I tried to speak another tooth would come loose, until I thought I'd choke on them."

The phantom feel of the falling teeth pressed in around her tongue. She swallowed, opened her mouth, sucked in a mouthful of air. Luna ran her tongue across her teeth set firmly in her gums. "Can you choke in your dream?" she asked.

Dillon blinked, eyes wide. "Uhh, yikes."

"Super creepy," Crystal noted, shivering beside her.

"That wasn't a nightmare—it was a warning. Some might call it prophetic." Crane's baritone voice turned grave. Leather crackled as he pulled his arm from around Dillon and leaned forward. He set his elbows on the table. Steepled his fingers so that his many rings glinted under the cafeteria lights. “Dreams have meanings. What you’ve described represents death, or to be more accurate, a fear of dying.”

Luna pulled a face. “How so?”

“The loss of teeth represents an inability to feed,” he said. “Without teeth—or being unable to use your mouth for consumption—you die.”

Consume. Stinging cold raced through Luna as, in the back of her mind, Edwin Boone’s tongue lolled and teeth snapped.

“It was just a dream,” she said.

Crane’s eyes didn’t leave hers. “I hope so, Moon Girl.”

CHAPTER 11

Ducey Evans

Plastic crackled under Ducey's finger as she hooked a digit in the break-room window blinds and tugged down to stare through the resultant gap at the patrol car parked at the back of Evans Funeral Parlor's small lot. It wasn't good, Deputy Taylor showing up two days in a row. Still, better him than Sheriff Johnson.

She snorted. Johnson would probably rather chew off his own foot than set foot on Evanses' property. Fine by her.

The deputy hesitated in the driver's seat before he turned off the engine, and Ducey watched him tap the steering wheel with his head leaned back against the headrest. She growled when her breath fogged up the glass. *Crap or get off the pot*, she thought, and finally, right about the time she was ready to march outside and give the man a piece of her mind for idling on her blacktop—he could waste gas loitering at Jimbo's if that's how he wanted to spend his afternoon—Roger opened the driver's side door, pushed himself out, and made his way toward the parlor's side entrance. Ducey let the blinds snap closed and listened for a knock at the side door.

Nothing.

She pushed her bifocals up into her hair and leaned in close to squint around the edge of the plastic strips, through the narrow strip of sun-streaked windowpane. Roger stood with his notebook clutched in his grip, speaking with Lenore beside her white rosebush.

The notebook gave Ducey pause. Nothing good came of a lawman writing down anything you said.

Lenore stood with dirt smeared on her pants and her hands on her hips, rigid as a raw ear of corn. Ducey smirked. Whatever Roger wanted, he was barking up the wrong tree if he expected to get more than a quick goodbye out of Lenore today. She'd been agitated when she'd stalked over to the cemetery after Mina Jean's service, clutching a wilted bloom from the woman's casket spray and a vial full of Edwin Boone's ashes in tow. By the looks of it, she hadn't come back any better off. When something stuck in Lenore Evans's craw, it stuck good.

She's like her daddy that way, Ducey thought. Royce had always been a little on the squirrely side, too. The man came up too poor to paint and too proud to whitewash, but he'd had a nose that went pink at its tip when she kissed him and a laugh so loud people two towns over could hear it. Man could get himself tangled into all sorts of knots, but he'd had a heart as big as his laugh and made of gold.

Ducey's left thumb bent to rub bare skin on her ring finger, jolting her out of memory and back into the Evans Funeral Parlor break room. She only took off her wedding band when she worked on the dead, never very long, but the body waiting out lunch hour on the lab's exam table had given her a fit all morning. She'd managed to get the eye caps on without too much trouble, but the lips kept sagging open, no matter how much wax she rubbed on them. The body wasn't restless, just stubborn. The woman it'd belonged to had been about as stubborn as a hot summer day was long, too. Ducey fished the ring out of her blouse pocket and wriggled it back onto her finger. Maybe there was some truth to Lenore and Grace's belief that something about a person stayed in their body long after their soul left.

Not that she'd tell them that.

Ducey peeled herself away from the window and let herself drop into her armchair for her afternoon ritual: a chicken salad fold-over, a cold can of soda water, and *Walker, Texas Ranger*. Whatever Roger Taylor wanted outside, Lenore could handle. Girl might be as temperamental as a pot of boiling water, but she held together like a diamond—could be cut into a thousand shapes and still wouldn't break.

"That"—Ducey bit into her sandwich, mumbling around the bread and meat—"the girl got from me."

The opening credits of *Walker* had barely begun to roll—all blue skies and steel guitar—when the side door of the funeral parlor creaked open. Ducey snatched the TV clicker off the table tray, mashed the mute button, and stopped chewing as Lenore and Roger made their way up the hallway toward the front lobby.

"I'll double-check the guest log just to be sure." Lenore's voice sounded tight when the pair passed by the break room. "But if she was here for Mina Jean's visitation, then I missed her."

"If you say she wasn't here, I believe you," Roger replied, sounding equally strained. "But, given the circumstances, I appreciate you taking a second look."

"Circumstances." Ducey slipped a fingernail under the soda tab and peeled the can open with a carbonated *snap*. Then she swigged to wash down the bite of sandwich and sighed out the bubbles. She'd seen plenty of *circumstances* in her eighty years, but she only got one hour a day with Chuck Norris.

From down the hall, Ducey heard the rustle of pages turning—the guest log from the previous night's sign-ins, she guessed. She snorted into her soda can. Lenore wouldn't miss an ant if it failed to show up for a visitation, much less a fully grown human.

"I'm happy to make you a copy if you like." Lenore's voice slid down the hallway again. "But like I told you outside, Snow left yesterday morning after fixing Mina Jean Murphy's hair, and that's the last we saw of her."

Snow.

With all the goings-on around the parlor, Ducey hadn't given a moment's thought to the beautician. Now she realized Snow hadn't been at the visitation, or the funeral. Well, hell.

"Sorry, Walker." Ducey dropped her unfinished sandwich on the plate and clicked off the set with a heavy sigh. "Guess you and Gilyard are gonna have to sort this one out without me."

Lenore sat ramrod straight in the chair behind the lobby desk and had the page of the guest log turned to the previous evening's visitation sign-in when Ducey trudged all the way back down the hall into the lobby, shuffling her feet so they'd hear her coming. The tension in the room made the little hairs on the back of her neck prickle. She stationed herself at the end of the desk, ran the palm of her hand around the spike in her apron, and popped a butterscotch candy between her lips. She shot a look at the deputy first, then Lenore. "What y'all doin'?"

The corner of Roger's left eye twitched and he pulled at his hat. He sucked in a deep breath and rubbed at the skin under his eyes. When he opened his mouth, a sigh escaped.

"Nobody has seen Snow since she left here yesterday morning," Lenore answered for him.

Ducey clicked the hard candy against her dentures. "And?"

"We've got a situation at her house which leads me to believe we might not be seeing her again," Roger said stiffly. He shifted, boots shrieking on ceramic. "I expect Channel Six'll be on it by the time I get back," he said. "It's . . . well, it doesn't look good."

Ducey sucked her teeth, reading between the lines. The deputy's *circumstance* sounded like a bloodbath missing its victim—which made the situation over at Snow Leger's house *both* their problems.

She pushed her glasses up her nose. "You think Snow is dead?"

Roger tugged at his hat again, then pulled it free and tossed it on the desk beside Lenore's open guest log. His eye twitched again as he leveled his gaze at Ducey. "Too much blood to think much else."

Ducey didn't blink. "Must be the same animal that got Edwin Boone."

"I've never seen anything the likes of what's in Snow Leger's den." Roger jerked his neck to the side, emitting a series of cracks almost sharp enough to distract from the sweat that beaded on his upper lip at the mention of the woman's home. "Probably shouldn't be telling you this, but a rabid animal's not at the top of my list of my suspects right now."

Ducey's hand traced the smooth, round curve of the trocar's head. "That right?"

The deputy's nod looked heavy. He started to speak then changed his mind, wiped his mouth, and started over. "Truth of the matter is, I've got more missing people than I do bodies," he said. "Edwin Boone confirmed dead and Snow Leger as good as—and both neighbors missing to boot."

"Neighbors?" Lenore slammed the guest log shut. She jumped to her feet so fast Ducey nearly swallowed her butterscotch from secondhand whiplash.

"Clyde Halloran's been missing since we found Edwin," Roger said, trying to make it look like he hadn't noticed the woman rocket out of her chair, "and Patsy Milner is currently unaccounted for."

Ducey made a show of rolling her eyes behind her wide bifocal frames. "Clyde Halloran probably got himself good and top-heavy and is holed up somewhere to dry out. Poor man's been drunk since 1961."

"And Patsy Milner has a daughter next town over," Lenore added, recovering. "Maybe she's gone to see Petunia."

Roger nodded the way people did when someone told them something they already knew. "Might be." He flipped a few pages backward in his notebook and read some of the scribbles on the page. "Did either of y'all notice anything strange about Edwin Boone's body"—he cocked his head to the side—"other than the obvious?"

Ducey pretended to consider the question. Other than the fact the dead man came back banging dents into her cooler she'd had to pop out with a hair dryer? "No."

"What about any other bodies that might have come through over the past couple of days?" Roger asked. "Anything unusual, any kind of pattern—something I should know about?"

Lenore shrugged. "It's been a slow week. Mina Jean Murphy came in first, then Edwin. We have a body in the lab. Heart attack, Quigg said."

Roger nodded and palmed the top of the desk before adjusting his belt. "Maybe I ought to take another look at Ed while I'm here."

"I'm afraid we cremated Ed's remains already," Lenore told him in perfect apologetic melancholy. "Within forty-eight hours, I reminded you."

"Often twenty-four," he added, visibly irked at the inconveniently narrow timeline.

More like five, in Ed Boone's case. All that remained of the man now was whatever ashes Lenore still hung on to, in the hidden stash Ducey pretended she didn't know about.

Ducey watched the man's eye twitch return. "Slow week," she repeated with a shrug.

"Well, might not be that way for long, at the rate things are going." Roger rubbed at his forehead, eyes closed, palm stopping so that his fingers pinched the bridge of his nose. His tongue made a dash over his teeth under his skin, cheeks going gaunt then letting go with a resigned pop. The deputy didn't have a clue what was happening in town, and it showed. Wouldn't take him long. Man might still be a deputy, but he was worth ten of Sheriff Johnson. "We're doing everything we can," he said. "In the meantime, if you see anything unusual, get wind of something not quite right, call me."

"You know we will," Ducey lied. She pushed her butterscotch along her teeth with her tongue. "Won't we, Len?"

Lenore's face slid into a smooth mask, her tone sweet as sugar. "Of course."

Nodding his farewell, Roger settled his hat on his head and made his way toward the front exit. "I'd appreciate it if you kept this between us. At least until we've got a little more information to go on. Don't think it's an animal, but I don't need people thinking worse thoughts and starting a panic." He pushed open the door and hesitated, index finger tapping time against the glass, and turned back. "And do me a favor," he said. "Lock your doors. Don't go out at night. Don't let anyone in."

Ducey pushed her mouth up into a smile. The moment Roger Taylor's backside was on the other side of the glass front doors, she let it fall. "Where's Grace?"

"Finishing cleaning up after Mina Jean's service." Lenore jerked her head toward the chapel as she slid the guest log back into the desk's top drawer. Her words came out stilted, each one a chip clinking its way down a Plinko board. "We need to get ahead of this, Mama."

Ducey nodded. "We always do."

"First Mina Jean, then Edwin Boone, and now Snow Leger." Lenore's voice rose with each name, then cut off abruptly. "That's three. Five if you add in Clyde Halloran and Patsy Milner."

"I can count, Lenore," Ducey snapped. "Lock the doors, and—"

Lenore's neck twisted so fast it was a wonder her head didn't spring clean off. "Lock the doors?" she repeated, incredulous. "Mama, we can't just ignore this."

"I'm not ignoring nothin'. I just don't need anyone strollin' in while you're raisin' hell, is all," Ducey snapped. "We need to get ourselves together and figure this out before Roger Taylor beats us to it—God forbid he opens his mouth to Johnson. We already know this road leads back to us." She watched as Roger's cruiser turned out of the driveway, drove away. Hopefully the deputy would be smart enough to take his own advice. Otherwise, he wouldn't be looking for his missing persons.

They'd be hunting him.

CHAPTER 12

Grace Evans

"First Mina Jean Murphy, then Edwin Boone—"

Lenore's words rushed out in frustrated knots that boomed through the insulated chapel walls from the front lobby as Grace finished tidying up the chapel following Mina Jean Murphy's service. The chore had taken longer than was typical, the deceased having been something of a paragon in the community, and Grace had waited until the last mourners pulled out of Evans Funeral Parlor's lot to start cleanup. Nothing destroyed a sympathetic scene like walking in on it being wiped clean. So much Kleenex had been stuffed between the pews that Grace's excavations had filled two trash sacks with the soggy tissues. After over an hour of trying to air out the small space, the room still smelled of Estée Lauder White Linen perfume and baby powder.

Better than the alternative, she considered. The dead, restless or otherwise, had a distinct, sickly sweet odor. Most people blamed the scent on funereal flowers, but it belonged to the dead themselves. It was also hell on upholstery. At least she'd instructed Luna to go straight home after school, which meant Grace could take her time. She'd prefer to have her daughter where she could keep a close eye on her, but Evans Funeral Parlor wasn't the place. Not today.

Not after yesterday.

"—and now Snow Leger." Lenore's voice rose to a crescendo in the lobby.

Grace felt the words' impact as she put away the last of her cleaning supplies into the storage closet. Her mother was the kind of woman who metered emotions, not thrust them all out at once.

Ducey's voice. "Now, Len, you need to calm down before you give yourself a conniption."

Grace sucked in a lungful of air and tucked a loose coffee-brown curl behind her ear. What did Snow have to do with Mina Jean and Edwin? The three didn't exactly spin in the same social circles—a single, middle-aged beautician who kept to herself, the head of the West End pecking order, a cantankerous widower from the outskirts of town. Grace had heard a car pull up, heard Roger's voice tangle with her mother's in the lobby, but she'd kept busy in the chapel, avoiding the adoring eyes of a man that she couldn't bring herself to love back. Now she was left with garbage bags full of old women's powdery tears and questions that would only have unhappy answers.

Every now and again a strigoi would rise, but rarely. This many so close made Grace's skin crawl. *It's not happening again. Not yet. Not again.*

A small voice niggled in the back of Grace's mind. *You always knew it would.*

Grace strangled the last garbage sack shut and tied it off. No, this was not like before—it was *nothing* like before. What had happened fifteen years ago hadn't started with old women rising from the dead, men having their necks nearly chewed off.

It had started with love.

"Love." Grace scoffed. The word didn't sit right, but she had loved Sam—and he'd loved her, no matter what anyone said. Maybe she should have known better. Should have seen him for what he was. She should have listened to her mother's and grandmother's warnings about strange men too interested in her for her own good—the same lessons she tried to instill in her own daughter. But if she'd have listened, she wouldn't have Luna, would she? Grace had known the sneaking around, the secrets, were wrong, but her heart had been on fire with forbidden love, and she'd been unable to resist the siren call of her own desire.

"But he's gone now." Grace said the words out loud, just like she'd done hundreds—*thousands*—of times over the past fifteen years, ever since that fateful night.

Gone but not forgotten.

Grace steeled her nerves, closed the storage closet, and turned off the chapel lights. She shut the door without taking a second look at the chancel, where Mina Jean had sat up in her casket. Grace had put down her share of the dead over the past many years, but Mina Jean Murphy had been different. The woman's rising was the start of something terrible. For her to come back after wasting away meant something had fed on her. For Edwin to follow as he did meant whatever that something was growing stronger.

No sounds of her grandmother's lunchtime routine drifted up the hall from the darkened break room as Grace stepped out into the hall. She pushed back her sleeve to look at her wristwatch. There was a cadaver in the lab, but Ducey didn't miss her daily hour with Chuck Norris. Not if she could help it.

But the lights in the lab were on, and her mother's voice was slicing down the hallway.

"*And* my bush is wilting," Lenore screeched.

Bracing herself, Grace slipped into the room. Lenore paced the length of the work area, each step quick and stunted as bits of dirt shook loose from the pleats of her pants, sprinkled into the tile without her notice. A body lay under a crisp white sheet on the metal examination table, all but the head covered. Ducey leaned over the body of a large woman and wiped a smear of wax off her lips. She grumbled something that sounded like, "Gonna have to stitch this one shut," but Grace couldn't be sure.

"What's going on?" she asked.

"No, not wilting." Lenore's hands raked into the air above her head, as if the overhead lights were scattered autumn leaves. "It's *rotting*."

Bile rose in Grace's throat. Darkness was like a disease once it got its teeth in you. A hungry thing that didn't let go. Sometimes you had to feed it, keep it satiated, to stop it from spreading, and Lenore fed what was laid to rest under her white rosebush every chance she got.

"Are you sure it's rotting, Mom?" Grace tried. "It's especially hot out this summer. Maybe—"

The look of cold fury in her mother's eyes turned Grace's words to ice water on her tongue. She drank them back in as Lenore's hand dropped to her lips, followed by the sound of her teeth biting at her nails.

It had been hot that summer, too.

Ducey's crooked fingers fed a black string through the eye of a large surgical needle and pulled the thread tight. Instead of returning to her task, she laid the needle atop the cadaver's chest, dropped her hand to her pocket, and emerged with a hard candy. She untwisted the cellophane wrapper of a butterscotch and shoved the nugget in her mouth.

"Lenore," she said, "I've got work to do and your words are comin' out of you faster than green grass through a goose. It's givin' me heartburn." She sucked at the candy with her eyes closed. "Why don't you sit down and get your breath? Then we can all put our heads together and discuss what's happening—and what we're gonna do about it."

Rather than inviting calm, Ducey's words made Lenore spin, glaring, on her heels.

"I'll tell you what's happening!" Lenore snapped. "The dead are rising, and this isn't a matter of a *hard* death or a *bad* burial. We can't contain this, Mama, not if there are others. Ones we didn't know about. The damage could be . . ." Her voice trailed off as she hunted for the right word. Her eyes lit briefly on Grace before she settled on, "Exponential."

The bitter fluid in Grace's mouth stung the backs of her teeth, and her pulse thumped in her neck. "Would one of you please tell me what is going on?"

Lenore looked as if she might speak, but Ducey loosed a deep exhale and beat her to it. "Clyde Halloran is missin', been gone since they found Edwin Boone." She picked up the needle, pierced the inner fold of the cadaver's lips, and pulled through. "So is Widow Milner, Snow Leger's neighbor. Taylor found a pretty ugly scene in Snow's house this mornin'."

Grace's heart sank to her toes. "How ugly?"

"They found a tongue in her den. A *tongue*." Lenore sank into a chair at the edge of the room, all the fight drained out of her. "Things are escalating quickly—*too* quickly."

"We need to get the lead out and get these ghouls in the ground. And we need to tell Luna," Ducey said. "*All* of it."

Grace shook her head. "She's only fifteen. She's not ready to hear any more secrets, especially this one."

Ducey pulled a stitch through. "You know what they say about secrets," she grumbled.

"You weren't much older than her when we told you," Lenore cut in, "and you didn't have half the stakes Luna does."

Shame crawled up Grace's thighs to burn right beneath her belly button.

"Stakes!" Ducey emitted a brusque laugh and clapped her hands together. "Perhaps if the girl had had more stakes growin' up, we would've had an easier time of this."

Lenore shot her mother a scathing glare. "Now is not the time for jokes, Mama."

"It's not a joke, Len," Ducey fired back. "Just because she doesn't know what she is doesn't change the fact any more than it changes what's buried under your rosebush." The old woman finished sewing and tied off the end of the thread for Grace to snip later. She pulled the sheet up over the cadaver's head and stepped away from the table, green eyes sparking through the lenses. "We did the girl wrong by not telling her sooner. We should have had the good sense to bring her up knowin' the truth—all of it."

"We couldn't have known how she'd take it, Mama," Lenore snapped. She pointed an accusatory finger at Grace, still standing in the center of the room, and dug her heel into the carpet. "We told this one early and look what happened."

The burning in Grace's belly moved into her chest.

"Oh, get off it, Lenore," Ducey said. "We all knew what was coming. We've just been countin' the hours different. Besides, the girl's an Evans."

Lenore huffed and shifted. She rubbed her hands along her arms, but didn't make eye contact. "She's only half Evans."

"We don't know that this has anything to do with Luna," Grace attempted weakly, feeling the hopelessness of the words in every syllable.

"Oh, like hell we don't." Ducey slapped a palm against cooler number three. "We've got two restless dead in two days, one of 'em gnawed up. We know it ain't no rabid animal out there, just like we know that Snow ain't missin', bless her heart. I betcha it was Clyde that took a bite out of Ed. Poor man's troubled enough that he could have drunk himself into an early grave and his body wouldn't know any better when it got back up for another sip. Might have been him that got Patsy Milner—who I reckon wandered over to Snow's house next door, in case you two ain't keepin' up." She huffed and sucked in a fresh breath, kept going. "If there was a mature strigoi in town, those ghouls would already be at the parlor by now, like they always wind up. But whoever drained Mina Jean is either lying low, takin' their time, or tryin' to hurry up and beat us to the punch. We need to get the lead out and get to work—and that starts with tellin' Luna."

"We protected her." Grace had been so careful—the curfews, the window locks, the constant badgering to the point Luna would barely talk to her. She'd damn near ruined her relationship with her daughter, and for what? For this to happen anyway?

"We did the best we could," Lenore agreed. "But this was always inevitable, and if we don't put a stop to it, it'll only get worse. We need to make sure what your Daddy died to bury under my rosebush stays buried."

"And then what?" Ducey's voice came out ragged. "Ain't nothin' under that pretty white rosebush that's gonna bring Jimmy back, Len."

Like the truth they'd hidden from Luna, this was a conversation they'd had before, so many times.

Every fiber of Lenore's body went stiff. A shadow slid over her face and her words came out as cold as ice. "I know that."

"Do you?" the old woman pressed. "Then why the ashes, Lenore? Why keep windin' that damn clock and frettin' every time you walk through the cemetery?"

Lenore sprung to her feet like someone lit a match under her chair. "Because we don't know everything, do we, Mama? You said it yourself: half of what we have to go on is hokum. Hell, we don't even know *why* we do what we do, other than it must be done." She pointed toward the side of the parlor, the other side of its walls. "Other than *him*, the strigoi we've encountered were just recently human and alive. We don't know how they go from that"—she swept her hand to point at the cooler Ducey's palm still pressed against—"to . . . to . . . something else. If there's anything I can learn from them, moving or not, then I have to at least try."

Grace's body had curled in on itself with each of her mother's words. By the time Lenore went quiet, Grace felt like origami, a sheet of paper bent and folded until it took on another shape entirely.

"This is my fault," she whispered.

Her mother said nothing.

"Oh, it ain't your fault, child," Ducey said, sighing. "But that don't mean it's not time to set things right."

Icy fingers coiled around Grace's wrist, tickled along the smooth edges of the scar. Her mother leaned close and Grace thought she might say something, but then she pulled away and stalked back to the lobby. Before Grace ruined her relationship with her daughter, she'd destroyed the same with her mother. Lenore said she didn't hold Jimmy's death against her, but Grace could feel it in every word she spoke.

Grace waited until Lenore's footsteps faded and Ducey returned to working on the cadaver under the sheet before leaving the room. She made her way back into the chapel, sat in the second pew, and stared at the place where Mina Jean had opened her eyes. The woman had called her name, voice as clear as day and not a scratch on her.

Her mother and grandmother were right, but that didn't change the fact that she had to find a way to tell her daughter that she was raising the dead.

CHAPTER 13

Deputy Roger Taylor

Roger's visit to Evans Funeral Parlor hadn't accomplished much, but it had confirmed that he and Lenore Evans were the last people to see Snow Leger. Whatever had befallen the woman had happened in the space of time between when she'd left her last appointment with Mina Jean Murphy and when Andy West had come by to deliver her morning paper. But *what*, exactly, had happened—and why did he get the feeling Ducey and Lenore knew more than he did?

It didn't make good sense to be aggravated about Edwin Boone's body already being cremated. Yesterday, there'd been no reason to hold on to it.

Yesterday, Lenore warned him they wouldn't.

Ducey wasn't wrong about Clyde Halloran's drinking, either. The man's benders were the stuff of legend, and it *was* plausible he'd simply tied on one too many and gotten himself turned around outside of town. Suspicion niggled at the back of Roger's throat. He couldn't put his finger on it, but something about the women's behavior had seemed off—which was saying something considering there was nothing usual about the Evans women. Normally, the Evanses' quirks were part of their charm. Today, they only added to Roger's mounting frustration.

Ducey Evans is the kind of woman who could look at a storm-cloud sky and convince you it isn't gonna rain, Roger thought. There'd be no prying anything out of the old woman other than what she wanted to share, and he'd be hard-pressed to find anyone else in town who knew as much as she did.

Mina Jean Murphy, maybe, but she was six feet under.

Roger's gut churned. He drummed his fingers on the steering wheel as he drove. Everywhere he turned, he kept coming up short. His mind jumped to the mess on Snow's living room floor. With any luck, Hinson didn't muck up collecting whatever evidence he could find in the woman's house. Roger should take another trip out to Ed Boone's, too. Look around again, maybe try to get a warrant for Clyde Halloran's place. Give Petunia Milner a call to check in on her mother.

None of those felt promising.

"Get your head together, Taylor," Roger ordered himself as he swung his cruiser onto Main Street, nose pointed back toward the sheriff's department. "Focus on the facts."

Facts. Fine. He could do facts.

The facts were: Edwin Boone had been mauled to death on his own property by something he'd shot, but either he didn't hit it or it didn't stay down. Ed's neighbor Clyde Halloran hadn't been seen since he'd shambled into church a week ago for the free luncheon put on by Mina Jean and the gals at the Symphony League. Mina Jean had since passed from cancer, but Snow Leger had been accosted in her home, and *her* neighbor, an elderly widow who only left home when her daughter drove into town to run her to the grocery, had walked out of her front door without her walker.

Fact was, Roger had one torn-up body, parts of another one, and a couple of old-timers nobody had known were missing to report. And, fact was, Sheriff Buck Johnson—a grade A Shit—was a good ol' boy who liked his small town quiet, slow, and predictable, not to mention he and Ed Boone had been hunting buddies. It didn't matter if it was a pack of rabid coyotes or a crazy serial killer, Johnson would demand somebody answer for disturbing the solitude of his quaint Southern town. If Roger didn't find someone to take the heat for what-in-the-hell-ever was happening around here, it might very well be him that ended up burning.

Hinson better have kept his mouth shut. Roger hadn't wanted to make it an order, but maybe he should have. Hinson was a fine kid and a decent deputy, but the last thing Roger needed was Johnson firing on all cylinders before he got a chance to load his gun.

Up ahead, just around a bend, a skinny skeleton of a boy wearing all black slunk along the side of the road. Roger checked the time on his dash clock and groaned. Really—half past one? Most kids who skipped school midday snuck out in cars or hopped on the city bus during lunch hour, squirreled themselves away in homes or at Parkdale Mall. Few had the gumption to boldly stride out the front door and down the street in broad daylight.

Roger blipped his sirens and pulled up behind the boy. He shunted the cruiser into park and pushed open the door, leaving the engine running to keep the car cool.

"Hold up there for a second, son," he said.

The boy's body twisted in Roger's direction, but if he was looking at the deputy through the shag of greasy black hair over his face, Roger couldn't tell. The confrontational tilt of the boy's posture irked him even more than the leather coat and pantlegs wide enough to fit in a second person. The kid's body language wasn't disrespectful, not exactly. If anything, it was smug, verging dangerously on arrogant, like a rock star nobody recognized.

Great.

The boy's tone matched his body language, but no Southern twang thrummed in his voice. "There a problem, Officer?"

Roger stepped back and crooked his head to the side so he could meet the boy's eyes without giving him the advantage. The kid had a few inches of height on him, not that it mattered.

"Deputy," he corrected, planting his hands on his hips in the stance favored by law enforcement. "You know the high school's back in the other direction. Mind telling me where you're headed this time in the afternoon?"

The boy smirked before he forced his face blank. "Obviously not the school."

Uh-huh. Roger tightened his lips into a scowl and felt his eyes narrow. "What's your name, son?"

"I'm known as Crane Campbell."

Known as? The odd manner the boy used to introduce himself didn't sit right with Roger. *Crane* didn't sound like a real name, either, at least not one used outside of literature or television. The word queued up images of the willowy, easily spooked pedagogue from Washington Irving's *The Legend of Sleepy Hollow*, Ichabod Crane. Given the circumstances, the character's close association with the Headless Horseman made Roger shiver, though the temperature on the flat stretch of scrub was perilously close to three digits. Southeast Texas was a long way off from Tarrytown, New York.

A tongue was bad enough. Finding someone's head—or their headless body—would be one more thing Roger just didn't need.

He cracked the tension from his neck. Sweat slipped below his collar, blotting his undershirt. "Unusual name for a boy your age."

"It's not a name," the kid called Crane replied. "It's an epithet."

"An epi-what?"

Crane lifted a hand, spindly pale fingers pulling aside the dark curtain of his hair to reveal dark eyes rimmed in black eyeliner. Roger grunted and shifted his weight from his right foot to his left. Apparently, the girl at the coffee shop and Snow Leger weren't the only ones sporting the new gothic makeup trend.

"A name I have chosen to use in place of the one decided for me at my birth," Crane explained, his voice more soothing in the hot summer sun than it had any right to be. "A new name opens the soul to new gifts and allows one to connect more deeply with their infinite selves." He let his hand drop so his curtain of hair fell closed, concealing his eyes. "The crane represents good luck and fortune through many cultures. Longevity."

"That so?" Roger's tone compensated by coming out overly gruff.

"There is much to be learned from nature as we look beyond the confines of the mortal trappings and into the realm of the spirit," Crane said.

"Uh-huh." Roger knew zilch about spirit realms. Must have skipped that class in school. His left eyelid twitched. "So, what's your real name, Crane Campbell?" he asked, rubbing at his cheekbone. "The one your mama decided for you at birth."

Crane lifted his chin and spoke down his nose. "Robert."

Roger took out his pocket notebook, flipped it open, and scrawled down the kid's name, real and assumed. "You new to town, Robert?"

"Do you interrogate every teenager you stop, Deputy?"

"Just the ones I don't know."

"And you know everything that goes on in your small town?"

"It's sort of my job." Roger rolled his neck, tapped his badge with the tip of his pen, then let the instrument hover above the little pad. "How long you been in town?"

Crane made to respond, but the radio on Roger's belt crackled to life. A familiar voice staticked across the line. "Come in, Taylor."

Hinson. Roger pressed the button on his shoulder mic. "This is Taylor. What's up, Hinson?"

"You might want to get down here." The rookie's voice sounded as wet across the radio as it had on Snow's back stoop.

"One second," Roger said. He pivoted away to muffle the radio's volume without letting Crane out of his sights and lowered his voice before pressing the mic. "Go ahead, Hinson."

"Station just got a call in from Petunia Milner. She hasn't been able to get in touch with her mother. Hasn't heard from her since Sunday."

Same day Edwin Boone was attacked. So much for that phone call. Roger cleared his throat and pressed the button. He hoped the rookie hadn't been fool enough to tell Petunia about what had happened to her mother's neighbor—at least not until they'd had time to get their facts together. And debrief Johnson.

"Roger that," he said. "I'm on my way."

He could feel Crane's eyes from behind the sheet of greasy black hair. With a sigh, Roger flipped his notepad closed and pushed it back into his pocket. One kid skipping school was far from a crisis, even if the kid in question was as strange as Crane Campbell. He'd heard about these types on the news from Austin and Dallas, with their black makeup and black clothes, but ugly outsides didn't always make for ugly insides. No need to go looking for problems where they didn't exist.

We got more than enough of those right now. Roger made a mental note to keep an eye on Crane Campbell. Spiritual or not, big city problems always found their way to small towns eventually.

His eye twitched. "Stay in school all day next time, okay?" Roger told the boy as he returned to his cruiser, opened the driver's door, and dropped into the seat.

Crane nodded, then turned as Roger swung the Crown Vic's door shut. The boy's black pantlegs billowed in the open curtain of his trench coat as he continued off away from the school without another word—a skinny scarecrow, tall, lank, and loosely strung together.

Roger shivered despite the sweat dripping down his spine. A newcomer in town hadn't given him the creeps like this since he'd set eyes on Grace Evans's old beau. Come to think of it, that guy'd had a weird name, too. She'd called him Sam, but that wasn't his whole name. It was something longer, not Samuel, but close.

Samael. That was it. Roger had looked it up once. An old name. Biblical—in the Old Testament way. Full of brimstone.

He slumped back behind the wheel of his cruiser, his elbow crooked against the warm window glass as he watched the kid called Crane make his way down the street until he was nothing more than a dark silhouette under the bright glare of the afternoon sun. Sweat dripped down Roger's forehead and he wiped it away.

Weird things were stacking up in his small town. First Edwin Boone and Snow Leger, and now this kid in his all-black costume. Another odd loner with an odd name.

Roger didn't like the looks of it one bit.

CHAPTER 14

Luna Evans

Luna didn't want to go straight home after school as her mother instructed. Nor did she want to go to the funeral parlor, as she was required to most days. She'd been so energized by Crane's unexpected attendance at lunch that she wanted to do something besides sit alone in the two-bedroom garage apartment she and her mother rented behind the laundromat. Or, worse, spend the afternoon waiting for another dead body to wake up at Evans Funeral Parlor.

With everything else going on, the last thing she expected to see after the final bell rang was the backside of Andy's letterman jacket. Lots of boys wore their jackets all year, but Andy always said the leather made him too hot. Even inside the air-conditioned school, Luna's armpits were damp from the mass of body heat, forget the sky-high temps outside. Maybe Andy really had been sick, then—a fever always made her run cold. Still, an uneasy feeling stirred in Luna's gut as she studied her boyfriend's disheveled, dirty-blond hair, watched as he hovered at her unattended locker, fumbled something between the slats with his fingers.

Why's he putting a note in my locker? The bell had already rung; surely he knew she'd be there any second. Luna lifted her hand to wave for Andy's attention, but realization struck before her arm made it too high. He'd probably come to school to pick up his make-up work and figured he'd dump her via note at the same time. Spare himself another phone call he'd have to ignore later. Why else would he slip a letter in her locker instead of just waiting for her to get there?

Luna crushed herself to the row of lockers to her right and watched

Andy over the top of her books as he turned and began to move away down the hallway. Restless dead and dark family secrets were enough. She didn't need the humiliation of a public breakup, too. Bitchy Bryant's locker stood only three doors down from Luna's. If the cheerleader got wind that Andy dumped her for Alison Haney, she'd make sure the whole school knew about it by morning.

Too bad Alison *isn't a restless dead*, Luna thought, then felt guilty for thinking it.

When Andy turned the hallway corner and the coast cleared, Luna sped to her locker, traded the Slipknot T-shirt she kept hidden from her mom for a safer Tori Amos concert tee, and stuffed the few books she'd need for that night's homework into her bag. The folded piece of notebook paper she'd seen Andy push between the slats slipped from between her pile of textbooks and tumbled to her feet. She squatted to pick up the little rectangle, glanced to make sure she couldn't spot Andy's retreating form, then unfolded the page and smoothed the note open.

Andy's familiar scrawl hurried across the paper as if he'd written with the wrong hand. Luna's stomach fluttered. After months of dating, she'd assumed he'd at least have the guts to break up with her in person, somewhere private, not scratch out his goodbyes on a crappy piece of wide-rule he hadn't bothered to even tear free of the spiral without leaving behind curly edges. Couldn't he have at least done this over the phone, where she could have the chance to get her two cents in, too?

Guess not, she answered herself. Not that he bothered to take her calls. An image of Crane washed up uninvited in her thoughts, but Luna braced, blinked, and read her probably ex-boyfriend's note.

The letter was only a couple of lines, scrawled at the center of the page.

Come see me tonight? I miss you.

He'd signed it *Love, Andy* and drawn a little heart with their initials in it, so that had to be a good sign, right?

She refolded the note and slipped it into her back pocket as the dismissal bell rang. Instead of the breakup she'd expected, Andy had sneaked her . . . what—an invitation? She'd sort out whatever was going on with her love life later. Now she had other plans. She fell into the throng of students moving toward the parking lot, singling Crystal and Dillon out among the herd.

"Are you sure you don't want to come with?" she asked, after both of her friends turned down her plan for an afternoon hang.

"Too much homework." Crystal hoisted her bulging backpack in a show of proof. "Ms. Davallier really loaded us up on AP biology, plus I have a paper due in English *and* a test in world history tomorrow. I'll be lucky if I get to bed before midnight."

Luna smirked, knowing how seriously Crystal took her studies—and prowled AOL chat rooms to talk to boys she was too shy to even look at in class. Of course, Crys would never admit she did the latter, and it would only hurt her feelings if Luna teased her about the secret screen name she hid behind—*ladybugz99*.

"Nerd," Luna teased.

Crystal's jaw dropped in mock insult. "Slacker," she shot back.

Dillon rolled his eyes at the two of them. "I *wish* I could go shopping with you," he said, "but the wardens demand I come home directly after school."

Luna groaned. "You can't still be grounded?"

The corner of Dillon's lip curled up and he picked an imaginary piece of lint from his tucked-in Ralph Lauren polo. "It's like my dad thinks if he keeps me under lock and key long enough, he can bore the gay out of me."

"Seriously?" Crystal fidgeted with a butterfly clip tucked inside her brown curls. "That's ridiculous."

"He thinks it's a phase, I guess," Dillon said. "If he gives it enough time, maybe it'll go away." He shrugged. "Until then, I'm just a pretty piece of home accent furniture."

"Your dad needs to get over himself." Crystal shifted her overly full backpack from one shoulder to the other as the trio made their way through the glass double front doors of the school and headed to the buses. "What does your mom say about all this? I can't believe she just lets him treat you this way and get away with it. It's not like you did anything *wrong*."

Dillon rolled his eyes. "You know how dramatic my mom is. Dad's mad that I'm gay, but Mom's embarrassed because I'm 'broken.'" He added air quotes around the word, then pressed both palms against his chest, feigning anguish. "How*ever* will Barbara Cole go on?"

"You're just being who you are—which is perfectly wonderful," Crystal argued. Both of her parents were lawyers and had passed their knack for rational thinking on to their daughter. "Your parents should be cool with that. I mean, they're your *parents*."

"Exactly." Dillon's scoff barely masked his pain. "Don't worry, they blame themselves. After all, they raised me."

"Oh, yeah. They're total martyrs." Luna pinched her lips together, exhaling through her mouth and resisting the urge to complain about her own parental problems. She and her mother didn't exactly see eye to eye, but Luna's struggle to find her own identity in a family run by women who'd done the same thing generation after generation paled in comparison to Dillon's home life. Hers differed from Crys's, too. Crystal's folks had to work twice as hard to prove their smarts in a town that measured everything by skin color.

The memory of Edwin Boone's gaping, pooling jaw rose up from the depths of her mind. Black liquid rushing from his mouth as he reached out from the cooler, grasping, yearning—

Luna pushed the memory down. The thought of having to take over the family mortuary business one day was difficult enough. Never in a million years had she expected her legacy to be something so entirely different. And gory. What was worse, there was absolutely nobody she could tell about it. Not Andy. Not Crystal or Dillon, either.

"Hello—Earth to Luna Evans." Crystal snapped her fingers in Luna's face, standing wide-eyed and open-mouthed beside the open door to her and Dillon's bus.

Luna bristled. How long had she been staring into space, caught up in waking nightmares of the restless dead? "Sorry, what?"

"I was saying"—Crystal drew the words out, motioning her eyes meaningfully at Dillon, who dug the toe of his sneaker into the ground beside her—"that we should have a girls' night this weekend. Just the three of us. We could watch *Ten Things I Hate About You* and eat, like, a metric ton of pizza and breadsticks."

Dillon's head snapped up, eyes glassy. "Uh, hello—permanently *grounded*, remember?"

"So?" A mischievous grin crawled across Crystal's round face. She bit at her lip and waggled her eyebrows. "It's not like your parents would kick us out if we just showed up. You could play stupid, like it's a total surprise."

"Are you proposing *mischief*?" Dillon asked, hand fluttering to his chest. "Who are you, and what have you done with Crystal Shipley? Wait 'til the rest of the student council hears about this—scandalous!"

The girl clicked her teeth and waved him away. "Right, Luna?"

Luna nodded. She forced herself to sound as positive as possible, though the idea of being out at night made her skin crawl. Her grandmothers had said that monsters came out during the day, too, but the idea of seeing one under sunlight felt a lot less terrifying than squinting into the shadows at everything that moved. "She's not wrong. We could pretend it was totally spontaneous."

"See?" Crystal nudged Dillon and winked. "They'd have no choice. They wouldn't want to seem *rude*."

Dillon's face cracked into a hesitant smile. "Okay," he said. "Let's do it."

"Let's do a three-way call later to talk about it," Luna said, waving goodbye. She'd have to walk down the road a bit, but a city bus stop a few blocks away ran to the town center. From there, a short trek under the sweltering summer sun would get her to the frigid, temperature-controlled icebox of retail paradise. "I'm off to the mall."

Where I'll be kept cool like Edwin Boone in cooler number three, she thought, and shivered. She pulled her long, black sleeves down into her fingers, and refused to think about the dead.

Worries about Dillon distracted Luna too much for her to think about much else as she made her way through Parkdale Mall. He tried to make light of it, but Dillon's home life had gone from bad to worse ever since he'd come out of the closet to his parents. He'd known they'd take it rough, but none of them had expected Mr. and Mrs. Cole to treat him like some sort of criminal. They'd been against the Clinton impeachment earlier this year, so it wasn't like they were prudes. Besides, this was 1999, after all, not 1899, and the Coles were Christians—

weren't they supposed to love everyone? Not lock him up in jail like he'd been accused of witchcraft.

After all, what was it Crane had said, to love others you first had to love yourself? Luna doubted very seriously if the Coles would accept such magical thinking, though it made perfect sense to her.

In any case, she didn't think about Edwin Boone and his gaping, pooling jaw in Claire's, where she picked up a bottle of black Wet n Wild nail polish, a tube of Crystal's favorite sparkly lip gloss, and a heart-shaped best-friend necklace broken three ways. Luna listened to a sample and then selected the most recent Type O Negative CD from the rack at Camelot Music. On the backflap, Peter Steele stood as tall, dark, and vampirically handsome as Crane had alluded to. Luna thought about Peter and not the reddish-black spot blooming against the white cloth over Edwin's body as he rode the gurney toward the parlor's crematorium. Her pager buzzed against her hip and she ignored the funeral parlor's number flashing on its narrow screen.

She checked the occult section in Books-A-Million for signs of Crane and made her way home. It was kind of ironic, wasn't it? Her mom spent so much time keeping Luna away from stuff like death metal and horror movies, when she was basically out fighting off all the scary stuff she complained about Luna liking.

Luna thought about Dillon's folks.

Were all parents such total hypocrites?

And, now that she thought about it, what else had her mom kept hidden from her?

The apartment was quiet when Luna opened the front door, two hours after she was supposed to be home. Last week's laundry still waited, piled high on the back of the sofa to be put away, her mother's lipstick-stained coffee mug cold where it sat half-full on the console table. A thin film had formed over the unfinished coffee.

"Mom, are you here?" Luna called.

Luna checked the kitchen, turning her nose up at the pile of dirty dishes still in the sink. She stepped down the hall to her mother's pink-wallpapered bedroom, the Jack-and-Jill bathroom they shared, the cramped living room that doubled as a dining area.

Nobody was home.

Of course. Tuesdays were delivery days at Evans Funeral Parlor, the time when all the critical, curious supplies needed to tend to the deceased arrived in large, unmarked cardboard boxes, their contents too discreet to be labeled. Mrs. Murphy's funeral had been this morning. Usually, Luna was tasked with cleaning up afterward, but for some reason her mom hadn't wanted her around.

Cool.

Unheard messages blinked from the answering machine that sat atop the phone book on the little side table by the front door. Luna deposited her keys in the bowl beside the phone, clicked the button on the machine. The tape spun, announced three missed messages, and her mother's voice filtered through the speaker.

"Luna, it's Mom," Grace said over the machine. "I'll be home a little later tonight than usual, possibly after dark. The . . . delivery was bigger than usual."

Luna heard the lie, wondered what sort of *delivery* might have come into Evans Funeral Parlor. Another body? Another restless dead?

She'd known Mrs. Murphy and Edwin Boone, but what if the next person to rise was someone closer—someone she cared about and didn't just yell at her about returning her shopping buggy or strong-arm her boyfriend into endlessly helping out with symphony events? Maybe Andy would still want to see her if Mina Jean Murphy hadn't gotten him so tangled up with debutantes like Alison Haney. Maybe the woman deserved what she got.

"There's some Hamburger Helper in the cabinet, and defrosted ground beef in the fridge for dinner," Grace continued. Her voice cracked, and she cleared her throat. "And, Luna, remember to lock the doors. Don't answer the door if anybody knocks, not even me. Stay inside, and keep the curtains closed. And don't forget to set the alarm."

The tape made a faint whirring sound for a moment, and the second message clicked on. "Luna, honey, you should be home from school by now," her mother said. A sharpness cut along the edge of her words. "Don't forget to call and check in."

Another click, and the third message, also from her mom—short and hard. "Where are you? Call me."

The answering machine clicked off. The blinking light went dark.

Luna dropped her bags on her unmade bed, kicked off her white-toed shoes, and crept into the kitchen in socked feet. When she opened the refrigerator door, the shrink-wrapped package of ground beef glistened on the top shelf. She gagged. The mashed-up meat made her stomach clench, eyes swim. Luna shut the refrigerator door, grabbed the Type O Negative CD from her backpack, and headed back to her bedroom. A few hours of sunlight remained, and with any luck she would be lulled to sleep by Peter Steele's dulcet baritone and dream a dreamless sleep, devoid of hungry men and looming shadows.

CHAPTER 15

Sheriff Buck Johnson

Sheriff Buck Johnson had spent the better part of the last forty years making sure the people of his town knew to obey the rules, and with the exception of a bar brawl or a husband getting too hot around the collar with his woman, things had been peaceful.

Easy.

And now someone's gone and stirred the pot, Buck thought from the quiet comfort of his unlit back porch. He chugged down a gulp of whiskey as he listened to cicadas sing their lullaby to the last sliver of sun slipping behind the horizon and watched the first stars prick through the twilight sky. Someone had gone and stirred the pot, all right, but they messed with the wrong town, coming into Buck Johnson's territory. Was a time when he would shoot first and ask later, but things changed, and—at least in Buck's opinion—not always for the better. The decade started off with cannibal serial killers, followed by a string of celebrity murders and a missing six-year-old beauty queen. Few months ago, a couple of kids shot up their high school.

Not a damn thing Buck could do about all that, but he could keep his town under control. That's all he'd done since 1954.

Buck sucked the last drops of booze from his glass, licked the taste of whiskey from his lips, and reached down to scratch his old hound Belle behind the ear. He had good men on his force, but every one of them was a damn fool when it came to doling out harsh justice, which just happened to be Buck's favorite kind. Not any one of them was better than Belle, either. In her prime, the old redbone had caught more quail in a day than his whole squad gave out parking tickets in a month. But those were the old days, back when Buck and Edwin Boone—

No. Buck stopped himself with a grunt. Only thing his old buddy was hunting for now was a pair of angel wings.

Buck tongued the edge of the glass and sighed. Men like him and Ed Boone weren't cut out for wings. They were better with their boots firm on the ground.

"Come on, girl. Let's go in and make some calls." Buck gave the dog another scratch behind the ear, then set his tumbler on the slatted wooden floor beside his chair. Stretched his arms up over his head. He thought about taking the glass into the house with him, but changed his mind. A couple of calls was all it'd take, just a few details to sort and asses to chew, and then he'd come on back out and finish the bottle. End the night with his two remaining best friends, Belle and Jack Daniels.

With another deep inhale, Buck pushed up from his chair, steadied himself—since when had a few swallows of whiskey gotten to his feet like that? He must be getting too damn old—and pushed the back door open. When Belle didn't twitch, he clicked his teeth and the old dog began to peel herself from the wooden porch one long ear at a time. Buck watched as she struggled to her feet, noting the way her rump had begun to curve in under her. How the red fur on her snout had run mostly to silver.

He rubbed his palm over the expanse of his flat, bald head. Patted the belly spilling over his belt. *Oh, hell,* he thought. *We're both gettin' too damn old.*

They'd been on him to retire since he'd hit his sixty-fifth birthday in '84. He almost had, too, if it hadn't been for what happened one night at Evans Funeral Parlor. It'd been fifteen years since that night, and peaceful since. He could have called it quits, traded in his badge, collected social security. But Buck swore to protect his town when he put on the badge as a cadet, and he'd wear that little brass shield to the grave—which, considering how his joints heat up every time the wind blew, probably wasn't too far off.

"Go on and lay back down, girl," he told Belle. "I won't be long."

The old's dog hearing was mostly shot, but at the command *down*, Belle let herself flop back onto the porch. Her tail thumped weakly behind her and she rolled thankful eyes up at Buck as he stepped over the threshold and into the house.

Buck thought about leaving the door open, just in case Belle changed her mind and decided to come in, but he knew she wouldn't, and so he closed it. Someone had once told him that dogs were like children. It didn't do to talk about certain things in their company—made them restless. Considering the call he was about to make, well, whether that was true or just some bit of women's foolishness, he might as well keep things quiet. Hell, he got bumps on his skin just thinking about the ten tons of hell going on in his town. Taylor tried to keep it hush-hush, but Buck was still sheriff. No one left him in the dark.

He hadn't been drinking just for the hell of it, not tonight anyway. What he'd seen happen to Edwin Boone was something he'd only ever seen once before. Fifteen years ago.

He'd hoped he wouldn't live to see it again.

He should have never let it go the way he did.

In any case, his old girl didn't need that kind of ugly in her bones, too, so he shut the door, grunting when he heard the knob click home. Buck's old rotary telephone was stationed on the dining table he never used, right beside the placemat where he kept his badge and weapon. The warped pine dining chair wobbled beneath his weight as he clunked down, picked up the receiver, and shook the kinks in the phone cord straight.

Buck dialed the number to the station.

Roger picked up on the first ring. "Deputy Taylor."

"Taylor, it's Johnson." He didn't feel the need to say why he was calling. Unless a screw had come loose in the boy's head, he already knew.

"Evening, Sheriff," Roger said. "I'm afraid I don't have much to report. Not yet. Forensics is still looking at the evidence from the Leger house"—he swallowed on the other end of the line—"and we're following up with Petunia Milner, putting together a timeline on her mother. With any luck, we'll have more to go on in the morning."

Buck's eyes darted to the cuckoo clock on his kitchen wall. The paperboy had called in about Snow Leger's place at 6:00 a.m., and it was already past 8:00 p.m. Fourteen hours. Fourteen goddamn hours, and not a damn thing to show for it.

"Listen here, Taylor," Buck growled into the phone. "I got one dead, another probably dead, and two more I ain't expecting to find this side of heaven." He tried to stand but the phone cord jerked tight and kept his rear end pinned to the pine. "I don't know if we've got a lunatic on our hands or if we're just suffering from total incompetence, but I expect results, and I damn sure better get them."

"Yes, sir."

Buck sucked his teeth. He put his thumb to his temple, rubbed, and thought about procedure. "You find the last person to see Snow Leger alive?"

Roger coughed. "Lenore Evans, as well as Ducey and Grace. Snow'd been down at Evans Funeral Parlor tending to Mina Jean Murphy. The funeral was this morning."

Of course, it would be an Evans. Everything about those women got under Buck's skin. Especially Ducey Evans, with her wild eyes and smart mouth. He'd loved that about her once, but wildfires had a way of burning loose.

The old sheriff licked his lips. Why hadn't he brought the bottle in with him?

He slapped his palm to his forehead, feeling the damp smear when it dropped. The sudden coolness made Buck's head spin. "You speak to her?" he asked, referring to any of the Evans women.

Roger cleared his throat on the other end of the line. "I stopped by the parlor earlier. Spoke with Lenore," he said. "Snow left after finishing up with Mina Jean and didn't make it back for the visitation. That puts our time of death anytime between one o'clock in the afternoon on Monday and five o'clock Tuesday morning."

"And the coroner's report?"

"Still waiting. Forensics should be on my desk in the morning."

Buck growled. "Tell Quigg to get the lead out of his ass." He eyed the cuckoo clock on his wall and watched the second hand tick. A few more turns, and the obnoxious little bird would come screaming out. "On second thought, I'll do it myself."

Roger's tone went curt. "Whatever you say, Sheriff."

Buck was just about to add that maybe they ought to get a warrant for the funeral home, take a look around anyway, when a strange noise jerked his attention away. The cool damp on his forehead slipped down the side of his face.

The noise came again, followed by the low gravel of a dog growling.

Belle.

He heard the flutter of wings, followed by a hoot, and Buck revised his verdict. Just an owl. A bird after all.

Buck curled his fingers in the phone cord and pulled it taut. "Listen, Taylor—"

Belle barked. Whined.

Shrieked.

The sudden noise squeezed the breath out of Buck's lungs, vising him in a grip of surprise and confusion. Belle's cry cut short and Buck jerked to his feet. The chair tumbled backward, and he dropped the receiver, the cord pulling the phone's base off the dining table. The bell clanged against the hardwood floor at the same moment the cuckoo clock erupted.

Buck grabbed his revolver and flung open the back door, slapping the porch light switch when the bulb didn't come on. The fluorescent 60-watt had burned out ages ago. He hadn't bothered to replace it, but Buck didn't need light to see that Belle was gone. He swept the gun's muzzle across the modest expanse of dry, dark night. The spot where Belle always lay beside his rocking chair, ears splayed out like lazy limbs. He inhaled the oaky scent of booze spilling from the overturned whiskey bottle, the coppery tang of the thicker puddle of wet beside it.

"Belle," he called. He held his breath and listened for the dog's familiar pant, the jingle of her collar.

Cicadas chirped. The cuckoo finished its time. But no Belle.

His precious girl had vanished, leaving only a streak of blood shining in the faint starlight illuminating his back porch.

CHAPTER 16

Grace Evans

Even if it was delivery day, Grace hadn't meant to leave Evans Funeral Parlor so late the day they buried Mina Jean. She hadn't meant to not go directly to the apartment. She'd intended to take the long route, maybe drive around and listen to the radio until the tension in her neck eased up, and still be home in time to chat with her daughter and get a bite of dinner before bed.

But Grace hadn't done any of that. Instead, she'd left a message for Luna on the machine and driven her late-model Mazda all the way out to Farm Road 121 with the radio off and parked in Edwin Boone's driveway. She'd rolled down her windows, cranked the Dixie Chicks, and smoked a cigarette from the pack of Virginia Slims she'd picked up on impulse at the 7-Eleven. By the time she'd sucked it down to the filter, she felt sick to her stomach and coughed until the nicotine passed through her system. When her five-disc changer rolled over to a new album and the streetlamps flickered on, she'd wadded up the pack of cigarettes and thrown them on the passenger seat, then backed out of Ed's driveway and drove over to Snow Leger's place.

Monsters were supposed to come out at night. Even the ones that moved about during the day. Knocked on your door and called your name.

Grace needed to be on watch.

Yellow caution tape snaked around the perimeter of Snow's carport, so she pulled to the side of the road in front of the house, turned off the headlights, and let the Mazda idle. She looked at Snow's small craftsman. At the window over the kitchen sink. Snow always left that light on, but tonight it was as dark as the rest of the house. As empty as the vinyl green chair on the porch where Snow spent her weekend mornings, watching church traffic and clipping coupons from the Sunday circulars. Snow would work her way through her phone tree every time the grocer ran a Blue Bell ice cream special in the paper. This was the kind of news Snow thought it important to share, never mind that Market Basket ran the three-for-ten special just about every other week.

"Just thought y'all should know," she'd say. "I'm stocking up on fruit special and rocky road. Got extra room in my freezer out back if ya need it."

"Snow," Grace said, tasting the woman's name as it slipped through her lips. Snow had been her first babysitter. Her first hairdresser. The first person to take her to try all thirty-one original flavors when the Baskin Robbins came to town, which was probably how Grace had earned her place on Snow's Blue Bell alert list. They'd been separated by a ten-year age difference, but Snow had always been a friend. At times, she'd been like a sister.

Now she was dead.

Likely restless.

And it's all your fault. The truth soaked into Grace's bones. She hadn't harmed a hair on Snow Leger's head any more than she had on Edwin Boone's, but that knowledge did diddly to stop her from feeling about as guilty as homemade sin. The women of Grace's bloodline had kept the dead buried for generations. And, though it didn't happen often, every now and then a body would rise, unfinished and hungry for a second bite at the life it had left behind. One or two every few months. They could usually tell by the way the person died.

But what was happening now? This was . . .

Punishment? Grace wondered. No. The thought was silly—silly and indulgent and reckless. She'd already paid for that Godawful Mess she'd created years ago, and dearly. The stain of that transgression left a mark on her as clear as it had left a scar on her wrist, one that couldn't be hidden under long shirtsleeves. Like the unlucky dead themselves, it rose again, clawed its way back to the surface of a world it no longer belonged in, and tried to feed.

"And we'll kill it again," Grace promised through gritted teeth. She rubbed the smooth section of scarred flesh. "Put it right back in the dirt where it belongs."

Put him *right back in the dirt*, she thought. Because it *was* him, right? It had to be. Who else would come back to punish her besides Samael? There were too many unknowns to destroy him completely, but they'd buried him just the same.

A patrol car turned onto the other end of Garner Road. Grace flicked her headlights on and shifted into drive, but the engine stalled when she pressed the gas pedal. She shifted into neutral and twisted the key in the ignition as headlights drew near. Grace had time enough to think, *Oh, I hope it's not Roger, or—worse—that asshole Buck Johnson*, before she recognized the young deputy behind the wheel.

Grace cringed. Johnson was the sort of man who'd sentence his own mother to the electric chair if he thought she deserved it. She'd never been sure exactly why the sheriff hated the Evans family. Maybe it was because they were women, or because he'd had to keep his mouth shut and let them go on with their business. Buck Johnson wasn't the kind of man who liked anybody holding anything over his head, no matter how much they did for his town.

That could be it, too: *his* town. Buck was a sheriff who'd rather be king.

The young deputy pulled his cruiser up alongside Grace, eased ahead, parked, and climbed out. He was a handsome kid—shaggy dishwater blond hair, good jawline, sweet eyes. Looked like the kind of kid who played football in high school, went steady with the homecoming queen. Grace smiled and tried to recall his name. Brandon something. She knew the rest, but it didn't come to her before he stood at her window, smiling down.

"Evening, Ms. Evans," he said without sparing so much as a glance at Snow's empty home. "Everything all right?"

The pale streetlamp light illuminated the deputy's badge. Grace read the name stamped on the gold bar above his heart and managed a weak smile. "As good as it can be, Deputy Hinson, considering." She nodded in the direction of Snow's darkened home. "Roger came by the parlor earlier," she said, in case the rookie found it strange she was parked in front of a missing woman's house turned crime scene. Surely he knew his superior had been by the funeral parlor to talk to Lenore—not that the whole town wouldn't know of Snow's disappearance by now. Police tape spoke for itself, and word traveled fast in the sticks.

"Guess I had to see for myself," Grace said. "Just saw her yesterday morning."

Hinson kept his back turned on the house. "We're still looking."

So am I, Grace thought.

The young deputy tapped his boot against the asphalt while Grace took another review of the house. She listened to the cicadas chirp, but the night was still. Safe enough for now.

"Well, I'm going to head on home," she told Hinson. She wanted to tell him to be safe, to lock his doors, but she couldn't, not without sounding every bit as strange as she felt, so she said, "You be careful, Brandon. Roger thinks there may be a rabid animal on the loose—might be that whatever got Ed and Snow is still out there."

"Might be," he said in a tone that seemed to signify neither of them believed an animal was to blame.

Poor boy looked green around the gills. He still hadn't looked at the house.

With a goodbye wave, Grace rolled up her window and started off down the road. She took a left off Garner, toward the apartment she shared with her daughter, but then changed her mind and turned right at the next light and headed down to Riverfront Park instead.

A decade earlier, Riverfront Park had been the place cool kids went to drink beer they'd sneaked from their parents. A decade before that, handsy boys took their dates to the little park at the bank of the Neches River and hoped to get lucky. These days there wasn't much left to recognize about the place. It still held the usual daytime community events—mostly picnics and local fundraisers—and there were still the occasional underage partygoers and groping teenagers, but the few empty beer cans and cigarette butts of yesteryear's nighttime crowd had morphed into dirty syringes and forty-ounce liquor jugs, the same way most places seemed to go eventually.

Places, like people, have their time to die, Grace supposed.

She pulled into a spot where the low lights of the streetlamps didn't reach, kept the windows up, and let the engine idle. Hers was the only car in the otherwise deserted lot.

"What am I doing here?" she mumbled to herself in the sudden quiet, tugging her shirtsleeves into soggy wads in her fist. "Luna will be wondering where I'm at."

No, she won't. Grace pulled the visor down to scowl at herself in the flimsy mirror—makeup kept her face fresh, but even cosmetics couldn't hide the worry line that sliced down between her brows, the ghosts that haunted her eyes. She'd thought she and Luna would grow closer as her daughter moved into her teenage years, but every day seemed to push them a little further apart, spreading the connection between them ever more thin. Mothers and daughters didn't always get along—Grace had enough experience as a daughter to know that firsthand—but the divide between her and Luna felt different. Deeper.

The Grace in the mirror rippled, distorted. *You're scared of her*, it seemed to say.

"Scared *for* her," Grace informed her reflection. "Been scared for her since the very first time you felt her kick in your belly."

For a moment, Grace and her reflection glared at each other in the dim mirror light. Two things could be true at the same time, she decided.

Grace felt the phantom gaze of eyes on the back of her neck from her empty backseat and fought not to turn and look. She flipped the visor up with a snap and the car went dark. Her night vision blurred, then adjusted. Just beyond the nose of her car, in the shadows beneath a droopy, moss-covered limb of an old oak tree, something stirred.

Not something, she revised as her eyes refocused. *Someone*.

A shadow emerged from behind the branches, the shape of a man, tall and walking with his head bent low and his right leg slightly crooked. He slunk through the tree line, one long, narrow leg leading him up to Grace's driver's side window at a time, like a skeleton come to life. Adrenaline surged in Grace's veins and sucked out all her frustration and fear, replacing them with energy. Purpose.

Just because she was scared for her daughter didn't mean she wouldn't give her last breath to protect the people of her town from the restless dead. In fact, that's exactly why she would do it.

She fingered the scar on her left wrist and thought of her daughter.

Not ever.

Grace kept her eyes locked on the figure coming closer and reached to her purse, pulling out the metal stake she kept in a concealed pocket she'd sewn into the lining. The steel was cool in her fingers. Her free hand brushed against the release handle of the driver's side door.

The figure shuffled in her direction but gave no indication it had noticed her. Didn't look up, didn't change pace. Just inched closer to her car, step after step, arms limp at its sides, head bowed to the ground.

Grace cracked open her door. The overhead light flickered on. Dim yellow light bathed the Mazda's interior.

It's a boy, she realized. A tall, lanky, teenage boy with long black hair, pale skin, and a leather trench coat at least two sizes too large for his rail-thin frame.

And he was alive.

She pulled the door until it clicked and the light snuffed out. *What is a teenager doing out here alone in the dark?* The answer came: *Nothing good.*

The boy lifted a pair of bony, milk-white fingers to his lips and the ember of a cigarette flashed in the dark, glinted off a collection of silver rings. Even after seeing her open and shut her car door, he didn't change direction or pace. He just kept moving forward, almost as if in challenge. As if she was his goal.

Grace's eyes narrowed. The park's nighttime visitors and the restless dead weren't the only reasons to be wary. The approaching millennium brought rumors of terrorist attacks and Y2K scares.

This boy's long black trench coat billowed like smoke behind him as he inched closer to her car. Goths had been around since the eighties, but something about this boy was different.

Dangerous. Not like the man she'd loved, but dangerous nonetheless. Boys this dark didn't come any other way, and she had the scars—literally—to prove it.

When his eyes found hers through the windshield, an unwelcome thought was written in them. *I know what you are*, it read.

The boy rapped his knuckles against the hood of her car and Grace jumped inside her skin. He moved to the window and gestured for her to roll down the glass.

She did without deciding to.

"Got a smoke?" He pulled the cigarette butt from between his lips, dropped it at his feet, stomped it out with the toe of his boot, still staring at her. A ring of black eyeliner framed his hazel eyes.

Grace started to say no, but then she remembered the crushed Virginia Slims on her passenger seat. She thrust the cigarettes through the window. "Here."

The boy took the pack, pulled out a long cylinder, put it between his lips, and sparked a lighter at its end. He dropped both the crumpled box and the lighter back into his jacket pocket.

"You're too young to smoke," Grace said without conviction. Mother of the year, she was not. "It's bad for your lungs."

He shrugged. Let loose a cloud of burn.

Grace held her breath so she wouldn't inhale and cough. Her stomach twisted. The boy looked about her daughter's age. Were he and Luna friends? Grace hoped not. "What's your name?" she asked.

His lips puckered around the cigarette as he inhaled. "What's yours?"

Her lips tightened into a line and Grace caught a glimpse of her reflection looking just like her mother, all thin lips and judgment. "You shouldn't be out here alone at night."

The boy smirked. "Neither should you."

He let loose another exhale of acrid gray smoke, then turned and disappeared back into the shadows. Grace waited until the last edges of the boy's outline had faded, and then she rolled up her window, locked her doors, and drove home.

Boys like that didn't come around often, and it meant trouble when they did. She needed to get home to her daughter.

CHAPTER 17

Lenore Evans

Lenore couldn't sleep.

Sleep had never come easy for her and closing her eyes had gotten even harder after Jimmy died, when she was forced to lay awake in a cold bed, staring at the empty pillow next to hers. Course, Jimmy had been gone fifteen years already. Men like Jimmy Stewart were few and far between, and the love she'd shared with him would have been enough to last a lifetime.

Longer, Lenore thought as she pushed the blankets back and climbed out of bed. She straightened the quilt and ran her fingers across her husband's pillow to gaze lovingly—longingly—at the framed wedding photo on the bedside table. How vibrant they'd looked on their wedding day, Jimmy in his crisp Marines uniform and Lenore in auburn curls and white lace. They had married young, only eighteen. Grace came two years later. Then, a blink, and Jimmy was gone.

I would have chosen longer, she decided. *I would have chosen forever.*

Lenore pulled on her silk house robe, checked her face in the vanity to wipe the crust from her eyes, and smoothed the wrinkles creasing the edges of her forehead. Then she made the rounds she always did when she couldn't sleep. First, she crept through the bedrooms and bathrooms at the back of the house, winding clocks and checking window locks in the dark before making her way through the long stretch of the living room. She kept the lights off as she floated through the dining room. Through the kitchen. Sometimes she checked the foyer, the secret spaces where she hid her most valued possessions, but not always, and tonight she didn't. She did double-check to make sure the garage was closed, though she knew it would be—she'd verified the metal door had come down before she ever got out of her station wagon.

Most nights Lenore ended up on her patio, staring out at the acre of land behind her house, sipping a cup of warm milk or a mug of hot tea, and thinking about her husband. Thinking about the list of regrets she'd managed to pile up in her fifty-five years. Fifty-six, if she made it to September.

But not tonight, she fumed. The night wasn't safe, not anymore. It wasn't the usual warm, comforting blackness because now, despite how much care Lenore had put into keeping the balance, the dead had become restless. Strigoi were rising. Soon, if the dead didn't make their way to the parlor, they'd have to go hunting. But there was nothing for it tonight, and so she checked the locks on the doors and stayed inside the protective walls of her home, drawing her robe closer around her, pulling the belt tighter until the space under her ribs ached and she could feel the silk band dig into her skin.

Lenore wandered back into the living room. For a time she sat in her rocking chair, then in Jimmy's old, overstuffed recliner beside the window. When she realized her toes had grown numb from tapping against the cool ceramic tile, she flipped on the lamp, snatched the winding key from her coffee table, and tended to her clocks.

Jimmy's clocks, she corrected bitterly. All these damn clocks had been Jimmy's, not hers—in their home, in the parlor. He was the one who'd bought them, collected them, babied them as if they were children and not just a bunch of wood and glass and metal.

And now look at me, she thought. *My husband's gone and all that's left is an old woman in a house full of clocks, constantly winding, winding, winding. Trying to keep the balance. Trying to keep time from running out.*

Lenore snorted.

"Time," she mumbled as she twisted the key in the face of the stately grandfather clock in her front room. "It was never about balance. Never has been. Clock's been ticking since the night that monster went into the ground, and all we've done in the years since is survive on borrowed time."

Him. Lenore bit her lip, hard, harder, until the taste of pennies filled her mouth.

Her mother had placed the mantle of caring for the restless dead on Lenore's head early. To Ducey, the dead were ghouls, soulless husks of familiar bodies. But Lenore saw the people they were before. She used their ashes to try to learn, to understand how to bury them with dignity so they didn't rise. To return them to the grave if they did. To understand how they changed as they fed. She'd raised her own daughter to respect the dead, and they'd told Grace about the family business early, but by the time she'd been ready to tell Grace everything she knew about strigoi, it had been too late. A monster had slipped under their notice, claimed Grace. A few months later, Luna was born.

A trickle of blood seeped from the corner of Lenore's lip, and she swiped it away with one hand and gripped the winding key in the other. They were Evanses. They should have been faster, wiser. How could they have been so foolish? They had waited too long to tell Grace, been too blind to the danger lurking at their backs. Too comfortable to see it creep in before it was too late, before it had already slipped its ugly hand up their blouses.

And now had they made the same mistake with Luna?

Lenore jammed the key into the second movement and twisted, forcing the little metal object to turn past the stopping point, choking past where the clock's inner workings shook and sputtered, past the taste of metal in her mouth. Past—

"Lenore."

The sound of her husband's voice spun Lenore, gasping, on her heels. "Jim?"

Part of her expected to see her husband there, standing barefoot behind her in the same faded denim jeans and starched white collared shirt he always wore. Bald head, long jowls, soft smile. One of her feet even slid out in front of her, her body already preparing to run across the room and throw her arms around his neck.

But there was nothing there. Nothing but emptiness and the echo of what had once been, so many years before.

Lenore's heart broke all over again as she clutched the clock key against her chest in the empty living room. She stood, and she breathed, and she waited to hear her name again.

Nothing.

Lenore jumped when the telephone rang.

With a sigh, she set the key back onto the coffee table and picked up the cordless telephone. "Mama," she said without looking at the caller ID. No one else would call this time of night.

"Saw your light on." Ducey's voice crackled close on the other end of the line, almost as if the old woman sat there in the room instead of in her own house around the corner, her backyard nestled up against Lenore's own. Almost as close as Jimmy's voice had been, just moments before. "Figured you was up windin' clocks."

It had seemed a little funny at first, mother and daughter living on the same stretch of road in a town where most everything was within walking distance. Having Ducey a few doors down was helpful when Grace was little. Tougher when she was a teenager. After, when Daddy passed and then Jimmy, having her mama so close was a blessing.

Lenore snuggled into Jimmy's worn recliner and brought her legs up under her. She pulled back the curtain on the large picture window by the chair and waved in the direction of the little lamp in Ducey's bedroom window. "Couldn't sleep," she said.

"Yeah." There was a wrinkle of cellophane and a pop as Ducey slid a butterscotch candy between her lips. "Me neither, Len."

The clock key had left an imprint on Lenore's palm, deep and red, where she had gripped the cold steel. She clenched, unclenched. Watched the shape of the key disappear from her flesh. "I'm not ready to go through this again, Mama," she said. "I'm just not."

"Don't reckon any of us are. Not that it makes a scrap of difference."

Lenore knew her mama had seen more than her fair share of heartache. She hid most of it behind jokes, or in the schnapps she didn't think Lenore saw her pour into her coffee. Ducey sucked down the sting of her pain with sweet candies, like she could build a hard shell around herself, pretend the hurt didn't reach her. And maybe Ducey could do those things, but Lenore never could.

Lenore's best line of defense was order. Control. Things she could touch and feel, could anticipate. And right now, control was slipping through her fingers.

"I have a bad feeling about this, Mama," she said.

"You have a bad feeling about everything," Ducey reminded her, correctly. "You always did have a way of seein' the glass half-empty, Len. Thought maybe you'd grow out of it, but it stuck."

Lenore wanted to argue but couldn't. "It's different this time," she insisted. Her fingers curled around the handset. Taking care of Mina Jean Murphy and Edwin Boone hadn't been so bad—just a quick, simple thing, really—but hard on the heart. Taking care of Snow Leger, whenever they found her, would be worse, especially if she'd fed. Clyde Halloran and Patsy Milner were unaccounted for. And another out there somewhere in the dark, the one who started this Godawful Mess all over again, was growing stronger with every bite. If the Evans women weren't careful, strigoi could overrun the whole town. *We're tired*, Lenore almost wanted to say, but instead, "We're different," she said.

Ducey breathed into the other end of the line. "Child, I've been the same woman I am now since the day I slid headfirst into this world. Only thing's any different is I've gotten prettier, is all."

Lenore closed her eyes. Inhaled patience. "You know what I mean."

"You just got your panties in a twist 'cause Jimmy's old rosebush has some rotten blooms, is all," Ducey continued. "It's ninety degrees in the shade, Len. If it gets any hotter, I'll have to take off things I ought to keep on—then we'll *really* be in trouble."

"Now, Mama—"

"Don't you 'now, Mama' me, Lenore Ruth," Ducey snapped. "We've got a job to do, and we're gonna do it—whenever and however it needs doin'. That white rosebush has been a second line of defense since it took root, but don't you forget who brought the shovel and dug up the earth beneath it."

Lenore remembered. She'd never forget. The memory flashed before her eyes—Grace, clutching her bloody wrist and her daughter to her chest. Ducey, eyes blazing. Lenore had screamed, and Jimmy—

No. She wouldn't remember that. Not now, not when his presence had just been so close.

Lenore's legs slipped from underneath her, and her feet touched the tile. She felt her spine straighten, her shoulders pull back. Ducey had never appreciated the sacrifice that went into that rosebush. The care. "If what I think is coming is coming," Lenore said, "we're going to need all the help we can get."

Another crinkle of cellophane. "You might be right about that," Ducey said. "But let's just hope what's in that dirt stays buried, for all our sakes. We've got enough problems without diggin' up the past, too."

This, at least, was one thing they could agree on.

"What about Luna?" Lenore asked. "Did we wait too long? Is this . . ." She sucked in air, then held it. "Is this our fault—did we miss something? I've done everything I can think of to keep them rested, to give them the burials they deserve, to repay the debt we took all those years ago when Grace . . ." Her breath shuddered.

"I know what you're thinkin', Len," Ducey cut in. "And this isn't that."

Lenore tensed in her armchair. "We don't know that, Mama. What about Mina Jean?" She remembered the woman's casket, covered with earth before she could take something to burn. To study. She thought of the things she kept hidden in the foyer.

The other end of the line went quiet. Then, the sound of liquid being poured and swallowed. Ducey didn't drink coffee past three o'clock, not unless it was full of brandy, and not unless she planned to burn the midnight oil.

"Listen, child," her mother said after another swallow. "There ain't exactly an instruction book for what we do. We make the best decisions we can, and we figure the rest out as we go along." Ducey cleared her throat in an effort to soften her tone. "That Godawful Mess fifteen years ago isn't something we can keep blamin' ourselves for—ain't a damn thing *guilt*'s gonna do but keep us holding on to things we're better off lettin' go of."

Lenore pulled back the curtain and stared at the little flicker of light from her mother's bedroom. She scanned the expanse of her darkened property. Checked the branches of the old oak that sprung in the center of her yard.

"And what about Luna?" Lenore asked. "She's at the center of this, and none the wiser. We can't know how she'll take it—what she'll do."

What she's done.

"Give her time."

"But blood is blood," Lenore pressed. "We don't know what she is, not with *him* in her. I've kept him fed, kept him buried, but he's alive, Mama. And Luna is his daughter."

"Don't matter," Ducey said. "No matter what else is in her, she's still an Evans. I'll die before I let anything happen to one of my own."

CHAPTER 18

Ducey Evans

Ducey hung up the phone, watched the long stretch of dark between her house and Lenore's until the lamp in her daughter's living room switched off, and then she pulled the blankets up to her chin and settled back into bed.

She took another swig of bourbon-spiked decaf, turned on her side, and returned her attention to the Harlequin romance she'd been reading before she'd noticed Lenore's light come on. On the glossy cover, a strapping young man, all golden curls and washboard abs, hung onto some floozy who had forgotten to lace her bodice. Washboard Abs's name was Phillipe and most of the words the author used to describe him could just as easily be applied to a slab of meat at a butcher's shop—muscled, marbled, veiny—as they could a man. Ducey clicked her dentures and flipped to a new page, skimming until she found a paragraph spicy enough to bother reading. Her eyes caught the word "throbbing" and held on for dear life.

"Oh, hush," she said aloud to no one in particular. "I may be old, but I ain't dead yet."

Two sentences later, a noise drew Ducey's attention back to her bedroom window. She looked out into the night, squinting behind her bifocals as an owl landed on a low-hanging branch on the oak outside her bedroom window. The bird hooted, staring at her with shining yellow eyes. Ducey held the owl's gaze until it gave up and took back to the sky.

"Go on now," she said as she watched it fly away and disappear into the dark sky. No, she wasn't dead. Not yet. And God willing—Ducey patted the trocar on the pillow beside her—she wouldn't be anytime soon.

The scene unfolding on the pages of Ducey's dime-store paperback had just started to steam when a pair of headlights flashed in her window, far brighter than the death bird's previous gaze. She barely had time to blink through the glare before a rumble of tires and a sharp screech of brake pads announced a vehicle flinging itself into park at the end of her long gravel drive. Ducey dragged her index finger under the last few words of the sentence she was reading before slipping the old butterscotch wrapper she used as a bookmark into place. She closed the tattered paperback. Phillipe would have to wait.

A shame, really, to keep a man like that on ice.

Ducey looked out her bedroom window to confirm Lenore's living room lamp was still dark, then threw back the quilt. Her toes touched the floor at the same moment a car door squealed open then slammed shut outside. Ducey set the book beside the framed photograph on her nightstand and sighed. "Oh, hell, Royce," she told the picture. "We got company."

Her trocar still lay on the pillow on her bed, but Ducey ignored the metal instrument, pulled her flannel robe over her muumuu, and stepped into her house slippers one foot at a time. Ghouls didn't drive, to the best of her knowledge, at least not the weaklings she figured were responsible for what was going on around town. Not that a powerful ghoul would announce itself crashing into her driveway like a bat out of hell anyway. Whoever had the gumption to invade her personal space nigh on midnight was human—and no shining example, either.

Royce's old Winchester Model 37 still stood on the side of the four-poster like it had when he'd been alive, and Ducey snatched up her late husband's shotgun without racking a round. Half the scare of having a gun like that was the noise it made before it fired—the *schick-shack* of a shell big as a tube of lipstick being pumped into the chamber. The first pellet was birdshot; the second, buck. Rest were all slugs. The thing would hurt like the dickens to shoot with her arthritis, but the racking noise alone should scare off anyone dumb enough to fool around in an old woman's driveway this far past dark.

And if it didn't, that was on them. It'd been a long time since a local prankster had toilet papered her trees or poured salt on her lawn, but if someone had grown fool enough to trespass on an old woman's peace, she'd see them back home with their tails tucked between their legs. Ducey was eighty years old, for crying out loud. She wasn't about to start letting her guard down now, prank or ghoul or otherwise.

She flipped the porch light on and threw the front door open, shotgun anchored at her hip. Hot, humid night air pulsed against her skin, sweat already collecting on her softer spots.

A rusted old Ford pickup sat crooked at the end of her drive, headlights on and engine running. A man stamped across the gravel, pebbles spraying in his boot's wake as he bowled up the driveway. The headlights' bright beams at his back bathed his face in shadow but didn't hide the fact that he was built like a square with legs—stocky torso, arms that pushed an extra inch out from his sides, neck a bolt holding the head on. A gait so stiff his knees didn't bend as he marched himself directly up the sight of the shotgun's barrel to Ducey's stoop.

Only one man—and the last one she'd expect to see come calling—carried himself with that amount of pent-up rage.

Sheriff Buck Johnson, off duty according to the Wranglers and pit-stained flannel illuminated by the bulb on Ducey's stoop, jerked to a stop inside the small circle of light. He glared at her like he could bore a hole clean through her head with nothing but his eyes. The man stunk, too, the stench of sweat and liquor a bitter cloud around him.

His words came out in a snarl. "Where is she?"

"Well, I'll be damned, Buchanan Johnson." Ducey kept her voice light and the unloaded gun level. "It's been over sixty years since you've set foot on my property. Didn't your mama ever tell you it's rude to show up at a lady's house uninvited after dark?"

Buck's boot nudged forward, and she was glad she'd kept the gun up. Man was a nuisance, but not dangerous—at least not enough to shoot. Still, it was best to keep him at a distance. Drunks made for poor judges of behavior. Bitter, angry, frightened drunks with a bone to pick could turn treacherous quick. This close, Ducey could see the veins in Buck's nose, a bright red map of booze and fury tracking trails across wrinkled flesh and watery eyes. Spittle mingled with sweat on his upper lip. No wonder he stank—man was so soaked full of booze he'd go up like a firecracker if he got too close to an open flame.

"*Where is she*?" Wet pauses punched the spaces between each word that climbed higher as they went. Three words, and by the end he was almost screaming.

"Where is *who*, you old fool?" Ducey snapped back. Surely he hadn't come here to badger her about Snow Leger. "Ain't nothing around here that concerns the likes of you."

"My dog's been taken." Saliva flew when he spoke, and Buck palmed away snot that dripped from his nose. He sucked in a breath that rattled down his throat. "Something drug her off, right off my back porch. Nothing but a smear of blood left of my girl."

Despite his rudeness, his blather, and his stink, Ducey was touched. It'd take an act of God to see Buck Johnson come to her for help. Or to accuse her face-to-face. Six of one, half a dozen of the other.

And here he stood, fuming and frothy, but his feet square on her driveway like he'd been planted there. Not looking for a person but for his hound, the only living thing Buck Johnson ever found it in himself to love maybe as much as he'd once claimed to love her.

Ducey lowered the shotgun and let its muzzle swing at her side as a bead of sweat slid off her glasses' arm and down her cheek. "Your dog ain't here, Buck."

The man's fists came up, his whole body squeezing. "There's two people dead, and now something's taken my Belle. I know it ain't no damn rabid animal." He took a step toward her, then two back. His voice shook. "You're behind this mess, Ethel. You and those freak daughters—"

"Careful," Ducey warned, her free hand going to her robe pocket, to the shape of the trocar that wasn't there. She patted the stash of butterscotch candies. "You'll go too far."

Buck either didn't hear her or wasn't listening. Rage and grief could do that to a person. "Give her back or so help me I'll—"

"You'll what?" Ducey jabbed the gun's nose against the porch hard enough to see the sound slap Buck across his bloated cheek. "Don't you dare come to my house in the middle of the night and threaten me with my Christian name, Buchanan Johnson."

"I'll get a court order and dig up that rosebush on the side of the parlor," he seethed, squaring up. "Let everyone see what you buried under there. I'll expose you women for the monsters you are."

Ducey snorted. The old fool.

"If you were gonna pull some stunt like that, you've had fifteen years to do it." She slid one slippered foot out in front of the other, smirked when Buck pulled back an inch for every one she gained. She'd never liked that about the man—all bark and no bite. "But you won't, because you know as well as I do what'll happen if you dig up that bush. Monsters come in all sorts of shapes, Buchanan." She took another step, letting the shotgun barrel rake against the ground as she walked until she'd pushed him back into the glare of his headlights. Gravel poked against the thin sole of her slippers. "You set that thing loose, and you'll have more hell on your hands than you can imagine," she said. "Then who do you think folks'll call a monster when we've got a plague on our hands?"

Her words landed solid in the night and awareness gathered around Buck as he backed himself against the hood of his pickup. His eyes finally peeled away from hers to glance over his shoulder at his truck, then at the house. At the shotgun pointed barrel down by Ducey's feet. Surprise washed over him, clarity breaking through his drunken stupor. He must have jumped in his old Ford and driven over before he ever realized where he was going.

"Get off my property," Ducey told him, suddenly tired. In her bedroom, anchored with a butterscotch wrapper, Phillipe awaited her return.

"Goddammit, Ethel!" Buck's rage was matched only by his fear and she saw it, glinting in his eyes in the dark, in the stiffness of his joints, in the way his eyes fell to the gravel and hung there. All the fight drained from him, and he stood there like the leftover skin of a wasted balloon. "She's all I got."

Ducey considered the man, tried to see the boy she'd known decades ago, when she'd lived in the back bedroom of this very house, her mother still in residence in the master suite. When he'd come courting and she'd shot him down. Was that man still in there somewhere, buried under decades of hate and fear and whatever else rolled through his veins?

"The dead don't take animals, Buck," she told him, turning back to her house, to her warm bed, to Phillipe. "Whatever got Belle, it wasn't one of them. Go home."

She stood in her doorway, watching as his truck retreated from her drive. She didn't go back inside until his headlights burnt out somewhere down the street.

CHAPTER 19

Luna Evans

"Hey, Moon Girl."

Crane's rich baritone slid over her shoulders as Luna hung the cafeteria pay-phone receiver in its cradle. She'd tried calling Andy again, and he still didn't answer. This was his third day out of school. Third day with nothing but that short note in her locker. When she'd called his house yesterday evening, Andy's mom—a single mom who worked nights and rarely parented—had said he hadn't felt well and went to bed early. Luna had thought about walking down the street to see if he might answer a knock on his window, but it had gotten dark and then Luna thought about Knockers. Spooked, she'd decided to wait to see if Andy showed up in their special before-school meeting place beside the Coke machines.

He didn't.

Maybe he just doesn't want to talk to you, Luna thought. She remembered the note—*Love, Andy.*

Did she care either way? She shrugged. She probably should, but she didn't.

Crane waited patiently behind her while Luna fished her unused quarters out of the pay phone change-slot and turned, a half-smile on her face. Her muscles were too tired to lift the corners of her lips any higher. Gaping mouths and gnashing teeth had filled her dreams again, her nightmares growing stronger every time she closed her eyes. Last night's terrors had been particularly visceral. Layers of white rose petals peeled like dead skin from an impossibly large, man-shaped shadow, and a dog—one of those big, floppy-eared breeds old men like Edwin Boone liked to hunt with—had growled, howled, snarled, so close she could smell the scent of its fur. Its sweat. Then, in the dream, she'd seen her own long dark hair flutter in her peripheral vision as she flung herself forward and sank her teeth into the animal's flesh while the shadow watched.

The late-night horror show in her subconscious had gotten so bad that Luna had resigned herself to talk to her mom about it, but Grace had come home after Luna went to bed and had been gone already when Luna got up this morning for school. She'd left the apartment's alarm armed.

Almost like Mom's avoiding me, Luna thought. *Just like Andy.*

But Crane wasn't ignoring her, or avoiding her. He was here, right in front of her, a still island in the swirling ocean of cafeteria noise, smelling like patchouli and stale cigarette smoke and looking down at her like she was special. Important. Could she hug him? Would that be weird? She kept her arms pinned to her sides.

Crane gave her an appraising look. He put a comforting hand on her shoulder that drowned out the din around her. "Everything okay?"

"Not really."

His gaze lingered on the circles under her eyes. On her unwashed hair. "Still not sleeping?"

"Not even a little. I mean, I *am* sleeping," she corrected, "but I don't think I'm actually getting any rest. It's like every time I try, it's just nightmare after nightmare and I wake up exhausted. And they're getting worse, like they're—"

Feeding off me, she almost said, but didn't. Luna wished she could tell Crane about the content of her dreams—about the *cause* of her dreams—but she couldn't. That part had to stay a secret, even from him. Perhaps especially from him. Everyone else would have said she was sick, or crazy. Even Crystal and Dillon would probably encourage her to talk to someone. Andy would, too, but he'd have to return her calls first.

Would Crane ditch her if she opened up to him? Luna didn't think he would. Crane might be the only person in her life who wouldn't think she'd lost her marbles. Who might be willing to listen, to try to understand the uneven churn of emotions roiling under her skin.

She wasn't sure if that would be better, or worse.

"Are you still dreaming about teeth?" he asked.

Among other body parts. "Yeah."

His face twisted into the same easy grin he'd worn when he kissed Dillon in the lunchroom the day before. Someone dropped a plastic cafeteria tray, prompting a round of jeers and applause, and Crane pressed in so close their bodies almost touched. "I've got something to help you," he said.

Something to help? Unless he had some kind of ceremonial magic to make her family's secret disappear, she didn't think anything would make the nightmares go away. Then again, it wasn't just nightmares, was it? She thought of Edwin Boone and shivered. At least a dead dog hadn't turned up.

Yet. She could still feel its silky fur against her palm.

"Let's go talk somewhere that doesn't reek of reheated cheese." Crane pointed at the doors that connected the school's cafeteria to an outside picnic area as a gaggle of students nearly knocked into him. They sneered over their shoulders, then, seeing who they'd bumped into, rushed away with their mouths shut. If their rudeness bothered Crane, it didn't show. "More privacy," he said.

Luna followed the taller boy through the double doors of the high school cafeteria and out into the afternoon sun. Squinting, they tucked themselves beneath the overhang of an adjoining school wing, away from the noisy chatter of the band nerds and sports jocks clogging the lunch tables.

Even though they were only on the perimeter of the crowded outdoor space, barely hidden away under the eaves, it felt as if they were the only two people in the world. Crane was so close Luna could see the little flecks in his eyes again, the small scar on his cheek the same shade of silver as her mother's. He reached for her hand, and she let him take it into his, enjoying how cool his skin was against hers as he coiled his fingers around her wrist.

Crane flipped her palm over. Traced the large crease across the center with an index finger, silver rings glinting in the sun as he read her lifeline. Then he reached into his pocket, pulled something out, and hung his balled fist over her hand as he inclined his head toward hers until their foreheads pressed together. Long, black wisps of hair tickled against the side of her face, and Luna's cheeks caught fire.

"Don't freak out," he whispered.

His voice was a caress, a deep, rolling lullaby, and Luna went numb. Her lips struggled to form words. "Why would I freak out?"

Two cold stones landed in her palm.

Luna tried to retract her hand, but Crane's grip held tight on her wrist. She stared at the oblong, slightly yellowed orbs against her pale flesh. For a moment she thought they were some of those little gemstones one could buy by the bagful at souvenir junk shops, or maybe hunks of peeled nuts, walnuts or Brazils. But then she noticed the curved undersides worn smooth from years of use. The small holes in the top where roots had once been.

Teeth. Luna gawked at the pair of teeth, clearly human, that Crane had deposited in her hand.

She wanted to be repulsed—she *should* be repulsed—but the little nubs shone in the sunlight. Something different moved in her stomach.

Hunger.

No, not hunger. *Desire.* She rolled her eyes up to Crane's.

"'Nature sends mankind into the world naked at first,'" he quoted with his gaze locked on hers. "'She then afflicts us with torture when she arms us with snow-white teeth.' Serenus Sammonicus, three AD."

"What?" Her voice came out breathy, a touch more 900-number than she'd anticipated. Heat crawled up her cheeks, but she couldn't tear her gaze away from Crane's even when it felt like her face might burst into flames. Did he see her, like, really see her? What did it mean if he did?

Crane smiled and Luna's knees turned to pudding.

"Remember, I told you how your dreams—losing your teeth—symbolized a fear of death, of dying?" he asked.

Luna nodded. How could she forget?

"Cultures throughout history have worn teeth as protective amulets," Crane said. "In the Middle Ages and through the seventeenth century, people used baby teeth to protect them from what they thought was witchcraft—that's where the Tooth Fairy legends come from, you know. Practitioners of magick, like myself, use teeth more figuratively in our spellwork. To bind, for example. To prevent harm." He looked her in the eyes. "These are a talisman, Moon Girl. Something to bring you good luck. To keep you safe."

Luna felt the edge of her lip twitch. Felt something shift under her skin. *Yes*, she decided. *Yes, I can trust Crane.*

"Where did you find them?" she asked. "You can't exactly buy teeth at the grocery store."

Crane grinned and released her, and she curled her fingers around the teeth. They were smooth against her skin, slicker than she'd anticipated.

"You'd be surprised what you can find if you know where to look, and I do," he said with a sly grin. He put his hand over hers, rounded his long, warm fingers over the small bud of her fist, and stepped into her as he bent to brush his lips against her ear. "I'll find anything it takes to keep you safe, Moon Girl."

CHAPTER 20

Deputy Roger Taylor

Roger had hoped today might be easier than the day before—and the one before that. Hump days brought a dependable lull to the middle of the week, bookended by slightly busier weekdays and only a mildly eventful weekend every now and then. But the heavy tangle in the pit of his stomach suggested this was not going to be anything close to a usual sort of week—not that it'd been any kind of usual so far. If the law enforcement veteran had learned anything, it was to trust his instincts.

"Easy, old boy. Pace yourself," he said aloud as he took a left at the edge of the forest by the movie theater and swung his cruiser into the Jimbo's Java Café parking lot, the same as he did before every shift. At least he was back on schedule this morning, though routine offered little comfort at the moment. The wheels of Roger's cruiser rolled over the streaks his tread had left on the asphalt yesterday. His stomach twisted. He'd forgotten to call Jimbo and apologize, but who could blame him? "Not gonna do anybody any good if you go on and get yourself all worn out this early in the game."

This early in the game? Hell, he still needed to get off the starting line. So far, Roger knew exactly zero more now than he did yesterday about what had happened to Edwin Boone and Snow Leger.

About what might happen next. He'd pulled another double chasing down every lead, every scrap of evidence he could. It wasn't much—nothing more than he already knew—and didn't amount to much of anything, either.

Hair freshly dyed and gleaming black, Kim leaned over the counter when Roger entered the café, chin cupped in her hand as she ignored the textbook facedown on the counter—swirling font on its cover read *Milady's Standard Textbook of Cosmetology*—and flipped fishnet-gloved fingers through the glossy pages of *Rolling Stone*. Angelina Jolie posed wrapped in black mesh lingerie that left little to the imagination, her sultry bedroom eyes and pouting lips gazing back at Roger from the magazine's front cover. The actress reminded Roger of Grace, though his sweetheart bore a closer resemblance to Geena Davis. A little softer around the edges, more girl next door. The thought of Grace brought Roger back to the present. Right back to Ed and Snow.

And Lenore.

Roger sighed and allowed his gaze to wander over the selection of sugary delights on display in the pastry case, the buttercream-topped delicacies and phyllo-wrapped treats making his mouth water. His sweet tooth ached about as much as his gut. Not everyone in town was as agreeable as Roger about the Evans women. Most folks thought they were a little too kooky for their own good and stayed clear as best they could. Except for Sheriff Johnson. The sheriff had harbored a special resentment for Ducey Evans for as long as anyone had known him, but any time Roger tried to bring it up to the old woman, she'd just laugh.

"Old Buchanan Johnson's been madder than a wet hen since 1943," she'd say. "I reckon the old fart's gonna die the same way."

If something came up that connected the Evans women to Snow's disappearance, that old bastard Johnson might actually smile.

Might see an opportunity to make trouble, too, Roger thought, and another layer of worry wound itself around the knot in his stomach. Still, he couldn't keep spinning his wheels on what happened to Snow. He needed to make sure it didn't happen again.

The sound of popping gum caught Roger's attention and he lifted his gaze to Kim, who stared at him with black-rimmed eyes and an expression of sheer aggravation.

"I said—" She rolled her eyes. "Another cream cheese croissant, Deputy?" Her hooded gaze took a quick detour to his waistline and hung there, as if she suspected how many pastries he'd already mentally gobbled down.

Roger patted his gut. "Just a coffee, please."

"Two sugars and cream?" Heavy emphasis on *two sugars*.

"Black, if ya don't mind."

Kim flopped the magazine on the register, poured the coffee, popped her gum. "Dollar fifty," she said.

Roger dug six quarters from his pocket and tossed them on the counter. By the time he raised his head to say goodbye, Kim had already returned to her magazine. He straightened his lips, tugged at his too-tight belt, and left.

Sheriff Buck Johnson was on him like white on rice the moment Roger walked into the station. He hadn't even clocked in for his shift before the man shot out of his office, a speeding gray bullet hell-bent on putting a hole through someone.

"Taylor," Johnson barked. The man's eyes were bloodshot, and a cloud of whiskey hung over him. The tip of his nose bloomed in gin blossoms so ripe they almost carried scent. "Where in the hell have you been?"

Roger swallowed. He was fifteen minutes early and already pulled two doubles, but it was best not to say anything when Johnson was in one of his moods. The old man showed up to work stinking of stale booze often, but never so much he'd fail a Breathalyzer. The deputy cast a quick look across the office at Hinson, who nodded in the direction of Roger's desk.

A thick file waited on the top of the wood surface, the envelope wrapped tight with elastic cord and thick red lettering. *Forensic report.*

"You'd better have something worth telling me this morning, Taylor." Spit flew from Johnson's lips and Roger squinted against the spray. "Phone's ringing off the goddamned hook," he hollered. "Petunia Milner's chewing my ass like grade A beef."

Shit. So far, they'd been able to keep the story contained, but any minute Widow Milner's next of kin would storm into the sheriff's station, raising hell. He was surprised she wasn't already, come to think of it.

Roger moved to his desk, picked up the file, and began to unwind the cord. "Looks like forensics already has the results on—" He couldn't bring himself to say the woman's name, so he said, "Garner Road."

The words twisted through Buck's sneer. "Let's hear it."

"Tongue definitely belonged to . . ." Roger stammered, the name lodged in the back of his throat the same way words had gotten stuck back when the teacher called his name to read aloud in elementary. He leafed through the stack of crisp Xerox pages, forced the words out. "Snow Leger."

"That all?" Johnson snarled, unaffected. "Lot of blood in that house for a tongue."

In fact, there'd been more blood in Snow's home than Roger had ever seen in one place in his life—not that he'd say so to Johnson. More than enough to fill one person, he'd think.

He scanned the page. "We were able to get a partial print off the handprint on the door, but the prints didn't match anything in the house," Roger said. "Forensics ran the DNA against some of the other names on our current missing persons list. We got a match."

He read the name but couldn't manage to force it through his lips. Again.

"Well?" The hard note of impatience in Johnson's voice stung between Roger's shoulder blades like the man had stabbed a knife in his back and left it there.

Roger's eye twitched. Felons weren't the only ones with prints in the system. Lottery vendors, truck drivers, healthcare workers, funeral directors, and even some celebrity talent agencies fingerprinted their employees. Kept them on file long after retirement, too, as evidenced by the name that stared back up at him from the report. "Patsy Milner," he said.

He thought of the handprint stamped on Snow's back door, of the walker Hinson had seen abandoned in the old woman's den. The trails of crusted blood leading into the grass off Snow's carport.

Johnson snorted. "You mean to tell me a ninety-something-year-old woman," he said, the words coming out so hot that he gasped between them, "who ain't walked on her own two legs unassisted for the better part of forty years"—the old man's sweat-slicked palms flew to his bald head, rubbed it like he might produce fire—"went on over to Snow Leger's house in the middle of the night, forced her way inside, and ripped the woman to pieces?"

Roger fought to keep his voice even. "According to the forensics report—"

"And then," Johnson continued, hands dropping from his head to form fists at his sides, veins bulging against the thick stump of his neck. Spittle began to crust in the corners of his lips. "When they was done doin' whatever the shit they was doin', they both just got up, walked clean out of that house, and ain't been seen by a livin' soul since?"

"I'm not suggesting anything like that." Roger cracked his neck. "But I'm not sure what to tell you, Sheriff."

Johnson sneered and his rebuke scratched out between gritted teeth. "Tell me you're doing your damned job."

The older man shifted his substantial weight as he advanced, tightening the space between them. He crossed his arms over his barrel chest, hands still balled into fists. His eyes narrowed into venomous slits so thin they were almost lost in the deep folds carved from decades of scowling. "You said the last person to see the Leger woman was Lenore Evans," he said.

"Lenore and myself, actually." This close, Roger was forced to suck in Johnson's whiskey-sour breath, taste the man's distaste for the Evans women. They had hardly gotten to this part in their phone call last night before something interrupted Johnson. He'd hung up the phone and hadn't called back. Apparently hadn't quit drinking since then, either. "Snow had been up at the funeral parlor earlier in the day, tending to Mina Jean Murphy's hair," Roger recounted. "I brought Edwin Boone's body in from the coroner's just as Snow was on her way out. Seems she went straight home and didn't leave her house again."

These cold facts did little to quench Johnson's fire.

"Well, *most* of her damn well did," he shot back. "All that's left of the woman is her tongue on ice down in evidence. Day before that, Ed's body showed up looking like something cut into him like Thanksgiving dinner. That's two bodies come in mutilated, Taylor. *Two.*" He shoved a pair of Vienna sausage fingers into Roger's face before balling his hand back into a fist and shaking it in the air. "We're not looking for a drugged-up lowlife here who's gonna leave his tracks all over town," he said. "This is an animal problem. I want you to get animal control, and you boys get your thumbs out of your asses and put your noses to the ground. I got a space on my wall for the head of whatever beast you find."

"I don't think we're looking for a rabid animal," Roger said. He rubbed at the twitch under his right eye with his index finger. "Things just aren't adding up that way. An animal couldn't have done all this, and even if it had, it's not in their nature to stick around."

Roger fixed his gaze on Buck Johnson's bulbous red nose. "Now, maybe a man, some sort of serial killer—"

Something passed across the sheriff's face Roger didn't recognize. His gun hand unfurled, lifted to the revolver holstered on his hip. Roger couldn't see Johnson's hand without breaking eye contact, but he heard the holster strap tick as it came unsnapped.

"Ain't a person done this. Whatever got Ed chewed him to pieces. I saw the bite marks on his throat." Johnson growled. "Unless, of course, you're trying to tell me we're dealing with one of those extra-crazy kinds?" His hot breath turned to steam against Roger's skin. "Sort that think they're possessed by demons or werewolves or whatnot?"

The way he asked made it sound so ludicrous that all Roger could do was shake his head, but the shine in the sheriff's bloodshot eyes and the way he stroked his gun made Roger's blood go cold. Lawmen's fingers shouldn't itch to pull their weapon; their eyes shouldn't glisten at the thought of squeezing the trigger. Booze-fueled or not, whatever thoughts ran through Sheriff Buck Johnson's whiskey-soaked brain didn't look like justice.

They looked like revenge.

No, Roger checked his assessment as a bead of saliva steam slid down his jaw. Not revenge. Fear.

Roger hadn't thought a man like Buck Johnson capable of such an emotion. Murders, even gruesome ones, happened every day, albeit rarely in their small town, but he'd worked with the sheriff long enough to know the man had seen his share. Besides, if Johnson was so insistent on rabid-animal attacks, then what in the hell was he so afraid of?

Johnson's body turned, his attention snapping to Hinson, who'd so far managed to stay out of the line of fire at his desk. "What about you, Hinton? You think we got one of 'em monster-movie maniacs in our town, too, or is any of that good ol' academy training kickin' in yet?"

Hinson cleared his throat and didn't correct his superior.

"N-nothing new to report, sir." The words tumbled gracelessly over his lips. "I watched the Leger house all night," he said.

A sudden thought made the rookie sit up straight in his chair. "Come to think of it, I did see something a little odd. When I got to the house, Grace Evans was parked outside. Said she'd heard about Snow and just wanted to see things for herself."

The sheriff made a smacking sound with his tongue, a denotator clicking to life. "I'll just bet she did," he mumbled. His thumb hooked against the hammer of his revolver.

Roger closed his eyes. *Oh, hell, Hinson. You've gone and done it now.*

"I don't see anything suspicious about Grace Evans passing by Snow Leger's place, given the circumstances," Roger ventured, trying to calm the storm before the bomb that was Buck Johnson went off and get his clumsy fingers off that gun. "The two are friends. Colleagues. Makes sense she'd want to take a ride over, see things for herself."

Too late.

Johnson's hand left his gun, but now his nubby middle finger stabbed into Roger's chest. "Now, you listen here, Taylor," he seethed, strands of spittle clinging to his lips once more. "I don't give a damn if it's a man or a coyote or goddamned orangutan running amok in my town. You need to get your head out of horror movies, do some good old-fashioned police work, and figure out what in the hell is going around chewing up people. And when you find it, I want you to put it *down*." The man sucked in breath that shuddered. "That's an order."

His finger fell from Roger's chest, leaving a burn mark where it'd been.

"Yes, sir."

"Oh, and Taylor," Johnson called over his shoulder as he marched back toward his office. "I want an eye kept on those Evans women. Parking infraction, speeding ticket, hell, if one of them so much as looks at you cross-eyed, I want them brought in, and it'll be your ass if I hear you're going easy on them. Understand?"

Roger sighed. Now he had two problems to manage—figuring out what the hell was going on in town and managing Johnson's petty grievance with the Evanses. Neither was going to be easy, and both would likely see him end up in a world of hurt. The Evans women were hiding something, and it looked like Buck Johnson was, too. The Jimbo's coffee churned in his empty gut. He should have gotten himself a croissant; at least then he'd have something in his stomach to soak up the acid. "Yes, sir."

CHAPTER 21

Kim Cole

At half past one, Kim untied her frosting-smeared apron, shook the boredom out of her long black hair, and grabbed her coffin-shaped purse from her cubby in the employee break room. She was halfway through the back door of Jimbo's Java Café when Rhonda, the chain-smoking day manager, trundled through the swinging partition door to call her back.

"There's a phone call for you." Rhonda's words came out in a rush before she hacked in a breath, muffled the resultant cough by biting into a donut pilfered from the day-old pile, and wagged the cordless phone in Kim's direction.

Kim sighed and rolled her eyes so hard she worried one of her contacts might get stuck. This was supposed to be an easy job, money earned to see her through cosmetology school and nothing more. The last thing she wanted to do was stay late to take a call from a needy customer about the inscription on their birthday cake order—especially after a five-hour shift that had already seen her through the breakfast rush and the better part of lunch hour. Things had been so much simpler when Jimbo's had just been java and not café, too. Pouring coffee, she could do. Frothing milk? No problem. But being forced to interact with indecisive customers who—like the deputy who came in every morning and drooled over the pastry case—couldn't choose between a red-velvet or Italian-cream sugar rush to go with their midmorning cup of pick-me-up?

Honestly, she'd rather die. Plus, she had a lunch date at the burger joint adjacent to the theater across the street.

Kim waved a dismissive hand over her head and moved a step farther out of the door. "I'm already off the clock."

Another cough. Another bite. A ring of chocolate frosting filled in the folds around Rhonda's jowls. "You sure? Sounds like your brother."

Dillon.

Kim froze. She blew a gust of breath out of the side of her mouth and dragged herself back inside the refrigerated chill of Jimbo's kitchen. Ever since her younger brother had told their parents he was gay, they'd made it their lives' goal to make Dillon's existence as close to hell on Earth as possible. So far it had been a lot of Dad yelling, Mom sobbing, and long-term periods of isolation in his bedroom, but sooner or later someone would try to exorcise a rainbow-clad demon out of her baby brother. Either that, or they'd do what everybody else's parents did—attempt to medicate him back to "normal." Such was par for the course in the Bible Belt. If you didn't fit in, you must either be possessed, crazy, or just plain *abnormal.*

In the event of the latter, it was best you left town. If you stayed, it was take two pills and see you at church Sunday morning.

Thank goddess for my crappy little apartment, Kim thought. She'd been there, too, when their parents had decided her black clothes and hard rock must be demonic influence. That was why she'd scrimped and saved and worked every morning shift at Jimbo's for eight months straight to sign her name on the lease for those few hundred square feet of bland white walls and peace. The ceiling had mildew in the corners and half the time the plumbing vomited up whatever it hadn't digested, but at least she didn't have to worry about her mom sneaking in when she was out and tearing down her Korn posters or torching her autographed headshot of Nine Inch Nails front man, Trent Reznor. More than a fair share of Kim's band memorabilia had met its end in Barbara Cole's barbecue pit over the years.

"Lucifer led the ministry of music when he was in heaven," her mother would pronounce as she held a CD booklet against the fiery tip of a long-reach butane lighter. "Now he sends Satanic rock music straight from hell to your ears."

Kim trudged back inside the kitchen to accept the phone. She put the receiver to her ear, holding the chunky plastic at an angle so her lipstick didn't smear against the mouthpiece. "Dillon?"

"Kim?" Dillon sounded like he'd been crying. "Is that you?"

"Yeah." She checked the clock. The high school cafeteria doubled as an auditorium, and background noise from the herd of kids should overwhelm her brother's soft voice and boom through the phone line. The quiet was unnerving. "What's wrong? Why aren't you at school?"

Dillon's breath came out in a shudder. "I am. I'm in Principal Brevard's office. There was an incident in PE, and . . ." His voice trailed off. "Can you come pick me up?"

It didn't take a rocket scientist to figure out what sort of *incident* landed her brother in the principal's office calling Kim for help rather than their parents. She felt heat move under her skin, crawl up her cheeks. The last time Dillon had an *incident* in gym, he'd come home with a swollen eye and a bloodied nose. *Those pieces-of-shit jocks.*

"Kim?" Dillon's sixteenth birthday was coming up, but when he spoke, he still sounded like the little boy who used to run around the backyard wearing nothing but his tighty-whities and a Kool-Aid mustache.

She fumed. Dillon had it bad enough at home; he didn't need the bullying at school, too. "I'm on my way," she said. She'd page Brandon and let him know lunch would have to wait.

"Don't tell Mom and Dad." The plea in her brother's voice was so raw it hurt Kim's ears.

"Cross my heart," she promised. "I'll be there soon."

Her heavy black eyeliner itched against her skin and the first bead of sweat was already forming on her brow the second Kim stepped out Jimbo's back door, like the heat could wring her body out like a sponge. The sunlight was blinding. The heat, blistering. She put one hand up to her face, shielding her eyes from the glare of midday sun as she rummaged in her bag for her sunglasses. Working the morning shift meant she was off in plenty of time to meet up with her boyfriend before heading to class to slather makeup on plastic mannequin faces. The downside, though, of getting to work at dawn was that she could look forward to clocking out at the hottest part of the day. She'd have to turn on the engine of her hand-me-down Buick LeSabre and max out the AC for a full four minutes before she could touch the shiny plastic steering wheel without scalding her hand.

"It's hot as hell out here," she grumbled under her breath to no one in particular. "I can't wait to get out of this armpit."

You've been saying that since eighth grade. Kim sneered at the reminder. She'd dreamed of putting rural southeast Texas in her rearview mirror for as long as she could remember, and the farthest she'd managed to get was the run-down Cornwall Lancaster Apartments four miles from the house she'd grown up in.

Still better than the Cole residence. The urgency in her brother's voice echoed in her thoughts and Kim picked up her pace, fishing her car keys from the bottom of her bag.

Jimbo's parking lot was little more than a patch of concrete nobody in town seemed to know what else to do with. Jimbo, his wife, Tammy—who only showed her face at the café on Fridays when she came for the weekly cash deposit—and Rhonda—who complained of an "old knee injury" no one really thought she had—were all allotted parking spaces at the rear entrance of the building. The rest of the employees, however, were left to park in a section of alley carved between the bakery and a small strip mall.

If it were a bigger city, or Riverfront Park, she'd worry about crossing paths with bums or drug needles. But this was small-town Texas. In the middle of the afternoon. On a Wednesday.

Still, a chill raced up Kim's spine as she moved into the narrow space between buildings. The blinding bright sunlight faded to dusky gray and a shiver breathed cold air across her skin. Her coworkers liked to tease her about the alley. They'd insist that because she was goth, she must like dank, gross places. She'd play along because what else was she supposed to do—admit she was scared? Not likely.

The alleyway gave Kim the creeps. Always had.

Water dripped down the exterior walls of the surrounding buildings to collect in shallow, slick, haphazard puddles. Humidity fogged the lenses of Kim's sunglasses as she splashed through one of the pools. A cockroach erupted from nowhere to scamper across the toe of her ten-hole Doc Martens. She bit back a whine and sidestepped the bug, the sudden movement upsetting a rat from its feast in an abandoned food container. The rodent stared at her from the belly of the pastry box, beady eyes shiny with malice.

Kim could feel its thin, sharp nails prickling against her feet, clawing up her shins—

Eyes on the prize, Kimberly. She locked her gaze on the hood of the peppermint-green sedan she'd inherited from her grandparents and bent her head, refusing to look into the dark spaces of the alley as she speed-walked toward her car. Goose bumps prickled her flesh with every step, dozens of unseen rodent and insect eyes stabbing into the back of her neck.

Something stirred in the shadows near a long-abandoned delivery truck with four flats.

Kim tripped. Recovered. *Just a rat.*

It moved again. A cardboard takeaway cup bearing McDonald's golden arches rolled across her path. Disappeared beneath a dumpster on the other side of the alley. Kim's breath caught in her throat.

Just a thirsty rat.

She took another step. The crunch of her boot against gravel sounded like bones breaking.

A low moan reverberated off the narrow walls of the alley, each rumble pulling the negative space between the surrounding buildings closer. Closer. Too close. The noise eclipsed the afternoon sun, pulsed under Kim's skin, balled itself into a lump at the back of her throat. Her boots stuck to the broken pavement. What the hell kind of rat made a sound like that?

Kim clenched her keys in her fist, leaving the business end of her car key to poke through her knuckles, the same way she learned to do when she walked alone at night. It wasn't much, but two inches of hard metal would make for an uncomfortable welcome should someone—something—try to take her by surprise.

The moan shifted into a growl. The dark mass in the shadow shifted. Stretched.

Definitely not a rat. Frost crept up Kim's arm.

"Who's there?" she called.

Were her feet moving? Kim's body inched forward of its own accord, pulling her to the twisted shape tucked inside the dark. Her heartbeat shuddered in her throat, her breath bleating in small, ragged bursts.

Turn around, her brain screamed as she took another step.

The thing in the shadows growled again, gathering up its legs to rise, and then it crumpled back to the pavement with a pitiful whine.

Kim's heart stopped, then restarted. *A dog.*

"It's okay. I'm friendly," she promised. She pushed her sunglasses up into her hair, squinting into the dark. The mass took on shape—a head, a body, four legs. A tail. It was a hound, somebody's pet judging by the shadow of the collar around its neck.

Her neck. The dog was female. She had a silver snout and her rust-colored fur was matted and filthy. One front leg twisted at an odd angle.

"Oh, babe, what happened to you?" Kim set her bag and keys on the ground, then dropped to her knees, murmuring to the dog as she crept closer, trying not to startle the injured animal. "It's okay," she cooed. "I'm here to help. I promise."

By the time Kim was close enough to touch the dog, the animal had stopped growling and watched Kim with wide, fearful eyes rimmed in white. This close, Kim could see the hound's coat was covered in blood—thick, tacky blood. Some of it had dried, clinging to the tips of her fur, but when Kim reached out a finger to stroke the poor beast her hand came back red. Whatever wound the poor old girl had, it was still bleeding. Badly.

"Oh, you poor thing. Who did this to you?"

The dog whimpered in response. Abruptly she stiffened. Her jowls rose into a snarl, baring teeth and a tongue stained scarlet from licking at her own wounds.

Kim barely had time to register the sound of footsteps behind her before a hand clamped down on her shoulder.

CHAPTER 22

Deputy Roger Taylor

The sound of his police radio buzzing to life on the dashboard nearly made Roger jump out of his skin. After he'd left the station, he'd driven in circles for a while, too agitated to even decide where to go. He hadn't intended to end up at the high school, but there he sat, parked under the blistering sun at the edge of the football field just like any other day on the job. Like a body count hadn't stacked up, left behind nothing but a bunch of clues that didn't make any damn sense and a dead woman's tongue.

A dead woman's tongue. A sour taste filled Roger's mouth.

When had he started allowing himself to think of Snow as dead?

"Probably around the time you read Widow Milner's name on the forensics report," he grumbled into the blow of his AC as he pictured the handprint stained on Snow's door. If a ninety-something-year-old invalid could rip out a healthy woman's tongue, Snow was dead. So was Patsy Milner. No one lost blood like that and lived.

Those women were just as dead as Edwin Boone. Probably as dead as Clyde Halloran was, too.

Of course, he'd known this already, hadn't he? Roger thought again of the scene in Snow's den. The gore. The blood. There'd been so much blood. No, wherever Snow was now, she wasn't alive. But where *was* she? And for that matter, where were Clyde Halloran and Patsy Milner—and who would go missing next? What was he missing?

Static crinkled on the radio and Roger jumped again.

"Come in, Taylor." Dispatch Darla's voice was packed tighter than the row of tall pines that bordered the road away from the high school.

Sheriff's probably still having a dying duck fit, Roger thought. The man was damn near unbearable in the best of times, but Roger had no idea what had crawled up Johnson's ass this morning. They were all on edge about what was going on in town, but the way Johnson acted it was like this was more than a crime, bloody as it was. Like it was personal.

Roger snatched the radio from the dash and braced for bad news. "You got Taylor."

"We've got another ten fifty-four. Uh, fifty-five." Darla's voice cracked. She swore under her breath without releasing the mic—"*Shit*"—then sucked in a breath. "Oh, for shit's sake, Roger. We've got another body."

Gravity hit Roger square in the gut. He pressed the mic. Let it go. Pressed it again.

Another body. He slid his thumb off the receiver and let his vision go fuzzy so the patchwork of greens and browns and yellows outside his Crown Vic's window mushed into a fluorescent swirl.

A crackle on the radio, then, "Taylor, you still with me?"

Roger forced his mouth open. His skin felt numb when his finger pressed the button. "I heard you, Dispatch."

Darla's voice was flat as she rattled off the details. "Young female. Caucasian. Teens, maybe early twenties. Dark hair."

"Any signs of trauma?"

The radio bled static as Darla hesitated, huffed. "That some kind of trick question?" The rhetorical question snapped across the line. "A local saw blood, phoned it in."

His eye twitched. "Anyone else on the scene?"

"Coroner is en route."

Roger could read between the lines. Quigg on his way meant the media wouldn't be far behind. Johnson had been pissed this morning, but the man would have a coronary if Channel Six beat them there. Not to mention the shitstorm that would hit the fan once they put two and two together and made a whole news story about the string of unexplained deaths. People would be out hunting rabid animals with pitchforks. Worse. "Tell me where I'm going," he said.

Darla recited an address and Roger scribbled it down on his notepad without registering the location. Two figures had come into view about a hundred yards ahead and walked up the gravel two-lane road toward his car—*away* from the squat blue-and-brick high school. One was tall, reedy, and dressed in head-to-toe black. Male. The other shorter, slighter, and female. Neither carried a book bag. Both were unmistakably students.

They turned, and the girl lifted her head. Even in the glaring sunlight, Roger recognized the profile. *Luna Evans.*

He knew the boy, too. It was the same truant he'd stopped the day before. Something Campbell.

Robert, Roger remembered. Boy called himself Crane.

The deputy's collar felt snug. He pulled at it, tugging the stiff fabric away from his throat. Something about the kid gave him the creeps, and Roger didn't think it was just because he reminded him of those boys from Columbine or one of those face-painted rock-star types. Course, he reasoned, that didn't help. Seeing Crane Campbell with Grace's daughter didn't sit well, either. None of the Evans women—not even the youngest—needed any negative attention, and hanging out with strange newcomers while the town's death toll rose wouldn't look good. Not at all.

Roger watched Crane lift a cigarette to his lips and exhale smoke. He dropped the butt and stomped the still-smoking stick under his boot, then put his arm around Luna as Darla's voice crackled back over the radio once more.

"You got that, Taylor?" she asked.

"Yeah, I got it. I'm on my way." Roger checked the address he'd scrawled on the paper. It was close. Even closer than Garner Road. Right in the center of town, the dead bodies practically working themselves right toward their eventual resting place at Eternal Flame Cemetery.

"Oh, and Dispatch," he added. "Hinson at his desk?"

A moment of silence while Darla checked. "He just got back from lunch."

"Send him back out. Have him meet me on scene." Roger felt half-guilty about sending the rookie out to another bloodbath, but only half. If this was anything like last time, he was going to need backup. Plus, the boy rubbed Roger the wrong way this morning opening his mouth to the sheriff, and he wasn't above being just a little bit petty.

Not when it came to Grace.

"You got it." Darla signed off.

Roger put the radio back in its cradle and shifted the cruiser into drive. He made to swing the car around, back onto Main Street, but Johnson's words came back to him. *I want an eye kept on those Evans women. . . . If one of them so much as looks at you cross-eyed, I want them brought in.*

He looked at Crane again.

"Oh, for cryin' out loud." Roger flicked his lights on and cursed under his breath, lifting his foot off the brake so his tires crawled toward the two teenagers. He didn't feel entirely good about detaining the girl just because of her last name, but if Luna was in his backseat, at least she'd be clear of trouble. Problem was, he wasn't so sure Grace would see things the same way. Ducey definitely wouldn't.

She'll skin my hide for this, he thought of the old woman. Still, if he could keep Luna out of Johnson's line of fire—it'd be worth it. The latest body belonged to a young girl with dark hair. They were about the same age, too. Roger couldn't see a pattern in the victims so far as he could tell, but he couldn't take the chance on Grace's daughter being next.

The teens stopped as Roger slowed the car to a halt and put it in park. He pushed open his door and stepped out, settling his hat on his head to blot out the sun. Was August always so damned hot?

Crane's voice mocked him in the bright glare of midday sun. "Afternoon, Officer. I didn't expect to see you so soon."

"Deputy," Roger corrected, automatically.

Luna kept her gaze downcast, but Roger noted the dark circles under her eyes. Her pale, almost sallow skin, like she hadn't slept in a week.

"Wasn't on my agenda for the day, either," Roger said, "but I can't help notice you two seem to be cutting out of school early." He glared at the boy under the brim of his hat. "Again."

The boy smirked behind his curtain of lank dark hair. Luna scuffed her shoes in the dirt on the side of the road but said nothing.

"What would your mom say if she caught you cutting school?" Roger asked, directing his question to Luna, who still hadn't met his eyes. "I doubt she'd be too happy."

The girl shrugged and the movement looked like it took some effort. "Wasn't planning on telling her," she mumbled.

One corner of Crane's thin lips pulled up into a smirk.

Roger glanced at his watch. Two minutes had already passed, and another was ticking its way around the clock.

"Why don't you kids hop in and I'll give you a ride home." It wasn't a request.

Luna automatically took a step forward, but Crane let his arm slide away from her shoulder and his hand land on her forearm, and she stilled. "Skipping last period isn't exactly an arrestable offense, Deputy."

Roger crossed his arms, sucked in his belly, and puffed out his chest in his best intimidation pose. Kid had a smart mouth. Maybe too smart.

"No, but unless you're eighteen, having a cigarette in your mouth is," he said. "Now, would you rather a free ride home, or a misdemeanor for minor in possession? Your choice."

A smile as greasy as his hair slid across the boy's face. "I didn't really feel like walking anyway," he said.

"Hopefully you don't have any interest in getting lung cancer before you hit twenty, either." Roger stretched his arm, flexed his palm open. "If you got any more cigarettes, I'll be happy to take them off your hands—along with anything else you might not want to be found with in a patrol car."

Crane's expression darkened and for half a minute Roger thought the boy might put up a fight, but then he grinned and stuffed his hands in his pockets. Pulled out a pack of Virginia Slims and thrust them in Roger's direction.

Roger eyed the boy. He accepted the pack, then slid it gently into his pocket, careful to keep the material from brushing against the cardboard sides. "Interesting choice."

"Got them from a friend."

"I bet you did."

Luna snickered, but her smile didn't reach her eyes. "My mom smokes those when she's stressed."

Roger raised an eyebrow and extended his hand again. "What about you, Miss Evans? Anything I should know about?" His eyes tracked the girl's hand as it slid to her hip. "Maybe in your pockets?"

Crane's eyes bugged when Luna's hand slipped into her jeans. He shook his head. "You don't have to—"

Sour words burned Roger's throat and curdled on his tongue. "There's a lot of strange stuff happening around town the past couple of days," he said, coaxing the girl along. What could she have—another cigarette, pills? "Sure would hate to see you mixed up in something you got no business being in."

The girl's hand balled under the denim. Hung there for a moment. Came out in a fist.

"They're not illegal or anything," she told Roger, voice small, fingers still curled into a tight ball. Her fist moved closer. Retracted. Dark hair eclipsed her eyes, traced along the angles of her cheekbones. "Can I have them back when you drop me off?"

Her last words came out so low they were almost a whisper and the little hairs on the back of Roger's neck prickled. His eye threatened to twitch. A movie scene flashed through his mind—Brad Pitt standing in a field while Morgan Freeman cut open a cardboard box.

Snow Leger's detached tongue in a pool of blood on her living room carpet.

For the first time in his life, even if it was only for a split hair of a second, Roger understood what it was about the Evans women that made others so damn nervous. He cleared his throat. "I don't have any intention of keeping anything that's rightfully yours," he promised.

Luna nodded and opened her fist, depositing two yellowed human teeth into the deputy's hand.

CHAPTER 23

Ducey Evans

Something nasty had prickled along Ducey's spine ever since she woke this morning, and she didn't think it was her arthritis flaring up again. The sensation had bothered her from the moment her eyes slid open, an unwelcome tick lingering just outside the edges of her vision, nestled in the space between her shoulder blades, where she couldn't reach to scratch. Course, the late-night visit from the sheriff hadn't done much for her mood. Not even Phillipe had been able to wash the bad taste of Buck Johnson's stale liquor out of her mouth.

She had gotten out of bed even earlier than usual, and by midmorning had already made her way through the stash of butterscotch candies tucked inside her apron pockets. By the time she'd settled behind the steering wheel of her old Ford Rambler to make her daily afternoon rounds to the florist, the truth had scorched up her skin like fire ants at a Fourth of July picnic.

It's time, she thought. Whatever was going to happen, it would be today. Course, she'd known that when she'd spoken with Lenore the night before, hadn't she? When she'd seen the death bird perched on the tree branch outside her window.

When Buck Johnson's headlights swung in her driveway.

Ducey had put down ghouls for nearly three-quarters of a century now. She knew their hunger, their eagerness. She knew something else, too—whatever made the dead rise in her small town, it had gotten tired of waiting. Frankly, she was surprised it had taken this long.

Every summer got a little hotter, a little more unpleasant. A little more suffocating.

A little harder to breathe.

Ducey felt it in every move she made. Sensed it the same way she knew before a storm blew through or if they were about to hit a dry spell. The inevitability ate at her bones and stiffened her joints. It picked at her until it became part of her as much as the arthritis and the wrinkles.

And so, she didn't question the urge to turn into Jimbo's Java Café as she passed the movie theater at the corner of Main Street on her return trip to the funeral parlor, backseat laden with roses and cremones and gardenias. Instead, Ducey pulled the old Ford Rambler through the parking lot to the edge of the alleyway between the café and the adjoining strip and shut off the engine. She rubbed the feeling back into her knees, stuffed a pair of oversized pruning shears inside the waistband of her trousers, and trudged past a rusted pay-phone stand and a sign pointing her to the café in the opposite direction.

Beads of sweat formed at the edge of her brow and trickled down the sides of her ears, but she heard the wet noises of death before she ever turned the corner. Sounds of shuffling. Panting. Ducey pushed her bifocals up the bridge of her nose, squinting into the damp darkness as she put one foot in front of the other. In the narrow walkway, a body lay twisted on the ground, covered in shadow. Limbs splayed out on either side like a broken doll. A second figure sat hunched down beside the first with its back to the alley, hovering so close it was hard to tell in the dim where one body ended and the other began.

Ducey pulled her right arm to her stomach, fingers gripping the shears' handle, and tugged the tool loose. She held her breath, watching as the stooped figure's hands reached out, rubbed the length of an outstretched limb.

No, not a limb. Ducey readjusted her glasses.

A paw.

A voice whispered in the darkness. "Who did this to you?"

"What in the blazes?" Ducey muttered. She crept closer and clasped the figure's shoulder.

A girl spun around.

A *living* girl. Black hair, pale skin. A bit heavy on the mascara, but otherwise not a mark on her.

Ducey recognized the girl's face, even if she didn't know her name. The Halloran apples didn't fall far from the tree, and even though that particular branch of the family sapling had cracked somewhere between Clyde's first and fourth wife, from his daughters on down, every generation with Halloran blood had the same look about them—wide mouths and heavy-lidded eyes. The man had hit every ugly stick on the way down from his own family tree, but his genes were about as pretty as they came.

"Your last name Halloran?" Ducey asked.

The girl blinked, her palm glued to her chest as she struggled to steady her breath. "My mom's maiden name is Halloran. My last name is Cole. I'm Kim." She pushed herself to her feet but kept her attention trained on the animal.

Ducey sucked her teeth. One of the Halloran girls had married a Cole, hadn't she? The youngest one, around Grace's age. "Your mama's name Becky?" Ducey asked.

"Barbara." Kim's brows twisted. "You didn't just scare me half to death or anything," she said, crossing her arms over her chest. "What are you doing in the alley anyway?"

Good Lord, I'm getting old, Ducey thought for the second time in as many days. *Old enough that no one bothers to ask your name anymore.*

"I'm Ducey Evans," she said, "but I'm guessin' you already knew that."

Kim flushed. Course she knew. Everybody did. Infamy was easy in small towns.

"My brother Dillon is friends with Luna," the girl said.

"Sweet kid." Ducey tucked the oversized shears back into her waistband, her gaze on the bleeding dog at her feet. Just like she knew Kim's features, she knew Buck Johnson's bony old hound. Ghouls didn't often go after animals—they must not have the same taste as humans—but something must have gotten to the poor dog for her to be out here, bleeding out halfway across town. No wonder the man had been spitting fire on her driveway last night. He loved the old dog more than he loved anything else. Neither of them knew it at the time, but she'd probably saved Buck from a fate even that old coot didn't deserve.

"Belle," she said.

The dog's tail lifted in one laborious thump.

"I just found her like this." Black eyeliner dripped in a sweaty streak down Kim's cheek, and her eyes were glassy. "It looks like something . . ."

Her voice dropped off as she fumbled for the right word.

Ducey peered over the girl's shoulder, trying to find the source of the ooze puddling on the stained concrete.

A bite mark bubbled bright with blood on the hound's hindquarters. Ducey retrieved a butterscotch from her pocket, popped it in her mouth, raked her tongue against the hard candy shell. The mark wasn't fresh, but it still bled. Only one kind of bite did that—the kind that was near impossible to stop once it got busy bleeding.

A ring of human teeth imprinted the dog's hide.

"I've heard there might be some rabid animals on the loose," Ducey said. Then, realizing such a claim might scare the girl even more, she added, "But she's not foamin' at the mouth, so nothing to worry about."

The sharp set of Kim's shoulders relaxed. "Can you help her?"

Ducey watched the dog's chest rise and fall in shallow waves. The poor thing had lost a lot of blood and was in terrible pain, but she was still breathing. Animals didn't rise like humans did, even in the rare instance they'd been chewed on by a ghoul, which was in itself desperate and unusual. Some said it was because animals didn't have souls, though Ducey's experience suggested not having a soul wasn't the problem. Half the people she'd known in her life had been soulless, terrible creatures, and a good number of them had needed some assistance staying in the ground. Most animals were made of sweeter stuff.

Either way, if they didn't get the old hound out of the alley and someplace safe, she'd be deader than a doornail within the hour. Buck Johnson would lay an egg.

"I'll do what I can," Ducey said. "Let's get her to the parlor."

Ducey pivoted toward the parking lot and stopped short, remembering the florist's shop filling her backseat. She looked at Kim, who still hovered over the dog. "You got a car?" she asked. "Mine's full of sprays for a service tomorrow."

Kim's face darkened. "I-I've got to pick my brother up from school."

"Parlor's on the way to Forest Park." Ducey jerked her head at the Rambler, a motion that tingled all the way to her toes. All that bending and squatting—she'd need the heating pad later. "And I've got a blanket in my trunk. We can wrap it around her, keep her warm. You just follow me back. I'll take it from there. Won't take but a minute."

The girl stalled.

"Well, come on, child. What are you waitin' for?" Ducey tapped the toe of her orthopedic shoe on the drippy, potholed pavement. "Skinny as that mutt is, I don't think I can pick her up all on my own." She clicked her dentures. "I might break a hip."

The remark earned a smirk from Kim. She took one more look at the suffering dog and pulled her purse up on her shoulder. Darn thing was shaped like a coffin. Now Ducey'd seen it all.

"Okay," Kim said, "but I better not get blood all over my car."

Ducey bit back a laugh. She'd had occasion to think the same thing a time or two. She'd also had to scrub the Rambler's vinyl free of bloodstains more times than she could count.

The blanket in the Rambler's trunk turned out to be a *Little Mermaid* twin-sized bedsheet. Kim rolled her eyes when she saw it, but Ducey would have bet money the girl liked the film. Sometimes the ones with the darkest exteriors had the softest insides.

Ducey didn't care much for either, but she was familiar with the type. The bedding belonged to Luna.

Together the two wrapped the bleeding hound. The tag on her collar was stained red, but Ducey passed her thumb across the engraving and squinted until she could make out the tiny lettering.

If found, call Sherriff Buck Johnson.

The dog's rabies tag hung behind the identification tag. It was current.

Well, at least there's that, Ducey thought. Not that rabies was on her list of top worries. Not even her top ten. Having Johnson's injured dog in her possession didn't exactly fill her with joy. The man had itched to get at her for the better part of sixty years, and harangued her ever since she turned him down for the homecoming dance and went with Royce instead. It hadn't helped matters much that he'd been around the night

Jimmy died and they'd put another body in the ground. Still, despite all his booze-filled blustering the night before, the man had kept their secret all these years. Didn't matter why.

"Come on, Belle," Kim said to the injured dog. "Let's get you into the car and someplace where we can take care of you."

Belle. Ducey smirked. Sweet name. Maybe there was something of the old Buchanan still in that grouchy stump Buck Johnson after all.

Belle moaned when they lifted her, but Kim patted the dog's head and she quieted.

"You're good with dogs," Ducey observed. "Says a lot about a person, you know."

Kim pulled her up shoulders. "They're easier than most people."

"You're right about that."

After securing Belle in the backseat of Kim's Buick, the girl situated herself behind the steering wheel and turned to Ducey.

"So, I just follow you to the funeral parlor and you'll, like, see if you can do something for her?" Kim asked.

"I reckon that's the plan," Ducey said.

"Will you call Sheriff Johnson?"

The butterscotch in Ducey's mouth had shriveled to the size of a penny. "Eventually. Unless you'd rather?"

Kim shook her head and looked at her hands, white against the green steering wheel. "I don't want this getting back to my dad."

"Your dad not an animal lover?" Ducey racked her head. Barbara Halloran had married some thick-necked boy from down the road.

"Something like that," Kim murmured.

She pulled the door closed and rolled down the window, letting some of the hot air escape. Then she peeled down the visor mirror and dabbed at the dried makeup humidity left smeared under her eyes.

Ducey sidled closer to the window. Men could be troublesome creatures, and sometimes fathers made the worst of monsters. "Would you take a piece of advice, from an old woman who knows?" she asked.

The girl shrugged, but didn't say no.

Ducey waited for the girl to meet her eyes. "All men are dust," she said, then leaned in closer, resting her forearms on the windowsill. "All of us, after we go into the ground and the worms get into our bones, we're nothin' but dust. All these little things that set us apart when we're aboveground don't make a lick of difference once we take our last breaths, so we might as well enjoy 'em while we got 'em. Ain't no sense feeling miserable about the things that make us special or wastin' our time with folks who don't appreciate them."

She paused again, blinking twice for punctuation. "You hear what I'm saying?" The girl shrugged again and said nothing. "What are you doing out in this alley anyway?" Ducey asked. "Not the kind of place I like to spend my free time."

Kim nodded in the direction of the café. "I just got off work."

"Not the kind of place I think I'd like to work, either." Ducey scrunched her nose. "Too sweet. Gives me a cavity just lookin' at the place."

"I'm just trying to get through school." A hint of a smile played on Kim's lips before a grimace twisted her features. "I take classes at the beauty college downtown, but I don't even know why," she said with a huff. "It's not like anyone in this town is going to let someone who looks like me do their makeup."

"My granddaughter used to say the same thing," Ducey said, fingering the tip of the pruning shears beneath her blouse. "But the livin' aren't the only ones who need to be beautiful, and I got a feelin' you wouldn't have a problem with a quieter clientele. Either way, don't you ever let anyone take *you* away from you, child. Because at the end of the day, that's all you got."

Ducey pushed herself to her feet, ignoring the stitch in her side. "Well, that's enough chitchat for one day." She clapped her hands against the window. "We better get a move on. Got a dog to keep from dyin'."

CHAPTER 24

Deputy Brandon Hinson

Brandon Hinson's stomach clenched as he pulled into the parking lot of the run-down, two-screen cinema behind the shopping mall. A large section of woodland backed up to the theater, and the trunks of tall pine and ash trees inked skinny shadows on the broken concrete. The ramshackle theater and piney trim were a common sight in this part of the country, but the pool of blood stretching from the pavement into the grass called in by a couple of matinee moviegoers wasn't exactly an everyday sight in Small Town, USA.

At least this time he wasn't the first on scene. The coroner's van was parked just ahead, right between the twin posters for Van Damme's *Universal Soldier: The Return* and a historical action flick starring Antonio Banderas. The sun's constant glow had already faded both film posters, wilting them with summer heat. Just last week, Brandon tried to bring his girlfriend to see one of the blockbusters, but Kim had convinced him to attend a midnight revival showing of *Night of the Living Dead* at the dollar theater the next town over instead. The vintage horror flick hadn't done much to scare him at the time, but now . . .

Hits a little too close to home, Brandon thought. A lot too close, actually.

Across the concrete, Quigg poured himself from his van, white lab coat blinding under the hot sun. He looked over his shoulder in the direction of Brandon's car and raised a hand in greeting.

Brandon waved on the other side of the dashboard glass. Even at a distance he saw the coroner's tongue dart out and lick at his bottom lip. Quigg approached a crime scene almost like he savored digging through the grisly remains of tragedy, documenting them on the thin green clipboard he carried everywhere with him.

Brandon swallowed back the bitter taste in his mouth and pushed out his driver's side door. He didn't want to see the scene awaiting him; still saw Snow Leger's tongue every time he blinked. Luckily, Kim had canceled their lunch plans at the last minute; otherwise, the burger he'd planned to have would've already bubbled back up his throat. Now he put one boot in front of the other until he arrived at Quigg's side. The coroner stood over the body, tongue pinched between his teeth, and scribbled notes on his clipboard as his assistants yanked a gurney from the back of the van, its metal legs clanging against the concrete.

The racket shuddered up Brandon's spine. Beat against his teeth.

"Afternoon, Quigg." Brandon imagined the blood pooling on the ground as spilled motor oil from some leaking pickup. The girl lying sprawled and split open on the pavement a morbid prop, the kind sold at pop-up party-supply stores every Halloween.

Quigg licked his bottom lip again and scribbled something else on the page as one of his assistants shook open a black plastic cadaver bag. "Hinson," he returned.

Brandon hated to ask. "Any early observations?"

"None that make a lick of sense," the coroner said and snapped his clipboard shut. "But cause of death is pretty clear."

Brandon hitched an eyebrow. *Motor oil*, he thought. *Motor oil spilled in a haunted house.*

Quigg aimed his pencil's tip at the body. "Blood loss caused by a massive laceration here"—he pointed to the girl's neck, where a deep red gouge glistened like a second mouth—"and here." He waved at her abdomen.

The girl's stomach had been ripped apart. Her innards spilled out of the open cavity, tumbled in heaps like wet scarlet noodles around her. The stink of meat left to swelter in the outdoor heat clung to the air, ruining Brandon's sense of smell.

He faked a cough to hide his nerves. "What in the hell could have done that?"

Quigg groaned himself into a squat, index finger pushing his spectacles up the bridge of his nose as he leaned in for a closer look. He licked his lip and Brandon's stomach lurched.

"No obvious blade marks. Doesn't look like she was cut." The man leaned close enough to the body that the few wispy strands of silver hair still attached to his scalp brushed the dead girl's arm.

Brandon's tongue swelled in his mouth.

"Well, looky here." Quigg's face was almost inside the girl's body. He snapped his fingers and wiggled them, and one of his assistants handed him a pair of tweezers and a Ziploc bag. The old man dipped the long metal prongs into the spongy red cavity of the girl's stomach, tweezed, withdrew. A gleeful smile played upon his mouth and his eyes glinted as he gave his lips another lick. "Looks like we found our murder weapon."

The coroner held his finding up so the light could cast a glow around the few inches of skin.

A finger. An honest-to-God *finger*, ripped free of its hand right below the second knuckle.

Brandon's eyes darted to the dead girl's hands, counted all ten digits. The remnant in the stomach wasn't hers. This time when his stomach lurched, Brandon turned to the side and vomited until his gut ran empty. Until dots danced before his eyes and he could almost forget the smokey red nail polish at the finger's tip.

When he finally managed to wipe his mouth on his sleeve and pull back up to his full height, Quigg gave him an apologetic look and passed him a small handbag. "Unless you want to wait around to give Channel Six footage for the evening news, we best be getting her loaded up," he said, wetting his lips with another lick.

Quigg's silent assistants covered the body with a cloth, then zipped it into the body bag and hoisted it onto the gurney. Dry gray pavement remained where the girl's body had lain, and Brandon watched as her blood rushed over the empty space, filling it in. He wretched again and redirected his attention to the handbag before he tainted the scene with his own bile.

Leftover vomit on his hands left a sticky orange thread on the pink fabric of the victim's purse. More than twenty years of life experience had taught Brandon it was impolite to rifle through a lady's handbag, and even under these circumstances, it still felt wrong. His fingers combed through cosmetic compacts, loose scraps of paper, two ticket stubs, and coins before landing on a wallet. He thumbed it open just as Deputy Taylor's cruiser slid into the parking lot, then thumbed out the girl's school ID. She was a sophomore at Forest Park.

Brake lights glowed red as Taylor pulled his car into the lot, turned around so the nose pointed at Jimbo's across the street, and put it in park. The man hoisted himself out of the vehicle but left his driver's door open and kept the engine running.

Figures shifted in the cruiser's back window as Brandon met his senior officer halfway between the cruiser and the crime scene, but the glare of sunlight on the glass washed them in shadow. "You got some-one in your car?" he asked.

"Two someones." Taylor watched the crew push the gurney through the van's open double back doors. One of the tray's legs stuck on the bumper and Quigg swatted his clipboard at one of the assistants, who jostled it free. "What's the story here?" Taylor asked.

"Young girl dead from multiple lacerations. Neck and stomach. The body is intact, but—" Brandon thought of her intestines swimming outside her skin, the slop of fluid on the ground, and clenched the wallet he'd forgotten he was holding. "It's not pretty, but Quigg found some . . . evidence."

"What kind of evidence?"

"A finger." Brandon swallowed another surge of fresh bile. "Might belong to whoever attacked her."

"He found a *finger*?" Taylor bit off the words.

Brandon nodded. Best he could do.

"Jesus H. Christ," the older deputy mumbled. "Get the finger into forensics for analysis. If there's nothing else, get the site blocked off and call in someone to clean it up." Taylor inched closer to the van, but Brandon hung back and the other man stalled. "There a reason we're not talking by the body?"

Brandon felt his face turn green. He shook his head.

"That bad, huh?" Taylor pulled his mudpie hat from his head and twisted it in his hands. "Make sure Quigg calls the parlor sooner rather than later. Lenore will want to know she's got an incoming."

"You sure you want to let the Evanses know?" Brandon asked, trying to keep his breath shallow in case the rank scent of death carried. He thumbed crusted vomit off the purse. "Sheriff Johnson seems to think there might be some sort of connection."

Taylor's sigh came out in a growl. "It's a small town, Hinson. You'd be hard-pressed to find two people who weren't connected, and those women have a job to do." He cast another look at the coroner's van, but he stayed put. His eyes swept the pavement, lingering on the wide red puddle. The leftover lumps of body matter still stuck to the ground. "Quigg will do what he can, but if the body's in as bad shape as I suspect it is, we want to get her cleaned up. Unless you think her parents deserve to see their daughter like we found her?"

"No, sir."

Taylor pinched the bridge of his nose like he was warding off a migraine. "Name? Any ID on the girl?"

"Alison Haney." Brandon read the name off the laminated student identification card, then put the girl's ID back in her purse, thumbing off the crusted line of vomit. He thought through all his friends, and their younger siblings still in school. An image of Kim's younger brother washed up in his thoughts and he shook it away. Dillon was also a sophomore.

Taylor set his hat back atop his head. "Find any ticket stubs in her purse?"

"Two." The coroner van's rear doors banged shut. Brandon opened his mouth to suck in a deep breath. His gaze landed on the stained concrete and his jaw clamped shut.

"Any leads on who she was with?"

"Haven't had a chance to ask," Brandon said. Alison hadn't stayed to finish the movie she'd come to see. The film would be ending soon, and her fellow moviegoers would trickle out, herded out of an inside exit so they wouldn't track right through the crime scene. "I'll go inside and ask some questions once we wrap up out here."

Taylor shook his head, then looked back at the teenagers in the backseat of his cruiser. "How old did you say our vic was?"

"Sophomore, so I'm guessing fifteen, maybe sixteen." Brandon shook the purse but didn't hear the jangle of car keys. "I'm banking on the former."

"Check the security footage," Taylor said. "Likely the second ticket belonged to another student, skipping school with her." The older deputy shifted, scuffed his boot against the concrete. He chewed at his lip for a little longer than Brandon found comfortable, then glanced at his cruiser and loosed a sigh so heavy his lips pushed out and fluttered like a deflating balloon.

He reached into his pocket and pulled out a crumpled pack of Virginia Slims. He retrieved a handkerchief from his other pocket, wrapped the package, and tucked the bundle discreetly into Brandon's hand.

Brandon eyed the cigarettes. "You . . . trying to quit, Taylor?"

Taylor's lips went flat, anchoring an eyebrow that shot to his hairline. "I smoked my last cigarette in '91," he said. "Take these over to forensics and keep it quiet. See if they can pull any prints. No one knows the results but me—got it?"

"Yes, sir."

Taylor turned to look back to his car and let go another sigh. His fingers rose to his breast pocket, thumbed open the flap, and sunk in. He paused with his fingers still deep in the cloth and set his eyes on Brandon's.

"This stays between us, Hinson," he said, holding the rookie in his gaze. "Now, I mean it. Johnson gets one word and you'll be clearing out your desk, you understand?"

Brandon swallowed. "Yes, sir."

Roger pulled two small rocks from his pocket, crooked his index and middle fingers so that Brandon would hold out his palm. Then he opened his grip to deposit two human teeth into Brandon's hand.

Brandon's eyes traced a line from his palm to his commanding officer. "You want me to run prints on teeth?"

The older man glared hard at him. "That a serious question, Hinson?"

Brandon closed his fist, trying not to let himself feel the sharp points of the teeth dig—bite—into his skin. "Right. No prints on teeth, obviously. I'll have forensics check dental records." He eyed the odd items in his hands. "You think these might be connected to our perp?"

His commanding officer watched as the coroner's van cranked to life, honked as it pulled away. "You heard the sheriff," he said. "We're dealing with an animal attack."

"But the finger—"

"I mean it, Hinson," Taylor said, "and I'm going to need those teeth back, so don't bag 'em. Just find out whose mouth they belong in. I want forensics on all three of these—the finger, the cigs, the teeth—by the time I get back to the station." He tipped his hat and turned away. "Nobody gets the results before me. That's an order."

"Yes, sir." Brandon swallowed. He stood with the crumpled pack of cigarettes in one hand and a pair of teeth in the other, watching as Taylor settled back into his cruiser and pulled out, the two faceless heads in the backseat swiveling to look back as the car drove away. The sour taste of vomit still hung in the back of his throat, but now a new feeling twisted in his chest. Deputy Roger Taylor was hiding something.

CHAPTER 25

Lenore Evans

The rod of steel running straight down Lenore's spine ached. She rubbed at her back with her right hand, fingering at the ridges of her bones. The space between her ribs. Her vertebrae. Each divot was nearly the width of her middle finger, deep enough to swallow her fingertip. When had she become so thin—so fragile?

She grunted and lifted her chin, pressed her loafers firm against the chapel carpet, and stared at the mosaic of multicolored stained glass that filled the chancel window. How many funerals had she overseen in this space—how many souls properly buried, returned to their graves? Enough that she kept a mental list of remembered names and remembered faces. She might be tired and she might be old, but *fragile* was not a word for Evans women. Not a word for *her*.

The phone in the lobby rang, the shrill noise in the quiet sparking like electricity under Lenore's skin. She cocked her head, listening. The telephone's ring pulsed through the space between the bones of her back and licked along the small hairs at the base of her neck. The phone at Evans Funeral Parlor had rung hundreds, thousands of times, and never before had the sound seemed so cruel, so desperate.

She set her left hand on the ledger in her lap, her pencil a sixth finger aimed at the page. "Mama, can you get that?" she called.

No answer. The phone shrieked again, sending another jolt of electricity down Lenore's spine. Her pencil hand jerked, scratching a messy line outside of the margin.

"Grace, honey?" Lenore flipped the instrument over, scrubbed at the erroneous mark so hard she nearly ripped the paper. "Phone's ringing."

Again, no answer, just the biting shriek of the telephone.

Lenore gritted her teeth and glanced at the watch on the chapel's back wall, its key pulling in her slacks pocket. It was nearly one o'clock in the afternoon. Where was everyone? Ducey had left two hours earlier to make a run to the florist, and Grace had been in and out all morning, bouncing around as if she had fire ants crawling in her underwear. Both should be back by now—*should* have been back already. It wouldn't be long, and the bus would drop Luna off from school.

The phone rang again, queuing another array of sparks to shoot across Lenore's arms. She set the ledger on the padded pew beside her and began to make her way to the front desk. She moved slowly at first, but by the fourth ring, she ran down the hall, scrambling in her sensible orthopedic loafers while the echo of her own footsteps chased after her.

Lenore's palm slammed down on the receiver half a second before the machine picked up. She wrenched the phone from its cradle and held it to her ear. "Evans Funeral Parlor."

There was a gasp in her voice and her words came out a little too sharp. She swallowed them both. Felt them cut against her throat on the way down. She counted to three and tugged the phone cord loose. "Lenore speaking."

The ringing left a phantom chime in her ear, an eerie tinnitus, and she struggled to hear the voice on the other end of the line. "I'm sorry, can you repeat that?"

Something wet, then, "Lenore, this is Jedediah Quigg."

Her heart hit her stomach at the same moment her bottom hit the cushioned desk chair. The painful ringing had subsided, but even without its interference she couldn't remember the last time the coroner had phoned her personally.

Long enough that she'd forgotten how loud the man's habitual licking sounded on a phone line. Not that they had reason to speak often. Their business was a wordless one, conducted in mournful transactions of cold bodies passed from one set of careful hands to another. Over the years, the two had developed a sort of dialogue between them—his, a few lines of text scrawled at the bottom of the surrender form attached to the gurney; hers, a copy of the memorial service program clipped to the paperwork and returned with one of the sallow-faced coroner's assistants.

Lenore forced a smile into her voice and shuffled papers on her desk in an attempt to sound nonplussed. To cover up the panic seeping into the places the phone's ringing had exposed and left open.

"Well, good afternoon, Jed." Lenore twisted a lock of her short red hair and tried to sound casual. The clock key hung heavily in her pocket, and she resisted the urge to pick up the cordless connection, return to the chapel, wind her dead husband's clock that she'd already rung tight twice this morning. "Didn't expect to hear from you today."

On the other end of the phone, Jed Quigg licked his lips. "Didn't expect to call," he said, "but the boys down at the sheriff's station figured you might want to hear this news from me directly."

Lenore leaned forward in her chair to finger her spine. Her back had begun to ache, jarred by the unexpected race down the parlor's long hallway. "Oh?"

Another lick.

"Got another body here," Quigg said. "Just picked her up from the theater."

Lenore breathed. *Her.*

"Another one chewed up like Edwin Boone." Quigg's voice caught, and he held the phone away while he coughed it free. He licked his lips before speaking again. "Worse, maybe," he said, "depending on your constitution. I'm not sure even you gals could do much with this one. Might want to talk to the parents about a closed casket."

"I'm sorry, Jed. Did you say *parents*?" The word stuck in Lenore's throat. In a rare moment of optimism, she'd allowed her thoughts to wander to Snow. Not that she hoped to find the woman dead, but if they had then it would mean she hadn't risen, wasn't restless. She'd be just another body, just another someone to put to rest.

"Well, you see, that's why I wanted to give you a call." Something heavy had crept into the man's voice. Pity, perhaps. He'd gone a full three sentences without licking. "Figured it might be easier coming from me before Roger Taylor or that young deputy of his makes their way to you. I've got a girl here. Young. Right around your granddaughter's age." He pulled in a breath. "This isn't going to be an easy one, Lenore."

Lenore let the man's words dissolve as she stared through the glass front doors of Evans Funeral Parlor. Ducey's old Ford Rambler pulled into the parking lot, followed by a mint-green Buick she didn't recognize. Both vehicles slipped through the front lot, past Ducey's favorite parking spot, heading around to the side of the building, toward the delivery door. What in the—

"Lenore?" The coroner's voice pulled her back into the lobby.

Lenore blinked as two sets of car doors slammed outside. "Burying a child is never easy," she agreed.

Seeing a dead one rise, she thought, *well, that's far worse.*

Quigg breathed into the line. "Girl's name is Alison Haney. She must have skipped school, taken herself out to a movie. Judging by the severity of the wounds, she'd have bled out in seconds, probably been unconscious immediately from the shock. It was fast, at least. Small mercy."

Lenore struggled for a question as she twisted her fingers along the phone cord. Her tongue felt swollen. "You said her body is in poor shape?"

"There's a deep gouge in her throat, right at the jugular. Stomach's spilled open."

"You think it was the same thing that got Edwin?" It was, of course, but Lenore needed more to go on. She needed to know how much to press to get the poor girl's body into the parlor before it woke up.

Quigg considered his response. Lenore heard his tongue pass through his lips on the other end of the line. The wet scrape of muscle against flesh.

"No," he said finally. "Whatever tore into Ed looked like an animal. This . . ." His words broke off in a sigh, followed by a lick. "Well, I've never seen an animal do someone like this. Whoever did this, it was like they knew where to pull her apart. Where to make her bleed out fast."

*Who*ever, he'd said this time. Not *what*ever. Lenore's thoughts raced as her fingers pressed painfully into her spine again, bruising her flesh. Not all those who found themselves fed upon by the dead came back, though they usually did. The death was so violent, so unexpected, the living hardly had time to accept it. So the cycle went. The more restless dead rose, the more living souls they pulled into torment with them.

And they were getting stronger.

The less predictable part was *when* they would rise. It could be as long as days, as short as hours, but usually the more violent the death, the quicker the return. She needed to get Alison Haney to Evans Funeral Parlor as fast as possible. They could have hours.

Less.

A new thought prickled through Lenore. Taking care of the dead as they came into the funeral parlor wouldn't be enough. Not anymore. Not with so many strigoi unaccounted for. Usually, the dead, even the restless, made their way to the parlor without much incident and the Evanses were there to welcome them home. But these strigoi weren't behaving like usual. Lenore thought of her rosebush, pale and rotting. Even if the monster was still buried, something else kept these restless from coming home, maybe the same something that had drained Mina Jean. The Evans women needed to find them and put them down. Perhaps they'd already dallied too long. Was it Clyde Halloran who killed Alison? Or Snow—Widow Milner?

Someone else?

Lenore's thoughts turned to Luna and the parlor went cold around her even as sun steam-fogged the glass-paned front doors.

"I'll get everything prepared," Lenore said as much to herself as to Quigg. "When will you bring her over?"

"That's the other thing." Quigg licked at his lips again. "We found something on the body that might explain what's been going on around here."

Lenore hardened to ice. She placed a hand on her side, squeezed at her ribs to force out the words. A delay getting the body to the parlor could lead to disaster just as quick as any explanation Quigg or the Sheriff's Department might arrive at by examining the remains. "Found something?"

There was wet victory in Quigg's tone now. "A finger."

The parlor's side door swung open. Slammed shut. Then, footsteps.

"Come on, let's bring her in here." Ducey's voice resounded down the hall, just loud enough to be caught over what sounded like moaning and a high, tinny whine. Another voice followed—a young woman's, unfamiliar. Her words were indistinct, ruined by the thud of something heavy dropping onto one of the steel tables in the laboratory.

A long, inhuman moan filtered through the funeral parlor.

Lenore shot to her feet and found herself anchored to the desk by the phone cord, the heavy base protesting as she pulled it into a thin line to peer around the corner, down the hall. Where in the dickens was Grace? And who—*what*—had Ducey brought back with her?

"A finger," she finally managed, hoping Quigg had mistaken her delayed response for shock rather than distraction.

"A *woman's* finger," he clarified. "At least, looked like a woman's finger. Even had a painted fingernail. The digit didn't look severed, though. Damn thing appeared to have been torn right off the hand, like it came loose when it ripped the body open. Couldn't tell you more than that, though; I only got a quick look before Taylor's boy took it down to forensics to run it for prints."

But Lenore had barely heard him as she saw Grace's car swing into the lot, followed by a sheriff's department cruiser. "What . . ." She swallowed, unable to complete the sentence.

Quigg licked his lips. "Excuse me?"

Lenore's own finger stabbed into her spine, but she barely felt it. Most of her body had gone numb. "What color was the nail polish?"

"Oh." Quigg emitted a small, nervous titter and his tongue slid across his lips. "Funny you ask. Nail was painted red so dark it was purple as a fresh liver, if you can imagine. Don't quite know what you'd call it."

"Oxblood." The word slipped out before she could stop it.

Quigg sniffed. "Excuse me?"

"The color is called oxblood." Lenore knew exactly whose finger Quigg had found on the dead girl's body, likely ripped free of Snow's fledging strigoi hand when she tore the poor girl apart. Lenore knew, and soon, so would everyone else because finding Snow's finger in Alison Haney's mutilated corpse wouldn't give law enforcement an answer, but it would confirm what Roger Taylor would already be thinking and Sheriff Johnson already knew: these deaths had nothing to do with animal attacks.

CHAPTER 26

Grace Evans

Grace had taken herself out for lunch. She'd needed something greasy to settle her stomach after a sleepless night wondering where Snow, Patsy Milner, and Clyde Halloran had got off to—how Mina Jean's life had been drained away when she'd done everything she could think of to prevent something like that from happening—and a fast-food cheeseburger and large order of fries served through a drive-through window had sounded up to the task. Now, as she swung her Mazda into the parking lot of Evans Funeral Parlor directly in front of Roger Taylor's cruiser, the wad of processed sodium and saturated fat sat like an anchor in the pit of her stomach.

When she saw her daughter's head in Roger's backseat through her rearview mirror, her lunch's aftertaste turned to acid in her throat.

It's happening, she thought. Whatever she'd been waiting fifteen years on, it was happening now.

Even if Luna had done nothing wrong—even if Roger was a friend—nothing good could come of her daughter being brought home in the hands of a lawman. Not now, when the dead had begun to rise. Not ever. History had handed down that lesson from generation to generation of Evans women, and the world hadn't changed much in the time between. It had perhaps gotten worse.

Grace thrust her car in park before it came to a complete stop, bit back the unpleasant taste that flooded her mouth when the vehicle jerked forward. She threw open her door, flung herself out, and marched to the cruiser, keys stabbing into her fist as she went.

Roger stepped out of his car, palms in the air. "Grace, before you go getting upset, everything is just fine."

The burning sensation in her throat grew hotter and Grace had to open her mouth to suck in cooler air. *Just fine* was another way of saying things were *just about* to go to hell.

Grace's eyes locked on her daughter through the rear window of Roger's car. She didn't breathe when he opened the door, when Luna crawled out of the backseat. She didn't even realize she was shaking until she heard the clatter of her car keys hitting the blacktop at her feet.

Her voice came out too high. Pinched. "Luna, what's going on?"

The girl shrugged, managing to look bored, though a faint wash of pink colored her cheeks. "Nothing, Mom," she said. "Everything's fine."

Just fine. Like hell.

Grace pushed her palms out in front of her, waved them at her daughter and the deputy. Anger had made her tongue numb, and she had a hard time putting the right words together, but when she did they came out red-hot. "How is you being dropped off in a squad car in the middle of a school day *fine*?"

Roger pulled his hat from his head, bending the brim in his fist. "Now, Grace—"

She pushed one hand, palm out, toward the deputy, but her eyes didn't stray from Luna. "I am talking to my daughter, if you don't mind."

The words were harsh, which made Grace almost feel guilty. Almost.

Silence descended over the parking lot. A lovebug tried to land on Grace's arm and she swatted it away. Luna shuffled and looked uncomfortable but said nothing. The growing distance between Grace and her daughter measured in miles now, acres of untouched forest impossible to penetrate. All these years she had tried so hard to keep Luna close. Safe. And all she'd managed to do was push her away while her worst fears came true anyway.

Roger took a cautious step forward, and when Grace didn't bite, he squared up. Sucked in a breath. "Luna, why don't you get on inside in the air-conditioning," he said. "I'll just have a word with your mother."

Grace watched her daughter tuck her chin under and speed toward the side door of the parlor without a second's hesitation or a single backward glance. *Well, that was nice.* She held her hand up to her eyes, blocking the sun's glare, and squinted up at the taller man as he closed the gap between them.

"Caught her skipping out of school early with a boy named Crane Campbell," Roger said. He mimed the boy's description, mudpie hat swinging from one hand as moisture ran down the side of his face. "Skinny fella. Tall, black hair, wears a leather trench coat even though it's hotter'n blue blazes. Ring a bell?"

Grace's thoughts slid to the boy she'd caught slipping through the shadows last night at Riverfront Park. He hadn't told her his name, but there weren't a lot of kids in town who fit the bill. She dared a quick glance at the cruiser's backseat. It was empty. "I didn't know picking up truants was a concern of the sheriff's department," she said.

Roger had the decency to look embarrassed. "Not typically. But something strange is going on around town, and—" The man stopped and palmed sweat from his brow. "Listen, Grace. There's something you need to know."

The tone of Roger's voice—firm but not harsh—extinguished Grace's ire as if someone had put a lid on a pot of boiling water. The man looking back at her wasn't a hard-boiled sheriff's deputy, or even one of the good ol' boys who occasionally came on to her in the grocery store, with pale stripes interrupting the tanned flesh of their ring fingers, looking for a fling to tell their buddies about over beer. This was the boy she'd gone to school with, the one she still caught looking at her when he thought she wasn't watching. Grace didn't love Roger Taylor. Not even close. In fact, she didn't think she'd ever love a man again.

But she did trust him. Not a lot, but enough.

A bead of sweat trickled down her spine, and she tugged her shirtsleeve over the scar on her wrist. "What?"

"Your girl had something odd in her pockets." Roger twisted his hat. Shifted his weight. "I don't know—"

"What did she *have*, Roger?" The words cracked out of her so fast the deputy staggered back like he'd been lashed.

"Teeth." He didn't look at her when he said it.

"*Teeth?*"

The deputy's head gave a single, quick nod. "Human teeth."

The fast-food wad in Grace's gut hardened to stone, burned up her throat, rushed into her mouth. She put her hand against her jaw in an attempt to keep the entirety of the number four from Whataburger's lunch menu from speeding past her lips. Why in the world was Luna carrying around teeth?

And more than that—who did the teeth belong to?

Roger clearly took her response as a sign of motherly concern, because his face relaxed and he patted the air again. "I don't want to have to do this," he said, "but I need to ask you a few questions."

Questions. Grace's left eyebrow inched up her forehead, pulled higher every time she tasted sick on her tongue. She cleared her throat and nodded.

The deputy's cheeks flushed and he wiped at his nose, then set his hat back on his head so its shadow covered his face. "Do you have any idea where Luna might have gotten a couple of human teeth?"

Roger's eyes flicked over Grace's shoulder to the funeral parlor, and he shook his head as if answering his own question. "Well, any reason she might want to go around carrying . . ."

Grace's eyebrow ticked higher.

Roger's eyes met Grace's and he rocked back onto his heels, pushed his hands in his slacks. "Oh, hell, Grace, I've got three dead bodies and some are missing parts. Last thing I expected to find on your girl was a couple of adult molars."

"I'm sure there's a perfectly reasonable explanation for whatever Luna had," Grace said, her anger burning like acid on her tongue. "Teenagers get into all sorts of things, but it's usually harmless. Just a phase."

Roger nodded, but his lips had pressed together so tight his chin puckered. "But teeth, Grace. You have to admit that's a little . . . strange."

She narrowed her eyes, feeling her faith in the deputy beginning to fade. Never once had Roger treated her any different for being an Evans. Maybe Johnson's poison had finally slipped under the man's skin after all. "And being strange is a criminal offense now, is it?"

"Now, Grace, you know I don't think like that, never have." Roger shook his head and sighed. "We go way back, and you know I . . . well . . ."

"I know you *what*?"

Long seconds ticked past before Roger answered. Luna saw a flutter in the break-room curtains of Evans Funeral Parlor, the floral fabric rippling like wind sweeping through a field of flowers. Someone inside was watching.

"You know I care about you," he finally admitted, words coming out barely above a whisper. The red creeping into his cheeks now had nothing to do with the heat. "But something wrong is going on around here, and it's getting worse." The man cleared his throat. "We just found another body down by the theater—a kid Luna's age, Grace. Something ripped her apart in broad daylight, and it wasn't an animal. People are dead. I can't shake the feeling there's something you aren't telling me."

Grace wanted to disagree. She wanted to say, *Of course, we've told you everything* or, *There's nothing to tell*, but she couldn't say either of those things. Couldn't lie to one of her oldest friends like that, not while he looked at her so intently, eyes full of acceptance, of concern.

"I'll talk to Luna about skipping school," she said instead. "And I'd appreciate it if you'd keep whatever she was carrying in her pockets between us."

For a moment it seemed like Roger would say something, but then he deflated like a punctured balloon. "All right, Grace."

Roger stepped back and turned to go. He paused, lowered halfway into his cruiser. "One more question, if you don't mind."

Grace forced her lips into a tight smile. "Yes?"

"Are you smoking again?"

"Smoking?" Grace remembered the pack of Virginia Slims she'd picked up, the butt she'd flicked out the window leaving Edwin Boone's driveway. The crumpled pack she'd foisted off on that strange boy at Riverfront Park. Had the cigarettes lay out in the open when she'd talked to Hinson? She didn't think so. "I haven't had a cigarette in years, Roger. You know that."

He nodded, settled into his seat. "Just thought I'd ask," he said, and then he shut the door, waved on the other side of the window, and drove away.

Grace watched the cruiser's taillights until the car took a turn and disappeared from sight. She sighed and rubbed at her temples.

Teeth. Ducey closed the cadaver's mouths, Grace painted them into soft smiles. They would have noticed a body going into the ground missing its teeth. The molars in Luna's pocket meant she'd been in contact with the dead, and not one that had passed through the funeral parlor. It meant there was more going on with Luna than they knew about.

It meant they were out of time.

CHAPTER 27

Ducey Evans

Ducey looked at the dog lying prone on the metal exam table in the back room of Evans Funeral Parlor and stuffed her hands in her apron pockets. She and the Halloran girl had only just gotten the poor thing situated, and already they'd used up all the gauze Ducey could find stuffed in the lab's drawers, along with damn near every rag she had on hand. All that, and blood still flowed from the bite on Belle's hindquarters. Dripped off the slab to pool in shallow red slicks on the linoleum floor. Ducey fingered her trocar while she stared at the animal. She watched the shallow rise and fall of her chest, the twitch of her closed eyelids. Even though the dog wouldn't become a ghoul, Ducey might still have to put it down. If it didn't stir soon—

Belle whimpered. Her pale pink tongue slid out to lick Ducey's hand, and she peeled open watery eyes as her tail began to thud lightly on the table.

Ducey released the trocar and fished a butterscotch out of her apron instead.

"You're going to be all right." She ruffled the dog's ears, then pushed the bedsheet they'd used to carry the old hound to the unoccupied end of the metal table. Belle nudged Ducey's hand for another pet and the bedsheet heaved off the slab, so saturated with blood and other fluids it hit the ground like an amputated limb. A heavy thunk and a wet slop. Splatter.

Ducey winced. "You're gonna be all right." She gave the dog's ears one last squeeze and patted her snout. "But I don't know if I can say the same about me once Lenore sees this mess."

At least something's got her preoccupied and out of my hair for now, Ducey thought as she kicked the soggy cloth under the exam table, grabbed her glasses where they hung on the chain around her neck, and set them on her nose.

The Halloran girl flitted around the lab like a hummingbird, touching and looking and giving Ducey heartburn. "Flip that big green switch on," she said, pointing first at the switch on the wall beside the door, then at the mobile medical lamp in the corner. "Then push that lamp over to me so I can get a better look at what we're up against."

Kim did as Ducey instructed, stationing the lamp at the head of the exam table. When Ducey leaned forward, Kim bent the lamp's gooseneck so that it shined on the pulsing red bite on the dog's hide. "Shouldn't you, like, be wearing gloves?" she asked.

Ducey *harrumphed* and ran her hands over the dog's body. Aside from the wound in her haunch, whoever'd gotten their teeth in Belle hadn't managed to bite off much else. None of her bones were broken. No scratches, no tears. But her gums had all but disappeared, and when Ducey felt along the left paw, Belle whined and pulled it away.

Poor thing was in bad shape. Her condition deteriorated by the minute, but she'd live—so long as Ducey could stop the bleeding and heal the bite. She adjusted the dog's body on the table and rolled her so the rump lay flat. The movement sent another red wave crashing against the floor, soaking the toes of both women's shoes.

"She won't stop bleeding." The whites of Kim's eyes showed, stark against the thick black eyeliner and mascara, and her voice came out higher than Belle's whimpering. "Why won't she stop bleeding?"

"Some blood don't clot," Ducey answered, which was only partially untrue. Bites were nasty things to begin with. Full of bacteria. Hard to heal without scarring. But a bite from the dead was different—a rip that tore all the way between one world and the next. Those kinds of bites never stopped bleeding, not until all the blood ran out. Every last drop.

Kim stared at the blood on her boots. "So she's just going to bleed to death?" she asked.

"Not if I can help it." Where were Lenore and Grace?

"What do we do for her?"

Ducey sighed. "*We* don't do anything." She traced her tongue along her dentures, grabbed another bunch of rags to keep her hands busy, to make it look like she had everything under control—which she did, if she could just get this girl out of the lab. "You go on and fetch your brother from school," she said. "I can handle things here."

Kim's eyes swung between the woman and the dog. She chewed at her lip. "But I can't just leave her."

"Sure you can."

The lab door swung open and a face popped into the room. Dark hair, wide midnight eyes. Luna . . . but it was too early for school to be out. Something else must have already gone wrong today.

The younger girl's eyes shifted from Ducey to Belle to Kim before understanding snapped into place. Her gaze fell on the bloodied rags as she neared the metal exam table. The dog. "What's going on?"

"We've got an injured dog to take care of." Ducey motioned her great-granddaughter toward the table and thrust the bundle of clean rags in her direction. Even *without* any training, even *with* Luna's role in the family legacy still uncertain, even *though* it was only a dog on her table and not a person, two Evans women in the presence of something half-dead was still better than one. "Where's your mother?"

Luna took the rags and started mopping up blood. "Outside talking to Deputy Taylor."

Ducey quirked an eyebrow. "Well, isn't today just turning out to be a peach," she muttered under her breath. First, she had to go and bring that old fart Buck Johnson's bit dog into the parlor. Now one of his deputies was out in the parking lot—not just any deputy, but the one sweet on Grace. If they weren't careful, they'd have another Godawful Mess on their hands by sunset.

Like hell. Ducey pulled a fresh butterscotch from her pocket, slipped it between her lips without letting her bloodied hands touch the candy.

Kim worked herself around the table in a series of red boot prints, one hand firm on Belle as she put the slab of metal between herself and the two Evans women. She opened her mouth to say something, but then Ducey heard the side door to the funeral parlor open and whatever the girl was going to say died in her throat.

"Luna, honey, we need to talk." Grace's voice carried down the hallway, arriving at the swinging lab door just as she did. She stared into the lab. At the dog on the table. At the blood.

At the girl who didn't belong.

Kim skittered in place, hopping from one foot to the other. Her pendulum eyes now swung in four ticks—Belle, Ducey, Luna, Grace. She bit her lip. "I'll come back after class and check on her—" Her eyes flicked to Ducey. "I mean, if that's okay."

Of course, it wasn't. Girl needed to go get a move on, before all hell broke loose and Ducey's day went from bad to worse. She made her mouth smile. "Course it is. Now go on, skedaddle."

Kim drew her fingers once more through a clean section of Belle's fur. "I'll see you soon, sweet girl," she said to the dog, then she jerked her sights toward Ducey, shouldered her bag, and left without meeting eyes with anyone else in the room.

Everyone kept quiet until they heard the parlor's side door swing open, closed.

Belle whined and panted on the table, and Ducey snatched one of the rags from Luna's arms and sopped up another spill of blood. "Well, come on, you two," she said. "Don't let me have all the fun to myself."

Grace's fingers fidgeted with the hem of her long shirtsleeve, then she hurled herself into the room. She grabbed a procedure tray and yanked open drawers to line it with a series of surgical blades, a pair of tissue forceps, a retractor. She set the tray atop the red smear the bedsheet left on the table, then raced to the steel cabinet containing the parlor's limited pharmaceutical supply. She pulled out a tube of gel anesthetic and twisted it open. "Where?" she asked.

Ducey dropped the bloodied rag and held Belle's head. "One bite," she said. "Hindquarters."

When Luna didn't move, her eyes locked on the run of blood dripping off the slab, the sharp instruments on the surgical tray, Ducey clicked her teeth. "Luna, mop up that mess before your nana finds her way back here and throws a hissy fit." She turned to Grace and watched as she dabbed numbing cream on the area around the bite. The dog whimpered but held still. "What did Roger Taylor want?"

"He caught Luna skipping school." Grace added another generous smear of gel, then tossed the tube behind her. It landed in the sink with a dull thud, and the two traded places.

"Hold the dog," Ducey said as she grabbed the forceps, spared an apologetic look at Belle, and plunged her fingers into the wound. The dog whined and jerked, but Grace held her firm and Ducey worked quick, finding then clamping the torn blood vessels. She nodded at Grace to release the dog. "Skipping school," she said, sighing as the bleeding slowed to a manageable drip. "That all?"

Grace leveled a steel gaze at Ducey. "For now."

Ducey scowled and wiped her hands on her apron. "I reckon Johnson's got the whole department spun up. Man likes to stick his big nose wherever he can find a hole to put it." She clicked her teeth and decided not to share that he'd carved tire tracks in her driveway last night. "Last thing we need is that man barging in here to find his hound on our table."

Luna's eyes went wide. "Wait—this is the sheriff's dog?"

"Her name is Belle," Grace answered. She twisted the pet's tag in her fingers before turning her attention to Ducey. "Where'd you find her?"

"Alleyway behind Jimbo's. Whoever bit her must have just woken up and wasn't strong enough to hold on, and the poor ol' thing got herself free and ran until she dropped."

Grace pulled back. "The dead don't attack animals."

"You noticed that too, huh?" Ducey snapped, wiping fresh smears of blood on her apron.

Luna took one small step backward, toward the door.

"Animals don't come back as ghouls," Ducey said, warding off the questions she heard in each of her great-granddaughter's backward footsteps—Do they become monsters? Do they feed on others? "Whatever it is that brings someone back, animals aren't affected the same."

"So they just die?" Luna asked.

The tiny nugget of butterscotch left on Ducey's tongue melted away, the sweetness evaporating along with the color in Luna's skin. "They just *bleed*."

"They suffer," Grace added. She held Belle's paw in her hand as she wiped red from the dog's nails. "And we have to take care of them, too."

The girl's skin went from pale to translucent. "We're going to kill her?"

"Oh, for heaven's sake." Ducey snorted. "We're going to *save* her. We just need a little help, is all. Can't stitch this one up."

At that moment, Lenore stabbed into the laboratory. "Mama, what in the—"

"Fetch some ashes," Ducey said before her daughter could moan about the blood spreading from the lump of fabric under the table. Raining off the edges. The dog's breathing had deepened, focus crawling back into her eyes. "I know you've got some of Edwin Boone squirreled away somewhere, Lenore, and I need it."

Lenore looked like she was going to argue, maybe say something about her damned rosebush, but then she saw what was on the table and blanched. "Is that—"

"*Ashes*, Len." Ducey snapped her fingers. "Don't rush on my account."

For a split second, the woman looked like her daddy—all Royce's thin fury and blazing eyes reflected in his daughter. Then she collapsed into the doorframe, sending the door smacking against the wall, and went as white as one of her roses. She peeled herself away and Ducey heard Lenore's loafers pad to the crematorium then scuttle back up the hallway.

She returned, carrying a baggie of soft gray flakes. Lenore sniffed, used the inhale to tip her head back and push her chin up. She straightened her spine, cleared her throat, and emptied the ashes into a small bowl, before adding in a drip of water from the faucet. She approached the slab, nose wrinkling at the mess.

"I've had an itch in my ass all morning, Len," Ducey warned, motioning the two younger women to step away from the table and let Lenore work. Belle whimpered when Grace's and Luna's hands fell away. "Don't come in here giving me grief over the mess. We've dealt with worse than a little bit of animal blood. It all washes down the drain the same."

Lenore bristled. "It's not the mess I'm concerned about," she said. "It's what you're going to tell the sheriff about why you've got his dog. I can't imagine Johnson doesn't know Belle's missing. He'll have the whole county out looking for her."

Ducey shrugged. "I've handled Buck Johnson before. I can do it again."

"Are those really Mr. Boone's ashes?" Luna's eyes were locked on the bowl in Lenore's hands, her voice nearly as high now as Kim's before.

"Yes." Lenore tipped a trickle of fluid onto the dog's wound. "The ashes of a burned strigoi mixed with water create a sort of salve for the infected. Like I told you the other day, there's a theory that the mixture can be used to heal a strigoi's victims, especially those drained over time."

Luna considered the dog. "Have you ever tried it before?"

The grim set of Lenore's lips was answer enough. Belle's head jerked and the dog lifted to lick at the wound, but Ducey patted her head with one hand and kept the other on her side, pressing the animal flat against the table. When the mixture soaked through her fur, Belle's rigid body went soft under Ducey's hands. She let loose a low moan that sounded a lot like *thank you.*

"You think it'll work?" Luna asked.

Ducey rubbed the hound's ear. "Guess we're about to find out."

"There's not a manual for what we do," Grace reminded her daughter. "We told you that before."

"I had a dream about a dog," Luna mused. Belle's tongue lapped out, licked her hand, and the girl stroked at the dog's snout. "But you said that strigoi don't attack animals."

"The dead don't always follow the rules." Ducey shook her head, watched Grace tug her shirtsleeve over her hand, and wished her hands were clean enough to fetch a butterscotch. "The only cured victim is a buried one, far as I'm concerned."

"In the case of an animal," Lenore spoke as she poured, dousing the dog's hindquarters with the liquid, "the mixture is the only thing that will cauterize a wound." She pointed at the bite mark. Still moist with the ashy fluid, the bleeding stopped, ragged flesh knitted together as if the ashes were tiny spiders, stitching sinew and flesh. Within moments, the outline of teeth had disappeared, the remaining evidence of the assault already absorbed beneath red fur. "We can't be sure it'll have the same effect on a human, but one day I hope to try."

Belle's tail thumped on the table. She let loose a heavy exhale and then closed her eyes. Within moments, the dog was snoring.

"Maybe taking care of his dog will earn us some kind of favor in Johnson's eyes," Grace suggested. "Roger said they'd found another body."

Lenore cleared her throat and tugged at a tuft of ginger hair. "Quigg called with a heads-up on another victim," she said. "A girl—a young girl—taken at the movie theater. Poor thing was torn wide open. Left for dead out in broad daylight."

Ducey slapped her knee. "Now, didn't I tell you we were behind the curve already, Lenore—"

"They found a finger." Lenore's voice sliced through Ducey's remonstration. "A woman's finger, with oxblood-red fingernails."

Snow. She'd been so damn proud of her new manicure. Ducey's eyes fell from Lenore. Her hand pressed against the trocar in her apron pocket as she stared at the bloodied floor. No one looked forward to putting Snow Leger to bed—not yesterday, when she'd have just risen, and certainly not now, when she was strong enough to fight back.

This time Ducey slapped her knee lightly, resigned. "We should have been out hunting," she said. "If ghouls are out running around town during the day, then we should be out there, too." The theater was just across the street from Jimbo's. Why had her gut taken her to the alley behind the café, and not the terror behind the theater?

Lenore's head gave a curt nod and her eyes shot toward her granddaughter. "You're home early. Did you have early release today?"

Pink flared in Luna's cheeks. "Deputy Taylor brought me home."

Lenore's eyes narrowed and the temperature in the room dropped enough to send goose bumps prickling across the flesh of Ducey's forearm. She balled her fist and pulled it away from her apron. Habits were hell to break.

"She wasn't at the movies," Grace said, as if guessing at the thought that washed across her mother's and grandmother's minds. She looked sheepish. "She was with a boy."

Ducey rolled her eyes. "Don't you and that boyfriend of yours have better sense than to skip school—especially right now, with everything going on?"

Luna bit her lip. "I wasn't with Andy."

Lenore glared down the bridge of her nose, and Ducey noticed her hand was in a fist, too. "Then who were you with?"

"A new boy in town," Grace said. "Someone named Crane."

Oh, hell, not again. Ducey rolled her neck against the back of the chair. A strange new boy with an unusual name taking a liking to an Evans—they'd been down this particular road before, and it didn't lead anywhere nice. "You were with this boy *Crane* the entire time?"

"Yes," Luna squeaked.

Lenore shot a sharp look at Grace as she brushed at her blouse. She set the little bowl in the lab sink, then opened the cabin beneath and pulled a biohazard trash bag from the roll. Without speaking, she plucked a pair of surgical gloves from the case on the wall, slipped them on, and began stuffing soiled rags into the bag, making a point of not looking at anyone else in the room.

Grace's left hand was lost in her sleeve while the other stroked the sleeping dog.

Luna's head gave a little jerk. "Oh my God, did you think it was me who got"—she fumbled for the right word before landing on—"hurt?"

Silence hung in the air. *No*, Ducey knew. That wasn't at all what they were thinking.

Luna shifted, uncomfortable when no one answered. "Who is it, anyway?" she asked. "Who got attacked?"

Lenore stopped cleaning. "Alison Haney," she said, studying the girl's reaction. "Were you two friends?"

What little bit of color had returned to Luna's face flared red, and she chewed at the inside of her cheek. "No." Her lips twisted. "Not even close."

Lenore looked at Grace, who looked at Ducey, who closed her eyes and pushed a gust of wind out of her mouth.

"What? It's not like I had anything to do with what happened to her." Luna wandered across the lab, sank onto a short metal stool tucked in the corner, crossed her arms over her chest. "Not unless the restless dead can hear my thoughts or something," she grumbled.

Silence enveloped the room, the only sound Belle's rhythmic breathing on the slab.

Grace and Lenore still stared at Ducey, who suddenly felt far too old for this shit. "Now that you mention it," she started, still wondering why the hard stuff always got shunted to her, "they just might. Hate to tell ya this honey, but truth is, the reason the dead are risin' is because you're pullin' 'em up."

CHAPTER 28

Deputy Roger Taylor

By the time Roger pulled his cruiser back into the lot at the station, he thought he might have discovered what it felt like to be a starving man. Throat aching, stomach churning, body heavy with a bellyache big enough to swallow him alive. Suck him down like an Old Testament sea monster.

Roger put the Crown Vic in park, cranked the AC, and left the engine on. He closed his eyes and let his head sag against the headrest. Two deep breaths later, he felt almost like himself again. Three, and his stomach growled. When he flexed his fingers against his midsection, Roger expected to feel nothing but brittle bone, but the girth of his gut was still there, still ample despite his best attempts at half a year's worth of dieting. Denying sweet breakfast pastries. Stepping atop the hard, plastic scale in his bathroom every evening before bed. All that hunger, all that sacrifice, all that *abstinence*, for what?

Perhaps it might finally be time to throw in the towel with Grace Evans.

Roger patted his gut again and didn't mind it so much anymore.

Truth was, he had better things to worry about than a little extra weight around his middle. What were a few pounds when people were going missing, being ripped apart? When parts of one victim were found on another and the man charged with protecting his town was more concerned about personal vendettas? They all knew whatever was going around tearing folks up had nothing to do with rabid animals.

Little things like dieting away a couple of unwanted pounds paled in comparison when life reminded you there were much bigger problems to worry about. And right now, Roger had too many of those to count.

A car door slammed somewhere near, but Roger didn't open his eyes. All his whining about needing to get into shape before he could gather himself up and ask Grace out had been just that—whining. A convenient excuse, a coward's justification for not taking the plunge, opening the door to the opportunity for Grace to say what she would probably always say.

No.

He'd seen the word written clear as day in Grace's eyes today, the one that told him she'd never love him back, never allow him access into her closed-off world. Never even consider doing so.

Did that make him want her less, or more?

More, I reckon, he thought, and immediately wished he hadn't. Loving Grace Evans, even from afar, made just about as much sense as trying to romance a moonbeam. You could see it shining in the dark, but there wasn't a chance this side of heaven you could reach out and touch it.

Of course, he hadn't been foolish enough to expect the woman to throw her arms around his neck when he'd driven up to her place of business with her only daughter in the backseat of his cruiser, had he? That would have been ridiculous. But he hadn't anticipated she'd be so . . . so what? Angry? Scared?

For sure, she had been both those things, but there was some deeper unease in her that he couldn't put his finger on. And that, above anything else, was what had started to sour like yesterday's coffee in Roger's gut.

Grace had lied to him.

He couldn't be sure about what, but he'd been in law enforcement long enough to know when someone wasn't giving him the whole truth. The question ate at Roger—what didn't she want him to know?

But Grace isn't the only one hiding something, is she?

Guilt stretched its spindly legs inside Roger's stomach, filling the sac of his gut with spider's eggs. He hadn't told Grace *why* he'd been asking the questions he had. Hadn't told her he'd found a pack of Virginia Slims, the brand she thought no one knew she smoked when life got to be a little too much, on the boy who'd skipped school with her daughter. Hadn't told her he'd given those—along with the teeth he'd pulled off Luna—over to forensics.

Put yourself in her shoes, Roger instructed himself, as he opened his eyes and scanned the parking lot for Johnson's cruiser, for Hinson's. *Things haven't been easy for the Evanses. Never have.*

He could vaguely remember Pie Evans, Ducey's mother, who'd by all accounts seemed to delight in being unlikeable enough to distance the Evans family from the rest of the community. By the time Ducey had managed to get herself out from under the woman's shadow, her own husband had passed away, leaving the family to fend for themselves. Locals always thought women running a funeral parlor was a little too odd to be normal, and having a man at the helm insulated the Evanses from the town's outdated ideas of what could be a woman's work. Regardless, Evans Funeral Parlor remained the only funeral business in town, and so people looked the other way about the Evanses, affording them a measure of respect and as much distance as they could without being outright rude.

For years, things seemed to settle, but then Grace's strange beau had shown up in town. He'd only stuck around for a couple of months, long enough for Luna to come along. There'd been some big fuss at Evans Funeral Parlor one night, and he'd left. Grace's daddy—Jimmy—passed away right about the same time. Lenore had damn near come apart, and the Evans women found themselves right back at the center of town gossip. The whole thing had been such a mess even Buck Johnson kept quiet about it, and didn't bother to debrief Roger on whatever happened at the parlor. Ducey Evans, who didn't keep her mouth shut about much, had kept quiet, too.

Still, even in the face of all that bygone tragedy, how could Roger just ignore the tickling in his gut as he waited to learn whose fingerprints he'd find on that pack of cigarettes? Roger hoped like hell that they didn't turn out to be Grace's. That those teeth in Luna's pocket didn't belong to any of their missing persons. He'd rather chew through his own fat than tell Sheriff Buck Johnson he had any reason to think the Evans women were involved with whatever was happening in town.

Problem was, Roger was having a tougher and tougher time believing he'd have it his way. His eye twitched and he tapped his fingers on the steering wheel, then killed the engine.

His boot hit the pavement. That's why he'd told Hinson to make sure no one else saw the forensics reports before he did: so he could decide what to do before someone else made the choice for him.

Johnson would fire up a witch hunt if an Evans name came up in his investigation, and there'd be nothing Roger could do to stop it.

Roger sighed as he pushed through the doors of the sheriff's department, nodded past Dispatch Darla, and made his way to the bullpen. Johnson's door was shut. Lights off.

"Thank Christ," Roger muttered. An altercation with that man was the last thing he needed, especially considering Roger didn't have any more information now than he had when they'd spoken this morning—

Not any you're willing to share, anyway, a dark voice niggled in the back of his mind.

—and that sort of update wasn't going to fly with Sheriff Buck Johnson. Not now. The man would want progress, he would want names, he would want *someone to answer for things*, and all Roger currently had was a belly full of creepy crawlies and a bad taste in his mouth.

In addition to the couple of chewed-up corpses and missing persons, of course.

Things in the small, quiet town were starting to become anything but quiet. Loud, it was all becoming too loud.

Restless, Roger thought as he recognized the shape of Brandon Hinson hunched over the interoffice-mail counter, scrawling on a Post-it Note affixed to a stack of corded brown folders.

Three slim folders, one for each: a finger, a pack of cigarettes, a pair of human teeth.

The sight of the files hardened Roger's gut. Forensics had processed the evidence he was least interested in seeing the results on faster than anything he'd brought in over the span of his entire career. He'd demanded it, but it'd be ironic, really, if it wasn't so damn sad.

Hinson finished his note and deposited the folders in the little wire basket on Roger's desktop as he made his way back to his seat. He sat in his faded office chair, elbows on the desktop, scratching another note in another file.

"That what I think it is?" Roger called as he approached his desk and sank down into his chair. His weight had deflated the cushion over the years, and the metal bar meant for lumbar support jabbed against his backside. "All three of them?

"Yes, sir." The rookie's pen stroke ended in a streak, an exclamation of black ink on yellow paper.

Roger shifted, tried to find a more comfortable position. "You look at the results?"

"Just the report on the finger, sir." He didn't look up. "The other two are for your eyes only, like you said."

Good. "Any match on the finger?"

A nod. Probably to keep from spilling his lunch, by the looks of his pinched lips, swollen throat. Green crept in around the rookie's edges and he pulled at his collar. Boy looked like he could use a snorkel.

"And?" Roger tapped his fingertip against the top folder but didn't open it.

Hinson shook his head, wiped imaginary sweat from his brow, and cleared his throat. "You're not gonna like it, Taylor."

"Didn't reckon I was going to."

"The finger belongs—" He cleared his throat without looking up. "*Belonged* to Snow Leger." The rookie lifted his head, met Roger's gaze. "There's something else," he said.

The insects in Roger's belly were back, swarming like a busted ant-hill. Images flashed through his mind—bloody, gory, nightmarish stuff. "Let's hear it."

"I don't . . . I don't know how it's possible," the deputy stuttered. "But forensics found matter under the fingernail. Skin. It's the victim's." Hinson's face went green. He swallowed hard. "Forensics also said the finger was torn from Snow's hand posthumously."

Roger tried, really tried, to string together a coherent sentence. Failed. According to the forensics report, the evidence indicated a dead woman had ripped the girl apart, leaving a finger in Alison Haney's body. The same bile Hinson had swallowed down crawled up Roger's throat. No, that wasn't possible. The dead only killed the living in horror movies. There had to be a rational explanation, something that led him back to a flesh and blood, breathing monster, a rabid beast he could shoot for Johnson to mount on his wall. Maybe a serial killer left Snow's finger behind as some kind of calling card—used it to dig into the girl's body as a taunt?

"Quigg called, too," Hinson added. "Said he'd finished up with his exam on the new vic."

Roger spoke around the lump in his throat. "So fast?"

"Didn't find anything other than what we already know." Hinson shrugged. "He's ready to release the body if you are."

It was Roger's turn to shrug. Was he ready? To let another body go to Evans Funeral Parlor without knowing for sure what was going on over there? To phone the parents of a fifteen-year-old girl and let them know their daughter had been found dead?

Not just dead, he corrected. *Mutilated.*

Truth was, he wasn't *ready* for either. Probably wouldn't ever be. Life—what was left of it, anyway—moved on. And there was only one funeral parlor in town, one set of women qualified to make sure the horror that awaited the Haneys wasn't what Hinson and the rest of them found splayed out behind the movie theater: their teenage daughter bled out in a puddle of her own insides.

"If Quigg's done, there's no sense in keeping the body in the morgue for the parents to identify. Let the Evanses do what they can before they see her. We don't need to make things any more awful than they're already gonna be," he said. "You got a number for the next of kin?"

Hinson nodded. "Parents are married. The dad, Brett Haney, works down at Blankenship's Auto. Mom's a Katherine Brooks-Haney, hyphenate. She's a nurse at County." He stood and stepped over to Roger's desk, a slip of paper clutched between his fingers. "I got a home phone and work numbers for them both. Address, too."

Roger knew which number he'd call first. He accepted the paper and waved Hinson off. Faced the other two neatly wrapped forensics files.

"I'll go out and see the parents when I finish with this paperwork," he said, "and then I'll drive the body over to the funeral parlor myself."

"You sure?"

Roger shot the young deputy as scathing a look as he could muster.

"There's something else." Hinson's voice shook, fractured. Back at his desk, he put his elbows on the desktop and leaned forward to rub his face. "I got a call from my girlfriend, and, well, you know the sheriff's dog?"

Girlfriend? Roger hadn't realized the boy had a special someone, but he damn sure knew Johnson's dog. "Belle."

"Right."

Roger's eyes darted to Johnson's darkened office window. "What about her?" Buck Johnson loved that old hound as much as life itself, maybe even more. If something had happened to her, well, it might explain why the man had been up in irons this morning.

Might explain the drinking, too. Then again, might not. Most cops were fueled by caffeine and purpose. Johnson's veins were full of booze. He didn't typically drink on the job, though. Not like he had today.

"Kim said she found the dog in the alley behind Jimbo's after she got off work," Hinson said. "It had been bitten, was bleeding out. But before she could do much about it, Ducey Evans showed up and took over. They carried the dog up to Evans Funeral Parlor to patch it up."

Roger swallowed down his surprise and fixed his attention on the first forensic file. "I'll check on that, too."

"What I mean is . . ." The rookie rocked back in his chair, seesawing the pen in his hand to thump the desk. "Do you think they could be related?"

Roger didn't look up. "How so?"

"You think maybe whatever got Alison Haney got Belle, too?"

Yes, Roger did think that. He also thought it was mighty suspect that Ducey Evans had been the one to come across Belle. He also wished he'd known earlier that his rookie was seeing the coffee girl at Jimbo's. Maybe then he'd have remembered sooner that Kim Cole was Clyde Halloran's grandniece, or something like that. And as soon as Roger thought this, he realized he didn't want Hinson thinking it, too.

"Hinson, get me a cup of coffee, would you?" he asked.

The rookie pulled back. He seemed to want to argue, but let it go and stood. "Half-and-half and two sugars, right?"

"Right." Had Hinson known that already, or had his girlfriend familiarized him with Roger's order?

Didn't matter. The rookie grabbed the dirty mug from Roger's desk and took off toward the coffeepot and Roger peeled open the first file. Its interior was thin, a couple sheets of paper about the contents of a half-smoked pack of Virginia Slims, nothing unusual. Two sets of prints were found on the wrapper. One was unidentified.

Probably the boy's, Roger guessed. Unless he'd been in trouble before, there'd be no reason to have his prints on record. Not a minor. Not a minor from out of state.

Breath caught in Roger's throat. The first pair of fingerprints had been a bust, but not the second.

Grace Evans.

Roger tasted the name on his tongue, rolled it around, bit down on it. So, she'd lied about smoking—so what? He'd known Grace long enough to know she only smoked when stressed, a nervous tick she kept private. But what had her so stressed she'd turned to her old, guilty habit? And how had Crane Campbell gotten ahold of the narrow cancer sticks? Did Grace lie because she worried she'd get in trouble if her cigarettes were found in a minor's possession?

Surely not, Roger reasoned. Kids lifted their parents' smokes all the time. Hell, he'd done the same himself. Luna could have easily taken them, given them to the boy. *But then her prints would be on the pack, too.*

Roger pushed the thought away and flipped open the second file, verified Hinson's statement on the finger found in Alison Haney's stomach, then turned his attention to the final file. This one was bigger, bulkier. Full of secrets. When he saw the name in smeared black type at the top of the cover page, though, he thought perhaps he'd give up eating altogether.

The god-danged teeth belonged to Clyde Halloran.

Shit. Roger leaned back in his chair, pressed the back of his head into the headrest, and returned once more to the facts.

Clyde Halloran was missing, and Luna Evans had two of the man's teeth in her pocket.

Edwin Boone was chewed up.

Snow Leger was dead, minus a tongue and a finger.

Widow Milner was missing and without her walker.

Alison Haney had been ripped open by a dead woman in the middle of the day, right outside the theater parking lot.

Johnson's hound had gotten a bite taken out of her, and Ducey Evans had come to the rescue.

And, prints on file or not, there was a strange new boy in town who'd been spending time with Luna Evans and smoking her mother's cigarettes.

Something hatched in Roger's stomach. He couldn't fathom what in the hell was going on around here, but now he knew without a doubt that the Evans women did—and as soon as he got through breaking the hearts of Alison Haney's parents, he was damn sure going to find out.

CHAPTER 29

Grace Evans

Grace's dark curls fell, casting twisted shadows over her vision as she retrieved a shovel from the supply closet where Lenore kept her gardening supplies. She traced her hands over the tools lined along the stainless steel shelving unit—loppers, pruning clips, soil knives. Something sharp pricked against her skin, and Grace fingered the teeth of a long pruning saw until they bit into her flesh. Her mother kept every blade in the funeral parlor sharpened, from the landscaping equipment to the lab tools. Even the scissors in the lobby desk's top drawer had an edge that could pierce skin.

Even the ones in her cosmetic case.

"We'll be outside," Lenore's voice called now, followed by the sound of the deadbolt in the parlor's glass front doors turning home. "Don't forget to bring a planter's pot."

Three pairs of feet tapped down the hall—the tense clip of Lenore's loafers, the soft pad of Ducey's sneakers, the thuds of Luna's Converse—and then the side door opened. Air sucked at the chapel doors, jostling them so the heavy wooden panels swished open and swung closed. Someone—probably her mother—flipped a switch on their way out. The front lights of the parlor went dark just as the side door slammed shut, leaving only the dim back-room overheads to light Grace's way.

Grace hesitated. She hadn't thought to ask how big the pot should be, how deep. How much room was needed to protect the roots of the rosebush her mother grew to keep the dead asleep? She tucked a spade in her waistband, wrapped one hand around the shovel's handle, and stooped to select a thick rubber planting pot from the pile of discarded containers in the closet corner. Footsteps padded behind her and Grace braced before she spun, the shovel pointed ahead of her.

Belle.

The dog rolled clear, liquid eyes up to Grace. Her tail gave one small swing.

Grace lowered the shovel and pat the dog's head. "It's good to see you up and moving around."

Another swing.

The dog nuzzled her hand, snout wet where it dragged across Grace's skin, and Grace thumbed one of Belle's long velvet ears. Wet was good. A damp nose meant a healthy dog. The ashes worked; Sheriff Johnson's hound was going to be fine.

Grace closed the storage closet door and made her way to the side door. She jumped and spun around when the shovel handle brushed her shoulder. For half a second, Grace saw a human-shaped image in the corner, but she raised the shovel and blinked, and it was only the ficus tree her mother kept in the lobby.

Keep it together, Grace. The doors were locked and the mortuary cooler was empty. The only thing restless in Evans Funeral Parlor was her.

Belle followed along at Grace's side, collar jingling as they walked and snout brushing against her pantleg every few paces. At the door, Grace slumped. She stared outside to where her family waited around her mother's rosebush.

"This is it, Belle." Grace had waited for this moment since she'd first felt her daughter kick in her belly. She'd pictured the day Luna would be ready to know the truth—the *whole* truth about that Godawful Mess fifteen years ago—dozens, hundreds, thousands of times. She'd wasted sleepless nights with her stomach full of acid, rehearsing what she'd say. Idled away slow days in the parlor daydreaming about how she'd steel herself—submit herself—to her daughter's inevitable anger, her scathing resentment, her loathsome shock. Because that was how Luna would respond. Of course, she would. How could she not?

How could she learn the truth about what Grace had done—what she'd kept secret—and not think her mother was anything other than a monster?

Belle's breath fogged up the side-door glass. She whimpered, but Grace didn't have enough experience with dogs to know if the sound was eager or nervous. "You should stay inside," she said. "It's safer in here."

The hound's tail wagged once, twice. A disagreeable huff flapped through her jowls, and when Grace stepped forward to open the door, Belle pushed herself through first.

"Okay then," Grace said. "Ready or not."

Grace emerged into the summer heat with one hand lifted to her brow to shield her eyes from the sun's waning glare, the other gripped around the tools they'd need to dig up the rosebush. The rest of her family had gathered at the edge of the building where they stood like mourners beside her mother's small garden, the large rosebush blooming over the tidy beds of starry blue aster and blushing begonia, camouflage for the poison hiding in plain sight. Lenore had planted white roses instead of red. Red showed pain. White drank it up.

"Took you long enough." Ducey stomped her foot, blades of dry grass crackling like brittle bones under her soft-soled orthopedic shoe. She squinted at Grace. "You forget where we keep the shovel?"

The ground seemed to grow mushier with each step Grace took, like she was walking on decomposing flesh, and the sensation licked at her heels. "No."

A few feet away, Luna shifted from side to side, arms locked deadbolt tight across her chest. Her eyes flicked between the shovel, the spade, and the pot, but never met Grace's. "What are we doing out here?"

"Gardening." Lenore squatted beside the bush, inspecting the blooms in a series of heavy breaths and sighs. The leaves around the base of the plant had curled in on themselves, and several buds had withered, fallen onto the dirt like shed skin. More gray petals shook loose as her fingers touched rose after rose. A manic sheen shone in her eyes when Lenore stepped away from the bush, the lines of her face etched deeper than usual.

"Gardening?" Luna's squint said she didn't buy it.

"Your nana likes to pick her words like she picks her damn flowers," Ducey said, blunt as usual. She let her bifocals hang on the chain around her neck as one hand descended to her apron, fingers searching for a butterscotch. "We're diggin' up a grave, child."

"A grave?" Confusion twisted Luna's features. Her gaze tracked Belle as the hound marched to sniff at the bush's base, nostrils quivering and snout so close to the ground that her fur bunched in thick folds around her eyes. Hunting dogs could smell dead things as easy as those living. "There's something buried beneath Nana Lenore's rosebush?"

Belle stopped sniffing. Dirt covered the dog's nose when she lifted her head. She sat back on her haunches, arched her back, and let loose a mournful howl. The sound pulsed under Grace's skin.

"Some*one*." The word caught in her throat and Grace coughed it free. "A master strigoi." Lenore nodded at the shovel and Luna held it out, grimaced when her mother's fingernails scratched against the wood.

Luna stared as her grandmother began to carve a wide circle around the bush, spooning heaps of dirt into a neat pile. "Here?" she asked, blinking wide. "I thought you, like, burned the restless dead, or whatever."

"Not this one," Grace said. "This one we kept."

"Why?"

Ducey groaned, impatient. "Because we needed to keep an eye on him," she snapped. "Right now we need to make sure this ghoul is still in the ground where it belongs." Then, to Lenore, "You gonna spend all afternoon romancin' those roots, Len? Just yank the sucker up."

Lenore leaned the shovel against the bricked wall of the parlor's exterior. "I need to be able to replant it properly, and I can't do that if I destroy the roots." Lenore motioned for the spade and when Grace handed it over, she sank to her knees and began to dig in the earth, using the tool to keep the hole from collapsing on itself as she separated roots from soil. Belle backed away, but her eyes stayed glued to the ground, a low growl rumbling in her throat. "Just trying to minimize the damage, Mama."

"'Minimize the damage,'" Ducey parroted, then clicked her teeth.

"If we wanted to minimize damage, then we should have done this days ago, Len. Right after Mina Jean woke up." She sucked too hard on the candy, choked, and cleared her throat. "Hell, we should have done it fifteen years ago. The girl has the right to know. She shouldn't have had to find out like this."

"Know what?" Luna asked, a tone of understanding now beginning to creep into her voice. "Find out what?"

Grace reached for her daughter, trying to close the space between them, but Lenore leaned back on her heels, stamped muddy handprints into her thighs with an exasperated grunt.

"We don't need to make this more difficult than it already is," she told Ducey, setting the spade on the grass to work at the plant's roots with her fingers. "We were trying to do the right thing. We still are." She gave the roots one last review before holding her hand out. "Grace, honey, give me a hand."

Grace edged toward the rosebush. She hadn't thought to bring gloves, and thorns sliced into her skin as she helped her mother lift the bush free of the hole—one hoisting from the top, the other making sure the roots didn't snag at the bottom—and set it gently on the ground. Lenore's fingers bled, too, and Grace watched as the bush's withered stems absorbed the blood. Drank it up.

"The *right* thing?" Ducey snapped. "You know as well as I do there ain't no such thing as right and wrong, Lenore. Not for us. It's all just a bunch of gray."

Luna used her hands to draw a loose circle around the group. The upturned rosebush. "I don't understand," she said. "Won't it look weird if we're all standing around outside, digging in the middle of an afternoon? Shouldn't we, like, wait until dark or something?" She shuffled, took a step forward, then two back. "What if whatever is in that hole gets out?"

"The restless are less powerful in the daytime," Grace explained. "They aren't strictly nocturnal, but they are slower during the day."

"Tell that to Alison Haney," the girl muttered.

She had a point. Grace watched as her mother gathered the rosebush's roots in a neat bundle and tucked them gently into the belly of the pot. She scooped in soil with her hands and tamped it down, anchoring the roots. "That's good for now," she mumbled.

Ducey peeled one hand from her hip and motioned at the spade on the grass beside Grace's foot. "The dead like the dark, and this one's been underground so long it hasn't fed properly in fifteen years, just sustained itself on the little bits of what your nana gives him." She clicked the candy against her teeth. "Assuming he's still where we left him."

Ducey realized she'd given the thing a pronoun. Hell.

"Him?" Luna asked.

Grace curled her shirtsleeve over her hand as she inched around the rosebush hole to retrieve the shovel. The wooden handle turned to bone in Grace's grip.

"Like I said, ghouls like the dark," Ducey continued without addressing Luna's question. She flipped her wrist at the hole. The shovel. Grace. "Now, let's get to digging."

"I don't understand." Dread filled Luna's voice. "You said that the restless dead have to be put down, even cut their heads off or burn them to ashes. Why did you keep this one buried, you know, *alive*?"

She looked at Grace, who looked at her mother, who was still fussing with the uprooted rosebush. Ducey's tongue popped against the inside of her cheeks and Belle's head swung at the sound, ears perked. "Because we didn't know what killing him would do," she said.

Grace fingered her scar. "We told you before that with every victim, every soul they take, the dead gain power. Some become the sort of monstrous creatures that inspire the caricatures you see in movies. Others become something more . . . human. It takes some time," she said, "legend says longer than a normal mortal lifetime for a baby strigoi to become a master. We put the ones that rise down before they can become so powerful, but the more mature and powerful they become, the harder it can be to recognize them for what they are."

Luna shrugged. "And?"

"And power like that doesn't just let itself be snuffed out," Lenore said. "It has to find someplace else to go."

"Or someone else to go to," Ducey added.

Luna looked at the scar on Grace's wrist and Grace hated the knowledge growing in her daughter's eyes. "So, there's a superpowerful ghoul buried under Nana Lenore's bush?"

The ground moved beneath Grace as Lenore pulled the shovel away from her hand. Her mother plunged the sharpened spoon into the dirt. The scent of summer scorch and fresh petrichor filled Grace's nostrils, and she closed her eyes.

Night.

The outside lights of the funeral parlor cast halos on the buds just beginning to peek through the freshly planted garden along the edge of Evans Funeral Parlor. Hair raven black, back straight, skin wrinkled but firm, Ducey stood in front of Grace. Her green eyes blazed with venomous fire as she raised her arm, a trocar poised like lightning in her grip. Lenore stood behind her mother, auburn hair loose around her shoulders as she clung to her husband's arm.

"You get away from my girls," Jimmy said, his collared shirt a white glare in the shadowed dark. "Leave this town for good, or I'll put you in the ground myself."

A laugh boomed at Grace's side, startling the infant asleep in her arms. The sound slid, a rolling, thunderous baritone, over her shoulders as Samael's arm snaked around her waist, held her close.

"They're mine now." Samael stepped in front of Grace, pivoted so he stood between her and her father. "And I will bleed the life from anyone who tries to take them from me."

Across the lawn, Lenore detached herself from her husband's side. She spread her arms wide, her hands pleading Grace to move away, step aside, run to her—but Grace's feet wouldn't move. She stood rooted in place, the baby a boulder on her shoulder, Samael's arm a vise at her back. She stared at the man beside her, his smooth white flesh, midnight eyes. Inhaled the scents of honey and rust. How could she not see it before, the way his features didn't move quite right when he spoke? How his long dark hair didn't shift when the breeze blew through. Or maybe she had seen and ignored what the signs meant. Love could be its own kind of monster.

"That's my daughter," Grace's father said.

Samael stepped closer to Grace. "And Luna is mine—ours."

Samael faltered, looked back at the baby in Grace's arms. He smiled and something deep in Grace's core, her heart, ached. "My moon." His midnight eyes lifted to Grace's. "My star."

Jimmy growled deep, a rumble that came all the way from his stomach through his jowls. "You're a dead man."

"Yes." Samael grinned, ran his tongue along the undersides of his teeth. "I am."

His arm dropped away from her back as he lunged.

Grace's mouth fell open.

Stop, she wanted to say. *Wait*, as her father rushed forward. But it happened too fast. Jimmy snagged the trocar from Ducey's hand and drove it deep into Samael's heart while his eyes still gazed at his daughter. The powerful strigoi twisted and fell, the sun-browned grass rushing up beneath him. His hands clawed for the other man on the way down, made purchase, ripped open Jimmy's throat.

Everyone was screaming. Lenore. Ducey. Luna. Grace couldn't hear her own voice, but she could taste it in her mouth—salty and thick, blood mixed with tears. Someone lifted Luna from her arms and Grace collapsed, hands sinking into warm, slick grass. She lifted her hands as two twin yellow lights illuminated the scene around her. So much blood. Coating her hands like gloves. Pouring in waves from her father's throat. Mingling together to pulse around the metal spike anchored in Samael's chest.

The lights bounced, grew larger. Tires screeched on pavement.

Headlights, Grace realized, but she didn't care as she watched the man—the monster—she loved bleed out beside her father on the grass. Blue and white lights blurred in the distance, bouncing as a sheriff's department cruiser screeched into the drive.

Samael's hand reached out, his fingers brushing hers as they passed, just out of reach. Grace crawled to him, blood and tears and earth soaking through her skin, her pants, her heart. His fingernails sliced into her wrist when she found his hand, and pain scalded her arm. Blood spilled down her hand, dripped from her fingers.

"Grace." Samael spoke with his eyes closed. "Tell her—"

His last words went unfinished, lost in a final exhale.

The sharp crack of twigs and roots slammed Grace back into herself. She opened her eyes to a mound of upturned dirt, to sweat trickling down her mother's face to form small, shallow creeks in the powdery lines of her cheeks. Lenore was panting, sinking deeper with each scoop of dirt. Everything below her waist was lost belowground.

Ducey snorted, hair gray, back bent, skin loose. "Welcome back."

Grace rubbed the silver scar on her wrist. "I didn't go anywhere," she said.

"Sure you didn't." Ducey slid her hand into her pocket, unwrapped another butterscotch, and stuck it between her lips. "How's it comin', Len?"

Lenore pushed herself out of the hole, pinned the shovel into a patch of grass. "Almost there."

Had they really buried him so deep?

Stop, Grace almost begged. But her mother was on her knees now, bent over and scooping out mounds of dirt with her bare hands.

"Wait." Luna's voice sounded so young, so innocent. So much like the child in Grace's memory. "Are you sure this is a good idea? If this one is really so powerful, is it safe to dig him up?"

Ducey chortled. "We put that beast in the ground." She snatched the spade from where it lay on the grass and thrust it into Luna's hand. "We sure as hell can dig him back up."

Grace's gaze swept from Samael's grave to land on Luna. Would he still be under the rosebush, kept satiated by the offerings Lenore brought, ashes and funereal flowers of the dead? Or had he grown restless and risen again to feed on the living?

And if he had risen, how long would it be before he came for his daughter? Had he already?

Either way, they'd have their answer soon.

Luna gawked at the tool, then crept forward to peer down into the grave as the first glimpse of flesh became visible beneath the dirt. "Who's buried beneath that rosebush?"

Ducey kept her mouth shut. This time, Grace would have to answer. She sucked in a deep breath, pushed her sleeve up her wrist to expose her scar, and let the words tumble from her lips. "Your father," she said.

CHAPTER 30

Luna Evans

Aside from the metal shaft still embedded in his heart, the man lying in the unmarked grave at the edge of Evans Funeral Parlor looked as fresh and alive as if he'd only just lay down in the dirt for a nap. Specks of soil crusted the spaces between his features and a dark stain covered most of the pale gray button-down shirt, but if Luna looked fast enough, she could almost see the rise and fall of his chest. Breath rushing in and out of the same narrow nose she saw reflected in the mirror every morning.

Her fingertips traced the edges of her brows, her cheekbones, her jaw, as she studied the dead man's face. She pressed her finger into the spaces where dimples would dot his cheeks when he smiled and outlined the curve of the ears, one lobe slightly more pronounced than the other. The sun's fiery glow filtered orange light into his burial plot, but Luna saw the silver halo on his shaggy, almost-black hair. If the man opened his eyes, they'd be midnight dark like hers.

The face was familiar, not only because it was her own, but because Luna had seen its shadow in the nightmares that had taken over her sleep. She recognized it now, watching her. *Following* her.

"Well, I'll be damned." Ducey's words floated on a cloud of butterscotch. Her right hand lingered on the trocar in her apron pocket, and she shook her head. "He's still there."

Nana Lenore sank to her knees, hands clutched at her mouth. A gravelly moan thrummed from under a fat rhododendron bush, where a rust-colored ear peeked out beneath butter-yellow blooms. When Luna's gaze slid to her mother, Grace's eyes shone like they were made of glass. Angry red smears covered the area where she'd rubbed her wrist raw like a sunburn.

"My father was a restless dead." She'd suspected there was more to her father than the few bits she'd tweezed out of her mother, darker truths hidden in the secrets her family wouldn't tell, in the little parcels they did. But now Luna tasted the full extent of it. She let it slide down her throat and burn inside her chest when she swallowed. Anger lit in her stomach, and she carved canyons into the ground under the heel of her Converse. "My father was a restless dead."

The words came out louder this time, almost a yell.

"Is." Her mother's voice sent a kiss of cold air against the fire in Luna's belly. "Your father *is* a restless dead—a master strigoi."

Ducey's lips opened, closed, opened, before she pushed air through her lips. An emotion Luna had never seen before moved across her face, but then her great-grandmother's expression settled. "Oh, restlessness ain't the only thing wrong with that man," she said. "But he's right where we left him, and that's a good thing."

Everything was hot, so hot. Blisters formed in Luna's mouth where words should be. She pushed her shoulders up, hands raised in frustrated claws on either side of her head. "How could you not tell me?" The words boiled out of her, and she moved as she spoke, circling her father's grave in short, angry steps. "How could you let me see Edwin Boone in the cooler? Tell me that people in our town are coming back from the dead?" She almost stepped on Belle's ear but stopped short. "How could you tell me the worst family secret imaginable, and still not tell me that my father is a *monster*?"

Nana Lenore diverted her eyes as she pushed herself up onto her knees and wiped her hands on her earth-stained slacks. "We need to get the rosebush back into the ground before the roots dry out," she said as she crawled to the edge of the hole and used her hands to shovel dirt back into the shallow grave. "Grace, get the pot."

"I'm so sorry we didn't tell you sooner." Grace's words pooled like they were made of tears, but she retrieved the planter's pot full of rosebush roots. She bent herself over the container, one hand clutching the plastic tub and the other keeping the bush upright as she dragged the plant toward the hole. Her words pushed out between breaths. "We wanted to keep you safe, for as long as we could."

Ducey shook her head as more gray petals fell loose with each step Grace took. Her lips pulled into a line, but Luna heard the click of hard candy against teeth. The old woman kept her mouth shut.

"You lied to me, hid this from me, to keep me *safe*?" Luna's throat hitched onto the last word, made it come out sharp and jagged, and her mother recoiled as if cut, bright red spots budding where the thorns had pricked into her skin. "I don't even know what that means—safe from what?"

"From him," Grace said. "And from yourself. It's—" She stopped pulling the pot and stood. Her eyebrows knit together, and she closed her eyes then rubbed her temples. "Complicated, and there's not a—"

"Not a manual," Luna finished. She huffed. "You've told me that already. A lot."

She stared down into the grave. A fine layer of dirt covered most of the man's face, and mounds had begun to form in the recesses of his limbs, around his head. Nettles poked under Luna's flesh. She'd always assumed her father had taken off, left her mother in the dust. She couldn't have imagined it might be the other way around.

"But how could you not know?" Luna stared at the face so much like her own. "How could you fall in love—have a child—with a . . ." None of the words she knew to describe the restless dead fit. Not ghoul. Not strigoi. She couldn't call the dead man either of those, because if she did, what would that make her?

Her mother shook her head and pink crawled up her cheeks, but she met her daughter's eyes. "We told you the old ones, the most powerful ones, look and act like the living," she said. "When I met your father, I thought he was unusual, eccentric. He was different than all the other men I knew around town, and I fell for him so hard that if there were signs, I didn't see them. None of us did." Grace's eyes tore away and she reached for the spade in Luna's hand, but let it fall away empty. "I didn't find out what he was until it was too late."

Her mother's shirtsleeves were still pushed up from digging, and Luna's eyes fixed on her wrist. "How did you get your scar?"

"Your mama got that scar the day we put your daddy in the ground." Ducey cleared her throat and snatched the shovel, began to dump in thick mounds of soil. "Luna, child, it don't matter how much he walked and talked like a real man, your daddy was a ghoul—a powerful one, and a hungry one to boot. And whatever blood ran in his veins runs in yours, too."

"What does that make me?" Luna asked. "Some sort of monster"—she winced—"like him?"

Nana Lenore bristled, affronted. Still on her knees, she met Grace at the pot and began working at the rosebush's roots. "It makes you part of two worlds."

"It makes you caught between," Grace said.

No one spoke while Ducey filled the grave. After, she poured a final heap of dirt into the grave and stabbed the shovel into the grass beside her. "It makes you an *Evans*," she spat. She crooked a finger at the brown blanket covering the dead man. "That thing down there might have helped bring you into the world, but whatever else is in you, you're one of us. Never mind the rest."

How could she ignore the rest, when *the rest* was the most important part? They were still keeping secrets, still not telling her the whole truth. "But why didn't you tell me what he is?" Luna asked. "What I am?"

Grace squatted beside her mother and used the spade to tamp down the dirt until it lay even, leaving the leftover dirt to spread around the garden. "Like we said," Grace tried, still tamping, "we aren't sure what effect his—"

"What's his name?" Luna interrupted. Emotions surged under her skin—anger, resentment, shock. Curiosity. Hunger. "Tell me my father's name."

Grace faltered, the spade going still. "Samael."

Luna tasted the name when her mother licked it away.

"What your mother is trying to say," Nana Lenore cut in, "is that we couldn't know what effect Samael's blood would have on you." She kept her eyes on the roots, arranging them in thick tangles on the grass. "There are legends, of course, of living children born from the seed of strigoi, but we've never seen it before."

"More legends." Cold had begun to creep into the spaces the heat had left in her body to bite at her ankles. Luna rubbed one foot against the back of her other. She thought of the nightmares, the images that waited behind her eyelids every time she closed her eyes. "What do they say?" she asked.

Unease built in the sudden quiet as her mother and grandmothers sealed Samael's grave.

A growl escaped Ducey's throat, and she glared at the other two Evans women. "Hokum. Those old legends are nothin' but hokum," she said. "And seeing as how you weren't born with a tail or pointed ears, we've had to just keep an eye on you. Wait and see what happened. Do what we could."

"You said you buried him to keep an eye on him," Luna began, "but why?

Ducey's hand slipped into her apron, the outline of her hand tracing the trocar before it plucked out another butterscotch. "Just because those stories are full of superstitious nonsense don't mean there isn't a kernel of truth in them."

Grace nodded in agreement, dark curls bouncing against the pink splotches in her cheeks that had begun to sour and turn green. "I couldn't risk losing you."

Luna noticed her grandmother's shoulders go tight. "Losing me?"

"Your daddy is the most powerful strigoi we've ever come in contact with." Nana Lenore set the last bunch of roots down and wiped at her face, her fingers marking brown stains on her skin. "Your birth created a bond between the living and the dead. Samael's death—his true death—might mean yours, too. If whatever animates the dead is killed, the part of you that is his could die with him."

Warmth flooded between Luna's fingers, and she realized her mother had taken her hand. "We couldn't know what Sam's death would do to you," Grace said, "so we put him in the safest spot we could think of, right here under the rosebush, so if ever he should wake, we would know—we'd see." She squeezed Luna's hand.

Luna hadn't considered what might happen if her father rose from his grave. Again. "What happens if he wakes up?"

Nana Lenore glared at the grave. "He won't."

"I told you before, if not total decapitation, a blade across the throat should keep 'em pinned down. We figured a stake in his heart would do the same thing," Ducey said. "And your grandmother keeps him satiated with bits of this and that from the other ghouls we put down."

Luna recalled her nightmares—the hunger, the shadows, the knocking. What did it mean if Samael didn't rise, but she saw death in her dreams? Something bumped against Luna's leg, and she looked down to see Belle beside her. The dog studied her with liquid amber eyes, then lowered herself to the grass and lay still.

"I don't understand," Luna said. Her mother had said they buried her father under the rosebush to keep watch, to know if he woke up. He was still where they left him, but something *had* happened, hadn't it? She tried to squeeze her mom's hand, but Grace had let go. "If he's still there, then how am I raising the dead—and why is the rosebush rotting?"

The three other women looked at each other, then at her, but no one spoke. The cold in Luna's ankles crawled up the backs of her legs, collecting behind her knees. They didn't know.

Luna could hear Belle panting by her feet, but otherwise, the day had gone as silent as her father's shallow grave. She shivered as her spine froze, one vertebra at a time.

"If Mina Jean was indeed the first to rise as we suspect," Grace said, "then someone had been feeding off her for some time. Perhaps even feeding off Samael himself."

"Some*thing*," Ducey was quick to clarify.

"Something," Grace agreed, turning to Luna. "But it wasn't you. I made sure."

Realization cracked the ice forming inside Luna's chest. "Your rules," she said. "The early curfew, the window alarm. That's why you made me go home straight from school or come here. You were watching me."

Tension squeezed the air. Let go when her mother nodded. "I had to keep you safe, even if it made you hate me."

"We need to figure out where this began." The set of Nana Lenore's jaw was so tight it looked like her teeth might crack with each word forced between them. The rosebush lay forgotten at her feet. "That's the only way we're going to put an end to it."

Ducey cleared her throat. "One of two things is happening," she said. "Either there's another powerful ghoul in town and he's got Luna in his thrall like Samael had Grace, or the part of her we hoped to heaven wouldn't wake up has been comin' out on its own." She squinted at Luna. "You been sleepin' all right?"

"I check on her every night, and ask her every morning," Grace said. "She says she is."

"That don't mean nothin'." The old woman pulled off her glasses and squinted harder. "I saw a death bird in my tree, couple of nights ago. Sat on a branch and looked right at me." She stared at Luna as if she could see through her. "You sure you've been sleeping good, child?"

Luna's teeth chattered when she tried to speak. "A death bird?"

"Owl," Ducey said. "Last time one sat outside my window like that was the night before we put your father in the ground."

Visions of dark dreams and loose teeth flashed through Luna's mind and she thought backward, fighting to remember things she hadn't thought important, things she'd passed off as nightmares and let slip into memory. Had those images been real—been some twisted shadow version of her prowling the night, hungry and feeding? She looked at Belle, remembered sinking her teeth into the hound's red fur.

Luna looked at her mother. "I wanted to tell you, but I thought it would just make me sound crazy." The words came out before she could stop them. "I've seen him in my dreams, too. My father. At least, I think it's him. A big black shadow made of rose petals, always hanging over me. Sometimes it feels like I'm flying." She swallowed, remembering the feel of her dream wings. "Hunger, too. The taste of blood."

"What about death?" Nana Lenore asked. Her eyes fell on the withered gray rose petals on the grass. "Think hard, Luna, honey. The strigoi that have risen, did you dream about any of them?"

"Mr. Boone," Luna admitted, "but that was after the cooler. I saw Belle, and a girl with dark hair." Her lungs tightened. "I thought it was me, but it didn't *feel* like me. Alison Haney has dark hair, too."

"What about Mina Jean?" Ducey asked.

Luna shook her head. Her mother's hand was in hers again, and this time Luna held on, clung to it like it were the only thing solid left in the world. Belle still panted at her feet. The dog licked her jowls and panted harder. "I'm so sorry I didn't tell you," Luna said.

She looked at her mother. "And I don't hate you, Mom. I promise."

Grace smiled at her—a small smile, but a strong one.

"So, there's another one." Ducey crossed her arms, cracked her neck. "Someone who hasn't come out of the dark yet." Her eyes locked on Luna's. "Someone keeping to the shadows, so to speak, draining folks dry so we don't find them out while they build up their power. Whoever it is, they're keepin' you close, tryin' to earn your trust. Anyone come to mind?"

Luna shook her head no, but already a name came stillborn into her thoughts. There was someone. Someone who sounded too close to how her mother described Samael—*I thought he was unusual, eccentric. He was different than all the other men I knew around town.*

Someone who'd given her teeth to help control her dreams.

"No," she said, even though there was a name screaming in her thoughts.

Crane.

CHAPTER 31

Sheriff Buck Johnson

The way Buck Johnson saw it, there was no sense in going home, not if there wasn't a soul there to go home to. Most fellas his age had a gal, maybe a kid or two, a grandbaby, but he didn't have none of that. All he had was Jack Daniels and Belle, and now he'd drunk all the whiskey and his dog had been dragged off.

Buck had lost the thing he loved most in this world, right off his own back porch.

Right out from under my damn nose, he thought, and sniffed. He'd lost one of his few remaining marbles and driven over to Ducey's, but all that'd done was make him look like a damn fool in front of the woman who'd already made a fool out of him a handful of times before.

He'd been driving circles around town, working his own perimeter, for the better part of the afternoon, and now his back ached, and the bottom of his foot had grown tender from all the gassing and braking. Dust flew up when Buck pulled his car onto an old gravel road, and he eased his foot off the accelerator until his speed dropped enough that he could hear the crunch of each pebble, smell the odor of hot moth-balls and rubber coming in on high through the AC vents.

Whatever'd come after Belle had some nerve, that was certain. Coming onto a man's property in the dead of night. Taking his dog. That sort of sin didn't get washed under the bridge; didn't get churned over like pebbles on a gravel road or passed by like the longleaf pines and tumbleweeds he'd driven by on the edge of town.

I'll find the sapsucker who took her, and make 'im pay, Buck thought as his back teeth ground together, pinching a piece of cheek meat. He winced as the taste of blood filled his mouth. His fists clenched against the sensation and he hit the dash. Once. Hard enough to crack his knuckles open.

Buck studied the red welling in the seams of his fingers. That'd been pretty much all he'd found of Belle, too. Just a smear, really, but enough blood to know whatever'd gotten a hold of her hadn't been gentle about it. Course, he'd known that just by the sound of her yelp. He'd heard the same high-pitched shriek drumming in his ears all day long. Couldn't drink that away, not with all the whiskey in the world.

Especially not when he'd heard it before. It'd been fifteen years, but Buck would never forget the sound of dying.

He pulled his cruiser over in the same patch of dirt he pulled into every Thursday. On a normal day, he'd sit in that spot, finish up his paperwork, then head a mile up the road to Ed Boone's and drink past dusk. But not today. No paperwork and no Ed. Buck flicked down the visor and tugged the photo he kept pinned to its underside free. His thumb traced along the curve of Belle's long red ears, the patch of white blooming on her snout. More dust must have come in through the vent because something stung in his eye, and Buck wicked away the moisture with his palm.

He'd followed Belle's trail of wet blood into his yard until the measly light from his kitchen ran out, then he'd gone in, fetched his Maglite, and tried again. His vision had never been good and wasn't worth squat now, but he'd sat on the back porch nursing the bottle 'til he'd gotten drunk enough to haul ass over to Ducey's. When the sun came up at dawn, he'd checked the grass again.

Nothing. Just a whole lot of scuffed-up ground and a few sprinkles of dried blood.

"That was all she wrote," Buck muttered. He thumbed the photo, then tucked Belle's picture back under his visor and flipped it shut.

All he'd wanted to do was search for his girl, but the day had been crazier than an outhouse rat. Another dead body, this one a young girl. Petunia Milner wedging herself so far up his craw he could damn near taste her perfume over the phone line every time she called to off-load another round of tongue-lashing about her missing mother.

Even the pretty gal with the nice tits from Channel Six had come by, all sugar and smiles, trying to wheedle a headline out of him. Buck snorted. He might have been fool enough to give a girl like Penny Boudreaux one a handful of years back—might have been fool enough to give her a couple other things, too—but right now all he cared about was Belle. He'd barely had time to call down to animal control, see if anyone had picked up a hound. Not that those boys would know a redbone from a basset. Half of them probably couldn't tell a dog from their own asses.

Ain't a fella left in this town who knows a damn thing about good police work, Buck chuffed. He shut off the car and cranked down the driver's side window so he didn't cook. The sun was already halfway set, the day still hot enough to make the trees shimmer. Wouldn't be long before twilight would come, and he'd be forced to go home to an empty house.

Buck snatched the radio from his dash and thumbed the mic. "Come in, Dispatch," he ordered.

Darla's voice crackled over the line. "Dispatch here, Sheriff."

"Any news on that finger?" Buck tongued the hole he'd bitten in his cheek.

The woman took too long to answer. Buck smashed the button down again and put a little more growl into his voice. "Cat got your tongue, Dispatch?"

"Forensics brought the file in just after you left." Darla's voice was terse when she radioed back. "Prints from the finger match Snow Leger's."

His boys had found the woman's tongue laying on her shag carpet. Buck winced at his choice of words before. Course the damn thing was Snow's. "Anything else?"

"No, sir."

Buck wiped his bloodied knuckles on his pantleg. "Anyone talk to the girl's parents yet?"

"Taylor's over there now."

"Better him than me," he said, without pressing the mic. Roger Taylor was the kind of man who cried in his beer. Still, Buck hated talking to survivors. The whole business ate him up inside, having to tell somebody that life had chewed up someone they loved. Spit them out dead.

And you know why, don't you? He shifted in his seat and tugged at the seatbelt strapped across his chest. *Because this has all happened before.*

The blood, the disappearances. Strangers lurking around town. Bodies turning up torn open. Buck knew he didn't have a rabid animal or rampaging madman on his hands. What was happening was far worse, and he knew how it would end, too. He'd seen it that night, at Evans Funeral Parlor. Heat churned in Buck's chest, and he put the radio back on the dash without signing off. Air stagnated in the cab even with the driver's side window down, so he leaned over and rolled down the passenger side, too. Maybe a breeze would flush the memory away. Then it wouldn't make him think back on things he'd tried like hell to forget.

"No such thing as forgetting, Buchanan," he muttered to himself. "You just put it away, lock it down tight."

Go on about your business, and we'll go on about ours. Those had been the words Ducey'd said to him at the end of that bloody night, spoken over a hot cup of coffee that had sobered him up and weighed him down at the same time. He'd always known there was something funny about her, something a little off, but he'd always thought it made her special, not . . .

Not *what*?

Hell, he didn't know what it made her. Maybe once he had, but he'd been so angry for so long he'd forgotten. Only thing Buck knew for sure was he could live a million years and never imagine he'd see what he saw that night over a decade ago when he'd gotten a wild hair and decided to go over to the funeral parlor and finally tell the woman how he felt. He'd pulled up just in time to see Jimmy plunge a metal spike into Grace's man's heart, and then that fella tore into Jimmy Stewart with his teeth and ripped his throat wide open.

Buck had learned that monsters walked the earth that night, dead things risen out of the ground, and there wasn't room for things like law and order then—just death and more death. He'd let a part of himself go that night, but he kept his mouth shut, and stayed the hell away from the Evans women. He'd focused on things he could control—could investigate, cuff, and put away for good.

"Anything else, Sheriff?"

Darla's voice scratched across the radio, and Buck jerked in his seat. The receiver bit into his skin when he mashed down the mic. "If I wanted something else, I would say so, Dispatch." Buck bit his lip until he tasted red. "Johnson out."

A breeze rolled like hot breath through the cruiser's open windows, carrying a sound.

"Buuuuck."

Something knocked against the outside of the car. Buck jerked and flashed his gaze to the rearview. Nothing.

He shook his head and reared his fist to hit the dash again. "You old—"

An arm reached upward through the open driver's side window, grabbing him by the scruff of his neck. Another crossed over his chest and pulled at his ribs.

Buck tried to holler, but the hulking shape pouring through his window pressed the wind out of his lungs in a ragged burst. He pushed at the thing with both hands, but his fingers sunk into decaying flesh that rained black fluid down into the cab. Whatever had hold of him raised his body off his seat with such velocity that the seatbelt cut into the soft protrusion of his belly before the polyester webbing snapped. Buck heaved, bile rushing up his throat. He barely had time to register that the hand gripping his throat was missing its index finger before his neck bent sharply, snapping bone and spilling vomit from his mouth.

Acid burned through the hole he'd chewed in his cheek.

"*Gerroff*," Buck managed to spit around the mess flooding through his lips, but the hand clung to him, clawed into him, and he cried out as his flesh split under his uniform shirt. Blood squibbed out between buttonholes, bright and red and mixing with the mucus-y mess in his lap. Something thick stuck between his body and the cloth. Guts. His body turned inside out, spilling open.

Buck reached for his gun, but his fingers slipped in a goo of sweat, and spit, and blood. Other fluids. His grip faltered, his vision fading like the twilight sky out the passenger window as the four-fingered hand clawed at his neck. Another figure moved on the other side of the windshield, a second groan joining in the chorus of wet, squelching noises inside the car. Something that might have once been a man pushed itself through the passenger window. Wet gums slapped together, but the sound of his name was unmistakable.

"Buck," the thing bleated. "Buck. Buck Bu—"

He's missing his teeth, Buck had time to think, *and Snow only has four fingers.*

For the briefest second, he knew who had killed him, but then Clyde's gummy mouth locked around his nose, pain burst through his head, and Buck Johnson was no more.

CHAPTER 32

Deputy Roger Taylor

From the moment he'd seen Grace Evans's name on the fingerprint report, everything about Roger's day had gone swiftly downhill. Considering how badly the day had started off—how badly his entire *week* had been going—this was saying a lot.

Five years, Roger thought, thumbing unshed tears from the corners of his eyes as he slid back behind the wheel of his cruiser parked against the curb of the Haneys' front lawn. He cranked the engine to life and reclined his head against the headrest. *Five more years and I'm trading in my badge for a subscription to* American Woodworker *and a fishing pole.*

"Getting the hell outta this job." The words came out hot under his breath, almost sour in the heavy evening air. He tossed his hat into the passenger seat and tried not to notice where the brim had begun to curl in on itself. Evidence of all the wringing he'd been doing over the past couple of days. "Five more years," he promised himself.

Roger's meeting with the dead girl's parents had gone about as terribly as he'd thought it would. Brett Haney had sounded like a gruff, stalwart sort of man over the phone, but nothing turned a hot-collared son of a bitch into a puddle of emotion like telling him that his baby girl had been found dead. Man had melted right there on the living room rug, and when Katherine arrived home early, she'd taken one look at her husband and gone off like a smoke alarm.

Mothers, Roger thought. They had a way of knowing when something happened to one of their babies, when something was *wrong*. And it didn't matter if they were one or fifty—when a woman's child hurt, she bore the pain. Katherine Haney's screams had been so loud, so full of agony, Roger knew they'd ring in his ears for the next month.

Now he sat in his car in front of the house, feeling the humid Southern evening heat thicken the air of the cruiser's cab as he watched the sun sink into a milky orange horizon and tried to collect himself. The trip to the Haneys' had taken longer than he thought, and he still had things to do before he headed home for the night—but the long shift wasn't the worst part. For the first time he could remember, Roger dreaded going over to the funeral parlor and seeing Grace.

Mothers, he thought again. When Grace had seen him drive up with Luna in his backseat, she'd had the same look on her face that Katherine Haney had worn when she walked in the front door and saw a cop in her living room. A pucker around the eyes, ears pulled back, jaw fixed. Roger's right hand shot out to snatch his hat from the passenger seat. He pulled it back and stuffed it under his thigh.

Had Grace reacted so angrily to protect her daughter? And if so, what sort of secret was she hiding that would explain why the girl was carrying around a pair of a missing man's teeth? And if Grace was protecting her daughter, what, for that matter, might Lenore be hiding to protect hers—and Ducey hers?

I want an eye kept on those Evans women, Johnson had told him. At the time, Roger had thought it nothing more than the old bastard's prejudices, but now . . . now he wasn't so sure. Regardless, whatever was going on with the Evanses—whatever was going on in this *town*—duty was duty, and Roger had to do his. Nothing about putting a pair of handcuffs around Grace's wrists would give him pleasure, but he was a deputy first and a man second.

Growling out a sigh, he pressed the mic on the receiver clipped to his lapel. "Come in, Dispatch," Roger said. His fingers felt slimy against the radio plastic, oiled up by the Haneys' tears. Those poor people would go to bed tonight in a house with a bedroom that would never see its person again.

No, he corrected. They wouldn't sleep. Grief was better than coffee that way, liked to keep you up and hurting.

White noise crinkled across the radio.

"Dispatch." He pressed the button harder, in case the pressure helped. Nerves twitched on his tongue. "This is Taylor. Come in."

Darla's voice was full of nails when it finally staticked over the line. "Dispatch here, Taylor. What's your twenty?"

"Leaving the Haney residence," Roger said. The last slip of fire slid over the horizon, and the skyline darkened into rust. It was still too bright for headlights, but he flicked them on anyway. "Give Quigg a call, let him know I'm en route."

"Roger that," Darla said, tone still shaky. "Over and out."

He let his thumb lift off the button, then mashed it back down. "Everything good, Dispatch?"

"Oh, just peachy, Taylor," Darla snapped back. "Up to my ears in dead bodies and missing persons, phone's ringing off the hook, and Johnson's gone and took off," she said. "Damn man can't be bothered to even answer his radio."

His head still against the headrest, Roger exhaled and let his jaw hang open. As much as he didn't love the old bulldog breathing down his neck, the sheriff going dark in the middle of a crime spree wasn't a good sign. People would notice, and they were on borrowed time keeping things quiet already. The man's feud with Ducey boiled in Roger's gut. "Got a location on his vehicle?"

"Parked out off Farm Road 121," Darla said. "Just like every Thursday."

Johnson had nearly blown a fuse when the state had insisted their department pony up what little budget they had to foot the bill for GPS tracking on their fleet cars. "Politics," he'd sneered, as if the mandate was a direct insult from President William J. Clinton, who'd been peddling the merits of geo-tracking. "An attack on small town privacy." The sheriff might spontaneously combust if he knew they'd use the newfangled technology to keep track of his weekly trips out for an early evening drink with his hunting buddy. The poor bastard had probably driven halfway out to Edwin Boone's before he'd remembered the man had taken up residence at Eternal Flame Cemetery.

Roger shook his head. "Is Hinson still around?" he asked.

"He's been out of the station a while," Darla said. "Shift's over."

"Call him back in," Roger said. "Have him head over to Quigg's and take the girl's body over to Evans. The parents will need to come in and ID her soon. I'll see if I can round up the sheriff."

The radio crinkled.

"Hang in there, Darla," he added, still affecting the soothing, bad-news voice he'd used with the Haneys. "Day's almost over."

Darla's laugh sounded like a bark. "Sun's setting, Taylor. Night's just getting started." She cleared her throat without leaving the line. "Keep me updated on Johnson. Over and out."

Without sparing another look at the Haneys' house, Roger released the receiver, shifted the lever into drive, and pulled the cruiser away from the curb—slowly, so the tires didn't shriek. He kept the stereo off as he wound his way out of the quiet suburban west end, past the Market Basket grocery store and the little row of boutique shops that catered to snooty women like Mina Jean Murphy.

Even in the warm silence, cold shivered under Roger's uniform. Every mile that crunched under his tires tightened the coil of his spine. By the time he pulled onto the lumpy gravel trail that made up Farm Road 121, he felt about as tight as he had back in senior year of high school when Ernest Deveraux had put him in the headlock that cost him the wrestling team win.

One more twist, he thought. *One more twist and my head'll pop clean off.*

But there sat Sheriff Buck Johnson's cruiser.

"Just where I thought you'd be," Roger muttered. The tension under his skin didn't lessen as he braked to a stop and put the car in park. He rubbed at the back of his neck.

Johnson's Crown Vic sat off to the side of the road, windows rolled down. Maybe he'd remembered Edwin Boone wouldn't be home, pulled off, slipped into a quick afternoon nap.

No.

Something was off about the car, something that made Roger forget about the stiffness in his body. Made his gut twist and push up his throat. Sweat slid down his spine and gelled against his lower back. His stomach turned over.

It took a minute for Roger to realize what he was looking at, but when his brain registered the sight, he barely had time to unhook his seatbelt and force open the door before a hot stream of vomit erupted from his mouth, spraying the dusty gravel with the remains of last night's supper.

Roger's throat clenched, then retracted. Still seated, he grasped at his radio receiver on his chest, even pressed the button, but every time he tried to speak the only thing that came out was a low whine, a thin whimper too weak to form syllables. There were no words to describe the thick streak of clotted red dribbling down the outside of Johnson's driver's door. Shiny white of exposed bone and deep purple of pulped muscle peeked through the scraps of the department-issued khaki shirtsleeves. Scraps of shredded skin hung limp over the windowsill, anchored by Buck's lifeless hand left dangling out in the open, red ribbons running down fingers bent at unnatural angles. His nails were stained a dark, dripping red and crusted brown at the edges.

Oxblood, Roger thought, *like Snow's nail polish.* He wretched again when he tasted the word, then pushed himself out of his seat until his knees hit the gravel and the door clanged open on its hinges behind him. He barely caught the acidic stench of vomit or felt the warm slush soak through the thin cloth of his pants. Red and copper. The world was reduced to red and copper.

Blood and bone and blood.

He crawled over the puddle of his own puke, looked up, saw the wet gleam of an eyeball, optic nerve frayed at the end, laying in the trench one of Buck's tires dug into the dirt. A lump of flesh that might have been part of an ear. A puddle of red, thicker and chunkier than his vomit.

Something had torn Buck Johnson to shreds, pulled his body apart right through the open windows of his damn car.

Roger crawled forward on all fours, giving the Johnson bits a wide berth. He dared a glance up inside the cruiser, at the odd-shaped lump behind the steering wheel.

The man's face is missing. Only a red splotch remained of Buck Johnson's head. Gray brain matter sludged down the sides and pooled in the wound where his ear had been ripped away. Filled the wound that had once been a mouth. Settled between the spaces his teeth left when his head had been pulled halfway off, mandible left hanging by strands of torn cartilage and meat.

The crunch of footsteps on the gravel thundered in Roger's ears. He felt the presence of someone at his back as he pushed himself up from all fours onto his feet, but no sooner had his hand found the revolver on his hip when a familiar voice rolled over his shoulder.

"Hello again, *Officer*."

CHAPTER 33

Luna Evans

Dusk settled over Luna as she sat cross-legged on the grass, watching her mother and grandmothers replant the rosebush over her father's grave. Belle had stopped panting once Samael had been fully covered, and now the old hound lay beside Luna, eyes closed and breath even. If any evidence of the bite mark still remained under her fur, Luna couldn't find it.

"The only thing worse than putting a body in the ground," Ducey said, "is digging one back up." The old woman made a show of fishing a butterscotch from her apron pocket. She pushed the candy into her mouth and licked at her lips. "Course, I guess it's first you gotta kill 'em, and that ain't much fun, either."

"Mama, enough." Nana Lenore's snap lost its sting in a gust of exhale as she rested the shovel's handle against one hip and put one set of long bony fingers atop the other. Her blouse and pants were covered in streaks of brown and green, and leaves caught in her short auburn hair. She pulled at one, her lips scrunched in disgust. "We have too many things to worry about right now to listen to any of that foolishness," she said. "Like transplanting a rosebush in the hottest part of the year."

The last came out in a mumble, but still clear enough that Ducey heard it where she stood near the side door, filling a watering can from the spigot.

"That bush will be just fine." Ducey lugged the heavy pail back to the rosebush and set it on the grass. "You keep the thing so well-watered, it's probably happy to shake out its roots." She tipped her head behind her. "Isn't that right, Grace?"

Luna looked at her mother. Grace hadn't flinched when Nana Lenore settled the white rosebush back into place and smoothed the roots under. She hadn't even bothered to pull her sleeves down into her fists, but maybe she no longer felt the need to hide her scar. Not after she'd already ripped open the wound that had caused it. Instead, she just stood there, staring down at Samael's grave like one of the weeping angel statues in Eternal Flame Cemetery.

"Mom?" The word was out of Luna's mouth before she realized she'd said it.

Long, quiet minutes ticked by before Luna gave up waiting for her mother to say anything. She watched her grandmother pat the earth around the bush's base. Snip off a few wilted blooms. Pour water over the rosebush. All the while, part of Luna wanted to throw her arms around her mom, tell her that she understood, that she forgave her, but another part wanted to yell and scream, to pummel with fists and tears, demand answers. But Grace said nothing, and neither did Luna.

Ducey snorted. "And what about you, child?" She cocked an eyebrow in Luna's direction as she gathered up the gardening tools spread across the small lawn. "I reckon you've got a bellyful of questions."

A chill crawled back up Luna's shoulders and she twitched it back. A thorny tumbleweed rolled around in the pit of her belly. She pressed a hand to her stomach. Luna wanted to answer, but her teeth felt loose, just like in her dream. If she opened her mouth, they might all tumble out, scatter like the wilted gray rose petals that still littered the ground.

She shook her head no.

Ducey stomped her foot hard enough that Luna heard the crunch of brittle, dehydrated grass. "You girls are gonna be the death of me," she said. "Go ahead and keep it all bottled up, but don't come cryin' to old Ducey when everything finally bubbles out—and it will." She snatched up the water pail and dumped out what was left. "Y'all can stay out here pretendin' like there's some kind of romance about all this business, but I'm gonna go inside, put this mess away, and get ready to hunt. Ghouls are walking, and if we don't find them, they're gonna find us."

The old woman spun on her heels and still muttered under her breath when Grace jumped alive as if she'd been electrocuted. The sudden movement made Nana Lenore jerk so hard the shovel at her hip clanged to the ground, and Ducey made a sucking noise like she'd choked on her butterscotch. One of Belle's eyes peeled open and her long ears twitched, but she stayed put.

"You know what, I *do* have something to say," Grace snapped, peeling her eyes from the refilled grave at her feet. "There isn't a day that goes by that I am not reminded of the mistakes I made all those years ago, and the Godawful Mess it caused. But even if she was fathered by a monster, I don't regret for a second anything I did that gave me my daughter." She plucked a rose from the bush, gripped the stem so the thorns pierced her flesh, then tossed the bloodied stem in the dirt. It sank beneath the soil, and Grace let out a laugh so sharp it looked like it hurt. "Both Sam and Daddy went to their graves protecting their families, and I will, too, if that's what it takes. I refuse to be ashamed anymore."

"You want to talk to me about *shame*?" Fury sucked the oxygen from Nana Lenore's skin and stretched it tight across her bones. "I held my husband while he bled to death and there wasn't a damn thing I could do to stop it. How do you think I've felt, tending to that monster every day while your father rots in an early grave?" A single tear cracked loose from her eye, slid in a muddy brown line down her cheek. "What would I have done if Jimmy had *risen*?"

Grace's dark coils jostled like a nest of angry snakes atop her head. "You're not the only one who lost someone that night, Mother," she snapped. "Just like you're not the only one who walks by that rosebush every day. I have to look at it, too, and try not to think about what's tangled in its roots." She stabbed a finger against her chest, held it there like the trocar stabbed into Samael's heart. "I'm the one who's spent the last fifteen years letting secrets and guilt eat away at her insides every time I look at *my* daughter, not you."

"I have my own issues with my own daughter. Mine can hardly look at me." Nana Lenore stomped across the grass. She pulled up so close to Grace that one of her feet came off the ground like she might step back. "Your daddy—"

"Daddy made a choice for all of us that night. One he didn't have the right to make." Grace shook her head but stood her ground. "He chose to confront Samael, to make demands on *my* life, and now he's gone, and we're the ones who have to live with it."

Quiet crept back into the small circle of women, punctuated with the song of cicadas, the soft breath of the dog asleep on the grass. Luna expected Ducey to say something, make some crack about the dead or the dying, but she kept quiet and let the words breathe. The ghost of a smile played on her lips.

She's been waiting for this, Luna realized. Waiting for everything to come out.

Nana Lenore wiped stray spittle from her mouth with one hand and took Grace's in the other. "None of it was supposed to be like this." She folded, collapsing onto the grass between her daughter and her rosebush. Her blouse puckered where a small tear pulled the fabric loose, and she pulled off her muddied loafers and tossed them aside. "We've done everything right, everything we were supposed to."

She wiped her eyes and looked at Ducey. "What did we do to deserve this?"

"Life isn't fair, especially not for Evans women. I've been tellin' you girls that for years." Ducey clucked, but her tone was soft. She gathered Lenore up from the dirt, pulled Grace into her arms, hugged their faces to her chest to blot their tears. "I wish it was different, I really do."

Ducey motioned for Luna to join the hug. She hesitated, but a space waited for her in the circle. Luna stood and allowed herself to be drawn in. Three sets of arms wrapped around her, holding her close until the tumbleweed in her stomach dissolved.

"Our job is to keep the dead in the ground," Ducey said. "That's what we've always done. It's what we did that night"—she jutted her chin at the white rosebush—"and, come hell or high water, it's what we're gonna continue to do."

Luna's pulse beat in her throat as a white van with CORONER emblazoned on the hood pulled into the parking lot. Her gut swung. Another mutilated body waited within those white steel panels, and even though Luna didn't care much for Alison Haney, the girl didn't deserve to die. Not like this, and not twice.

Was it her fault Alison was dead? Luna looked at her great-grandmother, but Ducey's eyebrow shot up and she spoke first.

"I know what you're thinkin'," she whispered so that only Luna could hear, "and it's not."

All the hugging and sobbing had knocked her glasses askew, and Ducey released the other two women, then situated the bifocals back onto the bridge of her nose and cleared her throat. "That must be the Haney girl comin' in now. Bless her heart," Ducey said, watching as the van circled around to the delivery doors and pulled to a stop at the far end of the parking lot. "Come on, girls. We've got work to do."

By the time the van's engine shut off, any evidence of emotion on Ducey's, Nana Lenore's, and Grace Evans's faces had disappeared, replaced with the somber, professional expression they always wore when a body came into the parlor. Long earthy smears still stained Nana Lenore's slacks, but her loafers were back on her feet.

Luna's heart stuttered when the driver's door opened and Deputy Hinson slid out instead of Deputy Taylor. She'd expected the older deputy to show up with the dead girl's body, to look at her with that same mixture of suspicion and fear as he had earlier today when she'd put Crane's "gift" in his hand.

Crane. Luna's stomach gurgled and she wished she'd never taken the teeth, never handed them over to Deputy Taylor just because he was a cop and she didn't know what else to do when he asked. Strange dreams had been a part of life long before Crane put teeth in her palm, but they'd only grown worse since she met him. Everything was worse since Crane arrived in town.

The dead had started to rise, and even if she wasn't directly responsible, she was helping. She was the daughter of a master strigoi, some kind of beacon for the restless dead. Luna snorted. Ceremonial magician. Yeah, right.

Deputy Hinson tipped his hat at the Evans women as he rounded the back of the van. He started to pull open the rear double doors, then stopped and looked over his shoulder. "Someone give you a call about this one?"

"Jedediah Quigg phoned a couple of hours ago," Nana Lenore

called back, already making her way across the grass to the parking lot to meet him. "We've been expecting her."

Something like relief washed across the young deputy's face. Luna heard him mumble what might have been, "Thank God."

Luna watched as her mother and grandmother received the deputy at the van. She turned to ask Ducey how long it might be before Alison woke up, but the old woman had vanished, along with the dog. The side door of Evans Funeral Parlor hushed closed. She'd gone in to prepare.

Resolve hardened in Luna's stomach. Whatever it took, she would put an end to this.

But how?

A mint-green Buick pulled into the funeral's drive and parked beside the coroner's van. The driver's door swung open and Kim Cole slid out, followed by Dillon from the passenger side. An idea bloomed in Luna's mind when she saw her best friend. A beautiful, perfect, wonderful idea.

Dillon winced when he ran past the open van doors and saw the body being pulled out on the gurney, but his sneakers thumped across the blacktop and he flung his arms around Luna's neck. "Alison Haney. Can you believe it?"

She could. "Crazy, right?"

Luna startled when Dillon pulled back and she could see his face. A small scab peaked at the corner of his lip and purple colored the space below his eye, but attention to these was largely stolen by smears of thick eyeliner and heavy eye shadow around his blue eyes, a heavy coating of magenta lipstick on his wide, smirking lips. "What happened to your face?" she asked.

Dillon smirked and nodded toward Kim. "My sister. I had to leave school early, and she took me to class with her to be her model. What do you think?"

Luna chewed her lip. "It's very goth," she said. "But I was talking about the scab and the bruise."

"Oh," Dillon dismissed the remark with a flip of his wrist. "I got into a fight."

"A *fight*?" Even among every strange and unusual thing that had happened today, the idea of Dillon engaging in a physical altercation still made the list.

"Ian Butler called me the f-word again. Sticks and stones, I know. But I'm done being bullied for who I am." He raised a finger to his lip, touched its tip against the scab, and smirked. "Don't worry. He looks worse than I do."

Luna grinned. "He always does." Crane might be a monster, but she had to admit that she was glad he'd inspired Dillon to stand up for himself.

The clang of the gurney's metal legs against the coroner's van shook both teens back to the moment. Luna watched over Dillon's shoulder as Deputy Hinson handed her grandmother a clipboard. The van's back doors shut and the gurney sat on the pavement now, Alison's body a humanoid shape tucked under a thick white cloth. She nodded so Dillon would look.

"Oh my God." He put his hand over his mouth. The sight was probably even more shocking for him, who'd never seen a dead body outside of one well-prepared for funeral viewing.

"Listen," Luna said as she watched the color drain from Dillon's face. "Remember that girls' night we talked about?"

Dillon managed to peel his gaze off Alison's covered remains. "Yeah?"

"Let's do it tonight."

"It's a school night." Dillon scrunched his nose and raised his upper lip, then looked at Luna like she must not know it was Thursday. "They'll never go for it. My parents are the literal worst, and there's no way your mom will budge on your curfew."

Nana Lenore signed off on Hinson's paperwork, and Grace began to push the gurney up the sidewalk to the parlor. Ducey emerged, charging across the grass toward the coroner's van.

Luna heard Kim's voice. "Can I come in and see Belle?"

"Oh, she's fine, honey," Ducey clucked back. "And we've got our hands full for the night. How about you come back by tomorrow?"

Kim made a face, but her boyfriend put his arm through hers, nodding at the gurney, and she relented. "Okay," Kim said. "Come on Dillon. Let's go."

The white cloth draped over Alison's body rippled. A dark red smear appeared on the sheet, somewhere around the dead girl's midsection, and Grace stepped in front of the gurney, blocking the stain.

Luna remembered the dark, blackish sludge pooling out of Edwin Boone's seal in cooler number three. If she was already bleeding, then Alison was waking up.

"Look," Luna whispered. "Tell your parents it's for a school project or something." The sheet bristled, another sickly red splotch appearing just below the first. "I don't care. Just . . . it has to be tonight, okay?"

Dillon fixed her with his best glare—eyebrow up, lips twisted. "Mhm, and what's this really about?"

Ducey had managed to fend Kim off, and now held the side door open for Grace as she pushed the gurney through. Luna watched her mother's back disappear down the hallway. Nana Lenore waited by the door, loafer tapping out the time. She stared at Luna.

"Look, you heard how Alison died, right?" Luna asked Dillon. Surely he must have, considering he and Kim had pulled up right behind her boyfriend who'd made the delivery.

"Not exactly," he said. "Just that she was dead. Although Stripper Cop *did* say something about several bodies being found with, uh, missing parts." A hand fluttered to his chest and his mouth formed a little *o*. "Oh my God, she isn't, like, in *pieces* is she?"

Luna shook her head and ignored the question. "I think I know what's going on—and how to stop it. But I can't talk about it right now. Girls' night." Her best friend's expression flattened into suspicion tinged with disbelief. "*Please*, Dillon," she begged.

He made her wait for it, but Dillon finally shrugged, lifting his palms in defeat. "Okay fine, but you're going to tell me what's really going on later."

Air rushed through Luna's lips. "I will. I promise."

"My parents will hate this," he added with a smirk.

"I know, but thank you." Luna gave Dillon a quick squeeze and release. She jogged to meet her mom at the parlor's side door, then turned to call back. "And call Crystal."

"She'll hate it, too!" Dillon returned, which was true. Crystal believed in a full eight hours of sleep on school nights.

Luna watched over her shoulder as Dillon slid into the passenger side of his sister's sedan. Hinson already sat in the driver's seat of the coroner's van. Two sets of doors clanged shut, two engines turned over, and Luna let out the breath she'd been holding.

If she could enlist some help, then she would have the army she needed to end this for good. She watched the van pull away and joined her family in Evans Funeral Parlor, sprinting back to the lab before Alison Haney woke up.

CHAPTER 34

Ducey Evans

Even in death, there was something ripe and alive about the girl laying on the metal examination table in the Evans Funeral Parlor laboratory. Her skin had paled and her lips turned blue, but if you didn't look at the mess under the cloth and just at the face, you could almost believe she was sleeping.

Not just yet, Ducey thought. But soon. A dark red spot bloomed through the center of the cloth where the girl's life had spilled out through her stomach. The body that once belonged to Alison Haney already grew restless. Wouldn't be long now 'til it rose.

Belle had followed along as Grace pushed the gurney into the room, but she'd wedged her bony rear end under a chair on the other side of the room right about the time the dead girl started to bleed in earnest. One thin, rust-red ear slid out across the tile, but the dog was so quiet that if Ducey hadn't just seen her hoof it under the chair, she might've thought the poor thing had curled up under the furniture and died after all. Animals always sensed the change first, even faster than Ducey.

At least I managed to save someone, she thought as she watched Grace squat down beside the chair and try to coax the dog out. Even if it was a half-dead old hound. Even *Buck Johnson's* half-dead old hound.

The pretty little dead girl's left fingers twitched under the sheet and poked out from beneath the cloth. On the other side of the room, Belle's legs shuffled against the slick flooring. Her ear disappeared under the chair, and Grace pushed her shirtsleeves up past her elbows.

"We've got 'bout three minutes 'til this one opens her eyes," Ducey said, hunkering down and leaning forward so her elbows rested on cool metal, just beyond the spill of the cadaver sheet turning ruddier by the minute. She let her glasses dangle from the cord around her neck and rubbed at her eyes. A faint gust of foul, stale air blew across her face.

Alison Haney—or what was left of her—had started to breathe.

Ducey fanned away the smell and spared a glance under the chair. Belle was gone.

Smart girl, she thought.

"Maybe less," she said.

"We're almost ready." Lenore slid into the lab and began pulling out cleaning supplies. Bleach, paper towels, trash bags. She tugged on a pair of dishwashing gloves and handed a second pair to Grace, who tugged them over her wrists with a snap.

"Here, Mama." Lenore offered Ducey a pair of yellow latex gloves, flipping them impatiently in the air. The old woman straightened her posture, shook her head, and stepped back from the table—close enough to reach out and touch the body, but not so near she'd have to smell its breath. "Not for me, child," she said. "I'm not going to need them tonight."

"And why not?" Lenore's arms snapped into triangles on her hips and she squinted, gloves stuck in her fist. She always looked like her daddy when she stood that way, like a kissing bug, ready to bite.

"Because I'm not puttin' this one down. And neither are either of you." Ducey nodded at the laboratory door as Luna slid into the room. She snatched the handle of the short trocar she kept tucked in her apron pocket, pulled it out, wagged it like a dowsing rod in the girl's direction. "She is."

Luna blinked, tripping to a stop so sudden her Converse squeaked against the floor. Her eyes swept down the family tree, passing from her great-grandmother to her grandmother to her mother, and then back again before landing on the trocar.

The metal rod wobbled in Ducey's hand. Dang thing was heavier than she remembered.

"Me?" Luna asked.

Fluorescent light cast a halo around the girl's dark hair, and the surprise in her voice was real enough, but Ducey caught the flash in Luna's eyes, the slight squeeze of her lips, as her gaze swung to the lumpy, bloodstained sheet on the table. Her eyes hung there and didn't blink. The sight unsettled Ducey, causing an uncomfortable twinge way down in the bottom of her belly.

Probably just a coincidence, Ducey thought. Coincidence that Luna had skipped school and a classmate turned up dead. Coincidence that Luna'd been squabbling with the girl ripped open in broad daylight. Weirder things had happened in small towns, and teenagers always had drama. World is ending one minute, crisis is forgotten the next. Still, *probably* was a long way from *definitely* when it came to the restless dead and Evans women.

Especially an Evans woman who had ghoul's blood running through her veins. Ducey lowered the trocar and slipped her free hand into her candy pocket. Came up empty. Too bad.

"Len, give Luna the gloves," Ducey said when no one moved. Not even the dead girl.

Luna finally peeled her gaze away from the body. "Did you say *I* have to do it?" She toed at the ground and didn't make eye contact. "Are you sure?"

Ducey's grip tightened around the trocar. Relaxed. Where in the dickens were her butterscotches? "That's what I said, didn't I?"

Lenore clutched the gloves to her chest. "Mama, I hardly think—"

"That's just it, Len. You hardly think." Ducey redirected her unsteady nerves to an easier target. Battling her daughter was simpler than worrying about what Luna might become if they didn't get a handle on things *fast*. They knew dangerously little about what happened when a monster bred with a human, but things caught between always had to choose a side. As Lenore had pointed out, the girl was only half Evans. "Now, we don't have time for ceremony," she said. "We need to put this one down and Luna needs to be the one to do it."

Another squeak of Luna's toe. "Why me?" she asked.

"Because you need to learn, child. And this is the sort of thing one learns by doin'." Ducey thrust the trocar, pointy end down, toward the girl. When Luna didn't take it, Ducey grabbed her hand, curled her bare fingers around the thin metal stem, and clamped them there until her grip stayed put. "You saw it done once. Now you can do it yourself."

Luna set her free hand on the gurney, bracing herself. She looked at the body, then the trocar. "Wh-what about the gloves?"

"Don't need 'em," Ducey said.

Lenore's head reared back and she opened her mouth, but Grace put her hand on her mother's shoulder. "Ducey's right," she said. "Luna needs to learn, just like we all did." She turned to her daughter. "I know we're asking a lot of you, hun. Putting down someone like this isn't an easy thing, and it's only harder when they were someone you knew when they were alive. Think of it as mercy. You're not killing them; you're freeing them. It's horrible in the moment, but helps you sleep better later."

Ducey smacked her lips. She didn't know about all that, but figured they each had their own way to cope with what they had to do. "At least one of you has some sense left." She motioned Luna toward the ghoul. "Come on, then."

Luna inched forward, edging along the table as she walked the length of the dead girl's body. She shuffled in place at Ducey's side, and pushed a thick shock of dark hair behind an ear. "She still looks like Alison," she said.

"No names." Ducey shook her head. "Callin' them by those only makes them talk back. Best to forget them fast as you can. If you can't do that, keep your mouth shut."

The sheet rustled. Luna jolted like she'd been zapped, but she stood firm. "Is it different," she asked, "when they died younger?" She considered the red splotches spreading over the body's abdomen. "Or when they're . . . mostly eaten?"

Lenore tried to answer, but Ducey shushed her with a motherly palm. "It's always different," Ducey said, "and always the same. Death's the one great equalizer, child. Don't matter what size, shape, color, age someone is, or what they got between their legs, death comes for us all."

The sheet shuddered again, and the dead girl's cold fingers tapped on the table. Wrapped around Ducey's wrist.

"Mama!" Lenore called.

"Ducey!" Grace's voice followed.

Her palm still lifted, Ducey patted the air. She might be eighty years old, but she was still strong enough to fight off a baby strigoi.

It'll be my turn on that table soon, she thought, looking at the ghoul's firm graying skin wrapped around her own loose, wrinkled flesh. *I just hope like hell I don't get up*.

The dead girl's grip tightened.

Luna raised the trocar over her head. She didn't flinch when the knuckles of the Alison-thing's other hand—the one *not* gripping Ducey—rapped across the metal. A knock. Almost.

"What do I do?" Her voice climbed as she raised the stake higher and wrapped both hands around the handle. "Head or heart?"

"Heart," Ducey said. "Imagine you're pinnin' it into a grave. One swift motion down, hard and fast as you can."

Luna licked her lips and blinked a bunch of times until Ducey's words settled in. Her hands trembled where they clutched the trocar, but she adjusted her stance on the tile. "Okay."

Ducey grabbed the stained cadaver sheet with her free hand. "Ready?"

Sweat had formed on Luna's upper lip, on the apples of her cheeks. She nodded, and Ducey wrenched her wrist out of the dead girl's grasp and swept the sheet back.

Luna's trocar hand plunged down just as the ghoul opened its eyes.

"Luna," the ghoul croaked, and Luna stalled, a beat away from stabbing the metal rod through its heart. It shuffled on the table, but the gaping hole in its stomach kept it from sitting up. Organs sloshed in the hollowed cavity. Eyes stretched open, wide and black. A hungry mouth snapped open and shut.

Luna stared down at the body writhing on the table. The trocar hung suspended in the air.

The ghoul's knuckles wrapped on the table, its jaw still sucking open and snapping shut. "Luna."

"Go on," Ducey urged. "Finish it."

"Alison," Luna's arm hovered in the air as she stared, wide-eyed and trancelike, at the body on the table. Her hand dropped to her side, and her words came out slurred, tangled with her emotions. "I'm sorry for hating you," she said, "but it's time for you to be still."

The creature on the table froze. Its blank eyes filled with something that made Ducey's skin crawl as it turned its head toward Luna. Ducey snatched the trocar out of Luna's hand and slammed it into the ghoul's heart before either of them could speak again. Blackened blood erupted out of its chest, splattered on the floor, coated Ducey's hands.

"Should have worn the gloves." Ducey stuck her tongue out at the thick sheen. "Go put on a pot of coffee," she told Luna. "It's gonna be a long night."

The girl hesitated at first, but then she took one last glance at the body on the table, at the blood, and nodded. She slipped out of the room without another word.

Lenore and Grace stood with eyes wide and mouths open. Grace was the first to speak. "What was that?" she asked. "Why did it respond to her?"

"Don't know for sure," Ducey said, though she had a pretty good idea—that the part of Luna that called to the dark could be heard and answered, which may have been what caught Alison Haney in the other ghoul's crosshairs to begin with. "But it's not good."

Lenore righted herself and hooked her finger around the nozzle of a bleach spray bottle. "The dead only respond to the dead. She heard Luna."

Ducey closed her eyes, and wished her daughter would shut up. Now was not the time to get lost in the metaphysics of it all. Now was the time to put an end to it. They could sort out the rest later.

"But Luna's not dead," Grace argued. Her voice came out high and sharp, edged on hysterical. Fury replaced the strength Ducey had seen in her before.

"Frankly, we don't know what she is," Ducey said, "but we're gonna figure it out." There were other legends, ones she would take to her own grave, God willing. Things she dared not think about with that scar on Grace's hand, or the vials of ashes Lenore kept squirreled away.

She wiped her hands on her apron and dragged the sheet back over the dead girl's head. Stared at the steeple the muddy red cloth made where it hung over the trocar. "Go get Luna," she said.

Grace slid out the door and padded down the hallway toward the break room. Ducey heard her granddaughter's footsteps take her to the lobby, heard the creak of the chapel doors open and close. The dull sound of the side door.

Grace reappeared in the laboratory door, eyes wide and white as wedding china dinner plates. "She's gone," Grace said.

CHAPTER 35

Deputy Roger Taylor

Roger stood even with the trunk of the sheriff's car, his back to the grisly scene behind him. To the bloodbath in the front seat. He'd never aimed his gun at a kid before. Couldn't even remember the last time he'd discharged his weapon in the line of duty. He had also never seen anything like what was left in the driver's seat of Johnson's cruiser, scattered across the gravel road. Too many firsts had piled up, crushing him under.

"Hold it right there," he instructed the boy, and tipped the nose of his police-issued Smith & Wesson Model 13, but didn't lower it completely. Damn thing didn't come with a safety, and a misfire would be the last thing he needed. "Don't take another step closer."

Crane leaned against the hood of Roger's Crown Vic and lifted ten long, bony digits. A dark curtain of hair obscured his eyes. A cigarette burned red-hot between thin lips, and his mouth danced as he nudged it to the side, totally at ease. "What happened here?" he asked.

Roger swallowed back salt and tried not to breathe. This was the third time he'd run into the newcomer, and every time, circumstances got a little stranger. But bumping into the boy at the gruesome scene wasn't truancy, wasn't a Class A misdemeanor for having a pack of smokes in underage pockets. This was . . .

Roger didn't know what *this* was.

"You tell me," he said.

One of the boy's hands dropped, swept aside a lock of hair to reveal heavy-lidded, black-rimmed eyes and a hooked nose. "What makes you think I know?"

The cig's ember flared, crackling as he pulled. The cruiser's headlights illuminated the black folds of the kid's trench coat, mixed red with the brake lights of Johnson's cruiser, making him look like some sort of demon, perched against Roger's hood. Crane's stare walked itself up the revolver's barrel to Roger's eyes. "Perhaps I should ask you the same thing," Roger said.

Roger's finger twitched, and he inched his aim to the right and lowered the gun to hang at his side. Kid had some nerve, but there was no blood on him. No red smear on his skin or clothing. Nothing that would indicate he'd done anything other than walk up on the scene, just as Roger had. The boy might not be involved in whatever had happened on Farm Road 121, but Crane Campbell still gave Roger the creeps.

"What are you doing wandering around out here at night?" Roger asked.

Crane smirked. "Is taking a walk at night a crime?"

"Not a lot of foot traffic out this way, especially after sunset." Roger noticed a smear of blood that he didn't remember getting on his hand. "No streetlights, lots of critters with teeth," he said. "Can't think of a good reason for you to be wandering these streets alone."

"Maybe I just wanted to get some exercise." The boy shrugged and made a show of looking around Roger to Johnson's cruiser and what was in it. He looked at the puddles of blood and upchuck on the gravel, and his eyes narrowed. "What happened, anyway? Someone hit a deer or something?"

"Nothing you need to concern yourself with," Roger said. He let loose a heavy sigh, and a whiff of hot, liquid copper hit him on the inhale, nearly bowling him over. The heat crushed against his chest. His revolver hung loose at his side, but he didn't decock it, and didn't holster it. Not yet.

A squelching noise from behind Roger—somewhere that might have been inside the cab of Johnson's cruiser—almost made his head turn. His own radio crackled before his brain could register the command, and the sound nearly scared the piss out of him.

"Come in, Taylor," Brandon Hinson's disembodied voice said on his shoulder.

Roger kept his gun in his right hand and used his left to press the mic on the receiver attached to his shoulder. His bladder needed emptying. Another scare like that, and it'd spill right down his leg. "Taylor here."

"Just left the funeral parlor," Hinson said. "Dropping the van off now and heading back to the station to clock out."

Crane lifted off the cruiser and took a step forward. Roger inched back, keeping his body at the midway point between the kid and the cars. He ignored the way the boy sneered at him when he moved. "Sorry, Hinson," he said into the mic. "I'm gonna need you to stay on duty. It's gonna be a long night."

A rush of static, then, "Any luck on finding Johnson?" Hinson asked, failing to hide the irritation in his voice. *Where the hell is the sheriff?* is what he really meant to say.

Unfortunately, neither of those was a question Roger wanted to answer in front of Crane. Police band or not, there wasn't a code in the book strong enough for what he'd walked up on.

"Oh, I found him, all right," Roger said, trying hard not to think about the slimy red stump waiting in the driver's seat of the cruiser behind him. The image rose up and he blinked to clear it, but still saw the cranky old man who'd been a thorn in his side since he'd joined the force, peeled open like a piece of rotting fruit right in his own damn car. Edwin Boone had been bad, Snow Leger—wherever the rest of her was—worse. Roger hadn't thought things could get more violent than Alison Haney.

He'd been wrong.

"Gonna need to put another call in to Quigg," he said into the receiver. "Tell him to get out to Farm Road 121, mile marker seven, and bring everyone he's got. And be quick about it, Hinson. We won't be able to keep this one quiet."

Another squelching noise. This time the wet, sucking sound was followed by a different sound—something heavy, trying to move.

"Roger that," Hinson said. "Over and out, Taylor."

Roger's hand dropped away from the radio the same second the cigarette fell out from between Crane's lips. Even in the crimson glare of Johnson's cruiser's brake lights, the boy's already pale skin turned white. Whatever Roger had heard behind him, Crane was seeing it over his shoulder.

Suuuuuck.

The heat that had stuck to the backs of Roger's knees gelled into cold, locking him in place as if it were cement. He tried to turn his head, but his neck muscles wouldn't budge, and he felt the crippling effect of his inability to assess the threat at his back all the way to his bones. But what would he have deduced if he'd seen what caused the sucking sounds, the sickening squelches of sound? There was no way Johnson could still be alive. No way anyone could lose that much blood, suffer that amount of trauma, and not kick the bucket. Hell, the man's face had been ripped clean off, brain matter splattered across the dash.

No, Buck Johnson was dead, dead, dead.

And yet, the wet, slurping sound at Roger's back would suggest otherwise.

The stink of copper was replaced by that of offal, and the sound of scratching on metal rang out into the dark quiet. The familiar thud of flesh against metal. A sharp blast of the car horn spun Roger like a top on the gravel.

Something was moving inside Johnson's car.

No, that can't be right, Roger thought. *There's a bag of blood and bones that used to be Buck Johnson sloshing around in the cruiser's front seat.*

Roger took a step backward, anchored his boot in the gravel. He stopped at the rear passenger door, held his breath, and took another step. He peered through the open window.

"For the love of—" Roger couldn't get the words out before footsteps rushed up, and Crane appeared at his side. The kid's breath was in his ear before Roger realized his revolver was already up, hammer now cocked to second position, sight trained on what sat in the driver's seat.

"Shoot it," the boy said. "Aim for the heart."

"The heart?" Roger barely heard his own voice.

"I'd say go for the head, but there's not much brain left," Crane mused, far too calm for Roger's liking. "But the soul lives in the heart."

"Shut the hell up, kid." Roger's finger grazed the trigger but didn't pull. "I can't just put a bullet in the man. He's still alive."

Crane inched closer, and Roger could smell the stench of nicotine and the earthy aroma of other less legal herbs. "Does he look alive to you?" Crane asked.

The seasoned deputy took in the monster in Johnson's seat. The ripped edges of where his skin had been pulled open, the sludge of black and red and purple that spilled from his head. The gray pudding where his brain should be, the clear imprints of teeth marks like a row of stitching up his one remaining arm. There was nothing alive about Sheriff Buck Johnson.

Then, a noise rumbled up from what was left of the dead man's throat.

The exposed muscles of what once was Johnson's mouth gaped. Half a tongue rolled behind busted gums and broken teeth. Roger heard something else in the wet slurping sound this time. Two broken syllables, barely comprehensible. "Tay-lor."

Roger closed his eyes and opened fire.

CHAPTER 36

Luna Evans

Luna knocked on the front door of the Coles' ranch-style house and waited for someone to let her in. She peeked through the stained glass panel and hoped Dillon would whisk her down the hallway to his bedroom before she had to face his parents. The last thing she needed was to answer Mr. and Mrs. Cole's questions about why they'd made plans on a school night or listen to a sermon on the proper times to address homework. Besides, Crystal should be in there by now.

Luna needed to get in there, too, before another restless dead rose. Ambled down the street. Staggered through the Coles' boxwoods.

She knocked on the door again. "Hello?"

Unfortunately, Dillon meeting her at the door was unlikely. Mr. Cole had actually said that it was a woman's duty to receive guests, which they all thought came off as both misogynistic and a skosh homophobic. Either way, Mrs. Cole typically answered the door, dependably polite even if she usually smelled of chardonnay.

Luna knocked again under the shadowy overhang of the Coles' one-story. She started to beat her fist on the door again, but then she remembered Ducey's lesson on knockers and callers and felt her pulse crawl up her throat. Her hand dropped to her side. After a heavy swallow, Luna rang the doorbell. Twice. Three times. When Mrs. Cole still didn't appear, Luna stepped back to peer at the window she knew hung over the kitchen sink. The light was off.

But Mrs. Cole was a one-light-stays-on-at-all-times kind of lady.

Luna's pulse was still too high, and now her skin started to prickle. "Come on." *Hurry up. Let me in.* Eyebrows knit, she surveyed all the other darkened windows. The whole house seemed quiet. Too quiet, like the flat brick home had already hunkered down for the evening. Told the cicadas to knock it off. Called it a night. Even the sconces on either side of the front stoop were turned off, and Luna wasn't sure how she hadn't noticed that when she could hear the neighbor's television wafting through the night.

Where was everyone? Didn't Dillon tell them she was coming? Or worse, did he tell them and his parents took him out for the evening just so they didn't have to be rude and turn her away? And where was Crystal? Anxiety itched up Luna's back, tickling her shoulder blades. If the Coles weren't home, that meant they were out, and if they were out, that could mean—

No. Luna pummeled her fist on the door. Even if they were out, it didn't mean they were in any kind of danger.

Something rustled at the far end of the boxwoods running beneath the Coles' front windows.

Luna thought of Alison under the sheet. The inky red stain spreading across the fabric.

"Dillon? Anybody home?" Luna cupped her hands over her eyes and tried to peer through the stained glass panel. Nothing. Just an empty entry that led into an empty living room. The lamps were dark, the television off. She couldn't see beyond that, but she knocked again, just in case.

Everything was still—

Except for that rustling. *What makes that kind of noise, anyway?* Luna wondered. A squirrel? Something bigger?

Something with more teeth.

Her stomach turned, shifting her voice into another octave. "Dillon!"

A thin shadow slunk across the living room and Luna heard the click of Mrs. Cole's heels tap, tap, tapping their way across ceramic tile to the front door. With each click Luna could breathe a little easier. She watched Mrs. Cole's distorted figure take shape on the other side of the stained glass panel. By the time Dillon's mom finally yanked open the front door, Luna felt almost normal.

"Luna, dear," she sighed, pulling Luna in and crushing her against her chest in a gust of perfume and hairspray. Tears had carved streaks into her perfectly applied makeup, and her breath smelled of butter and smoke. "Oh, honey, I'm so sorry to hear about your friend." Mrs. Cole pushed Luna back by her shoulders and held her at arm's length. "How terrible." She clucked. "How absolutely terrible. We're all in mourning."

Mrs. Cole squished Luna into another hug, and she spotted Dillon and Crystal hovering at the other end of the entryway. When Luna crunched her eyebrows at them, Crystal gesticulated something that looked like sobbing, shivering, and the word "lemons."

Luna scrunched her eyebrows harder. *What?*

Alison, Dillon mouthed. He wiped at his own imaginary tears.

Luna understood. Nothing put people on their best behavior like shared tragedy. No matter their feelings about weeknights or homework, the Coles would never be able to turn away a group of grieving teens.

When Mrs. Cole released her for a second time, Luna made sure her facial expression was appropriately dejected. Mustering up a tear for Alison Haney was a tall order—she hadn't known the girl well and had invested a lot of energy into disliking her—but remembering the way the girl had looked, twitching on the gurney with wide, hungry eyes, was enough to pull Luna's mouth into a frown. No one should have to die like that.

"Thanks, Mrs. Cole," Luna said, managing a small smile that passed for grateful and sympathetic at the same time. "I appreciate you letting us come over."

The woman's mouth pinched. "Of course," she said. "You kids are welcome here anytime."

Over Mrs. Cole's shoulder, Luna saw Dillon roll his eyes.

Mrs. Cole needed a hug from Crystal and one from Dillon before she released all three of them into the back of the house. When they finally made it to Dillon's bedroom, they closed the door, and all three sank onto soft surfaces. Dillon and Crystal took the bed, but Luna curled up in the wingback chair Dillon called his throne.

Her friends' stares pinned her to the seat. Crystal's butterfly clips were gone, and she'd already wrapped her hair for bed. Her dusky skin was flushed pink, and the few curls that escaped the bonnet twisted question marks around her head. Dillon crossed his legs and leaned an elbow on a knee, then winced when he brushed the scab on his lip and settled his chin on his knuckles instead. All evidence of Kim's beauty school makeover had been washed away.

"Your mom seems to be taking Alison's death hard," Luna said dumbly.

"We're on the same phone tree as the Haneys." Dillon's eyes flicked to the Backstreet Boys poster thumbtacked over his dresser. "And my dad is really good friends with hers. He's been over there all evening while Mom cries on the phone and polishes off a box of Franzia."

"In the dark," Crystal added, hugging a bed pillow. "It's kinda weird."

"I'm not the only drama queen in my family," Dillon said, "but whatever, we're not having a 'girls' night'"—he added the little air quotes for extra effect—"to talk about my parents."

"Right. There's something I need to tell you." Luna adjusted herself in the chair, trying to find an appropriate position to explain what was going on. How could she put everything into complete sentences and make it coherent? Her hand brushed against her jacket pocket before she realized she was feeling for a butterscotch.

Oh my God. I'm turning into my great-grandmother.

Luna looked at Dillon and Crystal again, then blew a sigh out the corner of her mouth. "So, like, you guys know what happened to Alison Haney?"

Dillon rolled his eyes. "Obviously," he said, "and I already told Crystal about all that anyway. Besides, she practically *lives* on Channel Six News—"

Crystal nodded, squeezing the pillow against her. "They said it was another animal attack, which is obviously a lie." Luna and Dillon looked at her in shock. Her eyes went big. "What? Animal attacks leave behind stuff like fur and claw marks," she said, picking at the corner of her pillow. "The police didn't mention any of that. Besides, animals don't kill just for fun. They kill for food."

Dead or alive, everything had to feed.

"This is going to sound crazy," Luna said, "but I need you to listen." Her gaze jumped around Dillon's room, from the bed to the plastic window blinds to the stack of schoolbooks on his desk and the clarinet his dad said was too feminine for him to play in the school band. "But Crys is right. It's not a rabid animal."

Luna closed her eyes so she didn't have to see their reactions. "It's the dead," she said. "They're rising."

She counted the ticking of Dillon's bedside alarm clock. When almost twenty seconds had passed and no one said anything, Luna peeled one eye open, then the other. Dillon stared at her, then shook his head and raked a hand through his curls. "I'm sorry, are we supposed to be taking you seriously right now?"

"That's not funny, Luna," Crystal murmured, visibly upset.

Perfect. Luna hadn't considered her friends would think she was pulling some kind of prank. She would've been offended, if it hadn't been such a completely reasonable reaction.

Luna uncrossed her legs, dug her heels into the carpet, and tried again. "See, sometimes they get buried wrong or just don't understand they're dead. They get restless, and then they come back." The words erupted from her mouth, a firehose she couldn't shut off. "That's why they haven't found all the bodies, just pieces of them. And why more people keep dying in horrible ways." She grabbed at the sides of her head and hooked her fingers in her hair until it hurt.

On the bed, Crystal tugged at Dillon's arm. The two shared a look, then Dillon slid off the bed and knelt beside Luna's knee. "We know you've been going through something, and I think seeing Alison today might have . . ." He shrugged. "Been the straw that broke the camel's back."

Crystal's cheeks lifted in an understanding smile. "But if this is the way you need to grieve, we're here for you," she said.

"I'm fine," Luna lied. "And this isn't about seeing Alison's dead body," she lied again. "Not *exactly* about seeing her body. Well, sort of." She let out a frustrated growl. "Look. I'm not making this up and I'm *not* having some kind of breakdown. The dead are chewing people up. And this isn't the first time it's happened."

Dillon pursed his lips and huffed through his nose. "You're telling us there's a zombie outbreak, and it's a rerun?"

"Yes!" Luna shook her head and put her hands out. "But they're not zombies. Technically they're called strigoi—" Dillon mouthed the word back at her and Luna continued. "But Ducey calls them ghouls. Sort of like zombies and vampires combined. You have to kill the heart, not the brain, and they grow stronger as they feed until they get so strong it's hard to tell that they're dead anymore." She paused to suck in air. "It happened before, when I was really little. My mom and grandmothers told me. And I've seen it for myself." She held up two fingers. "Mr. Boone and Alison. They both came back."

"And you, what?" Dillon asked. "Put a stake in their heart?"

"My grandmothers did." She decided to bite off another piece of the truth. "It's . . . sort of the family business. If a dead body gets back up, they—we—put it back down."

"Yeah." Dillon clicked his teeth and wagged a finger at Luna, his baby blues wide. "Now, *that* I could see. Especially your great-granny. Ducey is *intense*. Kim said she didn't bat an eye when they found the sheriff's dog bleeding out in the alley."

"Luna." Voice even, Crystal stuck to the facts. "If anything like this had happened before, don't you think we'd know about it? This is a small town. It's hard to keep secrets."

"Monsters never make the news," Luna countered, then reconsidered. "At least not nonhuman monsters. People already say the news is a joke. Imagine if Penny Boudreaux or Bill Kershaw went on the air saying that the dead were rising. People would lose their minds."

Crystal shook her head. "I don't think—"

"Come on, you two," Luna cut in. "You know what business my family is in, how much time Deputy Taylor seems to spend around the funeral parlor. And *everyone* knows how much Sheriff Johnson *hates* my family—there's got to be a reason for that. Maybe it's because they know the truth."

Dillon sighed. "Deputy Taylor is there all the time because he's obsessed with your mom."

"And the sheriff is a racist old jerk," Crystal added. "Trust me, he gives my parents so much crap every time they need to request something for a case."

"Maybe." Luna shrugged, turning to Dillon. "But you were there tonight. You saw how they acted when Hinson dropped off Alison's body. How quick they got you all to leave. Did anything about that feel normal to you?"

That worked. Dillon rolled his eyes, but his face grew softer around the edges. "Okay, I'll play along," he said. "The dead are rising, and the Evans women put them back in their graves."

Crystal fixed them both with a parental scowl. "Are you two seriously talking about how to stop a vampire outbreak?" she asked. "There's a test in trig tomorrow."

"There'll be time for math after the zombie apocalypse." Dillon reached to the bed and patted Crystal's knee, then motioned for Luna to continue. "What does this have to do with us? Sounds like your grandmas have it covered."

Luna gritted her teeth and opted for the truth, even if she wasn't sure she should say it. "Because they don't know what's causing it. Someone started this, and I know who."

Dillon crossed his arms over his chest, exhaled, blinked disinterested eyes. "Who?"

The name sat on Luna's tongue like a wet piece of black licorice—too gross to swallow, too bitter to spit out. Finally, she pushed it through. "Crane."

"Crane?" Crystal and Dillon repeated.

"It's the same pattern," Luna went on, ignoring the obvious disbelief in her friends' voices. "Everything that happened before is happening again, only before it happened to my mom, and now it's happening to me." She looked at each friend in turn. "I know it sounds insane, but I need you to trust me. *Please.*"

Dillon raised his hands in surrender. "So there are zombies or strigoi or whatever, and Crane is, like, basically Dracula. What exactly are we supposed to do to stop him?"

Dracula hit a little too close to home, considering the man she'd seen buried under her grandmother's rosebush, but she let it slide.

"The same way they killed Dracula in the book," Luna said, mincing details. "We put a stake through his heart."

Total decapitation works best, Ducey had said. "Then we cut off his head, and burn the body in the crematorium," Luna finished.

Her friends gawked at her like they'd never seen her before. Or worse, she thought. Like they were seeing her for the first time.

Crystal shunted to the edge of the bed and let herself drop onto the carpet on the other side of Luna's chair. Her friends wrapped their arms around her shoulders, and Dillon took her hands in his. "Luna, darling, I get that there's something weird going on around here, and I believe *you* believe what you're saying," he said. "But I'm gay. She's Black. We're the kids who die first in horror movies. Let's just sleep on this and see how things feel in the morning, okay?"

Luna almost reminded him that Alison Haney had been ripped open in broad daylight but decided against it. "Fine."

"Fine like you realize how insane this sounds and we'll chalk it up to grief and renting *The Craft* a gazillion times?" Crystal asked. "Or fine like you're going to do something crazy anyway?"

"Fine, like you're probably right." It was almost physically painful when Luna lied to her two best friends, but she bit down until her lip split open and her stomach churned as she tasted blood.

Luna lay on her makeshift bed of pillows and blankets with her eyes closed until Dillon's and Crystal's breathing settled into a slow, matching rhythm. When she was sure they were asleep, she opened her eyes and stared at the ceiling. Watched the fan swirl lazily overhead.

A plink against the window startled Luna. The wind. It was probably just the wind.

Another plink, followed by her name, deep and rolling, like baritone thunder. "Luna."

Luna pushed herself off the floor, crawled on her palms and feet over Crystal's sleeping form, and pinched down a row of plastic blinds. There was a pebble on the sill, and—her breath caught in her throat—someone standing just outside the reach of the streetlight. Someone wearing dark clothing whose face she couldn't see behind a curtain of hair. She glanced at Dillon and Crystal. Without taking her eyes off the figure outside, she reached backward and laid a hand lightly on Dillon's shoulder—

Then the figure shifted under the streetlight, and Luna saw that it wasn't Crane at all.

Blond hair, broad shoulders, layers of denim and flannel. She hadn't seen Andy in days and it was hard to make him out clearly in the spaces between streetlamps, but Luna would recognize her boyfriend's shape anywhere, and so she pulled the blinds to the side enough that he could see her. She put her index finger first over her lips—*Be quiet*—then held it in front of her in the universal gesture for *Just a minute*. Sneaking around on tiptoes, Luna laced on her Converse, then slunk out of Dillon's bedroom and down the hallway. She checked for stray shadows in the stained glass panel on the front door, then opened the door and slipped through. The boxwoods rustled behind her as she raced down the sidewalk, but she didn't look back.

Andy's arms opened for her, and she fell into them. "Where the hell have you been? Everything's crazy," she said into his chest. Warm. Andy was so warm and so soft and so safe.

"Just feeling a little under the weather the past couple of days," he said.

Luna grunted. His body didn't feel like it had been sick, even if the weird glow of the streetlamps made him seem more gaunt than usual, but a few days of being sick could do that. "You couldn't call?"

"I left a note in your locker." Andy tightened his hold on her. "Didn't you get it?"

She nodded into his chest.

"I heard about Alison," he said. "I went by your house, but you weren't home, and Crystal's parents said she was here. I figured you would be, too." He gave her a little squeeze. "I wanted to make sure you were okay, so I stole my mom's Lincoln and snuck out to check on you."

A gust of air pushed through Luna's nose before she could stop it. "I figured you'd be more upset about Alison than me," she said.

"Why would you think that?" Andy kissed the top of her head, and the touch sent electric waves down Luna's body. "You know you're the only girl for me, Luna Evans. I've never been more sure of that than I am now."

"I know," she mumbled. Whatever Luna thought before, Andy was here now. With his arms around her and his breath in her ear, Luna felt stupid for thinking things between them were over. For ever being interested in someone like Crane.

She pulled away from Andy's embrace.

"Listen, there's something horrible going on around town, and I think I'm the only one who can stop it," Luna said. If her friends didn't believe her, maybe the boy who loved her would. "I don't have time to explain, but I can show you. Can we go to the funeral parlor?"

Andy gave her a grin that made her knees feel like pudding. His green eyes glinted beneath long blond bangs. "Get in the car."

CHAPTER 37

Ducey Evans

Ducey refilled one of her apron pockets with a supply of butterscotch candy. She slid the infant trocar into the other, then set her wedding band into the soap dish on the lab sink and draped a leather baldric lined with metal spikes over her shoulder and across her chest. There was a small, locked box stashed in one of the laboratory cabinets, and after a second's hesitation, she pulled it out and twisted the combination lock to the correct sequence.

"I bet you've seen one of these before," she told the dog waiting by her feet as she thumbed the lid open. "Ol' Buchanan probably keeps one in every room."

Ducey had never been a fan of firearms. She'd never hunted the dead with Royce's gun, no matter how much he'd urged her to. Never even fired one, other than the old Winchester shotgun, and even then, so few times she could count them on one hand. But there were at least three ghouls wandering around town, and another powerful enough to hide in the shadows. While they fed and grew stronger, Ducey felt every one of her eighty years. Tonight, she'd take all the ammunition she could get.

She lifted the snub-nosed revolver from its case.

"Mama, we should be looking for Luna," Lenore said. "Not going out hunting." She'd been insisting the same thing for the past hour and getting more shrill about it each time. Yet, she'd gotten ready, too, trading in her loafers for a pair of smart sneakers and covering her filthy gardening clothes in a plastic poncho with a utility belt secured around her waist, laden with all manner of sharp, dangerous instruments. Lenore was a blade girl, like her mama, even if she did package herself up like lunch meat so she didn't ruin a good set of clothes. She tested the tip of a needle-thin dagger on her palm, and when the point drew blood, Lenore nodded and slid the blade into a sheath on her hip. "And please tell me you're not thinking about bringing the sheriff's dog with us."

"It's called multitasking, Len," Ducey said. "And, of course, I'm not."

She looked at the old hound. Surely Buck had taught Belle to hunt; the old dog had already proven she could sniff out remains under dirt and likely she could be trained to sniff out a ghoul, too. That'd be a help. Only so much humans could do with eyes and ears after all.

Lenore stuffed a vial of Edwin Boone's leftover ashes into her slacks pocket under the poncho, and Ducey rolled her eyes. Ashes might have worked on the dog, but they'd be about as useful as a chocolate teapot against a full-fledged ghoul, and they still knew squat about how the salve affected the living—if it did anything at all, or if it only made things worse. This, too, was a problem for another day. Ducey flung open the revolver's chamber and dropped five rounds in, naming the bullets as she went: Snow Leger, Patsy Milner, Clyde Halloran. Two more, one for the master and one just in case. Never a bad idea to have a spare.

After twisting the cylinder to make sure all the bullets were in tight, Ducey rolled the chamber shut, stuffed the gun inside the elastic waistband of her trousers, and winked at the dog. "Besides," she told Lenore, "we find one ghoul, chances are we'll find the others."

Lenore gritted her teeth but didn't say anything. She knew it was true. The dead always found their way to one another, collecting up like ants at the center of a hive. Usually, if the Evanses didn't get a restless dead before it rose, the risen ones made their way to the parlor without causing too much trouble. Maybe because something in them wanted to be buried. Maybe something else. It didn't much matter, so long as they came home. So far, these ghouls seemed to be making their way: Farm Road 121 ran the perimeter of town, all the way from Ed Boone's place way out on the far edge, to the first few mile markers a short walk from the edges of Eternal Flame Cemetery. The theater across the street from Jimbo's sat about smack-dab in the center between Snow Leger's place and Evans Funeral Parlor. Buck Johnson lived close enough to the parlor he could probably see it through binoculars if he wanted.

The dead were on their way. Problem was, there were too many, and they were too hungry. It might not be Samael, but something else out there drove these monsters. Ducey just hoped like hell whatever that was would show itself tonight, too.

Grace arrived in the lab and set a mortician's makeup case on the table. This kit was bigger than her usual one and black instead of red, its only tube of lipstick the kind with a razor blade hidden inside the cylinder. She kept quiet as she rummaged in her case, armoring herself in knives she tucked into straps on her arms, her chest, her ankle. Almost as an afterthought, she snatched a scalpel from a utensil tray and dropped it in the breast pocket of her long-sleeve button-down.

"You ready for this, Grace Ann?" Ducey asked.

"Do I have a choice?" Grace snapped the case shut, fingered the scar on her left hand. Her jaw locked. "I'm ready as I'll ever be."

When Lenore made no attempt to comfort Grace, Ducey sighed and put a hand on the girl's shoulder. "Listen," the eldest Evans woman said, "we take care of the immediate problem, and when that's done, we focus on Luna. Everything will be right as rain, you'll see. We'll all be dancin' around under the moon and drinkin' midnight margaritas in no time."

That got a smile. Ducey just hoped it sounded believable. She hated tequila almost as much as she liked dancing.

"But what if Luna . . ." Grace's voice trailed off, unable to ask the question niggling in the back of all their heads. *What if Luna takes more after her father than she does her mother?* If so, she might interfere, might find herself swept away in a bloodlust too powerful to ignore. The knowledge handed down on human-monster half-breeds wasn't extensive, but enough to know that Luna's fate was far from certain.

"We'll take care of her," Lenore said. "Find a way, just like we always do. No matter what happens, Luna is one of us. We won't let anything happen to her."

"That's right," Ducey agreed. "By the time the sun comes up, this will all be over. One way or the other." She waited until both other women nodded in agreement. "Now, we got everything we need?"

"Just about." Lenore spread out newspaper in the lab's corner for Belle and filled a bowl with water while Grace made a nest of clean sheets for the dog to lay in. "We need to let the sheriff know his dog is here," Lenore said. "We can't keep her. It's not . . . sanitary."

"We'll get to Buchanan when we get to him." Ducey rolled her eyes. "'Less he's dead, too," she added, "then I reckon maybe we *will* hold on to her."

"Mama—" Lenore started.

"Move your butt, Miss Priss," Ducey snapped, flapping a wrist at her daughter. "The dog's fine."

They waited until Belle had curled into her makeshift bed and started to snore, then made their way to the lobby and out the front door. Lenore twisted the deadbolt open, and they all slid out. She locked the door behind her, securing the key in the same pocket she'd put the ashes. Ducey saw the outline of the clock key still in her slacks.

"Let's start in the graveyard, work our way out," Ducey said, looking out over the expanse of cemetery next door. "Dead or not, ghouls always find their way to where they're supposed to be. Farm Road 121, Garner Road, the theater—they've been workin' their way this direction since it started."

Lenore nodded in agreement, a quick dip of her chin. "We'll start at Eternal Flame and fan out."

"We should go to Snow's, too," Grace added. "See if—"

The sweep of approaching headlights interrupted her.

Ducey moved instinctively in front of her girls, her gaze sweeping from the rosebush they'd just replanted to the vehicle that hopped the curb and squealed to an abrupt, crooked stop in the parking lot. Déjà vu slammed into her: a faint dizziness, followed by a swell of nausea when she registered the flashing blue and white lights.

Oh, hell. Ducey's fingers patted her trocar, then snatched up a butterscotch as Deputy Taylor stumbled out of his cruiser. His gun wasn't drawn, but even in the dark she could see how fear twisted the man's features. He yanked open the back door of the cruiser, and a figure slunk out. Tall and skinny and covered head to toe in bad news.

"That's the boy I met at Riverfront Park, Crane," Grace whispered.

"Roger mentioned him when he brought Luna to the parlor today. I bet he's the one that gave her the teeth."

"*Teeth*?" Lenore bit off the word. "You didn't say anything about teeth."

"It's been a busy day," Grace snapped back.

"Shut up, you two," Ducey said, cracking open the candy to get the bitter taste out of her mouth. "Can't hear myself think with you two motormouths."

"Stay here," she heard the deputy tell the boy. He left the tactical lights on and, hand resting on his holster, he strode forward in three purposeful strides.

"Ladies, we need to talk," Roger said as the lights flashed against his back and swam over the parking lot. "I need to know what's really going on around here, or so help me—" He swallowed back something thick and pulled at his jaw. A sheen of sweat covered his skin. "I just saw something I can't explain."

There was no sense lying about it now.

"Let me guess," Ducey sighed, noticing the specks of red on the man's uniform. She spared a look over the man's shoulder at the boy waiting in the shadows, who looked like he might have been propped there like some kind of lawn decoration. "You saw a dead man rise."

Roger only said, "Johnson."

Ducey felt Lenore's bony fingers wrap around her arm as the ground swayed beneath her. Her dentures felt glued shut and she had to force the words out. "Buck Johnson is dead?"

"He is now." Roger swallowed again. "Found him out near mile marker seven. He was torn open, gutted like the rest—hell, most of his face was gone. He was dead; I know he was. But then he started to . . ." Roger waved his arms to signify movement, then coughed to cover a gag. "He *moved*," the man finally managed. "He didn't even have a mouth and he said my *name*."

He nodded behind him. "Not just me. Kid saw it, too."

"Where is he now?" Lenore asked. Hopefully the deputy hadn't gotten into his car and raced off, left a restless dead man behind. If so, they'd have to get out there quick, before Johnson got out of his car. Before whoever Roger'd phoned to come clean up the mess arrived on scene and Buck Johnson moved again.

"Still there, but he's not moving anymore." Roger's chin dropped and he swallowed. "I emptied six rounds into what was left of him."

"Where?" Grace asked.

Roger's eyes slid over. "What?"

"Where did you shoot him?" Lenore prompted as her nails dug crescent moons into Ducey's flesh.

The man blinked a few times before answering. "Heart," he said, the word riding out through his lips like they'd traveled a bumpy road. "Kid said that's where the soul lived, and I figured it was as good a place as any. Seemed to work."

Lenore's thin lips pressed into an even thinner line as she looked beyond the deputy to the boy by the car. "Cheer up," Ducey told her. "We just inherited a dog."

Roger's face twisted in confusion, but whatever he might have said next went unsaid as a second pair of headlights swung into the parking lot. Ducey didn't recognize the late-model Lincoln. She did, however, recognize the girl who threw open the passenger side door and bolted out of it.

"Luna!" Grace called, panic and relief fighting for front position in her voice. She tried to run around Ducey, but Ducey threw her arms wide and held her back.

Luna wasn't alone.

"Mom?" Luna shielded her eyes from the glare of the blue and white tactical lights. The engine shut off, cutting the lights to bathe them in darkness as the driver's door opened. A second figure climbed out to meet Luna at the hood of the car at the exact moment her eyes landed on the tall boy who stood unmoving by Roger's cruiser.

"Mom, that's him!" she yelled, hand raised and finger pointed toward the other car. "The one raising the dead!"

The boy's dark hair hid his expression. He raised both hands, took a step back, and bumped into the trunk of the cruiser, but he said nothing.

Ducey glanced at her great-granddaughter, but her attention was on the boy whose arm wound tight around the girl's shoulders. Even cloaked in shadow, she recognized Luna's boyfriend from the last time she'd seen him—deep-set eyes, long blond fringe, strong jawline. But it was a good thing she had an iron gut, because she noticed a few other things, too: The way his hair didn't move in the breeze. How the moonlight did nothing to light his eyes. How his lips twisted into a sneer when he saw the cruiser's tactical lights glint off the blades strapped to the Evans women's chests.

The cop. The boy. The stretch of land between the oldest Evans and the youngest. Really, she should have seen this coming. History was an arrogant bastard. Didn't like anything better than to repeat itself.

"I'm gonna need you to scoot away from Andy," Ducey said as she popped a second butterscotch between her lips. "Get on over here by your old granny."

"What?" Luna's face contorted, but she didn't budge. "Why?"

Ducey pulled hard on the candy and slid the trocar from her pocket. She clenched it in her left hand as she pulled the revolver from her waistband with the other, cocked the hammer, aimed both at the thing currently wrapped around her great-granddaughter.

"Because I know a dead man when I see one, child," she said. "And it's time to end this."

CHAPTER 38

Lenore Evans

They'd already lived through this Godawful Mess once before. How was it fair they had to do it again? The dead rising, faster than they could put them down. A cop who knew. One powerful strigoi, feeding off their own. Lenore felt time ticking in her bones.

It was all happening again, and this time the Evans women didn't have any more men to sacrifice.

Andy laughed, and the sound rattled around inside Lenore's bones.

"Dead?" he said. "I've never felt more alive." The boy shook his head at Ducey as if she'd said something absurd, his long blond bangs sweeping across his forehead. The amber in his eyes sparked in the dark and dimples dotted his jaw like scars when he grinned. "I mean, at first I felt terrible, sure. But then it was like I woke up from a bad dream."

Luna flinched at the word. She squirmed against him, untangling herself from his grasp, and Andy let her go. He looked at Luna, staring at him with her jaw unhinged. "And it's all thanks to you," he said.

The littlest Evans stopped, frozen in place by her boyfriend's words.

Grace's voice rang like tinnitus in Lenore's ears—"Luna!"—as she stepped toward the Lincoln. Lenore wanted to reach out, comfort her daughter, but they had no time for coddling. Shadows had crept into the corners of her vision. She pulled the dagger from the sheath on her hip and closed her eyes to separate the shuffling sounds she heard coming from somewhere behind Andy.

Footsteps crunched on too-dry grass. Useless legs slithered on the ground. Gummy, toothless jaws snapped. Three strigoi converged on the cemetery, on Evans Funeral Parlor, just like Lenore had known they would.

"They're coming, Mama," Lenore said. Ducey waved her quiet. Grace had the scalpel gripped in her hand and her jaw set tight. Roger's hand was on his holster. The other boy—the one who'd, curiously, known enough to tell Roger to shoot Buck Johnson's strigoi in the heart—stayed put beside the safety of the patrol car.

The deputy pulled the revolver out of his belt, keeping its barrel pointed down as his eyes flicked between the women, then to Luna and Andy. "Who's coming?"

"All your missing persons," Ducey said. She made light as always, but now they could all hear the fear hidden in her words. "We're about to have us a party."

It's not enough, Lenore thought, and she realized she'd been wrong. This wasn't like before. Then it had been three Evans women, plus Jimmy, a baby, and only one strigoi strong enough to pass as alive. Four people with bullets and blades had barely been enough last time, and with more dead upon them now and Luna caught in the balance, the balance tipped even further out of their favor.

"Don't you remember, Luna?" Andy said loud enough for everyone to hear, his smirk now as sinister and unnatural as a jack-o'-lantern's. "All those nighttime visits, those stolen moments under the moon?"

"Don't listen to him, Luna," Ducey called. "Ain't nothin' but bad breath gonna come out of his mouth."

Lenore nodded. She spread her arms wide, waving to her granddaughter the same way she'd waved to her daughter fifteen years ago. "Just walk this way, honey."

"You're walking away after *you* did this to *me*?" Andy sneered as he watched Luna inch away from him. "You thought you were dreaming and the whole time you were drinking me up, Luna. You drank away my mortal life until there was nothing left. I thought I was dying, and then I think I did die, but then I learned how to do the same thing to others. I figured out how to drink from *them*."

"I don't—" Tears and frustration twisted the girl's voice into a growl. "I don't remember any of that." Luna's legs locked and she stopped, looked to her family, then clawed her fingers inside her hair. Shook her head. "It's not possible. I couldn't have." She looked to Grace. "Mom, I promise—"

"It's okay, Luna." Grace rubbed the scalpel's dull side against her scar, careful to not draw blood. "Don't listen to him."

Despite the comfort her mother's words offered, Luna's face cracked with understanding. Death was selfish, and greedy. It didn't let go of things it wanted easily, not even when they still breathed. Even with curfews and alarms, they'd been powerless to hold back the power of strigoi blood running through Luna's veins. It fed on her, and because of it she fed on others. Whatever had haunted the girl's nightmares wasn't fantasy but some sort of darker version of her slipping out into the shadows. Calling her home just as sure as the dead slunk toward Evans Funeral Parlor right this very second.

Andy laughed and Lenore righted.

"It's all very sweet." He looked at them each in turn and ran his tongue along the bottom of his top teeth. "Trying to keep Luna safe, when she was the monster all along."

Grace made a sound like choking. "My daughter is not a monster."

"I know a few people who'd disagree," Andy said, rapping his knuckles on the Lincoln's hood before advancing on Luna. "My mother, for one, but I'm afraid she's too ill at home to complain much—almost all dried up, that one, but I've kept her full enough to stay alive." He shrugged, a gesture that almost made him still look human. "I hadn't meant to finish Mina Jean off so quickly, but she made my life hell with her Symphony League bullshit. I figured no one would miss an old drunk like Clyde Halloran, when I found him passed out with his mouth hanging open at Riverfront Park. My first real drink was a little clumsy, I admit. Had to knock the old drunk in the jaw a few times to get him to hold still. But I got the hang of it with Widow Milner, who no one even remembered was alive anyway. Once I had them, I was strong enough on my own." He looked at Luna with possessive, hungry eyes. "Now Luna and I have many children, and I will bleed dry anyone who tries to take them from me."

Lenore's knees wobbled. They'd heard these words before, almost the same ones, word for word, the night Jimmy had faced off with Samael.

"Over my dead body," Ducey snarled beside her.

Andy grinned, and there was nothing human left about him now. Nothing of the sweet boy Lenore had met several times before. Nothing the ashes in her pocket could hope to heal.

His voice came out in a growl, any human quality long gone. "If that's what you'd prefer."

Lenore watched the shadows at the edge of the parking lot form limbs. Arms, heads, legs. Roger's hand shook and his trigger finger twitched, but Grace grabbed his arm before he could squeeze off a round.

"Save your bullets," she said. "We need to make sure Luna is away from him first." She glared at the boy standing too close to her daughter. "The powerful ones move fast. Just because he's claimed her doesn't mean he needs to keep her alive."

"What about that one?" The deputy jerked his head in the direction of his car, where Crane still lingered by the trunk. "He one of them, too?"

Grace shook her head. "No, he's just a creepy kid—but luckily, he's our kind of creepy."

Roger waved his gun, flagging the boy's attention. When they made eye contact, Roger jerked his head left, toward the parlor's entrance. Crane cast one look over his shoulder, then bolted to the doorway, his long black coat fluttering out behind him. He tried the door, and Lenore felt the key's weight in her pocket with every rattle of the bolted pane. Locking it had felt like the right thing to do, the proper thing to do, but now she wondered if it might have been better to lock the innocents in with Belle, and the strigoi out with them.

"Mama." Her heart skipped in her chest as a bead of sweat slipped down the bridge of her nose. The figures were close enough now that she could make them out. Snow, Clyde, Widow Milner. The old woman dragged herself across the ground, all arms and elbows, while the other two followed close behind her, forming a semicircle behind Andy.

"We need to move," Lenore said, tightening her grip on the dagger's handle. Not much longer now, and the dead would be upon them.

"I'm old but I'm not blind, Len." Ducey's knuckles were white around the trocar, but steady. "Don't get your panties in a knot. Here they come."

Snow broke forward first, lumbering past Andy, so close Lenore could see the gap where the woman's finger had been torn off.

"'Enore," she slurred, tongueless.

"Luna!" Grace screamed. "Go!"

Luna fled in the same direction Crane had gone. He pulled his coat open as she approached, and she tucked herself in under his arm. Lenore felt breath rush into her lungs as the two huddled together under the awning, covered in a shield of black leather.

Widow Milner came next, her hands curled into fists, knocking on the ground as she pulled herself forward. Clyde staggered past, a thick, black muscle hanging through the gaping hole of his mouth. He was missing half his teeth, and had a hole so big in his chest that the graveyard tombstones were visible on the other side. Had he aimed just a few inches higher, Ed Boone might still be alive.

"Well," Andy said, clapping his hands together. "It is a party after all. Too bad Alison couldn't join us," he added when he noticed one among his throng missing. "I had so hoped to see her again after Snow finished her meal."

Roger cocked the hammer of his revolver. The thing that had once been Snow turned at the noise, the gummy hole in her face making eager sounds as she shuffled in his direction. A tremor raced up the man's arm and Lenore made to rush forward, but Ducey blocked her with a hip.

"Stay behind me, Len," she said. "Remember, aim for the heart," Ducey told the deputy, nodding at the hole in Clyde's chest. "Anything else is a wasted shot."

Roger pulled the trigger.

The revolver clicked dry.

Realization seized Lenore.

I emptied six rounds into what was left of him. In all the panic, he'd forgotten to reload.

"Ducey!" Fear flooded Roger's face as Snow's four-fingered hand reached for him.

Everything moved too fast then, as if Roger's yell had been a gunshot that rang out at the starting line.

Lenore watched Snow's remaining fingers latch onto Roger's sleeves, then rake the fabric to shreds. He held her back, but almost lost his balance when Widow Milner got near enough to grasp his boots. She pulled herself up his leg, smacking gummy lips as she tried to fit her mouth around the man's ankle to gnaw through the thick leather of his boots. Lenore pulled a knife from her belt and went for Snow, but then she saw Clyde's tongue lick at the air between his missing teeth as he spotted the kids cowering in the doorway. He veered toward them, and Crane pushed Luna behind him, brandishing a wad of sage like a sword while Luna twisted to grab Lenore's shovel they'd left at the door. She swung it at the old dead thing like a baseball bat.

Andy's lips curled in a vulpine snarl when Luna's shovel connected with Clyde's rib cage. He lunged toward Luna, but Grace raised her scalpel and readied to throw herself between her daughter and the oncoming threat.

"You girls stay behind me." Ducey pinched the gun under her left arm and used her free hand to yank Grace backward so hard she nearly hit the ground. Lenore pitched forward in Grace's sudden wake and Ducey used the trocar's pointy end to nudge them both back. She pulled the gun free of her arm and thumbed the hammer back. Her eyes shimmered wet behind her glasses as she looked at Lenore.

"You'll always be my baby girl," she said.

Lenore's throat wouldn't work. "Mama. No."

"Remember what I said, Len." Ducey pushed one last butterscotch between her lips, closed her eyes, and sucked so hard her cheeks hollowed. "Don't bury me in my brassiere."

She raised the gun and fired until the barrel clicked empty. Five shots rang out, but Ducey's arthritis got the better of her. One of the bullets blasted through the Lincoln's windshield, another stabbed into the cruiser's tire. Compressed air shrieked, the flashing lights tilted, and Snow hit the ground. Roger fell over the body and didn't stop kicking at Widow Milner with the tip of his steel-toed boot until her head caved in and disconnected from her shoulders.

Lenore looked up just in time to see her mother alive one last time as Ducey raced toward Clyde Halloran. She dropped the gun and grabbed the dead man by his collar, pulled him away from Luna, and sank her trocar into his chest—but not before his remaining teeth had already torn the softest part of her throat wide open.

CHAPTER 39

Grace Evans

Staring down at her grandmother's lifeless body, Grace had no time to think.

No time to grieve.

Not even time to cry.

Ducey lay in a sea of her own blood on top of old Clyde Halloran, who stared up at the stars with dark, dead eyes. Lenore collapsed beside her, the poncho a slick red sheet saturated in her mother's blood, while Luna screamed somewhere in the distance.

It took a few tries for Grace to clear the tears from her eyes enough that she could see, but when she finally managed, she found Roger in front of Luna, swinging Ducey's trocar at what had once been a sweet young man. Blood poured in red waves from Roger's forearm, and he looked like he might pass out at any moment, but he stood in front of Luna, between her and the monster. There was a red slash across the top of the girl's forehead and her nose was bleeding, but Luna pointed the shovel at her boyfriend, her teeth clenched in determination. Crane stood at her side. He'd traded the sage for a knife.

Andy snarled as he paced in front of them like a caged wild animal, curving a wide arc around the dead bodies that now littered the parking lot of Evans Funeral Parlor. Snow, Widow Milner, Clyde. Ducey. Blue and white lights flashed ghostly specters over the scene, made the boy's bloody footprints gleam against the pavement.

"Get away from my daughter!" Grace yelled, the moment her throat decided to work.

The dead boy laughed, high and cruel, but his eyes didn't so much as twitch in her direction. "Make me," he said.

Grace had always liked Andy, thought boys like Crane were the dangerous ones. But the tall boy clad all in black stood at Luna's side, while the one Grace had thought safe licked his lips at her daughter.

She took a step toward Luna and felt her mother's fingers tug at her pantleg.

"I can't lose you, too," Lenore begged. She thrust her key ring into Grace's hand, the parlor and clock keys smearing red on her palm. "Get Andy to the crematorium. If Luna leads, he'll follow. Burn the whole place down if you have to."

"It won't work. He knows what we do—he'll never follow her in," Grace said. She looked at Samael's rosebush and thought about the night she'd lost him, lost her father. "I'll die with Ducey before I let what happened before happen again. The only thing that matters now is Luna." She let the keys drop to the ground and reached down to pluck her mother's dagger from where it had fallen on the grass.

Lenore looked at the keys on the grass. Something clicked. "The ashes."

She climbed to her knees, Ducey's body settling on the ground as she dug in her pocket and pulled out the vial of Edwin Boone's ashes.

Grace shook her head while Lenore pulled open the vial, spit inside it, sealed the bottle closed. She shook the tube in her fist, mixing the two together until a thick gray batter formed. "She's gone, Mom," Grace said, understanding. "It won't work."

Lenore fisted the bottle and shook harder. "We don't know that."

Belle barked inside the building—loud, panicked yelps—as Grace toggled her attention between her mother and grandmother, the swarm facing off on the lawn. Luna had always wanted a dog. Grace should have gotten her one, shouldn't she? Or a cat, maybe. A kitten with black fur and a white bib, white socks. There were so many things, so many silly little things, she could have done different.

She blinked long enough to feel the hard metal of the scalpel's handle in one hand, her mother's dagger in the other. Then she opened her eyes to find Andy watching her.

He grinned at her with predator's eyes before his gaze swung back to Roger, then Luna. Andy peered at Crane as if noticing him for the first time. "You're standing too close to my girlfriend," he said in a snarl.

Curtains of lank black hair hid the boy-in-black's face from view, but he stood ramrod straight at Luna's side. "I don't think she belongs to anyone but herself," he replied.

The white rosebush glimmered in Grace's peripheral view, and as the first tears slid across her vision, she saw the memory again—her and Samael and her father. She knew what came next, remembered how things ended before. She turned her back on her mother and her fallen grandmother. So much was lost already. She only had moments left to save what mattered most.

"Roger," Grace whispered, loud enough so only the deputy would hear.

He answered without taking his eyes off Andy. "Grace, you get Lenore and you two run."

"This isn't your fight," she told him. Her daughter still had her shovel trained on Andy, but the tears pooling in Grace's eyes broke free to join the blood on her cheeks. "It's mine."

The monstrous boy narrowed his eyes as Crane put one hand where the shovel's shaft wobbled in Luna's grip, helping her keep it steady.

Behind her, Grace heard the crinkle of her mother's poncho as Lenore pushed Clyde's corpse to the side and gathered Ducey's head in her lap. A wave of blood still poured from the old woman's throat, but Lenore worked the gray mixture into the flesh around the wound. Red washed down her fingers, but Lenore worked until the vial was empty. Grace frowned as Ducey's blood drained the mixture away. Nothing could be done to save Ducey now, not even if her mother used every bit of ashes she had.

Lenore tossed the empty vial aside, and Grace looked away as she slid a thin surgical knife from one of the straps on her arm and aimed it over Ducey's heart. They didn't burn Evans women, but they couldn't let them rise, either.

"Mom, go inside," Luna called, breaking into Grace's concentration. "This is my fault."

Andy shifted, his attention pulling away from Crane to land on Luna.

"No, sweetheart." Grace shook her head as she bent to retrieve the empty vial, then stepped forward. "I told you we didn't put your father down because we wouldn't know what effect his death would have on you. That wasn't the whole truth—at least not *my* whole truth." She ignored the sting behind her eyelids as she tried not to squirm under Andy's stare. "I loved Samael, even after I knew what he was. I thought killing him would make me a monster. My daddy died to save me from that."

She crept forward as she spoke, sidestepping Roger's hand when he reached to stop her.

Grace extended her arm, angling the vial so it glimmered in the flashing cruiser lights. Andy glared at her, but the dead were curious, hungry things, and she waited until he turned in her direction, took a small step toward her and away from her daughter. "These are strigoi ashes," she said, gripping the glass in a way that hid the contents. "Mixed with water, they could give back the life that was drained from you."

She waited for Andy to register the lie—that it was nothing but an empty bottle in her hand, that she knew nothing about the power of ashes other than it could heal a wounded dog—and took another step closer, making sure to let the dagger hang harmlessly at her side. "You have a choice they didn't have." Luna stepped over the twisted shape of Patsy Milner. "You can stay as you are." Over Snow Leger. "Or you can drink the ashes and get your life back."

So close. Almost close enough to touch.

Andy's fingers reached out, but then he slapped at Grace's hand. The vial flew up and landed in the grass near Roger's feet.

Grace lifted her dagger as Andy opened his mouth and lunged.

There was a scream, and the scraping sound of wood and metal, the flutter of leather. Crane threw himself in Andy's path, attempting to tackle the other boy to the ground, but Andy flung him aside as easily as a scarecrow. Grace heard the sharp slurp of metal in flesh as the edge of Luna's shovel made purchase in Andy's stomach. Then Crane wrapped himself around Andy's knees and the two barreled in a heap to the ground.

The shovel clanged against the pavement, blood dripping from its rim. Crane's long body pitched into the air. There was a crack, and he lay crumpled on the blacktop, arm twisted at an unnatural angle.

Grace saw the rise and fall of his chest. "Roger, get the boy!" she screamed.

The dead boy didn't look at Crane, and didn't acknowledge the deputy as he scrambled across the grass to pull the black-clad lump into his lap. He pulled himself to his feet. A thin line of blood dripped from where his shirt had torn open over his stomach, but he kicked the shovel aside and set his sights on Luna.

Grace couldn't think. There wasn't time to think.

Andy charged.

Luna's voice stabbed her heart. "Mom!"

Grace's head hit Andy's midsection as she rammed herself against him. His fingernails raked against her flesh, and she felt him flay her skin into ribbons. One of his hands forced its way through her stomach and pulled at her insides.

Agony seized Grace's body. The snap of breaking bones echoed in her ears as one of Andy's hands clawed its way through her, followed by the churning crunch of ligaments and cartilage as he forced her body open. She was on fire, heat crackling through her arms, her legs, her stomach in each squelch of muscle, splatter of blood. The pain ate her whole, swallowing her screams before she could lose them. The weight of her own agony crushed against her as black spots edged around her vision. Her lungs constricted, unable to suck air, and with her last inhale, she connected her hand with something solid. A hot wash of liquid, a new surge of fire, raced over her hand and up her arm.

Her eyes rolled down to see red dripping from the hilt of Lenore's dagger where it stuck out of Andy's heart.

He spluttered, words lost in a series of bloody pulses through his lips. His hand slipped from Grace's stomach, and by the time the sentence was over, Andy was gone.

Grace didn't feel her body hit the grass. Just the cold freezing its way through the invading hot in her body, under her skin, over her eyes. The night went silent, like Grace had been pushed underwater—all noise reduced to dull beats like distant thunder.

Arms wrapped around her. Something pressed against her back—Roger's chest, she realized, but she couldn't feel his heat.

Luna's face rose to the surface in front of Grace's. Luna's mouth was moving but Grace couldn't hear what her daughter was saying. She watched tears slip down Luna's cheeks and roll inside her lips. Grace looked over her daughter to see Crane sitting up on the pavement, Andy sprawled facedown among the other lifeless bodies in the parlor's parking lot. Lenore hovered just out of reach, mouth opened wide in what must have been a silent scream.

Grace's head rolled back. A tug in her neck. She saw her mother's face, closer now, as Lenore worked at wounds Grace couldn't see or feel. Shards of glass sliced through the skin of Lenore's long fingers as the vial broke in her hand, and Lenore tried desperately to find residual ashes to rub into Grace's skin, into the river of blood running down her throat, across her chest, into her lap. Roger held a wad of black fabric against her stomach, and Grace realized too late that it was his brown uniform hat, turned black with her blood.

Sound rushed back to her in a rush of wind against her ear. "Mom, Mom, Mom." Luna's voice, hot where it touched her neck. "Don't leave me, Mom. Please don't leave me."

Grace smiled. *It's worth it after all*, she thought. *Dying for love.*

She lifted one hand and the scar on her left wrist shone bright silver in the moonlight. Grace brushed her palm across her daughter's face. And then she closed her eyes.

CHAPTER 40

Luna Evans

Belle's snout pressed wet and cool against Luna's shin, and Luna reached down to scratch behind the hound's ear. The sun had just begun to peek over the horizon, but even the blazing colors of sunrise seemed pale and unremarkable. Within the span of a few hours, everything had changed.

With Deputy Taylor's help, Luna and Nana Lenore took care of the bodies belonging to the restless dead. Snow Leger, Clyde Halloran, and Patsy Milner were given a thoughtful farewell before their bodies were fed to the furnace. They burned quickly, as dead things are wont to do, and no one spoke when Lenore harvested their ashes, then hid them away somewhere deep in the heart of the funeral parlor. She put a small amount in a vial in her pocket, and no one said anything about that. No one said anything, either, when she wound the clock at the back of the chapel until her fingers bled.

It took some time to decide how to handle Andy's remains, but eventually they interred them to the fire, too. Roger didn't say much, other than he'd handle the rest. Andy had told them that he'd fed on his mother but left her alive, and the deputy promised to drive over to the West's later—right after he sorted the mess out by mile marker seven.

"The drained don't turn if they don't die," Nana Lenore told him. "Tanya West won't be the same after what she's been through, but she'll live. If you get there and she's not breathing, call me." Nana Lenore worked a washcloth over a stray drop of blood spatter on the deputy's uniform sleeve. She sighed when it smeared. "Or I suppose you know what to do."

The last turned Roger's skin a pale shade of green but he nodded. His promotion to sheriff after Buck Johnson's death would be a matter of procedure, but he knew now that the job description also came with the mantle of guarding the Evanses' secret. Luna didn't think the secret would turn him bitter as it had his predecessor.

She kind of thought it made him proud.

They patched up Deputy Taylor's and Crane's injuries on the same metal table where they'd put down Edwin Boone and Alison Haney, and treated Sheriff Johnson's dog, Belle. Luna tried not to notice Ducey's wedding bands still in the soap dish, or her dog-eared romance novel left unfinished on the lab's counter. It was too hard to believe the old woman was really gone, and these little signs of life kept her close so that her presence still filled the space around them. Nana Lenore put Grace's cosmetic case and Ducey's glasses on the bookshelf, while Luna wrapped a bandage around Crane's elbow and Roger wrung Grace's blood out of his hat in the sink. He set it on top of Grace's case when he was done and shrugged when Luna caught him looking.

Some of the ashes in Nana Lenore's pocket became a salve for the various cuts and scrapes on Crane's skin. None had been caused directly by a restless undead, but safe felt better than sorry. "I don't think we have to tell you how important it is that you tell no one what you witnessed here tonight," Nana Lenore told Crane as she smeared the mixture, then covered it with a Band-Aid. "Can we trust you to keep our secret?"

Crane took Luna's hand and squeezed it before he answered. "I will take it to the grave," he said, and that was enough, even for Nana Lenore.

No one asked how he'd come to be in possession of Clyde Halloran's teeth, because no one had to. "I found them at Riverfront Park," he explained. "Just lying in the dirt. I thought maybe they belonged to an animal or something, so I picked them up, cleaned them off, and brought them to Moon Girl. I thought they'd make an amulet to help with her nightmares, and what I saw tonight makes me believe in the power of magick even more."

This wasn't the strangest thing someone had found at the sketchy park by the river, and since Clyde was dust and Andy had essentially confirmed that's where he fed on the old man, they decided to trust him. Besides, Crane's ceremonial magic paired nicely with the Evans family folklore, and they needed all the knowledge—and the help—they could get.

Both Deputy Taylor and Crane had put themselves between the dead and the Evanses, and that made them friends, if not a kind of family. Not all family was blood, and—as far as Luna was concerned—not all blood was family.

Under the guiding light of dawn, two fresh graves were dug at the edge of Evans Funeral Parlor, directly beside Samael's white rosebush—one for Ducey, one for Grace. Nana Lenore laid Ducey's trocar on her chest and filled her apron pockets with butterscotches, while Roger and Luna wiped Grace's skin clean. Crane volunteered a ring from each of his hands, and Lenore strung these on silver chains that she affixed around the dead women's necks.

Roger and Crane gave Luna and her grandmother some space as they wrapped the bodies of their fallen loved ones in clean white sheets. Luna covered her mother's face last.

"I love you so much, Mom," she whispered against the cloth. "Thank you for keeping me safe."

Nana Lenore held Luna close while Deputy Taylor and Crane, with his one good arm, lowered the bodies into the ground and covered them with earth. Her grandmother's arms were stiff and not the sort accustomed to hugging, but they were safe and warm, and the only home Luna had left. Roger sat for a while by Grace's grave, and when the sun finally slipped full into the morning sky, he tipped his hat and took his leave. He nodded at Lenore and clamped his hand on Luna's shoulder as he left, Crane in tow.

It was over—at least for now.

Luna stood next to her grandmother at the edge of the small garden. Just hours ago, they'd used the same shovels and spades to dig up the grave of the monster who was her father. She'd hit Clyde Halloran's ghoul with the same shovel, held it in front of her against the boy she'd once thought she'd loved. Then she'd used it to bury her mother next to the man who—for better or worse—Grace had loved, and the old woman who'd loved them all most.

"Shouldn't we have buried them in the cemetery?" Luna asked her grandmother.

Nana Lenore's lips curved into a wistful smile. "Evans women stay close in life and in death." She patted her blouse over her heart and turned to the white rosebush that guarded Samael's grave. "Here, both our mamas can stay with us. Besides, maybe if we put enough love into the ground, it'll help control some of the other darkness we have to worry about."

This was still there, too. Luna's past was out in the open, but her future remained uncertain. There would be hard days ahead, full of grief and remembrance, but also full of learning and preparation. Soon, Luna would face a choice and take her place in the Evans's legacy, but now she needed to finish burying her family.

Seed packets waited among the gardening tools still propped beside the fresh mounds, and Luna squatted to consider the colors. A rainbow of choices awaited her, none of them the white blooms of her father's rosebush.

"Blue roses symbolize peace," Nana Lenore said in a small, breakable voice. "Red for passion."

Luna nodded. "Which color goes to who?"

"You pick," Nana Lenore said, then clipped two cuttings from Samael's bush and pulled a small vial of still-warm ashes from her pants pocket. The ashes went to Samael, the blooms to Ducey and Grace.

Belle padded between them. The old hound's nose dropped to the ground, and she sniffed at the graves, long red ears dragging the churned dirt as she moved back and forth between Ducey's final resting place and Grace's. She stayed close while Luna and her grandmother planted the seeds, and when they were finished, she crept back to Ducey's grave, sniffed long and hard and full, and then let loose a mournful howl. Afterward, she walked three circles and lay down, refusing to budge when Luna turned toward the parlor, patted her thigh, and tried to call the dog home.

"Just let her be," Nana Lenore said. "She lost people she loved, too. Besides, it's a lovely day outside."

Luna eyed the dog who stayed behind to grieve. "We'll keep her, won't we?"

Nana Lenore huffed, but she smiled. "Of course, we will. She's an Evans now." She laughed like it hurt and took Luna's hand. "It's funny, isn't it? All those years of Ducey and Buck Johnson hating each other over old reasons and buried secrets, but I like to think they did right by each other in the end. Ducey saved the thing he loved most, and now she's a part of us, which is what the old grump ever really wanted, too."

Luna gawked at her grandmother. "That mean old jerk *loved* Ducey?"

"Oh, honey, the Evans women are full of secrets." Nana Lenore shook her head and slipped the clock key from her slacks to admire under the morning sun. "Let's go put on a pot of coffee."

Hand in hand, Luna and her grandmother made their way into the parlor. The doors closed behind them before either caught the scent of butter and caramel that floated on the crisp dawn breeze. They didn't see the dirt rustle under where Belle still lay on the old woman's grave. Didn't see the hound's tail give one quick, joyful thump.

They didn't see the white rosebud laid atop Ducey's grave sink into the soil.

Acknowledgments

Writing a book that's this close to your heart is a little bit like practicing magic: full of surprises. Mostly it's like ripping yourself open to expose your most vulnerable bits, which isn't all that different from what the ghouls in *Bless Your Heart* do as they eat their way through this fictionalized version of my own hometown—rip them open, gobble them up, and leave behind traces to tell their story. After all, just as Luna notes right as she's about to spill her proverbial guts to her best friends: everything, dead or alive, has to feed.

Sometimes we are fed, and sometimes we are feasted upon. Sometimes, dear reader, we're both.

While *Bless Your Heart* is, of course, a work of fiction, it's more than a little autobiographical. Every character and every setting is inspired by someone or someplace I hold dear. And though the Evans women aren't strictly true-to-life, from their pockets full of butterscotch candies to their collections of clocks and scarred left wrists, they represent my favorite parts of my great-grandmother Ducey, my Nana Linda, and my mother—three of the strongest and most capable women to ever stake their claim on Southeast Texas.

And Belle, of course. There is simply nothing more beautiful than the love of a dog.

The Evans women aren't the only family, nor the only friends, who appear in *Bless Your Heart*, and while I am indebted to the people who inspired this story (especially the many who've passed from this life into the next), I am tremendously grateful to those who have been part of this journey—from clawing its way out of the ground as a concept

("I want to write a story about a monster-hunting granny," I once told my ever-patient agent) to chewing through draft after draft to finally become the book in your hands.

First and foremost, my biggest thank-you goes to Christopher Brooks, my book husband, writing partner, most trusted editor, and favorite road-trip companion. *Bless Your Heart* would simply not be the book it is without you, and I appreciate you more than I can say. I am so grateful to have you in my life, and for the many more books and the pieces of pie we will eat together (in our Princess Room, while I try very hard not to spew Little America all over your car, and you molest the windshield wipers).

Thank you to my agent, Italia Gandolfo, for believing in me, supporting my harebrained ideas, and always checking in to make sure I get enough sleep. Also, for introducing me to Christopher!

My heartfelt thanks to George C. Romero, Josh Malerman, Rachel Harrison, Clay McLeod Chapman, Nat Cassidy, Maureen Kilmer, Christopher Golden, Gwendolyn Kiste, Kristi DeMeester, and Darcy Coates. Your friendship and support mean the world to me, and I am grateful for and inspired by you folks every single day.

Thank you to Alexandra Sehulster, Cassidy Graham, and the amazing team at Minotaur Books, for opening their arms and hearts to the Evans women and their world.

To my mom! For sharing fun family memories (that Lady Clairol story is real, folks!) and only being slightly fussy about being killed off in the end.

To Robbie Campbell for becoming Crane, to Carrie Sonnier for helping me remember the details of our high school cafeteria, and to Crystal Coleman for being a rock-solid friend since 1998. I could never fit all my oldest and dearest friends on the page individually, but you're all here in the memories we made at Riverfront Park and Parkdale Mall.

To Pearry Teo, gone but never forgotten. Thank you for the dream interpretations, the anatomy lessons, and the unflinching answer to every completely bizarre, middle-of-the-night question I lobbed at you. I hope you and Ducey are partying it up right now in the afterlife.

Special thanks to everyone who helped build the playlist for this novel to keep me sane while writing, including but not limited to: Jessica McHugh, Monique Snyman, Ryan Groff, Nadia Hasan, and Brent Snyder.

Bless your hearts.